MANLY PURSUITS

MANLY PURSUITS

ANN HARRIES

BLOOMSBURY

First published in Great Britain in 1999
This paperback edition published 2000

Copyright © 1999 by Ann Harries

The moral right of the author has been asserted

Bloomsbury Publishing Plc,
38 Soho Square, London W1V 5DF

A CIP catalogue record for this book
is available from the British Library

ISBN 0 7475 4544 8

10 9 8 7 6 5 4

Typeset by Palimpsest Book Production Limited,
Polmont, Stirlingshire
Printed and bound in Great Britain by
Clays Ltd, St Ives plc, Bungay, Suffolk

for
my daughter
Sophie Brown
and
in memory of
my friend
Peter Lundwall

ACKNOWLEDGEMENTS

For the information about Cecil Rhodes' ill-fated British songbird project, I have many of Rhodes' biographers to thank; in addition, Appollon Davidson offered an unexpected sub-plot by linking the Jameson Raid with Oscar Wilde's trials of 1895 in his extraordinary *Cecil Rhodes and his Time* (Progress Publishers, Moscow, 1988). I have also drawn on details from: Robert I. Rothberg's monumental volume *The Founder: Cecil Rhodes and the Pursuit of Power* (Southern Book Publishers, Johannesburg, 1988); Elizabeth Pakenham's insights in her *Jameson's Raid* (Weidenfeld & Nicolson, London, 1960); Brian Roberts' description of life in the New Rush diamond-mining camps in *Kimberley, Turbulent City* (David Philip, Cape Town, 1976); and the research of the many biographers of most of the characters in *Manly Pursuits*. Their revelations have provided me with the historical framework of this novel, which is narrated by practically the only character in the book who exists only in my imagination.

I should also like to thank those friends and family members whose enthusiastic support has encouraged me so much, and whose printing equipment was responsible for the original hard copy of *Manly Pursuits*.

LADY CAROLINE: I don't think that England should be represented abroad by an unmarried man, Jane. It might lead to complications.

LADY HUNSTANTON: You are too nervous, Caroline. Believe me, you are too nervous. Besides, Lord Illingworth may marry any day. I was in hopes he would have married Lady Kelso. But I believe he said her family was too large. Or was it her feet? I forget which.

Oscar Wilde, *A Woman of No Importance*

Generally, the most vigorous males, those which are best fitted for their places in nature, will leave most progeny. But in many cases, victory depends not on general vigour, but on having special weapons, confined to the male sex. A hornless stag or spurless cock would have a poor chance of leaving offspring.

Charles Darwin, *The Origin of Species*

Part One

CAPE TOWN 1899

This morning he asked me if it was true that blackbirds can hear their worms moving in the earth. No apology for his five-day absence; no enquiry about the voyage; no reference to my nervous collapse or the reports of my Oxford physicians; not even a how d'yc do and good to meet you at last. (We had communicated entirely by telegram.) Above all, no explanation as to why the arrangements had changed so suddenly; why, in complete contradiction to the previous plans, I had been ordered to bring forward my date of arrival from spring to autumn – or autumn to spring, depending on which hemisphere you happen to occupy.

I was warned about this, of course. He'll take you by surprise, the Captain said. That's how he's made his millions, by coming in at an angle. He was like that as an undergraduate over twenty years ago, as I remember. Tall and gauche, in his habitual blue sailor tie with white spots, he shambled uneasily among us pale academics, startling us with sudden displays of the diamonds he carried in his waistcoat pocket when he registered our sneers. He'd lived rough beside the Kimberley mine, and enjoyed talking dysentery and fleas. Rumour has it he read his Aristotle and Marcus Aurelius in English! His library is full of translations, shelves of them typed and bound in red morocco: every reference made in

The Decline and Fall of the Roman Empire. They smell of smoke and ash when you open them (which I frequently do). Miraculous that they were saved from the fire, and by the butler at that.

You'd think his architect would have encouraged him to make the new place more of a home – along the lines of the dons' cluttered comfort – but this place is a museum piece, built in the Stoic mould. All teak and whitewash, flags and firearms, and a bath eight feet long hollowed from a slab of granite. Every hinge and handle is hand-wrought, yet the symmetry of the house is such that it could have been fashioned by a machine, with no feeling for the imperfections that create a home. And if he'd built the house a few hundred yards higher up the mountain slope he'd have ensured a magnificent view of a distant mountain range, and caught the morning sun. Instead we freeze in these great dark rooms, inhaling the bitter aroma of tropical hardwoods (six shiploads brought in from the East Indies) just because he wants historical continuity. As if building your house (twice) on the ruins of an old barn that stored the First Settlers' crops gives you some sort of sacred power – a mantle of belonging. And he a vicar's son from some provincial market town in England, with plans to ruin and subjugate the descendants of those very Settlers he admires so much.

I'm particularly annoyed about the position of the aviaries. When the matter was first raised, one of his so-called secretaries assured me – by telegram – that the birds would get at least ten hours' sunshine a day. They won't sing unless they're fooled into thinking it's spring, it's as simple as that. Now I find the aviaries have to be at the rear of the Great Granary because certain members of the public are allowed to wander freely in the gardens (in spite of the fire) and would frighten or tease these nervous British birds. So we're right at the back of the main building, impinging on the drive that leads to the kitchen, and in the shade all day – either cast by the Devil's Peak mountain, or the shadows of these wretched conifers that have been planted all over the mountain slopes. He sees himself as some sort of Capability Brown of the Cape, grooming the mountainside to look like the gardens of a stately home. The natural habitat of the mountain is this scrubby *fynbos* – the odd thorn bush throwing out a torrent of hot perfume; flowerheads that sprout fur and feathers instead of petals; lilies that burst into bloom only after a savage mountain fire; and silver trees with leaves like daggers. But we see little of this from the Great Granary, hemmed in on all sides, as we are, by dark forests planted a mere twenty years ago, as if in preparation for my songbirds. They wouldn't survive in the heat of the *fynbos*, it's true, but who knows what ghastly predators lurk in the plantations? My telegrams informed me that the purpose of the songbird introduction is '*to improve the amenities of the Cape*'. Presumably the kangaroos, llamas and zebras enclosed in adjacent meadows perform the same function. I believe my employer is commissioning some sort of Temple of Theseus, with colonnades, for his lions.

I am attempting to rest, in obedience to my physician's stern orders. Rest does not come easily to one whose entire adult life has been stretched on the rack of chronic dyspepsia. And since my collapse (of which I remember little) I feel that the convolutions of my brain are but a microcosm of the coils of my abdomen where ancient ulcers erupt and poison disseminates, so that orderly thought is replaced by chaotic outbursts (of which this observation is a telling example). I have therefore asked to be excused from the Great Granary's indigestible evening meals.

My medical supervisors in Oxford agreed that the turmoil in my head would best be quietened by a complete change of environment, as far removed as possible from the claustrophobic confines of my college. A rest home in Eastbourne was mentioned. I refused to budge. An eminent psychologist under the unfortunate influence of Vienna suggested hypnosis. I turned my face to the wall and declined to move from my bed. My elderly scout, Saunders, unpacked my cameras in a row at my bedside in the hope that this reminder of my lifelong hobby might encourage me to take a photograph. I groaned impatiently. So when the request came from the Cape Colony for two hundred British songbirds to be selected and delivered personally by the world's leading authority on birdsong to an anonymous diamond tycoon, it was considered to be the perfect excuse for me to venture out of my shuttered rooms and sail into the brilliance of the Southern hemisphere. Needless to say, I had no interest in the whim of some tycoon, and communicated my displeasure by refusing to eat.

It was Saunders, grown pale and drawn with the effort of tempting me to sip at bowls of gruel specially prepared in the college kitchens, who whispered ramshackle stories of Africa into my ear: potted accounts he had read in our national broadsheets of the travels of G.B. Challenger, that famed elephant hunter and explorer, whose ambition it was to retrace the zigzagging steps of the Reverend David Livingstone, and erect a monument in his honour at Ujiji. (Funds had been raised through public subscription for a leading Pre-Raphaelite sculptor to produce a statue of the doctor pointing his finger at the African landscape, with the inscription: *I leave it to you!* on its plinth.) It is true to say that Saunders was less interested in Challenger's achievements than in the antics of Mary, the female poodle who accompanied the explorer wherever he went, and had endeared herself to the nation through her playful acts of bravery and devotion, which included rescuing her master from the fury of a wounded rhinoceros by jumping in its

6

path, and twirling a coloured ball upon her nose. Who will ever understand how this gentle manservant (who had never travelled further south than Basingstoke, to visit his sister and her unruly family) managed to instil into my consciousness the wild plains of Africa, sharp with shadow and yellow light; the mangrove swamps that lift a stinking frill of roots as the brown Zambezi estuary rises and falls; long, lean peoples in round huts beside inland oceans turned pink with one-legged flamingos? – for Saunders had no idea of geography and imagined Cape Town to be swarming with the elephants, crocodiles and mosquitoes which Challenger met and killed on a daily basis in central Africa. Perhaps his trembling voice awoke in me memories of the eventful career in the New World of my tutor, Mr James, who had roused me from a childhood inertia with his ability to rattle off the binomial nomenclature of cats that barked, dogs that hung by their tails from trees, and plants that opened and shut like umbrellas in Amazonian forests and African jungles, with photographs to prove it. Whatever the reason, I found myself agreeing – by telegram – to supervise a cargo of songbirds that would leave Southampton in time for the Cape Town October spring.

Then, out of the blue came the cable requesting – *commanding* – me to leave immediately. Because very large amounts of money would be paid to the zoology department for the project, the university insisted I agree to this change of plan, even though I had only just vacated my sick bed, and, in doing so, had contracted the unpleasant bronchial infection which still plagues me. The month was April, and the nightingales, chaffinches, robins, starlings *et al*. I had ordered from a reliable farm in Sussex were singing and laying eggs for all they were worth. I argued that if we arrived in Cape Town in autumn all mating would cease and there would consequently be no birdsong for the nameless millionaire who required it so urgently. My feeble voice was powerless against the imperative of a sum of money large enough to subsidise the building of a new laboratory. Saunders packed my bags almost overnight.

It was not until I boarded the *Northampton Castle* that the identity of the bird-loving tycoon was revealed to me. It came as a shock. The Colossus, they call him now. After one of the seven wonders of the ancient world: the hundred-foot bronze statue of the sun-god Helios guarding the harbour entrance of an Aegean island. Let us hope my diamond entrepreneur does not follow the example of the original Colossus, which was toppled by an earthquake and sold for scrap, in forty-seven wheelbarrows, eight hundred years later.

Yesterday morning my breakfast was ruined by the arrival of a flirtatious mother and her sly daughter. They seemed incapable of perceiving that I require silence for successful digestion, and clearly regarded my lack of response as a challenge to their feminine wiles.

The mother (whose husband is an administrator up in the north of the Colony and who speaks in a guttural Boer accent laced with pantomime gentility): 'Come on, Professor! You need building up! I'm going to put a fried egg on your plate next to that teeny little piece of bacon!' And she brushed her bosom against my shoulder as she leant over. I shuddered, but could not bring myself to tell her that I cannot eat eggs first thing in the morning.

The daughter (aged sixteen): 'Oh, leave the poor man alone, Mother. Just think how fat Daddy is compared to the Professor. You overfeed everyone you see!' And she coiled herself round her chair, sliding her eyes to see if I was grateful for her support.

She is biding her time until the return of the noisy young men who appear to play some sort of secretarial role in the life of my absentee host. They rise at five, bathe noisily in ice-cold water, gulp down some rough porridge and coffee, then tear up the mountain on horseback. They are out all day; they ride straight into town to conduct company business or run the Colony, or plot the downfall of the old Boer in the north, who is undoubtedly plotting theirs. I wait for the shouting to subside into the distance, then heave myself out of my hard but warm bed. The Negro manservant – I cannot bring myself to call him Kaffir, for that is the name my mother gave her favourite dog when I was a small child – brings me the great jug of hot water on which I insisted after the first disastrous morning. I ask him if his employer has returned from his election campaign. He replies, *Not yet, baas*, in a voice drenched in apology, then seals his lips. I want to ask him whether it is an African custom for the host to be absent when his guest arrives, but I contain my pique. I've been in this mausoleum for nearly a week, and still not a sign of the man who has employed me, I want to say to this manservant in frock-coat and high collar, the tribal markings etched in parallel lines across his cheeks. He has no tip to his middle finger. His name, by some devious route, is Orpheus. I am disturbed by his silence.

In fact, I am already homesick for Oxford. I long for the claustrophobia of my rooms and the soothing murmur of donnish gossip. When a new guest, usually a woman, wanders into the dining-room, I pray she will be British. You know after the first two words they speak. I like my Good Mornings crisp and rectangular like my bacon rashers, not an operatic aria as these colonial women will make their greetings. Usually with a garish display of teeth as they linger unnecessarily on the final syllable. They ask enthusiastic questions about British birds. The air is sprayed with exclamation marks as they respond to my dry pronouncements. They gabble on about the fire: a couple knew the house before it was gutted. All the oil paintings and some valuable tapestry had been destroyed, as well as period furniture which has been painstakingly replaced. They wonder whether the fire was accident or arson. The general opinion is arson. The Colossus, though worshipped by the present company, has many enemies. Since the Raid four years ago, there have been a dozen further attempts at burning his house down. They accept his absence with smiling tolerance. I learn he is touring the north of the Colony, making speeches: in spite of his disgrace he fills halls with supporters who would forgive him anything.

After my experience with the mother and daughter I rose an hour earlier today in order to be alone with my bacon and slice of toast and pot of China tea. The coffee here is monstrous. The secretaries drink it by the gallon, especially when playing billiards in a vast smoky room at the back of the house. I can hear them shouting with caffeine-inflamed voices which they lower when I pass by. I collided with one of them in a corridor once: he stank of coffee and brandy and Turkish tobacco. He looked at me with bloodshot blue eyes (every young man in this house has blue eyes of a particularly vibrant hue), and murmured an apology in Dutch.

This morning the clatter of the early risers didn't disappear down the avenue for once, but shut itself up in the drawing-room, like a giant trapped animal trying to claw its way out. The noise had continued for a good hour when I descended for breakfast. A piercing female voice rose above the rumble of male dialogue (and clash of coffee cups) and I wondered if it might belong to the Colossus' formidable sister, who had been rescued from the flames of the Great Granary by the butler (only after he had rescued the library books, saving what he thought his master valued most). It was certainly a voice at home with male company, breaking into high-pitched giggles through the gusts of masculine badinage.

I had just swallowed my first sip of tea – the best moment of the day, in my opinion, as the smoky fragrance of the East rises from the back of the throat and stimulates the olfactory nerves – when the dining-room door shot open. I tried to control the spasm of annoyance which I am told momentarily contorts my otherwise bland facial features, and replaced my cup (surely not genuine Ming?) delicately on its saucer, though with shaking hand. For some reason my place had been laid at the head of the long dining-table – a table, I may say, which had been carved in its entirety from one massive trunk of Yellowwood, an indigenous tree which grows in the Colony's little rain forest. I could thus hear several people burst into the quiet of the dining-room, but could not see them, the door being behind me. A billow of cigar smoke immediately wreathed itself round my head; I coughed discreetly, a mere sparrow's cheep. The chatter was dominated by the woman's strident voice. Her talk was distinctly unwomanly.

'I tell you, if we change to a four-foot-eight-and-a-half-inch gauge we will go through Africa at a rate of fifty miles an hour rather than twenty. In other words, we'll get from Cape to Cairo in 110 hours on the wider gauge instead of 270 on the standard southern African rail gauge. More than twice the existing speed, and for the same price!'

This pronouncement was followed by a sharp pause in her chatter, as my self-effacing presence was registered.

It is in pauses such as this that long-inactive memory cells come suddenly to life.

'I say, Wills,' came the Colossus' now familiar falsetto voice, now just behind my back, 'is it true that blackbirds can hear their worms move in the earth?'

As if a question of national importance had just been posed in the House, the secretaries fell silent. No one moved. It appeared that my interrogator expected me to turn round to face him. This I proceeded to do at considerable strain to my neck muscles, as some inner rebellion at this treatment compelled me to leave my feet firmly planted under the table and thus pointing in the opposite direction. I raised my eyes.

He had doubled in size since his undergraduate days (needless to say, he did not recognise me). He was as crumpled as the photographs and cartoons had led me to expect: an enormous fleshy man with a bloated face and cold blue eyes. His thick hair was unbrushed, even untidy, but his moustache had been carefully shaped and his skin shone with the soap of a recent shave. I remembered the dimpled chin. Could he be wearing the same spotted sailor bow of twenty-five years ago?

I watched him study my own pink and white features, my neatly clipped grey beard, the paucity of my hair, which had treacherously receded to the back of my head, the rosiness of my too-full lips. Something in his piercing stare made me shrink from him, to wriggle in that gloomy tapestried room, like the blackbird's victim worm itself. But even in my discomfort, I could feel pity. Although I am not a medical doctor, my interest in the zoological field (and, let me admit it, in my own physical ailments) has made me observant. I know an ill man when I see one. Heart malfunction and hard living were etched in the myriad purple veins on this man's face. His forehead was beaded with perspiration. Yet he continued to stare.

His acolytes had gathered round him, handsome young men in the main who, by contrast, exuded the ruddy glow of good health, some slumping in vacant chairs, others peering over his shoulders (he was taller than any of them) to fix me with their energetic blue gazes. I could feel the phlegm (the aftermath of my prolonged bronchial attack) gather in my throat, and cleared it with my sparrow's cough.

'Well,' I stammered, marvelling nevertheless that I was able to produce a fully formed sentence under these trying circumstances, 'it is true that the blackbird has remarkable auditory powers.'

This evasive answer seemed to satisfy the great man. I believe it was the sound of my voice he wished to hear rather than any ornithological information I could impart. To my relief he moved from behind me and I was able to straighten my position, administering at the same time a deliberate massage to the twisted muscles of my neck.

He sank into the chair on my right hand and honoured me with a surprisingly limp handshake, using only two fingers (the house is filled with Masonic emblems of one kind or another). At once the white manservant, a grim-faced fellow of military bearing, provided him with a mug filled with odious coffee. Fastening me again with that look of peculiar intensity, he pronounced, still in that queer soprano voice of his: 'Wills, it is my dream to fill my forests with the sounds of all the birds of Oxfordshire and Gloucestershire.' He ran his fingers through his thatch of greying hair, an affectation designed, I felt sure, to draw attention to its quantity, and continued: 'Do you know what it is I miss most in this mighty African continent?'

I raised a polite eyebrow.

'I miss the early morning song of the blackbird, the thrush, the little wren: that dawn chorus which in my opinion far exceeds any human opera or oratorio in musical beauty. Their music is nothing less than the song of civilisation!' His already moist eyes reddened and glazed; the young men looked downwards. His fleshy chin sunk into his hand, his profile was that of a melancholy Roman emperor.

I felt that this was not the moment to remind him that the dawn chorus occurs only during spring and early summer, and that the Southern hemisphere was about to enter the silent months of winter. Nevertheless, I was compelled to confess an unfortunate development.

'I have to tell you,' I murmured, 'that half the blackbirds died on the voyage out.'

I could have sworn that a minuscule serpent's tongue flickered out of each of his watering eyes as I spoke. A secretary gasped.

'And are the other half in mourning?' he enquired sharply, with no hint of melancholy. 'There are over one hundred songbirds caged in my grounds, and I am told that every one of them is silent. I hope, Professor Wills, that they are not the subjects of your experiments?'

I could feel my face flush even more crimson than my interrogator's. 'I can assure you . . .'

So he knows, he knows. Does everyone in this great household know?

'We release them Saturday. Jot that down, Joubert!' snapped the Colossus to the nearest secretary. 'I shall invite a hundred guests. The Kaffirs can play their minstrel music on the lawns and every child shall have ice-cream. Then the Professor here will open the aviary doors and – voosh!' – hands flapped from wrists in imitation of a bird in flight – 'my forests will fill with a halleluiah of birdsong!'

I felt faint. There had been no mention of this in the telegrams. I cannot abide celebration of any kind, and this one would assuredly be celebrating failure.

'What time will that be, sir?' The secretary's pen was poised.

'Make it midday, Joubert,' replied his master. 'And have fifty bottles of Veuve Clicquot up from the cellar, will you?' He pulled his fob-watch from his waistcoat pocket and frowned. 'And tell our High Commissioner I'm ready for him now.'

Draining his coffee mug in one ill-concealed gulp he began

to rise from his chair. The acolytes rushed to stand by, without actually assisting him, and as he floundered upwards he turned to me and smiled briefly. It was a smile to penetrate my bones and warm my blood: in a moment of brilliance I felt my flesh grow young.

'Welcome to my home, Professor,' said he. 'You are an honoured guest.' His eyes were suddenly azure. Their brightness seemed to illuminate the gloom, even after he had swept out of the dining-room to the clanging of two Javanese gongs which stood on the bureau nearest the door, responding with their fierce metal vibrations to draughts caused by passers-by.

The gongs kept up their ominous rumble for some time after the Colossus' exit. I dabbed my lips cautiously with my unstarched table napkin and felt for the handle of my tea cup. The massive grandfather clock, with its cut-out galleon tossing on mechanical waves, reminded me it was time to visit the birds. The manservant was collecting used crockery in thoughtful silence. I decided to risk a conversation to deflect the panic I could feel rising from the pit of my stomach.

'Were you a soldier once, Huxley?' (The extreme erectness of the spine can also denote a long spell in prison, I have been told – though I can't say Oscar's posture improved much after his incarceration.)

The man smiled modestly. 'You can tell, sir?'

'My brother's in the army, you see. One brother in the Army, one in the Church, and then there's me – in the University.' The man looked impatient, so I returned to the topic of his former career. 'And what made you leave? I suspect you made a fine soldier.' (I do not intend to sound patronising, but know no other way to talk.)

Huxley, whose accent sounded South London, overlaid a little with the rasping Boer intonations, pulled himself up even straighter. 'The master picked me out, sir,' he said with pride. 'He's a man who makes his mind up quick. Saw me one night at the Wynberg barracks when he came drinking with his friend. Took a fancy to me there and then. Next thing I know I'm his butler – of sorts.'

'He's treated you well.' (I was careful to state rather than to question.)

'Couldn't find a finer employer, sir. He respects the fact that I was once a sergeant major.' He hovered a moment, then brought himself to utter: 'Sir, could I ask you something?'

'Depends what it is, Huxley.' (This is the way I reply to my scout's respectful questions.)

'Sir, I've been thinking. It's May, right?'

'Yes, Huxley.'

'May's spring back home, but it ain't spring here, sir. In fact, it's getting on for winter in these parts. It's like that, in the Southern hemisphere,' the innocent explained.

'I know that, Huxley,' I said patiently.

'So then, how's them birds going to lay their eggs, sir, what with them being all muddled up, like?'

How indeed? 'Well, we might have to wait till your spring arrives, Huxley,' I replied, less patiently. 'We'll just have to wait and see.'

I could feel another question brewing, and pursed my lips in preparation.

'It's a pity about them nightingales, isn't it, sir?'

I flinched. 'How do you mean, Huxley?' I enquired in my gravest voice, laced with the slightest hint of warning, which I expect was entirely lost on this simple man.

'They ain't lookers, are they, sir? I mean, I was expecting a beautiful bird, not a little brown thing, you wouldn't look at it twice!' (I will not attempt to reproduce the glottal stops that drilled holes through Huxley's speech.) 'And to think she sings more lovely than any other bird in the world!'

'"She", Huxley? Have you been reading those silly tales by Mr Wilde?' (I will never forgive Oscar for the ornithological misinformation he has disseminated in his children's stories.)

The man was thrown into confusion, so I said more gently: 'It is the male of the species who sings, Huxley, not the female. He sings to establish his territory. Or to advertise that he wants a female partner to provide him with offspring.'

'You're having me on, sir!' exclaimed Huxley, rapidly gathering the remains of my breakfast. 'I always thought they sang because they enjoyed singing, like, sir.'

'I expect they do, Huxley,' I said, taking pity on him. 'And you may be interested to know that the subject of my research in Oxford has been exactly what you have just queried, Huxley – whether birds ever sing just for the fun of it or not!'

But the brisk manner in which Huxley gathered together the marmalades (each made from different species of orange that our master had imported from California, according to the ladies) suggested to me not only that his interest in birds was exhausted but that he had also dismissed me as a person of dubious education.

In any case, someone was running into the dining-room. A secretary. A handsome young chap whose golden moustache perfectly outlined the edge of red lip above ivory teeth. He waved an opened telegram at me, and collided with Huxley. The priceless china cup in my hands flew into the air (my startle-reaction has always been extreme), and just before it would have shattered into pieces upon the uncarpeted floorboards the athletic secretary extended his body sideways and caught it with a deft hand. Huxley fell to his knees, gathering fallen cutlery and swearing with some violence.

'Oh, I am so sorry, Mr Huxley!' cried the secretary. 'That's the second time this week!' He turned to me and grinned. 'A message for you, sir.' His pale blue irises, the colour of the plumbago which riots in all the hedges here, beamed goodwill.

I frowned at the proffered telegram and made no attempt to accept it. The understanding with my physician had been that there were to be no communications of any kind with Oxford: I was not, in any way, to be reminded of the disastrous sequence of events that had preceded my departure.

As if reading my thoughts, the young secretary smiled reassuringly.

'He uses them as scrap paper. The message is on the back, sir!'

My hand shook as I accepted the telegram. I raised my reading glasses to study the well-nigh illegible scribble: *Sorry I won't be dining at home tonight must speak to you, please come to my room 9 a.m. tomorrow.*' No signature was necessary.

By the time I had read these words, lifted my head, and replaced my glasses, the messenger had vanished, though I could hear his footsteps pounding, diminuendo, down the corridor. A pair of female footsteps pattered after him, probably the young girl's. Huxley, too, had disappeared. I turned over the telegram to read its original message.

ARRIVING MORNING TRAIN – STOP – JAMESON – STOP

The date was today's.

I could not prevent a reluctant frisson of excitement from running up my spine. This could only be the Dr Jameson whose image, cast in Staffordshire clay, rode doggedly across a thousand British mantelpieces; the Jameson who, at his trial, argued that he had illegally entered the Boer Republic with his five hundred troopers, not to raid, but to *aid* helpless British women and children while their husbands rose up against the wicked Boers. Unfortunately, the uprising didn't materialise and Dr Jim was obliged to hoist, not the Union Jack, but a Hottentot servant's white apron on a wagon whip . . . The cunning old Boer president, rather than create a martyr through public execution, shipped the failed raider (previously known and loved as the swashbuckling family doctor of Kimberley) back to his mother country, to appear before a special jury at a trial at bar.

My interest in these imperial intrigues, though distant, had been triggered by the fact that this trial followed hard on the heels of Oscar's; in addition, Sir Edward Carson, the counsel who had precipitated my friend's downfall and humiliation, now presented Leander Starr Jameson to the public as the chivalrous knight who had redeemed the manhood of Britain by daring all. While Oscar, for love of boys, was sent to work the treadmill in Reading Gaol for two years, Jameson, for leading a military expedition against a friendly state, spent a few months in Holloway, without hard labour. His bungled Raid was celebrated in every London music-hall. The very Poet Laureate had composed the words to the song that now began to beat, uninvited, in my head:

> *'There are girls in the gold-reef city,*
> *There are mothers and children too!*
> *And they cry, 'Hurry up! for pity!'*
> *So what can a brave man do?*
> *If even we win, they'll blame us:*
> *If we fail, they will howl and hiss.*
> *But there's many a man lives famous*
> *For daring a wrong like this!'*

Needless to say, money, or, more precisely, *gold* was behind the whole story. Had Jameson's madcap dash succeeded, the wealthiest goldfields in the world would have become the property of Great Britain. This not irrelevant fact wasn't even mentioned at the Committee of Inquiry held at Westminster a year or so later when the Colossus was called over to be publicly interrogated about his role in the Raid. There was of course no question but that the Raid had been his master-plan to grab ultimate wealth and a further chunk of Africa for the Crown – he'd resigned his Premiership of the Cape the day after it happened – but all that emerged from that farcical *Lying in State at Westminster* (as the wits would have it) was a dense fog of ambiguities, nods, winks, misunderstandings, evasions, half-truths and partial replies, out of which miasma shambled the bloated figure of my host, a not unheroic villain in the unlikely role of sacrificial lamb.

It was generally known that a number of telegrams had gone missing – telegrams, it was whispered, implicating our Secretary of State for the Colonies – up to the neck! Could it be possible that Joe Chamberlain, the self-made man from Birmingham with a home-grown orchid in his buttonhole and a monocle in his steely eye, had really *backed* the very Raid he had so roundly *condemned*, both at the time of the crisis and throughout the Inquiry? Far be it from me to seek logical behaviour in political animals. One needs proof before one can accuse: the variables must be eliminated. But it is true that Uncle Joe's orchids continued to bloom in his buttonhole and the Colossus, in spite of his disgrace, was able to keep intact his Chartered Company, and to continue to build his Cape to Cairo railway.

In the world of Art and the Emotions, a different set of criteria operate. Three months after the Westminster Inquiry, Oscar was released from Reading Gaol. He slipped over to

France twenty-four hours later to escape the full fury of the nation's outrage.

'The public is wonderfully tolerant. It forgives everything except genius.' (Oscar)

OXFORD 1870

An unexpectedly long queue, a millipede queue, wound through all four corridors of the museum's upstairs galleries, past the collections of crustaceans, each with a name as long as itself penned across a label in minute copperplate; past the boxes of small fossils that Gosse claimed had been created by God simultaneously with the earth; past the six-legged insects and eight-legged spiders of a thousand different species, each pinned in order of size inside gigantic display cabinets. Alice doubted the value of giving names to insects if they wouldn't answer to them, but the newly-built University Museum was to be read as a book of Nature, and labels were thus everywhere, even upon the gallery columns, each made of a different British ornamental rock, and supporting cast-iron girders between whose ribs blossomed metal branches of leaf and flower. The remarkable synthesis between iron, stone and glass, to say nothing of the range of Natural History exhibits, made of the museum a miniature Gothic Crystal Palace in which it was impossible not to be educated, even while dawdling in a queue.

Mr James and I had arrived early, having caught the 6.05 that morning from Clapham, and changed at Reading. The lecture was due to begin at midday but Mr James wanted me to get a taste of the colleges, as it was generally considered

I would continue my zoological studies at Oxford. In fact, this introduction to the City of Spires was unnecessary, for even as I stepped off the train on to the Oxford railway platform and lifted my eyes to the cold sky-line apparently pierced by inverted icicles, I knew I had found my home. A few snowflakes materialised out of the grey air, as if in welcome.

This overwhelming sensation of arrival, of return to a place I had not yet visited, was interrupted by the practical necessity of removing Mr James from the compartment we had shared. As arranged, the wheelchair was rushed to the door of our carriage, and, with a great deal of heaving and general advice from passengers, we succeeded in transferring my guardian into his chariot (as he called it), the train's engine panting out clouds of impatient steam as we too panted under James's great weight. I was thankful we had dissuaded him from bringing his photographic equipment, which inconveniently included a range of pungent chemicals, a handcart and a portable dark-room.

Mr James knew the colleges well, having once supplied them with exotica from foreign lands. He directed me to Christ Church Meadows, Magdalen Deerpark and Trinity Gardens with an assurance that disregarded the considerable effort involved in pushing him to these far-flung spots at top speed, if we were to arrive at the museum in good time.

It turned out that we had dramatically misjudged the hour which would allow us entrance, for the queue already extended from the museum's front door a good hour before the lecture was due to begin. I stood with my guardian in the bitter February wind, underneath a window arched in the Venetian Gothic style, the stone flowers and leaves at its edges ending half-way down, on account of the peremptory dismissal of the wild Irish stonemasons. While the queue inched forward my guardian pointed out to me the stone monkeys which had displeased the authorities (still sensitive about their ancestors) and which had been converted into cats – until we at last passed through the outer archway into that extraordinary edifice which was the museum. Some members of the public removed their hats. And in the diaphanous light of the glazed courtyard, as we enjoyed the skeletons of giraffes and dinosaurs and examined the oak cabinets of shells and stuffed birds, it occurred to me that we had entered a futuristic glass cathedral in which the bodies of animals replaced the body of Christ and his martyrs. Indeed, the filigree nature of the cast-iron ribs supporting the transparent roof seemed to me but an extension of the gigantic animal ribcages on display, the visitor thus being able to enter the very body of Science and becoming as much an exhibit as the butterfly pinned inside its display box.

I knew only too well that Mr James had visited the museum with my late father shortly after it had opened its unfinished doors to the public, ten years earlier, in order to attend a debate on Mr Darwin's inflammatory Theory in the very lecture theatre we were hoping shortly to occupy. On that occasion the family gardener had accompanied the two men, in order to lift Mr James up the flight of stairs that led to the lecture theatre. Now it would be necessary to find a muscular gentleman who might help me transport Mr James in his wheelchair up the stairs, as I was of too slight a build to carry him over my shoulder, in the manner of the gardener, without a great deal of assistance.

We were by this stage at the bottom of the staircase, next to a glass box which, according to its label, contained '*The Head and Foot of the last living Dodo seen in Europe*', which had been of especial interest to my father. Beside the remains was displayed a portrait of the flightless bird whose physical ineptness had resulted in its extinction. The doleful eyes were the same as those that stared at Alice in Wonderland in the

Tenniel illustration, and attracted much interest from the members of the queue as they passed beneath it. It was rumoured that Charles Dodgson himself was present among the flurry of dons who scampered up and down the stairs in some agitation as it became increasingly apparent that the lecture theatre was not large enough to hold the ever growing audience.

A slender youth of my own age, but considerably taller, with a pronounced Adam's apple, lounged against a door behind us, pensively fingering the fret-cut foliage of its brass lock. While the rest of the queue chattered and quibbled in a state of high animation, this young man seemed at ease with his own company, and made no attempt to communicate with the members of the public who stood on either side of him, locked in argument over the genius of the newly-appointed art professor whose inaugural lecture was about to commence within the half-hour. He raised his head abruptly as I addressed him: I felt a slight shiver as his large pale eyes focused themselves with appalling intensity upon my face, as though he were emerging from the solidity of some dream, and wondered if I was yet part of it. However, as he heard out my stammering request, and followed my gaze to Mr James, smiling encouragement from his wheelchair, the expression on his features relaxed and he nodded agreement. No doubt attracted by the weather-beaten, manly face of my tutor, so at odds with the lower half of his ruined body, the now-alert youth even abandoned his more advanced position in the queue and came to join us in readiness for the moment when it would be necessary for us to lift the chair up the steps. At once Mr James engaged him in furious debate about John Ruskin's challenging political and social views. The youth, not much more than an overgrown boy, replied haltingly in a light, girlish voice which made me wonder if his vocal cords had yet undergone the rites of adolescence; I tested my own with a quick but reassuring growl, disguised as a contribution to the dialogue.

Mr James had been a disciple of John Ruskin ever since reading his slim volume on political economy some eight years earlier. I had thought Ruskin was an art critic who had rescued Turner from obscurity and abuse, but it seemed he also had strong views on social reform for ordinary working people enslaved by the factory hooter and living in miserable poverty; Ruskin's solution was free education, fixed wages, and pensions. Mr James announced his support of these views in a voice booming with the confidence that everyone would agree with him. To my surprise, the dreamy boy had an opinion on these topics and dared to differ with my tutor over the issue of free wages.

A man who stood behind us with his wife, their eyes bright with excitement, interrupted the argument: 'Ah, but they do say his brains is affected now – too many grand thoughts hammerin' away inside them, I'll be bound. I'm told he suffers from bouts of the madness quite regular these days.'

His wife giggled nervously: 'He must have his brains addled to fall in love with a ten-year-old girl, I'd say!' She lowered her eyelids and bit her smiling lip as proof of her own demureness. The couple, local innkeepers, had heard much about the celebrated Mr Ruskin's performances upon the lecture podium: they hoped he would 'rave like a loony', as, apparently, was his wont.

Mr James rolled his head towards our new acquaintance, his mouth twisted with satire. 'It seems we have all come to witness a different aspect of Mr Ruskin's personality!' he said cheerfully. 'May I ask what *you* hope to gain from this afternoon's lecture, young man?'

A slightly feverish light entered the youth's eyes as he exclaimed in his soprano voice: 'Sir, I seek my destiny!'

At this moment a pink and plump don in flowing academic

robes clapped his hands in the middle of the courtyard, directly under the grinning jaws of a dinosaur skeleton, and begged for our attention. So many people would be disappointed of admission into the lecture theatre, he announced, that it had been decided to move the venue to the much larger Sheldonian Theatre, just down Parks Road. Professor Ruskin himself had volunteered to lead the way, and would be found waiting on the lawns outside the main entrance.

In the excitement we lost our young man, whose services by now were in any case no longer necessary, and rushed with the crowd to join the lean, stooped conger eel of a professor. Mr James pointed out to me the slight figure of the Reverend Dodgson himself, with whom he had corresponded on the topic of wet collodion plates. Dodgson, smiling with only one side of his mouth and walking with a quick unevenness that almost amounted to a hobble, led the way with Ruskin. So keen were the two men to arrive at the grand new venue that they soon broke into a run, which induced something of a stampede in the flock that followed them.

More snowflakes fell, but did not settle.

CAPE TOWN 1899

On opening the side door of the Great Granary, one is immediately confronted by an acre of dead hydrangeas. I am told that in the summer this acreage becomes a lake of blue petals: the ladies call them 'Christmas Flowers' because December is the month when they are at the peak of their brilliance. Our host distributes a million blooms to the local hospital on Christmas Day, they tell me. And the poorest members of the community are allowed to come and pick one bunch each, also on Christmas Day.

Other than the shrivelled hydrangea heads, there is little to tell the English eye that we are well advanced into autumn. Certainly there is no sign of the reds and yellows that illuminate that glorious season in Europe. In any case, the only British trees immediately visible are oaks and pines. The oaks, about to drop their crisp leaves, have already pushed out the buds of spring. British leaves, I would venture to suggest, are more sensitive creatures altogether: more supple, more silken, more willing to tremble even when the air is utterly still. More green, too, and more of them. The equivalent Cape leaves are, by contrast, tough and leathery, as if they will soon evolve into perennials and remain forever gripped on to their rugged twigs.

My feet dragged a little as I approached the aviaries. I

have employed two small black boys to guard the cages with their lives, and have renamed them, their real names requiring a mastery of clicks in the throat that would choke my bronchial tubes. Chamberlain at once presented me with the corpses of two song thrushes and yet another nightingale, while Salisbury lay on his stomach in the sun, his preferred position for profound sleep. I cannot determine whether these birds are dying of a mysterious disease (they look perfectly healthy to my practised eye) or if the shock to their fragile systems has been too great. It is at moments like this that I am tempted to unlock the aviary doors and have done with the whole foolish business.

There is something different about the aviaries today, something which I do not know how to interpret. They are positioned on a patch of sand on the driveway, beneath the conifers. Until today, this sand was unremarkable, bearing only the footprints of myself and my two young helpers. Now there are lines and circles etched into it, with smooth stones from the forest dotted around upon the tracery. I know not if this design is some work of tribal art, or if it possesses more sinister, talismanic properties. It has certainly been devised by my helpers, who frown anxiously when my foot displaces a pebble or flattens a groove, but I feel it is wiser not to query its purpose. Nevertheless at the back of my mind I think of voodoo and black magic and wonder what other secret rituals might be performed on these well-groomed slopes.

Both boys speak a little English, being the sons of my upstairs manservant, who, I believe, once laboured in the diamond fields of my employer. (Orpheus has assured me that his son will never leave the cage door while in my employment, and brings food for the two children to eat on the site.) 'Wake up, Salisbury,' I command. 'It is time for your lesson.'

I am a prim man, about whose behaviour people have certain preconceptions. So, even when nothing in my face moves but my lips, I am used to the incredulous stares I receive when I first begin to whistle – rather as if I were uttering obscenities, or speaking with a sudden provincial accent. I long ago mastered the art of speaking to birds in their own language, and it is true that neither bird flageolet nor flute can mimic their song better than I. I am aware, too, that the production of these sounds involves somewhat extravagant contortions of the lips and tongue in order best to regulate the passage of air between my teeth. It has been known for my (accidental) audiences – men, women, children – to have difficulty in holding back their mirth as my whistling grows more elaborate, though I know my facial expression is impassive, as always.

However, neither Chamberlain nor Salisbury laughs at my whistling. Instead they produce a very creditable imitation of my performance, even though the shape and inflection and rhythm of the blackbird's song are clearly foreign to their ears. I am teaching them the art of duetting. Chamberlain must whistle the question, and after an appropriate lapse of time, Salisbury must whistle the reply. This is supposed to stimulate my birds into instant song but so far, as an exercise, it has proved quite useless. As we pipe and flute into the cages I am reminded of the lunatic George III in dressing-gown and night-cap, struggling to teach his caged bullfinches the popular songs of the day by means of a miniature mechanical organ. It is said that when they failed to respond he resorted to throttling them, snapping those little throats in each of which lay an obstinate syrinx. Pray God I am not tempted to do likewise.

After half an hour spent in futile singing practice, I examine the dishes of fresh snails, worms and insects which Salisbury and Chamberlain have gathered from the gardens for my birds' gastronomic delight, and then order them to clean out all four aviaries from top to bottom.

'Yes, *baas* Wills,' they chant, sullen but obedient.

There seems no way one can prevent these Negroes from using the term '*baas*'. Even if they know no other English word (and I have come to think of the word as English, though it has a Dutch flavour to it) their speech is studded with the brutish monosyllable. It seems to me that a blatant irony is distilled in this word when uttered by a Negro: sometimes I have overheard a distant mocking harmonic in the British 'sir', even when on the mild lips of my dear scout Saunders, but this '*baas*' slices through the air like an assegai: I find myself dodging.

Feeling somewhat stronger after this pretence of work, I elected to stroll along the woodland path which runs up a mountain gorge filled with the strangest assortment of flora, and into which the birds will be released in a matter of days. Champagne and minstrel music had disappeared into the nether regions of my conscious mind. Since my collapse I have trained myself not to think about matters over which I have no control, even if I am to be held responsible for their outcome. In among the oaks and pines standing side by side with banana and avocado trees it is possible to be diverted.

I opened the gate in the fence which runs around the perimeter of the garden, and began to walk upwards.

It is indeed a curious pathway that wends its way, I am told, to an old Dutch summerhouse, a mile or so along the mountain foothills. Just within the gate there is an arch of purple bougainvillaea, linking this southernmost tip of Africa with the brilliant flora of the Mediterranean. Then, a few yards further up grow a number of ancient trees, the likes of which I thought survived only under glass. But these cycads, no different in appearance, so the fossils tell us, from their ancestors of some hundred million years ago, thrust their palm-like branches across the path along with the oaks and pines and plumbago. Some are tall with heavily armoured trunks; others keep their trunks buried so that their crowns of compound leaves protrude from the ground like the heads of giant green feather-dusters. And in among this exotic flora scampers the familiar grey squirrel, introduced to this country only a few years ago by my indefatigable host. Already they have multiplied enough to make their presence felt wherever you go on this estate – whether on the open stretches of lawn where they quite fearlessly devour their acorns and run up to passers-by in the hope of a piece of bread, or in the forests which echo with the sounds of their harsh chatter.

The Colossus has installed magnificent teak benches at intervals about his garden and along this path for the pleasure of the public, and it was on one of these that I intended to rest after the particularly strenuous uphill gradient. In fact, one does not see many members of the public about as there is now some measure of security since the conflagration: I believe a hundred trustworthy citizens have been presented with keys to the gates of the estate, though it would be easy enough to enter the grounds from the upper mountain gates, which are not locked. (I have to confess that I am exceedingly grateful to the arsonists for ensuring a degree of privacy in these gardens which is much to my taste. I never could bear the push and shove of the Botanic Gardens in Oxford.)

The bench towards which I laboured was placed underneath tall Corsican pines, which by now had become the predominant tree on the mountain slope. (Strange to think that only ten years ago these slopes were covered by nothing but the aforementioned *fynbos*.) Although I do not much care for the appearance of this tree, I enjoy the warm, resinous aroma released by its needles, and remembering that pine fragrance is supposed to be good for the lungs, I inhaled deeply a few times, in an effort to control my breathing pattern. (One day some entrepreneur will find a way to capture and sell this smell so that people may create their own illusions of pine forests.) There can be few places on earth where Corsican pines grow side by side with banana and palm trees: a sudden grove of these specimens bulged out over the path I was following. It was possible to see my bench through the tangle of their great split leaves.

To my annoyance, the bench was occupied. The occupant evidently had very sharp ears, for a mere second after I had laid eyes on her, she rose to her feet and hurried up the mountain path. I had time only to register a cloud of dark hair round a small pale face which surmounted a shortish body, sombrely clad. A heavily laden hat seemed in danger of sliding off her head. Although her movements were quick, a certain heaviness, perhaps a weariness, told me that she was no longer in the prime of her youth. My reflexes had not been quite quick enough for me to catch her in the binoculars which I always hang round my neck while in the gardens in an attempt to look like a busy ornithologist. Assuming that she must be a citizen with a key, I dismissed the incident from my mind and hastened to the bench before anyone else should claim it.

It was indeed pleasant to be seated among clusters of blue plumbago and pink mountain lilies, listening to the rustle of assorted leaves, feeling the occasional shaft of sunlight warm my cheek as the foliage shifted in the morning air. In amongst the creaking pine tops, indigenous birds of prey squawked and howled but I did not allow them to disturb the growing mellowness which fresh air and exercise so often promote. The unpleasant sensation in my diaphragm had completely disappeared, and was replaced by something resembling pleasure. I have long reconciled myself to the fact that I feel happy only when alone, or in the company of birds. Even dear old Saunders back home, whose entire purpose in life is to attend to my creature comforts, has always caused me small spasms of irritation through his harmless personal habits, for example gulping, sucking his teeth, sniffing – indeed, even breathing.

My thoughts drifted randomly, lulling me to the point where the physical body with its aches and twinges seems almost to melt away, and the brain takes wing. (This surely is the purpose of the geometrically arranged Fellows' Garden enclosed within the corridors and quadrangles of my college, wherein all the petty anxieties of daily life arrange themselves in perfect perspective and open the door to inspiration.) From my vantage point I could see across the terraced lawns of the Great Granary; beyond the banks of moulting hydrangeas; across the sweep of driveway leading to the colonnaded entrance, surmounted by a bronze cast of the first disembarkation of Netherlandish gardeners dubiously surveying a group of nomadic Aboriginals, some two and a half centuries ago, I believe. In a flurry of dust a Cape cart drew up before the entrance; Orpheus ran out of the front door and down the short flight of steps to unload the suitcases of a small, balding man, who bounded out of the coach as if fired from a cannon, at the same time extending his arms towards someone who awaited, unseen, inside the doorway.

Though the new visitor had leapt up the steps at a speed not normally associated with men of his middle-age, I was able to catch a glimpse of his face with the aid of my convenient binoculars. His smooth features were at once familiar, having stared out at the British public from broadsheets and satirical journals at the time of his trial, and had resurfaced a year or so later when his friend, the Colossus, was publicly interrogated at Westminster.

> *'There's many a man lives famous*
> *For daring a wrong like this!'*

Just as I feared that this ditty was about to re-insinuate itself into my brain, out of the thickets a little further up the mountainside, without any warning, poured forth the unrivalled fluty piping, the *jug-jug-jug of Luscinia megarhynchos*, most musical and melancholy of birds.

Had a nightingale escaped from the aviaries? Acute pleasure at the sound of the warble was replaced within seconds by even more acute anxiety. Reminding myself of the necessity of nervous equilibrium, I rose to my toes and moved as silently as my age would permit in the direction of the tumbling song. The suddenness of the outburst was indeed strange, and it was the wrong time of day – still, no doubt the birds were disoriented, and one could not predict any aspect of their behaviour with certainty.

The song took me deep into the heart of the pine plantation, which now resembled the inky depths of the *Schwarzwald*, where not even a ray of sunshine can penetrate the dense needles. My binoculars would be of no use in this almost total darkness, and before long total silence had set in as well. I stood motionless for a full five minutes, straining to catch a waft of the nightingale once again. Nothing. Nothing except the sudden strident clatter of a triangle rising from the gardens below: it beat out a six-quaver pattern several times over, angrily, it seemed to me, as if announcing the end of an unnecessary performance. When it too had ceased sounding, I resolved to return to the safety of the sunlit garden, and berate Salisbury and Chamberlain.

But while I stood and listened in vain, I had become

aware of a dim path which opened up among the trees and beckoned. Along it I could begin to hear the startled movements of indefinable and invisible creatures further up the steep slope – perhaps the misplaced offspring of the imported fallow deer that wander in the fields above, or birds struggling out of the silence of their nests. At the same time something stirred in my own dark soul, perhaps an atavistic curiosity to know where the path led, and something more: a sudden desire to abandon myself to danger. Yet what lurked in those sunless woods was unlikely to be a leopard, or a lion, or a hyena, and as my feet placed themselves (without my permission) on the pathway, crunchy with pine needles, I felt more like Hansel without his Gretel than the intrepid explorer Livingstone.

The footpath, such as it was, evidently led to the upper regions of the stream which bubbled so peacefully in the Colossus' garden. Rocks and boulders heaved among pines; squirrels scuttled; a pinecone hurtled, with some malevolence, on to my shoulder. I wondered about snakes.

The path stopped abruptly at a mossy bank beside the stream. I gazed into its clear, dappled waters, feeling foolish, but nevertheless straining my ears. It was a quite delightful spot: Titania herself would not have looked out of place among the wild orchids and ferns peering between the rocks. The cool aroma of mountain waters, mingled with the scent of pine, at once cleansed away the impurities of mind and lung, causing me to inhale deeply, as instructed by my physician. But even as I hesitated in this pleasant place, the melodious trill of the nightingale floated up from lower down the ravine, not far from the gate which opens on to the path. I cursed aloud, and was about to start running down the path back to where I had started, when I noticed something bright among the tall ferns by the stream. A stray shaft of light had caught what appeared to be a humble glass jar: the nature of its lid suggested it must once have contained some kind of fruit preserve.

I hovered over my find indecisively; then turned on my heel and hurried down the mountainside.

OXFORD 1870

John Ruskin's ample gown fluttered against my cheek as he raced up the central aisle, his bowed head now crowned with a velvet college cap. He turned to confront his vast audience, an expression of timid pleasure and surprise on his face. He laid his notes on the table before him. Now he settled a pair of spectacles on his nose, opened the notes, rose up and down on his toes a few times, and cleared his throat.

Above our heads a number of fat *putti* rolled back ropes and awnings to reveal Geography, Arithmetic, Botany, Astronomy, Law et cetera driving British Scoffing Ignorance out of the South Door, through the organ case of the Sheldonian Theatre. Truth himself, a writhing golden cherub, occupied the central panel, in which he descended from on high on a vast bank of sunlit clouds. Considering that the topic of this inaugural lecture was 'British Landscape', a subject that would normally attract perhaps twenty art students, the audience of men and women, maidens and matrons, artists and scientists, covered as wide a range of representatives as that depicted on the ceiling. Now they fell into a motionless silence, as if already mesmerised by the tall, stooping figure before he had even begun to speak.

But if they were expecting the wild words of a prophet from the wilderness – such was his reputation – they were to be disappointed. Ruskin began speaking quietly, his eyes following the written words on the paper before him with an intensity that suggested he had already forgotten about the thousand people who had travelled in bad weather from all over England to hear him lecture. His voice had a penetrating, other-worldly timbre, as if conceived and cultivated in an atmosphere where the vocal cords were the vessels of higher thought only, and had never been used for the humbler modes of communication essential to the survival of the common man. A long sentence was unfolding itself, loop upon measured loop, polite, respectful, an old-fashioned roll of the 'r's shimmering in the perfect harmony of his thoughts:

'The duty which is today laid on me, of introducing, among the elements of education appointed in this great University, one not only new, but such as to involve in its possible results some modification of the rest, is, as you well feel, so grave, that no man could undertake it without laying himself open to the imputation of a kind of insolence, and no man could undertake it rightly, without being in danger of having his hands shortened by dread of his task, and mistrust of himself.'

While he spoke, his downcast face had been furrowed with sadness, but now he lifted his head and presented his audience with a radiant smile, artless in its sincerity, which at once quenched the sorrow in his piercing blue eyes. He returned to his notes; great clouds of words billowed forth as he gently explained the relationship between art and labour, and that it was our moral duty to ensure that beauty and labour went hand in hand. A thousand pairs of eyes were fixed on him with hopeful rapture, whether as an aid to understanding his convoluted speech or merely with a view to judging his performance, I could not say. I discovered that I myself was scrutinising every aspect of the great man's appearance and memorising details of his clothing and mannerisms as if he were some rare species of bird that might flit away and be seen no more. Beneath his academic gown he wore a double-breasted waistcoat and a blue frock-coat, with a tall Gladstonian collar and blue tie which seemed to intensify the blueness of his eyes. His entire outfit made no concession whatever to fashion, but so lean and graceful was his figure that there was almost the air of the unconscious dandy about him. His hands were peculiarly delicate, with tapering fingers which ever opened and closed in nervous gesticulation, as if preparing for some larger movement, perhaps flight. He spoke about the need for art to follow nature. But it was the exquisite modulations of his voice, punctuated with many artificial pauses and cadences, that seemed to me more compelling than the torrent of words that poured forth so musically, yet so relentlessly. Now and then his eye would meet that of the rosy don seated next to me, who nodded discreet encouragement. Ruskin was behaving himself.

The first rule of art is that art is work; conversely, work must become art again. 'Life without industry is guilt, and industry without art is brutality,' declaimed he, unaware of a growing restlessness among his listeners. They were not interested in the morality of art: they were waiting for Ruskin to boil over. Instead he told them that the art of any country was an indication of that country's social, political and ethical life. And the most moral thing you could do was leave Nature intact. 'You cannot have a landscape by Turner without a country for him to paint; you cannot have a portrait by Titian without a man to be portrayed. I need not prove that for you, I suppose, in these short terms; but in the outcome I can get no soul to believe that the beginning of art is in getting our country clean, and our people beautiful!'

Mr James nudged me. '*Railways!*' he whispered in excitement.

At that moment a strange afflatus began to flash in the Professor's blue eyes, and his spirit appeared rapt in a sudden ecstasy. Abandoning his notes, he strode back and forth behind his table, pouring forth a positive rhapsody of exalted thought in rhythmic phrases which piled upon each other so thick and fast that he seemed to have achieved the impossible: a kind of vocal polyphony, almost fugal in effect, where ideas overlap and blend with each other, producing ever richer resonances, ever more complex textures, as in some mighty chorale. Now his hands flew upwards and, his arms becoming hopelessly involved in folds of black cloth, his gown was flung on to the majestic chair as he began to chant:

'The England who is to be mistress of half the earth, cannot remain herself a heap of cinders, trampled by contending and miserable crowds; she must yet again become the England she once was and, in all beautiful ways, more: so happy, so secluded, and so pure, that in her sky – polluted by no unholy clouds – she may be able to spell rightly of every star that heaven doth show.'

Next to me, the plump don stirred uneasily and looked about him. Further down the academic row I could see Dodgson's mild, watchful face, his lips puckering in controlled astonishment at the performance that held the audience spellbound. I most earnestly hoped that Mr James would not confront him about wet-plate collodion afterwards.

Ruskin had stopped pacing. His gaze swung solemnly round the amphitheatre. His voice dropped to a kind of moan, all the more powerful for its monotonous intensity.

'And this is what she must either do, or perish: she must found colonies as fast and as far as she is able, formed of her most energetic and worthiest men; seizing every piece of waste ground she can set her foot on, and there teaching these her colonists that their chief virtue is to be fidelity to their country, and that their first aim is to be to advance the power of England by land and sea.'

He paused for a full minute. The audience held its breath. Then he narrowed his eyes and repeated thoughtfully: 'Her most energetic and worthiest men.' New thoughts were passing through his mind, thoughts that were not penned in the pages before him.

He flung his arms up into the air once more. 'And how do the energetic young men of this university expend their energy? They fruitlessly slash the river waters' – and here his arms descended to pull at imaginary oars, to the delight of his audience – 'or they kick a ball and run after it!' His voice trembled with incredulity. Now he leaned across the table, his eyes imploring us to understand. 'Can they not see that muscular effort can be directed towards useful and ennobling ends?' His melancholy face gave an abrupt spasm of disgust. 'Such as pulling down monstrous railway embankments and building lovely human pathways in their place, rightly adorning them with wildflowers and shrubs – this is what I shall teach my students!' He had abandoned his desk again. 'For a nation is only worthy of the soil and the scenes that it has inherited when by all its acts and arts it is making them more lovely for its children!'

The Professor at my side was shaking his head and groaning, but Mr James, on the other side, was ecstatic. He slapped his knee in delight at this spontaneous outburst and, to my acute embarrassment, even called out: 'Hear, hear!'

Ruskin ran back to his desk. I became aware that the pale sunlight that had filtered through the long windows was now supplanted by the gloom of approaching dusk, but so completely was he absorbed in his message to us that he, like his audience, was quite unconscious of the flight of time. Yet there was something final in his cadences as he leaned across his desk and seemed to address each one of us personally.

'Will you, youths of England, make your country again a royal throne of kings; a sceptred isle, for all the world a source of light, a centre of peace; mistress of Learning and of the Arts; faithful guardian of great memories in the midst of irreverent and ephemeral visions? You will think that an impossible ideal. Be it so; refuse to accept it if you will; but see that you form your own in its stead. All that I ask of you is to have a fixed purpose of some kind for your country and yourselves: it is the fatalest form of error in English youths to hide their hardihood till it fades for lack of sunshine, and to act in disdain of purpose, till all purpose is vain.'

Up until this point I had felt, with all the cynicism of my youth, that I had merely been witnessing a great performance by a renowned professor, which had no possible connection with my own life. But such was the intensity of his words, and the precision with which they had been chosen, that I felt myself straighten, as if his message was aimed at me alone. My eyes shifted to see if others were thus affected.

The entire audience was transfixed. Row after row of faces, young and old, male and female, gazed in silence at the sweet-faced man whose transparent sincerity and intensity of conviction could leave no one unmoved. A young woman who sat in the front row, her hand clasped in that of her lover, gave a low moan and burst into sobs.

And then I saw the tall young man we had met at the museum. He was leaning forward in the upper circle of the theatre, his mass of hair standing on end, as if his fingers had pushed through it in unconscious fervour; his blue eyes were aflame; his mouth had dropped open. If the cherub of

Truth had dropped down from the ceiling, the expression on this youth's face could not have been more astounded, more ecstatic, as if his fate had just been revealed to him, and the rest of his life accounted for.

CAPE TOWN 1899

Chamberlain and Salisbury were on their hands and knees drawing lines in the sand as I approached the aviaries. I was thus in a position to kick at least one backside and shout angrily about escaped nightingales, but one look at the cages told me that the bird who had sung on the mountain had not come from my collection. The two boys expressed indignant innocence, at the same time casting worried glances at the damage my feet were wreaking upon their dusty patterns. Finally I stamped back into the house in a state of some confusion: why had the Colossus hired me to bring nightingales to the colony when a nightingale already sang in his forests, and in the autumn at that?

To distract myself from the anomaly of this state of affairs, I took refuge in a pastime that has been a source of pleasure to me since childhood. Originally I had had no intention of bringing my cameras with me to Africa, even though I realised that there would be much of interest to photograph in the Colony. However, at the last moment before my departure from Oxford, I gave in to the urging of my physician, who assured me that a resumption of my only leisure activity would have a soothing effect upon my shattered nervous system. On arriving at the Cape I discovered that Saunders had packed not only all my photographic equipment, but most of my photograph albums as well. Though displeased about this at first, I gained some solace by unloading the cameras and albums into a lavish dark-room a few doors along my bedroom corridor. Originally intended for the use of the Colossus himself, this haven of darkness remained at the disposal of guests once his interest in photography had waned. In fact, it had become a source of pleasure for me to hide away in this little distraction-free room and turn the pages of those albums which so vividly preserved the images of friends and familiar landscapes.

On the other hand, till this moment, I had had little desire to photograph anything in my new environment, in spite of the majesty of the mountain which formed a perpetual backdrop to my every move. (Actually, it is the *back* of Table Mountain which overshadows our estate. When my ship steamed into the harbour of the fairest Cape, I was struck, as were all the passengers, by the extraordinary formation of this rectangular mountain which towers over the rather scrappy little city of Cape Town, and resolved to unpack my camera as soon as I had arrived at the Colossus' home. But this sudden surge of energy soon fizzled out, to be replaced by the usual inertia, and the ruggedness of the nether side of the mountain did not hold the same mathematical charm for me.)

There is comparatively little of ornithological interest in this area. I am already irritated by the constant calls of the doves and pigeons, the only birds I know who can sing in strict 3/4 time and strut about the lawns in stumpy sarabands. The raptors keep to the upper slopes of the mountain. Probably the most unusual species is the male Cape sugar bird, *Promerops cafer*, a creature composed almost entirely of beak and tail. I had watched the behaviour of this bird (it has no song: it clacks and hisses merely) in the *fynbos* and decided to photograph it in its natural habitat when I felt inclined to do so. So it was that I found myself in the upper reaches of the Colossus' garden, hiding in a structure made of sacking, my head under a black cloth, my new, untried telephotographic lens trained upon this curious creature.

The sugar bird's feeding behaviour is interconnected with his mating behaviour: he perches on the furry heads of the *fynbos* and screeches for a mate, then leaps into the air and flicks his streaming tail (twice or even thrice the length of his body) over his back. After thus advertising his territory he plunges his long curved beak into the cup-shaped sugar bush and extracts its nectar. He flutters off to the next bush covered in pollen, a perfect example of co-adaptation in nature. I was able to photograph several examples of each one of these stages, though doubted whether I had been able to capture the bird in flight.

Many bird-watchers may find this display of interest, but I find myself comparing it unfavourably with that of the South American humming-bird, a creature which holds some fascination for me even though, like the sugar bird, it squeaks and twitters in a very irritating fashion. However, to see this minute little fellow hovering before the flower of his choice, his tiny wings a brilliant blur reminiscent of a delicate, extended piano trill, is to wonder at the extent to which the species is prepared to modify. Well do I remember that extraordinary release of humming-birds into the greenhouses of the Botanic Gardens when the members of the Oxford Zoological Society were allowed to observe at first hand such varieties as Loddiges' racket-tail, slapping its spherical feathers together during its courtship flight, a more exotic performance altogether than the sugar bird's. A well-known mathematician in our midst calculated that the tiny creature's wings beat seventy-eight times a minute. *Mirabile dictu!*

After photographing these antics for precisely one hour, I noticed what I at first thought to be a very large sea bird swaying among the shrivelled hydrangea heads. Sometimes it is possible for the brain to be entirely mistaken in its perception of objects viewed through the glass plate of the camera: like the retina of the eye, the plate receives its image upside down, and although it is remarkable that the brain can instantly invert this image, visual errors are easily made. I removed my head from the cloth and on closer inspection with the aid of the pair of binoculars which accompanied me everywhere, I was obliged to conclude that the black and white shape was, in fact, a well-worn white Panama hat encircled by a black band. Further inspection revealed that a couple of women and two very young children were moving about on the colonnaded verandah or stoep which stretches along the back of the house (and which reminds me, perversely, of a giant centipede waiting to scuttle off on its multitude of whitewashed stucco legs). One child was a mere baby, the other a smocked creature scarcely yet steady on her feet. A nanny figure clapped hands with the child while the mother bounced her baby on her knee. I was about to pack up my equipment, already planning to enter the Great Granary by way of the front verandah, and thereby avoid an exchange of pleasantries with women and children, when I heard a voice murmuring in the hydrangeas. An adult male voice. An English voice. A private, lowered voice, speaking intimacies.

Floating out of the hydrangeas from under the Panama hat came a stream of love-words. Not the language of inflamed passion or romance, but words suffused with such tenderness that, though the subject matter was trite, I felt myself to be eavesdropping on the beatings of a human heart.

'. . . who was full of 'satiable curtiosity, and that means he asked ever so many questions. *And* he lived in Africa, and he filled all Africa with his 'satiable curtiosities. He asked his tall aunt, the Ostrich, why her tail-feathers grew just so, and his tall aunt the Ostrich spanked him with her hard, hard claw. He asked his tall uncle, the Giraffe, what made his skin spotty, and his tall uncle, the Giraffe, spanked him with his hard, hard hoof. And *still* he was full of 'satiable curtiosity! Just like you, O Best Beloved!'

'Mother has an ostrich fevver,' piped a juvenile voice, of the age when it is impossible to distinguish gender.

'O is for Ostrich and Mother's new bonnet Has lots of fine fevvers of Ostrich upon it,' came the grave reply.

'Go on about the effelen's child,' commanded the genderless voice.

Needless to say I disapprove of the anthropomorphism of animals, yet I have to admit, unwillingly, that nowadays this literary technique seems an essential ingredient of children's stories *q.v.* Dodgson's March Hare and White Rabbit; Oscar's Nightingale and Swallow. Why cannot these animals, miraculously endowed with human speech and clothing, at least exhibit species-specific behaviour and thus educate as well as entertain their young audiences? In this story it seemed that everyone was spanking the elephant's child because he kept asking what the crocodile had for dinner (though why this should remotely interest an elephant is beyond me, particularly as the African elephant is the only form of wildlife immune to that ghastly predator's jaws). A bird with a nonsense name advised him: 'Go to the banks of the great grey-green, greasy Limpopo River, all set about with fever trees, and find out.' These words were delivered as a kind of mournful howl, and the Panama hat rotated wildly among the hydrangeas.

The woman on the verandah rang a little bell. 'Tea's ready!' she called as Huxley's stiff military form retreated. I could hear hints of New World intonation coiled in her voice.

Out of the blue hydrangea sea shot the Panama hat, beneath which dimpled a little red-faced man with a massive walrus moustache and beetling eyebrows. His features were almost as familiar to me as those of the Colossus, through cartoons and lithographs attesting to the success of his Indian stories. His eyes glittered behind thick wire-framed spectacles. Kipling was jubilant.

'Dens!' he shouted to the group on the verandah. 'Every child should have one! And you, O best beloved' – he bent to scoop a small smocked girl out of the shrubs – 'will have a den of your werry own when we come to live here once upon a time. Until then – your steed awaits you, madam!' And he fell on all fours, regardless of the creaminess of his flannels, and bore the child on his back across the lawn to the waiting teapot and hot scones.

Rendered invisible by shrieks of pleasure or horror, I packed my equipment and fled to the silence of the front verandah.

The hand of Northern Europe has twisted this house into a misalliance of shapes and styles. Whitewashed Dutch gables, tapering Palladian columns and Jacobean barley-sugar chimneys reflect the brilliance of African sunshine and dazzle the eyes, so that on entering the vestibule one is quite unable to see the carefully constructed Dutch interior until one's vision has adapted to the sudden darkness. Was this a deliberate ploy by the architect, I wonder, to plunge the visitor into an environment such as one might have witnessed in Holland three hundred years ago, but which manifests itself only as the baffled eye adjusts? The ghosts of tall-hatted men with flowing locks and baskets of green vegetables grown in the Hottentots' grazing land melt away once the after-image of bright light has disappeared. I feel there is something deliberate about everything in this house, even its illusions, arranged by male hands to overwhelm rather than delight.

Unaided by vision, I was nevertheless able to creep into

the silence of the famous library which has afforded me much solace over the past few days. Not only is there a remarkable range of histories, ancient maps, biographies and translations of every kind (though very little in the way of *belles lettres*, other than all of Kipling's and Ruskin's works), many other items of historic interest are openly displayed on shelves and cabinets for anyone to handle. Prominent among them is a large, somewhat menacing soapstone bird, referred to as the 'Phoenician Hawk', and acquired from the mysterious ruins of Zimbabwe in Central Africa, along with a selection of objects associated with phallic worship, in which my host has an evident interest. However, it is the bird which has caught the architect's fancy and has been reproduced in wood at regular points of the banisters (where it causes considerable inconvenience to the trailing hand) and in various gloomy corners where its accusing glare converts visitors into trespassers.

Today a new book, recently published, had entered the library and was ostentatiously opened upon a fifteenth-century Buhl bureau, to display its frontispiece image: a truly shocking photograph of a number of dead Negroes dangling from ropes in a foreign-looking tree, while a larger number of white men pose for the picture beneath it, smoking, and at ease, as if unaware of the corpses in the boughs above them.

Curiously enough, I was familiar with this book, *Trooper Peter Halket of Mashonaland*: written by a woman, a Miss Schreiner, it was certainly not the sort of text to arouse my interest in normal circumstances. In her story – more of an allegory than a novel, with much ranting in the Biblical style – she denounces my host by name, calling him amongst other things 'death on niggers' and accusing him of murdering and enslaving the Matabele people so that he could possess their land and give it his own name. In fact, the whole purpose of the book seems to be to expose the sins of the Colossus to the world: quite what Miss Schreiner hopes to gain by her accusations I cannot imagine, other than land herself in a great deal of legal trouble, for surely he will sue. Nevertheless, it is always pleasant to read shameful things about the rich and famous, whether they are true or not, and although I had entered the library to gaze at quite different texts, I found myself stretching out my hand to open the book in order to find the libellous paragraph – when a sonorous greeting floated up from an armchair in the shadows.

'Hello, Wills.'

My brain worked furiously to resurrect the owner of this familiar voice, without having to turn to face him and expose my disadvantage.

'Well I never!' it continued. 'How long has it been – quarter of a century?'

Twenty-five years ago, as a young Natural History student at Oxford University, I found myself in the laboratory of the Botany department, confronted by a number of cassava plants newly arrived from Mexico. My task was to cut open and examine a slice of the bulbous cassava root under the microscope, with a view to examining the elements within it which are converted by the natives into tapioca, flour, starch and alcoholic beverages. (I was then of the opinion that the Spanish invaders would have done better to introduce *this* tuber to the European public, rather than the glutinous potato without which no British meal is now complete.) I suppose there must have been about half a dozen of these stemless plants, part of a consignment of exotic creepers, ferns and miniature palm trees destined for the drawing rooms of the middle classes, together with several species of rare parrot, fated for the cramped laboratories of the Ornithology department.

The cassava project was hardly challenging: I was aware that the investigation of tropical plant behaviour was standard fare for undergraduates in their first year. With a singular lack of enthusiasm (for Botany was to me the least interesting of the natural sciences) I selected a particularly well-developed plant, emptied it out of its pot, and inserted my laboratory knife into its tangled tuber.

The blade had no sooner penetrated the outer skin than what appeared to be a jet of dark liquid sprayed out from the base of the plant, and attached itself in a hundred gleaming globules to my white laboratory coat. I was about to wipe away the mess with a nearby cloth when I noticed that the globules had sprouted tiny appendages, which were beginning to move in a rather lively fashion. Fortunately, my reflexes have always been quick, and I was able to brush off these surprisingly tenacious creatures (now clearly members of the animal rather than the vegetable kingdom) into an energetic pile in the middle of my table. A large glass dome, always on hand for trapping animal life that might escape from foreign foliage, enabled me to observe the burgeoning insects with proper scientific objectivity. Fellow students gathered round.

Within half an hour it became certain that these were no insects, as no fewer than eight segmented legs arched into angular struts, minuscule flying buttresses to lift the two central body parts into the air. Less obvious than the spiders' legs were the diminutive jaws and pedipalps that now emerged below the eye area of the head region; at the same time, all appendages were slowly becoming covered in a brilliant orange and brown fur which gave them the illusory appearance of warm-blooded vertebrates – like eight-legged, venomously-fanged tortoiseshell kittens, perhaps. The undergraduates began to guess the precise identity of these exotic arrivals; we were able to recognise the order Araneida and invertebrate arthropod class Arachnida, but the suborder, class and species were as yet unknown to us.

As luck would have it, our tutor happened to have spent two years in the Amazon basin collecting varieties of tropical fungus, and, on being brought over to the seething glass dome, was able to identify its contents as belonging to the family Theraphosidae, and known to the world as the species *Tarantula celerrima*, so named on account of the extraordinary speed with which the spiderlings increase in size.

A hush fell over the undergraduates as Mr Finnegan Jones made this announcement. We could not fail to remember that the left half of his face was partially paralysed as a result of the bite of a venomous Amazonian spider, and one or two of us stepped backwards. But Mr Finnegan Jones was unperturbed.

'They make fine pets, y'know. A tarantula will grow to the size of an adult hand – with spread fingers – and a female can live for up to thirty years. Any takers?'

'But, sir,' interjected the younger son of the Earl of Lancaster (now a leading authority on the reproductive system of seven-toed newts), 'how true are the reports that the bite of the tarantula can cause a man to spin into a wild dance from which he might never recover?'

'If ye'll believe that ye'll believe anything!' retorted Mr Jones, smiling with the unparalysed side of his face. 'Those rumours come from Southern Italy, where I believe the male population is much given to wild dancing, whether bitten by tarantulas or not.'

I do not know what made me speak just then. Perhaps it was the sight of the anaesthetic that a laboratory assistant produced in order to curtail the careers of these multi-segmented creatures who by now had almost filled the glass dome with their fat, furry bodies; perhaps it was the sudden yearning to tame a wild animal and keep it in a box.

'In the interests of science,' I said, 'I should be interested in rearing a tarantula.'

Finnegan Jones could not disguise the revulsion in his eyes (a response not stirred by the spiders) as he listened to me, but with deft, gloved fingers he proceeded to disentangle the most conveniently-placed tarantula from the turmoil of its siblings, who were then quietly executed by the waiting assistant.

'It's a male,' said he, placing the brown and orange spider in a box reserved for soil samples. 'You can see the enlarged tips of the pedipalps form copulatory organs. You'll find he'll attempt to build a sperm web when he's ready to mate, but presumably you do not plan to breed?' And my tutor, a father of six, gave me a cold, sideways glance. 'He'll want feeding, though. Mice, birds, insects. But bread and milk and porridge will suit him just as well.'

Of a sudden, I knew that this tarantula could be my friend. I began at once to search for an appropriate name for him. I was to find it soon after meeting Oscar.

'Hello, Alfred.'

At Oxford Alfred Milner had burdened his youthful upper lip with moustaches inspired by Bismarck. Born, and to some extent brought up, in Germany, he exuded the disdainful air of a Prussian prince, and won every academic prize on offer while an undergraduate at Balliol. He and Oscar became close friends during this period: Oscar assured me there was an exotic side to Alfred that certainly was not apparent to me. He was one of those intensely ambitious men whose lack of imagination combined with sabre-sharp powers of logic creates about them an intellectual *cordon sanitaire*, discouraging to humbler mortals. Last heard of he was streamlining the national budget: what on earth was he doing in this curious library, six thousand miles away from the Athenaeum?

'Yes, I thought it must be the same Wills. Still carrying your cameras round with you, I see. When did we last meet? You were photographing the Hinksey Road, weren't you?' A slight movement on the edges of his heavy moustaches, now streaked with grey, suggested he might be smiling.

It was these very moustaches which had inspired the name for my unexpected pet of twenty-five years ago. Tarantula fangs are hairy; they fall from the head like a pair of hirsute brackets, suggesting dignity. However, it was not only large moustaches that the two Alfreds had in common.

'We were very young then.' To my disgust, I spoke in a meek whisper.

'And idealistic. The only time I've ever known Oscar to indulge in manual labour. Scant preparation for the hard labour that awaited him in prison, poor chap. Do you hear from him?' Milner's voice was rich as the flow of good gravy; you heard in it the scrape of Athenaeum cutlery and the gurgle of claret from cut-glass decanter to crystal goblet.

I paused. 'No.'

'What a tragedy that was! What a waste of a brilliant mind! Polite society will not mention his name. He is utterly finished. That is what happens when one cannot repress one's baser urges. One is extinguished. It cannot be other.' An expression of distaste flitted across his lean face. 'I believe the name "Oscar" has become a term of abuse among the lower classes.'

'I beg to differ,' I said with sudden boldness. 'I am willing to bet that the name of Oscar Wilde will still be invoked with admiration in a hundred years' time, when names which are now on everyone's lips will have been long forgotten.'

'Oh really? You think disgrace outlives solid achievement?' He leaned back, extending his too-long legs.

'I would imagine that generations to come will be appalled by the nature of his punishment.' My voice shook with emotion. 'And I believe his epigrams and aphorisms will be repeated as often as Shakespeare's. An apt phrase may be more valuable and more enduring in its effects than a long campaign and a dozen victories.'

Milner surveyed me down the length of his aquiline nose. 'What an unpredictable chap you are, Wills.' The leisurely drawl of his voice was not unlike Oscar's. But he had had enough of this dangerous topic and sat up straight again. 'Well, as neither of us will be in a position to see if you are right, there seems little point in arguing with you.' His sharp gaze moved to the book I was clutching.

'A lot of slanderous nonsense, that. Don't bother to read it. The woman should have stuck to writing about Boers on their farms. I've probably learnt more about the intractable Boer psychology from her first novel than I have from the Boers themselves. Primitive lot. Phlegmatic, crude. But wily, wily.' He narrowed his eyes as if trying to drill into the secrets of the wily Boer mind with his pupils. The eyebrows knitted more ferociously than I remembered from his youth; he appeared to have forgotten I was there. But innate good breeding made him suddenly glance at me and ask: 'So what brings you here, Wills, to this cultural desert? It must be the most tedious spot on earth. You can't surely have come here voluntarily?'

Without enthusiasm I embarked upon the somewhat ludicrous explanation as to why I found myself in Cape Town. Upon my asking him the identical question, he replied coolly: 'Oh, I've been sent here to pick up the pieces after the Jameson débâcle. A task not dissimilar to cleansing the Augean stables, on the scale of things.' He stretched out his long spidery legs, and gazed at the shine on his boots. 'Do you know, Wills, I find it absolutely astonishing that a country on the edge of war can actually be *dull*! Those British foreigners in the Boer republic who run the goldfields – and therefore the economy – are no better than a bunch of barbarians: there aren't a dozen of them who can tell a vegetable from a violin. As for the Boers . . . You know that most of them believe the earth is flat. Need I say more?' His eyes glazed over.

'So war is really imminent?'

'Oh, almost certainly.' One of his legs swung over the other with elaborate gracelessness. He rotated a foot, unembarrassed by the protest of clicks from its ankle. 'It's not altogether Jameson's fault, though quite frankly I don't rate him highly. It all comes down to the issue of franchise. That old Boer isn't going to let the foreign Uitlanders vote unless they've been living in his wretched republic for seven years – fourteen years – he keeps changing the number, but it's never the right one. He's a wily old fox if ever there was one. As for our host, I have to say – if men are ruled by their foibles, then his foible is *size*. Not his own size, you understand – which is vast enough – but land-size. Territory. Crown territory. He can't get enough of Africa for the Crown – and after Africa there are four other continents . . . yes, Huxley?'

That great slab of a man had materialised in the doorway.

'Your cab has arrived, sir.'

'Thank you.' Milner stubbed out a cigarette, and then appeared to forget this piece of information at once. 'But I'm afraid his foible has led to his downfall. The Raid has united all the Boers in the country against him – at one time the Boers in the Cape were very wisely becoming Anglicised, but it's goodbye to all that now – and the Imperial position has been horribly weakened. And we can't allow that.' He grinned beneath his load of moustache. 'He still seems to believe that every man has his price. His idea of diplomacy is fat cheques slipped under the table. If anything, he's even more slippery than Oom Paul, as I believe they call the President of the Boer Republic.'

'I assume,' I said evenly, 'that your job is to achieve some kind of compromise.'

Milner inhaled deeply, allowed his eyes to explore the ceiling, then sighed. 'Wills, let me give you a piece of advice. In South Africa it is necessary to be incredulous. This country breeds a special bacillus, nourished on whisky – or, even worse, Cape brandy: the habit of telling lies. Therefore I say to you: don't believe a thing you hear. I certainly don't.' He laced his fingers beneath his chin and looked melancholy.

There was a pause, during which I attempted to relate his reply to my earlier remark. 'How soon?' I asked.

He laughed outright. His teeth, revealed for the first time, were long and narrow and tapered inwards. 'Don't worry, old chap, you'll be back in Oxford long before we've jumped through the last hoop. I'm meeting a delegation of Transvaal Boers in Bloemfontein in two days' time, and I hear conciliation is once again in the air . . . or delaying tactics.' He rose to his feet. Alfred Milner had never known what to do with his arms and legs: beneath the stiff cloth of his dark suit there seemed to be a series of erratically arranged appendages over which he had incomplete control.

His eyes strayed to my photographic apparatus near the door of the library. The hawkish features suddenly softened. With embarrassment. For a moment the possibility occurred to me that he might be human. Could those be dimples at the edge of his great, fanged moustache?

'I say, Wills, I wonder if you could do me a favour?'

(Why do I have this feeling that as the end of the century draws near, the human race is about to slide off the edge of the world, into the abyss to which it rightfully belongs? And once again the land will be occupied only by fish, fowl and four-legged flesh, and Darwin's Theory, God help us, will be given another chance.)

After leaving Milner, I had a bowl of nutritious gruel and fell asleep upon my bed. I cannot survive without an afternoon nap, and the morning had been particularly eventful.

I awoke at 5 p.m., dreaming of crocodiles. The crocodile, I am told, has consumed more missionaries, hunters and explorers than all the other African predators put together. Challenger told me this on the voyage out, waving the stub of his arm as some kind of proof. His eyes are yellow with malaria, his skin chewed to rags by armies of red ants. He plans to return to Ujiji next year. I believe he knows Stanley.

VOYAGE

I chose to travel with my twittering cargo through Suez, and thus down the east coast of Africa, a somewhat lengthier route, but one that offered the wonders of the ancient world along the Mediterranean Sea. Our ship picked up colonial administrators from Portugal, France and Italy, so that I was able to take advantage of organised tours around the famous ports and harbours of these bastions of civilisation. Like all Englishmen, I feel at home in Italy. Perhaps it would have been wiser for me to spend a few weeks prodding among ruins, drinking good coffee in the sun, slowly piecing together my own breakages . . . At that stage my birds were happy, purring in their cages, even laying eggs. They gave me no warning.

To my annoyance, I was obliged to share a table with a young Cambridge man and his wife. He had been employed to help administer the building of a railway from the port of Mombasa to Lake Victoria. He was tired already: his cabin was too close to the steerage class with its cargo of settlers and soldiers (why so many soldiers?) who kept him awake at night with drinking songs and unseemly revelry. He could furnish me with no very clear explanation as to why it was necessary for the British to build a railway from Mombasa to the Great Lakes, other than that railways were the key to civilisation on a continent filled with people who still lived in the Stone Age. With one exception, we met only at the dining-table. We spoke mainly of the wonders of the Suez Canal and the brilliance of de Lesseps, who had so elegantly detached Africa from Arabia for us travellers, and his foolishness in trying to split the two Americas by the same method.

The young woman could speak only of the possibility of malaria, and consumed her quinine tablets with a tragic intensity which suggested that she had already contracted the disease. The fact that the cause of this dreaded scourge has at last been attributed to the bloodlust of the female anopheles mosquito (and not to sleeping in the African moonlight, as Burton opined) did nothing to allay her fears: I gave up trying to explain to her the various species of the Protozoan blood parasite which belongs to the single genus Plasmodium.

We kept away from the dining-table during a series of squalls that hit us just south of the Equator. The release from tedious conversation more than compensated for the uneasiness in my stomach. One night, as I tried to regain my sea-legs by strolling on the now steady upper deck, I bumped into the young couple whose faces were strangely radiant. The woman laid her hand on my arm and bade me look up. The sky flickered with a fiery life never visible to those who live in the Northern hemisphere. I averted my eyes from the shooting stars.

The young woman pointed. 'The Southern Cross!' she breathed. 'Now we really have left Europe behind!'

A new constellation blazed on the horizon, an asymmetrical cross of five bright stars. I am not a spiritual man, but this moment took me unawares. For a dizzying minute the five points of my own bodily extremities swung up into that busy firmament and I found myself giddily crucified among the galaxies. Call it a religious experience: perhaps it prepared me for my new role of father confessor to the Southern hemisphere.

*　　　*　　　*

G.B. Challenger was carried on board in a cloud of pale-blue butterflies. As our ship nosed towards Zanzibar, the sky had scissored apart, and those who knew Africa suggested locusts. The flock of Lepidoptera descended silently on to every available space on the upper and lower decks, and shimmered on handrails, doorways, coils of rope. (This phenomenon mirrored almost exactly the young Darwin's experience on the *Beagle* en route for Patagonia, even to the exclamation made by the seamen: 'It's snowing butterflies!') A day earlier we had dropped off the young couple at Mombasa, together with some hundred young men who had been given millions of acres of excellent land to farm in central Kenya. While reloading in Mombasa, the captain had received an SOS to pick up Challenger from the spice island a hundred miles south, whence he had been forced to return after having lost both an arm and all his porters in a bloody onslaught somewhere between Lakes Albert and Victoria. Challenger was himself suffering from at least three tropical diseases and had to be borne up the gangway on a stretcher, followed by an endless stream of Zanzibar ex-slaves who carried on their sullen heads unimaginable bundles of booty. A strong smell of cloves wafted upwards with them. The hapless butterflies, with no regard for their own survival, were crunched underfoot. They made no attempt to fly away. Their genocide was unobserved by the horizontal Challenger, who bellowed out a torrent of instructions, curses and queries, as he bobbed across the sky-blue deck.

Once he had disappeared into his cabin, the tusks arrived. These were carried in huge caskets by a fresh set of Negroes – probably porters who had accompanied him on his expeditions into central Africa. They had already been grouped according to size and weight; the passengers (including myself) watched with awe as casket after casket of tusks, ten feet in length, descended into the hold of the ship, followed by as many containers of smaller tusks of the purest ivory. The ladies among us demurred at the number of elephants that must have been shot to provide such vast quantities of ivory, but the gentlemen were quick to remind them of the keys of their beloved pianos, their fans, and the knife handles with their intricate inlay work.

The next day, to my astonishment, Challenger invited me to his cabin. He had observed my cages of birds and had something to tell me. A mere skeleton of a man, with wild, protruding eyes, he was nevertheless in feverish good humour, dismissing his condition as a temporary inconvenience.

'I spotted your birds, Wills!' he exclaimed jovially as I edged into his cabin, which was already crammed with gigantic teeth, antlers, hoofs, horns, tails, beaks and feathers. Leopard skins hung on the walls; a couple of monkeys screamed at me from cages, but of Challenger's poodle, Mary, there was no sign. 'Find yourself a space, man – push those snakeskins aside – I shot that cobra between the eyes myself – the last bullet I fired before the croc got me!'

Great beads of sweat rolled freely down his face as he spoke, and his shivering was so violent that I feared he was suffering an epileptic seizure. From the tumble of his suitcases the head of a full-grown lion bared its teeth hopelessly at the rigid carcass of a young zebra.

'You have an interest in birds?' I murmured.

'Not so much for myself, old chap – I'm a big-game man as you can see – but I saw something you as a bird person might find interesting. Ever been up to the Lakes?'

For one foolish moment I thought he was referring to the spiritual and physical home of William Wordsworth and his sister, and recalled a day trip to Grasmere with a colleague. But Dove Cottage was not what Challenger had in mind.

'I'm talking about Lake Bangweolo, which poor old

Livingstone thought would prove to be the source of the Nile. He died in the surrounding swamps, you know, convinced that the four fountains of the Nile described by Herodotus were just around the corner. My God, what a place! Up to my waist in swamp and mud for the best part of a week. Had to carry my guns and bullets over my head – thank God I had both arms then! Now I've seen, oh, a thousand different species of beast up there – shot most of 'em too, by Jove! – but the strangest creature I ever laid eyes upon was the bird of the Bangweolo swamp!' His voice had modulated into a different key: the key men speak in when they sit round campfires in Africa or smoking rooms in the clubs of Pall Mall. Even the monkeys were affected by his change of pitch, and clung to their bamboo bars, watching first his face, then mine, with their bright eyes.

During the pause that followed, Challenger lit a cigarette with his five remaining fingers and blew out a stream of smoke into whose blue depths he stared as if winged phantasms might appear within them. When he spoke again, his voice had dropped a full minor third.

'I'd thought that the Dodo was dead, Wills. We'd been told the Dutch sailors shot them off the face of Mauritius: poor beasts were too fat and short legged to run for it. Stumps for wings, as you'd know. I have to say I wouldn't know what a Dodo looked like if I hadn't read *Alice in Wonderland* at my nurse's knee and goggled at Tenniel's illustrations along with a million other brats of my age. Care for a cigarette?'

I shook my head.

'One day, having finally reached a piece of terra firma on the swamp, my men and I sat picking the leeches off our arms and legs, and swatting away the myriad mosquitoes that breed in this kind of swampland. I heard a kind of grunt, and motioned to my men to be quiet. Strutting from its nest, in an awkward, pigeon-toed sort of way, was none other than Alice's Dodo! Of course, my automatic response was to reach for my rifle, but then I thought, hold on, old chap. Remember nanny's tears: this might be the world's last Dodo. Damn fool, actually. The swamp's crawling with 'em.' He drew on his cigarette, awaiting my response.

'Dodgson died last year,' I said. 'Dodo Dodgson. Or Lewis Carroll to the world outside Oxford.'

'You knew him?'

'We shared an interest in photography.'

'Tell you what, Wills.' Challenger's eyes swivelled in their sockets. 'When I return to the Lakes next year with a new arm, damme, you must accompany me and we will capture that Dodo. We'll bring back cages full of 'em, Wills, alive – *alive* as a Dodo, what d'ye think? We'll show 'em!'

I thought his eyes might start right out of his head as he extended his lips into a livid line about his teeth, and howled. The sound was as wild as any that might come from the jaws of any of the animals whose carcasses crowded around us. For a moment I felt myself turned to stone, as if by black magic. But when Challenger's famous poodle (whose sleeping form I had mistaken for a stuffed monkey) leapt upon her master's lap and bared her sharp, cat-like teeth at me, a high-pitched growl throbbing in her throat, I screamed aloud in panic so profound that every hair on my body uncurled and stood on end, while a ghostly mewing sound escaped my own lips. I knew I must escape at all costs and extended a shaking hand to ring a bell placed at hand for emergencies.

Afterwards, when I felt calmer, I considered Challenger's invitation.

To photograph the Dodo – that would be something. A gesture of reconciliation, perhaps, towards poor dead Dodgson.

Our ship bore a treacherous cargo. The Captain told me

straight out when he heard where I was going. Or rather, when he heard who would be receiving the birds. He promised to show me a sample after dinner one night.

One evening the heat was such that I forbore to attend dinner, and leaned over the deck rails in my shirt-sleeves, grateful for the small movement of air I could enjoy in this position. The sun was low in the sky, which had assumed a reddish hue, reflected in the brimming waters of the Indian Ocean. A certain mistiness dissolved the horizon, but I guessed we must be near land because of the large numbers of seagulls (a species of bird in which I have no interest whatsoever) that screeched and fluttered above the steaming funnels of the boat. In spite of the oppressiveness of the weather I felt strangely at peace, suspended as it were among all four elements, a passive product of sun, water, land and ether. It was then that a most sublime vision began slowly to emerge from the rosy haze.

One by one, spotlit by the brilliant rays that emanate from the sun only at dusk, the spires of Oxford appeared against the skyline: Tom Tower in all its Wrennish glory; the bronze dome of the Radcliffe Camera; twenty different spires and steeples of churches and colleges and libraries – even the newly built Town Hall with its weathervane in the shape of a horned ox. I actually fancied I could see Her Imperial Majesty seated in the apex of the central pediment! Needless to say I realised at once that I was the victim of a superb hallucination, a mirage such as rises mysteriously before the eyes of over-heated desert travellers. But then I heard the church bells. Not the glorious cacophony in the fine English tradition of bell-ringing, but the more orderly, some would say more melodious, chimes that tumble from the steeples of Italy, France, Portugal. Passengers began to emerge excitedly from the dining-saloon, blotting their still-chewing mouths with their table napkins, in their desire to view this phenomenon off the coast of Africa.

'Ilha de Lisboa!' cried a small Portuguese man, upon which a great purple mist enveloped both us, and the island, and for a few moments we held our breath, confused by the improbable mixture of fact and fantasy and waiting for the cloud to lift like a curtain. When it did we found we had drifted close to the shores of the island and were nudging the base of a massive flight of white marble steps that led, in a triumphant esplanade, to a magnificent Baroque *piazza*, in which played a fountain composed entirely of spouting dolphins.

The whole frontal slope of the island was covered in patterned pavements and intricately structured courtyards and archways, above which swelled those towers, domes and cupolas which I had mistaken for the dreaming spires of the most beautiful city in England. And sauntering along these elegant byways were fashionably-dressed men and women, both black and white. Our boat was so close to the island now that one could hear the murmur of voices, and the clink of chisel against stone, as black labourers fashioned lumps of green and white rock to be laid in symmetrical patterns within the delicate pavements. It was difficult to believe that we were several thousand miles from Europe, but the lush flora which tumbled from balconies and sprouted from the sweep of marble steps suggested a climate more tropical even than that preserved in the hothouses by the Isis.

The boat drifted on, around the walled curve of the island. Now the inhabitants could lean over their wall and gaze at us face to face. One man smiled and waved.

A deep groan ran through the crowd of passengers, who suddenly crumpled and swayed as if hit by a sudden cyclone. Glasses of claret and champagne shattered as the stampede began.

Curiously enough I have no fear of lepers. In fact, I have to confess that I rather enjoy resting my eyes on their grotesque deformities, much as one actually pays to stare at malformed freaks in travelling fairs. These lepers were all the more interesting in that their disintegrating limbs protruded, not from the usual beggars' tatters, but from what I would imagine was the very height of *haute couture*. They seemed content.

The passengers remained below deck until the ship had returned to an empty sea. I alone remained, exactly in the place where I had positioned myself earlier, when the vision of Oxford first appeared. I caught the eye of a man who waved to me with his handless wrist.

With all the gravity I could muster, I mimed the gesture of raising my hat. He bowed, evidently satisfied.

Occasionally I sat at the Captain's table. Here the conversation was much concerned with the possibility of impending war in South Africa. I learnt there were several hundred Royal Irish Fusiliers on board, ready to decant at Durban. Naturally this talk was not good for my digestion, but the Captain soothed me by saying that the old Boer president was giving in to British demands over the franchise question: the wounds opened by the Jameson raid still had not healed, but there was hope that war between the Boer Republics and Great Britain would be avoided by compromise.

One night after dinner the Captain revealed his secret to me. Along with Challenger's tusks, the cargo held two thousand copies of a slim volume, an allegory by the South African authoress Miss Schreiner, whom the Captain had met on an earlier voyage from Cape Town to Southampton. I had heard her name through Oscar, who admired her work very much, being smitten by the same semi-Biblical style in his own parables. The Captain told me with some pride that those slim volumes in his hold were the equivalent of two thousand sticks of dynamite. He pointed out to me the very lines in which she personally attacks the Colossus: they are spoken by an English soldier and employee of his beloved Chartered Company, who helps put down a rebellion in Matabeleland, using the usual brutal tactics of warfare. The soldier admires his employer's ability to force the native's unwilling nose to the grindstone: 'They say he's going to parcel them out, and make them work on our lands whether they like it or not – just as good as having slaves, you know; and you haven't the bother of looking after them when they're old.'

Quite frankly, I'm not particularly interested in these issues. But the Captain was much stirred, and seemed to think I should know about these things. He remembered her very clearly, and with some awe.

'A mannish little woman, very highly strung,' was his verdict. 'She told me he could finish her, but she had to speak out. It was her duty to expose his brutalities, she said. Very high-minded lady. Said he was laying the foundations for a national tragedy. She became very animated when she spoke of the native question.'

I thank heaven she was not on my boat.

CAPE TOWN 1899

The sun sets abruptly in this part of the world. One minute it's day, the next it's night. After my rest I realised I would have to hurry to pay my final visit to the cages, and reluctantly rose from my comfortable bed. As usual I turned to my photograph albums for consolation. They are safer in the dark-room, which is visited by no one but me. I cannot imagine that the charms of Oxford would appeal to Orpheus or Huxley but I do not like to think of strangers poring over my precious pages, and leave nothing to chance.

Chamberlain and Salisbury were fiddling about with their patterns and pebbles in the sand when I arrived to check up on the well-being of the birds, all of whom sat sullen and silent in the gloom. The guilty start given by both boys reinforced my suspicion that these loops and trails around the cages were the manifestation of some primitive belief in the powers of magic. Deliberately kicking one of their carefully placed stones so that it clattered against the starling aviary, causing a group of huddled birds to shake their black feathers at the disturbance, I demanded to know how much the birds had eaten during the day. Not much, seemed to be the answer. I opened my mouth to lecture the boys on the necessity of vigilance, when the heart-stopping trill of the nightingale bubbled from the forest above.

I looked at my two helpers. The song was now flooding through the gardens, glorious melody which I had taught them to reproduce in the hope of stirring the collective syrinx of the caged birds, but the boys were strangely indifferent to the miracle pouring from the mountain slopes. I waved my hand in the air. 'Listen!' I exclaimed. The boys lowered their eyes, at the same time chewing their lips to stifle their grins. Their bare feet dug into the sand, their toes exploring its textures like fingers.

It was clear that no bird could have escaped through the fine wire mesh that covered the cages. I found my legs running of their own accord across the lawns towards the gate that opened on to the mountain path, as if the bird were calling me upwards, even as the sun shot red spears above the horizon. To my finely tuned ears there could be no doubt but that the birdsong came from the mossy spot I had discovered in the morning; excitement made me race up the steep path without noticing the stabs of pain in my leg muscles. But by the time I had reached the dim path that led to Titania's grove, the sublime music had stopped, disturbed, perhaps, by the thud of my feet.

With a stealth that surprised me – one needs supple limbs for stealth – I crept down the darkening path, aware of watchful eyes in bushes and upon branches. A squirrel froze in mid-ascent of a tree trunk, a crucified carpet with a visibly beating heart; a bird of prey whined from above; a small snake thrashed among the pine needles.

I reached Titania's grove and raised my binoculars.

The small girl was sitting on a rock far to my right. Her head was bent over something she was holding in her cupped hands, something she must have only just reached out for. So absorbed was she in retaining this object that she did not hear the twigs snapped by my trembling foot. The overtall pines creaked behind her, and my own stiff, motionless knees creaked in sympathy. I tried to control my panting.

The girl wore the white apron of childhood, thick black stockings and sturdy black shoes. Underneath the apron peeped the sleeves of a demure cotton frock, dark green in colour, as far as I could tell in the twilight. Then, mysteriously, she began to stretch her clasped hands upwards, sacerdotal fashion, and her ringlets fell back from her face to reveal plump cheeks of a deep colour, and glittering eyes. Her tiny mouth had dropped open with excitement as she gazed at her uplifted hands.

For a few moments the child held this position, as if partaking in some pagan rite of nature-worship; then, with a sharp intake of breath, parted her chubby hands to release a speck of light that floated and darted erratically about before disappearing into the foliage of the plumbago hedge. At this, she rose from her rock and began burrowing between the mossy pebbles beside the stream.

I racked my brains for some whimsical remark with which to open a conversation with this creature, such as would have dropped effortlessly from the lips of Dodgson, who always travelled with a black bag full of small puzzles to capture the interest of young ladies at moments like this. I have a good memory for verse, and summoned Edward Lear's genial limericks to my aid. Entertaining as these rhymes undoubtedly are, I realised that the sudden intonation of lines concerning an old person of Ealing who was wholly devoid of good feeling, or a young person of Bantry who frequently slept in the pantry, would terrify the child out of her wits; I was therefore obliged to remain frozen to the spot, risking problems to my circulation, while I watched the delightful child probe and poke among the stones.

In fact, something far more spontaneous than a *bon mot* was about to spring from my lips. A good five minutes before the sneeze exploded, I felt sure that, in addition to the encumbrance of a foot now entirely devoid of sensation, I was catching a cold. The back of my throat was suddenly on fire; my blood seemed to have turned to water; a slight sweat tickled through my beard. It is that monstrous house which has done this to me, those icy shifts of space between open windows. Dare I reach for my handkerchief?

The sneeze reached my nose before my handkerchief did; my numb foot skidded forward on the damp stone; and I found myself on my posterior, a sharp pain jabbing through my coccyx. My eyes being now level with those of the little one, I expected her own to fly open in alarm, and a whimper of fear to escape her lips. Instead of which, she frowned severely and pronounced in stern tones: 'Sssh, or you'll frighten the fairies!'

Though relieved at her composure, I now found myself caught in another dilemma which certainly would not have posed a problem for the likes of Dodgson or Lear. Do I inform her that her fairies are really glow-worms and fireflies, which are neither worms nor flies but lampyrid, elaterid or coleopterous insects, or, to enter the sublimely ordered world of Linnaeus, more specifically are the larvae *Lampyris noctiluca* and *Phrixothrix genera*. Even I drew the line at the latter, and retracing the variety of nomenclature at my disposal I found myself back at the species of winged creature which she herself had named, and pressed my forefinger against my lips in conspiratorial though anxious silence.

I was well acquainted with the larvae which she groped after, Coleoptera being particularly fine prey for migratory birds, especially when they shine in the dark. I could have told this angelic child how some so-called glow-worms emit a greenish gleam but bear a red headlight in addition; that their rhythmic flashes are no more than signals to bring the sexes together; how some frogs eat so many fireflies that they themselves give off a greenish glow. Instead of this, I concentrated on not sneezing, in total obedience to her command, a task which absorbed most of my energies.

After a few minutes of searching she said reproachfully: 'They've all flown away!' The child's voice had a strong colonial intonation, with its sharp falling cadence and slithering vowels, not at all like the refined accents of an Alice Liddell. Her eyes, still level with mine, were grave with accusation.

Humbly I raised my clenched right hand and opened it just beneath her chin. A perfect spray of microscopic fireworks flurried before her eyes and caused her face to light up, both literally and metaphorically.

'Do it again!' she implored, her pupils still zigzagging after the vanishing insects.

I had not known, when I performed my trick, that a child's greatest accolade is to ask for more. In my effort to escape repeated and unattainable encores, I suddenly entered the world of the imagination.

'I am allowed to perform that magic only once a day.' I certainly sounded very grand, even though I must have looked absurd. 'If you happen to be here tomorrow at the same time I may be able to do it again.' From whence this inspiration came I am utterly unable to tell.

'Hmm.' She now seemed indifferent to the trick. 'Are you p'raps the Englishman with the birds?' Again the curious intonations, almost as if English were her second language.

I felt it was time for me to rise to my feet but feared my knees and ankles might let me down.

'Yes, I suppose I am.' I gave myself a tentative push with both hands and found my joints still operated.

Her eyes were mischievous. 'I've got a bird.'

'Can I see it?'

In reply, she ran across to the stream and clattered about. And there it was again; in the silence of the forest rose the pure, soaring song of the nightingale, now chirruping, now gargling, now embarking on an exquisite melody in lopsided 5/8 time, and causing my heart to contract with forbidden pleasure.

The music stopped short and she scampered back.

'May I see your bird?'

'Here's my bird. You've got to put water in it.'

She held out the little clay bird-whistle carefully, so as not to spill what remained of the water. It was a finely modelled instrument, unlike the cheap tin models the children of England perform upon.

'His name is Oom Paul. My mommy made it out of clay.'

I smiled at this. 'You're quite right. It is only men birds who sing so beautifully.'

'You talk posh, hey?' Her eyes were wide with astonishment.

Relinquishing the spoken word, I pursed my pink lips together and began to whistle. Her astonishment turned to admiration at the full-throated ease with which I reproduced the nightingale sounds, and her gaze settled on my busy lips with envious curiosity. When I had finished she continued to stare at my mouth with great concentration, and then slowly, uncertainly, began to draw the rosebud of her lips into a tiny circle. I did not smile at the pathetic little whisper she produced, no more than the rush of air needed to blow out a candle.

'That is a start.'

She raised her eyes to mine, evidently still overawed by my performance.

'I want to whistle like you.'

'I'll be here tomorrow morning. Perhaps you can practise getting your lips into the right shape – like this.'

The obedient child squared her face with mine, and attempted to mirror the movements of my mouth.

'That's more like it. Put the tip of your finger into the hole you have made with your lips, and try to make it as round as possible.'

I could see that nothing else in this child's life now existed except the desire to whistle. I had yet to learn that childhood obsessions approach the crystalline qualities of genius.

Held in her spell, I tried to exclude an intrusive sound. A sharp clatter of metal from the world down below began to assume the summonsing call of an exotic percussion instrument. I had heard it the day before, and had wondered at its message: a rhythm of six beats and a pause, played again and again with no variation.

The girl unpursed her lips. 'That's my mommy calling me for my supper.'

'You must go then.' Already she seemed about to run off, forgetting her promise to meet me the next day. I resisted the impulse to grab her by the arm, and said instead: 'You haven't told me your name.'

She stared at me, amazed that I could be so ignorant. 'Maria!' she exclaimed reprovingly.

'Maria who?'

'Maria van den Bergh.' She chanted the pretty Dutch name shrilly, as if she had memorised it with some difficulty.

'Maria of the mountain,' I translated. 'That is a good name for you. Now shall I tell you my name?'

But the child had lost all interest in me and was anxious to get away. Clearly she had not been introduced to the rules of etiquette that an English child of her age would have dutifully obeyed at this point. Frowning, she opened those well-exercised lips and snapped at me: 'No thank you!'

'Maria – before you go – just wait a minute – why haven't I heard your bird before? Do you come here every day?'

I was overloading her with questions. She stared at me

77

blankly, as if I had spoken in a foreign language, then said in a plaintive voice: 'I been sick.'

The triangle rattled out its command again; Maria gathered up her skirts and leapt off the rock. She was taller than I had imagined, her head reaching almost to my hip. Then, with blank eyes, she stretched up her arms towards my neck, planted a kiss on my startled lips, and said politely: 'Thank you, uncle.'

With that she disappeared into the undergrowth, leaving me still bent over into an unaccustomed shape, reluctant to abandon it. When did I last stoop to kiss a child?

I unfolded myself bit by bit back to my normal upright position and called out to a faint rustle in the undergrowth: 'I'll see you tomorrow!'

CAPE TOWN 1899

Orpheus has finally understood that I prefer to take breakfast in my room. This morning I was awakened with a tray of toast and tea, together with the morning newspaper. The front page was almost entirely devoted to a dispute between the Colossus, who heads the Opposition Party, and the Prime Minister who had replaced him after his Disgrace. It is, of course, an absolute mystery to me how a man of his obvious ill-health, to say nothing of his Disgrace, should actually want to undertake the responsibilities of state in addition to his vast business enterprises (he has control over ninety per cent of the world's diamond production, I am reliably informed) and Chartered Company. Surely what he needs now is rest, rest, rest?

I waited for the fragrant aroma of the East to do its work with my olfactory nerve endings before attending to the dense text which made up the speech delivered by my host, and which even a cursory glance told me altogether lacked the easy fluency of your average British MP. He was holding forth on the topic of franchise within the Cape Colony, a different affair altogether from the franchise question in the Boer Republic. A new bill was being introduced which would permit the educational qualifications of voters to be examined; my host claimed that civilisation rather than education should be used as a criterion. 'I have always differentiated between the raw barbarians and the civilised natives,' declared he to hoots of derisive laughter from the Ruling Party. 'My motto has always been – Equal Rights for every civilised man south of the Zambezi who has sufficient education to write his name, has some property, or works. In fact, is not a loafer.' This opinion obliged the Prime Minister, who shares his surname with Miss Schreiner (I know not if they are related), to remind the erstwhile Premier of an earlier version of this motto, first mouthed during the previous year's election, which expressed his views more accurately: 'Equal rights for every *white man* south of the Zambezi.' Jeers from the Ruling Party, who understand only too well the need to boost the number of voters in individual constituencies.

At least there was no comment on the issue of female emancipation, a topic which, I feel, receives far too much attention in even the most respectable of British broadsheets. In my opinion, only graduates of Oxford and perhaps Cambridge should be allowed to vote in England; it is quite absurd to expect a man of little education to understand the complexities of running a country. I have no doubt my host would thoroughly agree with me, but of course in these days of liberal reform and Marxian stirrings one dare not voice such opinions publicly.

It was ten minutes to nine. I consulted Orpheus on the whereabouts of the Colossus' bedroom. I have to confess that, momentous as the prospect of this meeting should have been, my thoughts lay more with the meeting I hoped would follow it. The image of the little girl Maria danced around the bedroom: she pushed her face up close to mine and planted kiss after kiss upon my lips. But I pushed her out every time she appeared: after all, I do not like children. How had she managed to trespass into the sanctum of my entirely adult thoughts? Orpheus pointed to the other upstairs wing of the house which I had not had cause to enter, his face as impassive as my own.

In fact, the route from my side of the house to the wing containing my master's bedroom was not as direct as one might imagine, and I found myself moving cautiously along whitewashed corridors that seemed to take me away from my destination rather than towards it. Old Dutch still-lifes of fruit and vegetables piled on kitchen tables hung at intervals on the walls. A number of dark, heavy looking doors, identical to my own, all firmly shut, lined the corridors on either side. Just as I supposed that I had wandered into the secretaries' quarters, one of the doors slowly opened and out of it tiptoed the woman I had seen on the back stoep the day before. Sensing I was about to speak to her, she placed her forefinger over her lip to silence me, and closed the door gently behind her with her free hand. Then she bustled me down the corridor past several more doors and whispered: 'They're all still asleep and I want them to stay that way! We've had a bad night.'

Her voice had the quiet inflections of the New World in it, and made me feel suddenly comfortable: I found myself blushing as I confessed I had lost my way. 'Oh, you've had one of his summonses!' she laughed, and with matronly confidence led me out of the maze and into a passage which opened on to a panelled landing. 'There you are,' said she, pointing at a massive yellowwood door. 'Good luck!' And touched me lightly on the shoulder before she pattered off down the stairs. She did not enquire after my identity.

Having cleared my throat for well over a minute, I took the proverbial deep breath, and lifted my hand to knock on the yellow door, framed in chocolate-coloured stinkwood, a combination very popular in this colony. But I paused as I heard my host's soprano voice raised in argument; a one-sided argument as the unseen listener kept entirely silent during the rattle of words that rose in both pitch and volume together with the speaker's passion. He appeared to be repeating the phrases I had first heard from his lips the day before: *railway gauges, Cape to Cairo, twice the speed.* And as I listened – was I being fanciful? – I heard the regular beat of metal wheel against track, interrupted now and then by a kind of braying howl, as if he were himself some great engine of steam and energy upon which we mortals depended for our own momentum; without which inertia would take over.

Then, silence. I awaited a response. None came. I fisted my hand to knock – just as another torrent of shrill argument burst through the stillness. How long did I hover thus, waiting for the right moment to present itself? It became clear to me that only a rap on the door would release his dumb prisoner. I knocked. The monologue ceased at once.

'That you, Wills?'

'It is.'

'Open the door, man, and let yourself in!' cried the Colossus.

His bedroom was a great net of latticed glass and wood, flung out to capture as much of the mountain view as possible. There is no doubt that his architect fully understands how the window frame can intensify and simultaneously tame a powerful landscape, and by designing a multiplicity of lattice frames, he has indeed augmented the power of the mountain. The eye naturally travels upward, from the wide stone stairway that cuts through the geometry of the Dutch garden, through the terraced lawns and crescent of hydrangeas, to the pine-forested foothills wherein graze zebra, llamas, fallow deer and kangaroo in apparent harmony, and finally up the purple rock-faces of the central mountain, untouched, as yet, by my master's hand.

For a few moments I stood as if trapped in the window-net, unable to drag my gaze to the seated figure at his desk beneath the great bay window. No one else was in the room. But then my host continued to speak, this time in those final cadences which signify the end of a conversation. 'G'bye!' he snapped into the mouthpiece of the telephone, which he replaced with a great deal of noise; then turned his attention to me.

'I think no other man can have a view to match this one.' His voice was reverent. Far from looking exhausted after the acrimony in the House the day before, he appeared ten years younger. The puffiness round his eyes had subsided, the eyes themselves were clearer and sparkling with good humour. Clearly this man thrived on stress and confrontation.

Looking at the view through the window I resorted to rhyme:

> *'Great things are done when men and mountains meet,*
> *That are not done by jostling in the street.'*

'I like that, Wills, I like that very much!' His voice soared upwards again in his excitement as he scrabbled among a heap of telegrams on his desk. 'Let me take that down at once, if I can find a blank piece of paper. Perhaps I can find some woman to work it in cross-stitch and I'll hang it next to my window. Shakespeare, I presume?'

'Actually, William Blake.'

'I'll take your word for it. The words are strangely appropriate: I happen to get my Greatest Thoughts on the mountain. Most people go to church for their religious experiences, but my church is Out There, where I'm alone with the Alone, where I can dream my dreams . . .' As he spoke he scribbled on the back of a telegram, while I allowed my eyes to wander round the room.

More of an office than a bedroom, further flags, firearms and photographs adorned his whitewashed walls. Next to a large photograph of himself in the company of grinning young men, inscribed *The Conqueror of Matabeleland*, a pair of large crossed flags was ostentatiously displayed, both of which, a label beneath them told me, Jameson had carried during the first Matabele War, and one of which was riddled with shot. Further along this wall an old-fashioned blunderbuss, evidently taken from the heart of an oak tree on the estate, hung above some links of an ancient Arab slave chain: all arranged for my host to view from his bed.

In the midst of these trophies hung two pictures within a single frame. The etching on the left was familiar to me, having appeared in many newspapers at the time of the great Diamond Rush, and having also been revived at the time of the infamous Commission of Inquiry in London, to illustrate how the Colossus had made his millions. Labelled *Colesburg Kopje*, in the same brown copperplate that marked all the other pictures and souvenirs, it depicted an opencast mine operating on many levels, in the various chasms of which several thousand men clustered thick as ants, while above them baskets of ore swung along fantastical webs of aerial tramwires, and mules pulled carts along the very edge of the crumbling abyss. The artist had contrived to give almost every ant a pickaxe or shovel: those who were not digging deep into their disintegrating claims were scuttling up vertiginous ladders or staggering towards the mule carts with bucketloads of earth in which their fortune might lie.

The photograph beside this etching, also marked *Colesburg Kopje*, by contrast appeared to be nothing more than a flat-topped hill in an empty landscape. The juxtaposition of these two pictures was certainly very striking.

An old photograph of himself in the centre of three rows of his Chartered Company men hung above his bed, together with a recent picture of himself propped up horizontally on a mattress somewhere in the veld, the omnipresent secretaries grinning around him; and a portrait of the Matabele king who had sold his country's mineral rights to the Colossus for a thousand breech-loading rifles and an armed steamboat on the Zambezi. The bed itself was simple and narrow, with no hint of the luxury one might have expected from the richest man in Southern Africa. Next to the bed, a table fashioned from an elephant's foot was adorned with a photograph of an elderly woman, presumably his mother; a well-used copy of the Marcus Aurelius meditations; a biography of Napoleon; and the collected Sherlock Holmes stories. A variety of pills and potions, such as one would expect a man of an invalid disposition to rely upon, were clustered next to the books.

He was rising from his desk, his great girth blotting out much of the vista behind him. 'I must apologise for my absence over the past few days.' Though his eyes suggested a bland regret, his mouth expressed scorn. It was a masterful mouth, with a full lower lip which twitched with every passing thought, beneath the curve of his neat moustache. 'I have to travel all round the Colony at the drop of a hat – keep the members of my constituency happy and all that. But I've called you here for a very specific reason, Wills.' He strode over to the frame of the Colesburg Kopje pictures, and with a flick of his hands caused it to swing open. A small safe was embedded in the wall. 'I'd like you to see my collection of little treasures.' He was rotating a complex safety lock backward and forward: it emitted a series of musical clicks, and the heavy metal door suddenly swung open. I tried to prevent myself from peering inside it in the expectation of glittering precious stones and priceless jewellery. In fact, the safe seemed to be disappointingly empty, though my peripheral vision (upon which I increasingly rely for much of my visual information) noted a shadowy hoard of stone relics, small carvings and several piles of papers, carelessly stacked.

'You can see I'm not a man for ornament,' he said, withdrawing from the safe something so small as to be entirely enclosed in his huge hand. 'But I have in my time been given valuable gifts – some might call them sweeteners – which I have not wanted to sell or store in a Swiss bank. This is one of them. I have reason to regret having accepted this gift, but it is a cunning one, and I cannot bring myself to return it, as I should.'

He opened his hand. In its palm lay something about which I had heard much but had never seen. Peter Carl Fabergé's jewelled Easter eggs, designed for the Tsar to present to his Tsarina on the most important day of the Russian calendar, had achieved mythical status in Britain, where only the wealthiest in the land were able to commission the goldsmith to create *objets d'art* on a miniature scale of such exquisite detail. The egg in the hand of the Colossus was encrusted with gold, diamonds and Lilliputian pearls, one of which, when pressed, caused the crust to crack open and reveal its inner treasure. Coiled inside the shell like a long earthworm was a diminutive model of the Orient Express, complete with two steam engines.

'How well she understood my passion.' His voice whined upwards. 'Probably a copy of the original, but priceless, nevertheless. I believe she has staked her entire fortune in giving it to me. They tell me she hasn't a penny.'

'She?'

'A Russian princess who has set her heart on marrying me . . . not the first, I can assure you. I was fool enough to be taken in by her title and flattery. She was intelligent enough, and vivacious . . . but marriage!' He snorted and snapped the egg to. 'I hope she's got the message. Used to spend a lot of time here and at my dining-table, but I thank God she's returned to Switzerland.'

'You are fond of railway trains?' I enquired, in an attempt to discourage further intimate revelations.

'Not as much as I love railway *lines*, Wills, and one line

in particular: that which will extend from Cape to Cairo!' he exclaimed, burrowing into his safe for another exhibit. 'That is my dream, Wills. My heart is riveted into those lines of steel that now run right through the colonies named after me, and all the way to Ujiji!'

I feared a lecture on the economic opportunities to be opened up by the advent of rail, and a debate as to the advantages of a broader gauge, but he had judged his audience correctly and changed the subject with customary abruptness.

'Now I come to a treasure closer to your ornithological heart.'

It was clear that the great man had structured a piece of sequential theatre for reasons that I could not begin to fathom. With some reluctance I allowed myself to look at the next miniature he held in his hand. And tried not to gasp.

The pistol which he pointed at my heart was decorated with enamel and precious stones. At its mouth hovered a humming-bird which quivered its wings and sang, not with its own unmusical voice, but with the pure warble of the goldfinch. Even though my poor heart was beating at twice its normal rate I at once recognised the exquisite flageolet as the work of the Swiss music-box manufacturer, M. Jaquet-Droz. 'Worth a pretty penny, eh Wills? I won't tell you who gave me this pretty thing – or why he gave it to me!'

Well pleased with the fright he had given me, my host replaced his two miniatures, and, between sniggers, withdrew a third and final item. Suddenly solemn, he motioned me across the room so that we could stand in the magnificent bow window and inspect the contents of the simple box he held in his hand.

'I have another apology to make to you, Wills,' he said simply. 'The original arrangement was for you to come in spring. I very much appreciate the fact that you were able to come at short notice several months earlier.'

'I must say that I am curious as to why the plan was changed.'

'I suppose you know the Hans Andersen story about the emperor and the nightingale?'

Warning bells jangled in my head, but I said calmly enough: 'I confess I know only the Wilde story. About the nightingale and the rose. Based on a Persian fable, I believe.'

At the mention of my friend's name, the Colossus gave a violent start. For a few moments he seemed lost for words, though the tremor in his underlip indicated that his thoughts were racing. Finally he whispered: 'You are referring to – Oscar Wilde?'

'He was – he is – my close friend.' Was.

My host glowered at me with his red-rimmed eyes. 'You believe in absolute loyalty to your friends, even in the depth of their disgrace?'

'I do. Though absolute loyalty requires a courage of which I am not always capable.'

His gaze softened. 'I'm glad to hear it, Wills.' He seemed to have forgotten about the box in his hands. 'One must not abandon one's friends in the time of their greatest need. This is the cornerstone of my personal philosophy.'

Were those bright, pale eyes filling with liquid? 'Absolutely!' I agreed with a fervour that was calculated to calm him, to dry his tears. I do not care for open emotion.

'It might sound extraordinary to you, Wills, but I identify with Wilde in a number of ways. I was at Oxford with him, you know.' Certainly I could think of no two men I knew who were so much the opposite of each other. Quite apart from matters of lifestyle, ambition and politics, it was apparent to me that my host thought and expressed himself exclusively in the *literal* mode, altogether lacking the musical ironies of Oscar's discourse – and yet, I could recognise that, mysteriously, my host, for all his stumbling staccato prose, was able to mesmerise those around him by the power of his dreams in the same way that Oscar had once bewitched his audiences through the dazzle of his words.

'One minute your friend is at the peak of his career, the toast of London, the darling of society. The next – well, even I have difficulty in saying his name. I followed the case, of course, but the thing that struck me most of all was – here today and gone tomorrow. Little did I know that by the end of that very year I too would be thrown into deepest disgrace. Doubtless you know the details.' He winced at his memories. 'And both your friend and I were toppled because we valued our friendships more than even our countries or our own personal fame. I could have put the blame squarely on Jameson's shoulders. I could have avoided humiliation.' He sank into a brief, bitter reverie. Then: 'I believe Wilde is out of prison now. Will he have the strength to rise to his former heights, I wonder. He is an artist, and most artists I know are weak, self-indulgent. I doubt he has the discipline to pick himself out of the mire.'

The Colossus had sunk into a dreamlike state. He spoke without meeting my eye. 'Sometimes I wonder, Wills, and you may laugh at me for this, whether our society is being dragged down by the end of the century. It's as if we have to arrive at a solution before the twentieth century overtakes us: public figures have to be sacrificed like offerings to the gods. I worry about this war that Milner's going to drag us into. I feel he wants to cleanse the air with bloodshed to start the new century with a *tabula rasa*, even if it means sacrificing the whole Boer race!'

He gave a shuddering sigh. 'But there is one thing I wish most profoundly, and that is that I shall live into the twentieth century, if only for a year or two.' The man turned to face his mountain. 'That is why I sent for you.' He lit a foul-smelling cigarillo.

'You flatter me . . .' I stammered, scarcely believing this last remark. But he was telling me a story, or, more accurately, telling the mountain a story, pulling deeply at his cigarillo all the while.

'There was once an emperor of China who loved nothing more than the song of the nightingale in his forests. One day his enemies presented him with a mechanical nightingale made of pure gold. It sang the same mechanical song over and over again, but the emperor was seduced by its golden beauty and drove away the real nightingale. Eventually the mechanical bird broke down. The emperor became ill with longing for the real bird, whose song, he realised too late, sustained his spiritual life. The real bird returned and sang to the emperor on his deathbed and miraculously restored his health.' He swung round to face me with a dreadful intensity. 'I too am a dying man, Wills. I spoke yesterday about dawn choruses and suchlike, but I, like the Chinese emperor, am in need of a nightingale. Last month my doctor assured me I had only a year or two left to live – mind you, I've heard that story before, but then I had youth on my side. That is why I sent for you at once.'

I looked at him incredulously. 'But it is very unlikely that the nightingales will sing until springtime – if, indeed, they survive in this alien environment.'

The vipers' tongues flickered in his moist eyes. 'But, Wills, you are the world's leading authority on the nightingale's song. You have written books, performed experiments. You know more than anyone in the world what makes a nightingale sing. My advisers were unanimous about that. But in my mind your greatest asset is that you too have been touched by disgrace! As a result you are not merely a cold Oxford scientist. You have suffered! You will understand my position.'

I remained silent as a surge of emotions did battle in my breast. Was this an invitation for me to speak of my collapse?

If so, my host did not know his man. I cleared my throat, and wondered if the *Northampton Castle*, due to sail that afternoon, might have an empty cabin.

'So you are relying on me to restore your health?' I glanced at the potions at his bedside: clearly the drugs he was taking for his heart had affected his brain.

'I'm relying on you to get those birds to sing,' replied he. 'There is something about birdsong that purifies the system. My mother used to tell me that as we listened to the nightingales and blackbirds in the little forest across the meadow.' He glanced demurely at the floor. 'It was she who told me the blackbird could hear worms moving in the earth. I used to crawl on my hands and knees in the mud to listen for worms: I fancied I could hear them too.' He looked up at me, his lower lip quivering. 'I've become quite the expert at hearing the worms crawl, you could say.'

'B-but − are you aware that a nightingale sang on the mountain slopes just last night?' I was flustered.

He frowned. Then remembered. 'Oh, you mean little Maria? Yes, I got her mother to make a clay nightingale. I pay Maria sixpence a week to play in the evenings, before sunset. She's been ill over the last week. Measles, I believe. So she's started again?'

'I have to confess that I was completely taken in by the whistle. It sings as well as any bird in my cages, and is probably more reliable.' I tried to control the panic that had gripped my stomach by breathing deeply, in the manner demonstrated to me by my physician.

He shook his head vehemently, like a spoilt child. 'No, Wills, I want the real thing! Remember the story I've just told you. Imitations aren't good enough. In any case I want the whole mountainside flooded with British birdsong. That's after all what I've paid you to provide.'

It seemed to me that we had spent long enough on this

topic. I dropped my gaze to the box among his papers. 'Is there a golden nightingale there?'

A cunning smile spread over his features. 'Better than that, Wills. There is a *diamond* nightingale in here. It is the most precious thing I own for it represents the consummation of my achievements . . . yet it can never see the light of day! This may come as a surprise to you, Wills, but you are the first man to see this bird, apart from myself and the man who made it.'

'You pay me an extraordinary compliment,' I murmured uncomfortably.

'It is essential that you understand the importance of this project. Look.'

He stubbed his cigarette into a full ashtray, picked up the box (his hands shook a little) and opened it. If I had expected to be ravished by the brilliance of gigantic diamonds, I was to be disappointed. The model of the small bird he now held in his hands appeared to be made from a reddish clay, and was studded with about a hundred opaque stones. It could have been the work of a child.

'You say this is a diamond nightingale?'

'Made out of the clay in which they were found.' He was clearly enjoying my confusion. 'Ever heard of the model compound system up on the diamond fields, Wills?'

'I'm afraid we academics . . .'

'The compound system is one of my Great Thoughts, conceived on the mountain slopes. What do you do with hundreds of thousands of natives from all over Southern Africa, all wanting to work on the mines so that they can buy guns? And drink? They bring their women with them and next thing you've got is whole families of Kaffirs outnumbering the Europeans, wandering about the town at their own sweet will, drinking at Kaffir canteens, smuggling out uncut diamonds which they sell without a qualm to the illicit diamond buyers, the scourge, the IDB scum of the earth!'

Mistaking the distaste which had settled on my face for outrage at his views, he attempted hasty placation. 'Don't get me wrong, I like the natives – but they're children with simple minds. Primitives. They've got to be disciplined and they've got to be watched or they'll play right into the hands of the IDB scum. They've got to be outwitted.' He threw his massive head back and turned his lips down in an imperious smile. 'That's where the closed compounds come in, Wills. Once the miners enter into contract with us, they know that they have to stay in the compound for the length of their contract – two or three months, perhaps. We provide them with everything they need – food, beds, a hospital, baths – good God, man, we've even given them a swimming pool!'

'I'm wondering what this little nightingale has to do with the compounds,' I smiled primly.

The Colossus smirked.

'How long does your food take to pass through your body, Wills? We estimated five days, that's going by British standards. A pair of leather mittens were a further security. Then we let them go home.'

I gazed down at the creature in his hands, my stomach heaving as comprehension dawned.

'Yes, Wills, all these stones have passed through the bodies of my miners. They'll never be released on the market, or go to Amsterdam to be cut. Yet they are my most precious stones, known only to me – and now to you as well.' As I was bereft of speech, he continued, all the while staring at the little model in his hand, his flushed features working. 'I thought this imitation was good enough for me, Wills. But, like the dying emperor, I want the real thing now.' He stretched out his hand and grabbed my arm with a sudden urgency. 'That's why I've brought you here, Wills, all expenses paid. I'll pay you more, man, if you can get those birds to sing. Look round my house – there are priceless antiques – yours for the choosing, Wills!' He waved at the safe. 'You can have the egg, the pistol – all I ask is that you save my life.'

I was trembling. 'You ask too much,' I quavered as I made my way to the door. 'There was no mention of this in the instructions. I am not a well man myself.'

He paused, then spread his lips into a powerful smile. 'I've been meaning to ask you, Wills. Do you play bridge whist? Wonderful game. I've only recently been converted. It takes your mind off all your problems, quite remarkable.'

'I'm afraid I've never been one for games of any kind,' I said faintly. 'Now I must attend to the birds. Good morning.' And I slipped out of the door before he could pounce again.

But he had already reached for the telephone.

To slit open the throat of a nightingale – under careful laboratory conditions, of course – is to embark on a voyage of discovery infinitely more thrilling than those of the early Portuguese and Spanish navigators who inevitably misunderstood the territory they observed. For I have chartered the voyage of song: under the bright flare of the hanging gaslight I have pegged out a rosy fabric on my dissecting table and found within it the two independent chambers of the syrinx wherein the nightingale can sing with two or more voices, controlling the antiphonal flow of his melody with six minute pairs of muscles; pumping, pumping, pumping music into the wet air of Europe, and filling the ice-blue eyes of the Colossus with pink tears. Yes, I have carved open the breast that Oscar set against the Rose's thorn until it penetrated 'her' heart and the rose became crimson as the eastern sky; and within that breast I have found a strong set of bronchial tubes admirably adapted to regulate, reverse and rotate the passage of air that attempts to escape the labyrinthine columns and chambers of the syrinx.

Oh Oscar! Why didn't you consult me before immortalising

your sexual solipsism! You would reply, of course, that gender identity has its ambiguities, whatever the scalpel might reveal; that in the body of every male there lurks a female unseen by anatomists, and only this age of elaborate respectability represses the man in the woman. Such paradoxes have bubbled from your lips 'like water from a silver jar', to use your simile, and you have now paid the ultimate price for the indiscipline of your tongue: it is your breast, dear Oscar, that has been pressed against the thorn of the public, and the red rose of your love has been tossed into the gutter in the cart-wheel's path!

Did I write the above? I sometimes wonder if in my scientist's brain there lurks an artist. I too write books about birds, to my cost.

And now I have three days in which to induce my birds to sing. Perhaps I could bribe a troop of piccanins to whistle in the woods on the day of the Release as the birds struggle out of their cages – to be fed to waiting predators.

OXFORD 1874

My first meeting with Oscar occurred in the Succulent House of the Oxford Botanic Gardens. More accurately, Oscar first acknowledged my existence as I tested the reflexes of a set of sticky insectivorous plants newly arrived from some tropical rain forest in Brazil, and allocated to me, as a student of Natural History, to classify. For my part, the conspicuous style of dress and affected mannerisms of the young Irishman had on several occasions offended my sensibilities, for, as undergraduates in the first Michaelmas term, we had been assigned rooms on the same staircase at Magdalen. His great bulk, often the worse for drink, had more than once battered past my considerably slighter and entirely sober frame, causing me to shrink against the medieval staircase panelling so that he might ascend. Now he leant against the greenhouse doorway, resplendent as a tropical bloom in his violently checked tweed jacket, brilliant yellow necktie, tall collar, a large hat with an upturned brim angled over one ear. He was fiddling with something behind his back.

I recognised him at once, of course, but continued tapping the sharp end of my pencil into the jawlike leaf-blades of the Venus's flytrap. Beside the plant lay my notebook, into which I had ruled (with the same pencil) a grid of taxonomic possibilities pertaining to the two families Nepenthaceae and

Droseraceae. By no means did I underestimate the challenge of accurate classification, for in the world of science the greatest discoveries have sprung from the precise observation of minutiae, whose complex relationships with other levels of minutiae in the hierarchies of the natural world reveal themselves only to the meticulously trained eye. Did Mr Darwin himself not spend eleven years in the patient study of the humble barnacle before releasing to the world his cataclysmic theory of descent by modification? And the last work he ever wrote, as if in anticipation of his own death and burial, was a loving study of the recirculation of organic matter: *The Formation of Vegetable Mould, through the Action of Worms*, in which we learn that, every few years, the whole of the world's top layer passes through the bodies of earthworms.

The green jaws snapped shut and I moved my pencil to mark a tick in a column. The figure in the doorway stirred with evident interest. No doubt mistaking me for a literate gardener he called out, in admiration: 'My dear man, would you be so good as to do that again?'

In those early undergraduate days his voice still had an Irish lilt to it. His smiling charm was dangerous. Pretending to ignore him, I nevertheless removed a small fly from my specimen jar of insects with a pair of pincers. In silence I placed the fly upon the sensitive hairs within the plant jaws: the fly struggled; the trap sprang shut and contracted so tightly that the outline of the writhing victim bulged within the lobes.

'Does this creature have a throat – a stomach? Though green, is it partly human? And if one were to eat this carnivore, would one be eating meat or vegetable?'

I considered my reply. Incapable of the cut and thrust of Oxford badinage, I could, at best, deliver a lecture on plant-trapping mechanisms, the details of which would soon discourage my visitor. Instead, I continued filling my columns with details concerning the habits of insectivorous plants (shape of leaf, activity of tentacles, production of viscous fluid), and heard myself say:

'You may be interested to know that Mr Darwin feeds his insect-eaters with roast beef and strong tea.'

'Thereby proving them to be little animals disguised as leaves!' exclaimed Oscar, suddenly gauche.

Something about his benign presence inspired me to continue this absurd conversation.

'You may also be interested to know that these plants can count from nought to two.' My voice was so faint that he would have had to strain his ears to hear me.

'Indeed? How truly remarkable!' He bounded over to the tray of plants with wide eyes as if expecting to see each of them equipped with a small abacus.

'Look in here.' I pointed to the inside of a hinged trap. 'Three sensor hairs. If I tickle one – like so – with my fly, nothing happens. But if I touch it again within thirty seconds, the trap will snap shut!' The plant obliged by swallowing the specimen. 'It can tell the difference between nought, one, or two taps – more than most mammals can do.'

'I find this more fascinating than you can ever imagine,' declaimed Oscar as if to a great hall of enchanted listeners. 'I have in my head poems – and stories – upon this very topic: a beautiful continuum between plant, animal and man, in which each experiences identical emotional states. My ambition is to erase the barrier between human and non-human animals, and to prove that love and suffering, anxiety and joy, are not unique to the human race.' He tilted his head towards me, and smiled hopefully.

I allowed this froth of thought to settle in my brain for a few seconds, and was about to dismiss it as aesthetic claptrap, when I became aware that something odd was stirring in my heart. That throbbing organ, the sole function of which had been, till this moment, to circulate the blood in my thin white body, now appeared to be swelling with a sensation that I had never before experienced. I bit my lip to prevent myself from bursting into gales of inexperienced laughter, and, in a flash of euphoria, I understood that the greatest gift one human being can give to another is that of *joy*. Oscar gave me that priceless gift. He gave it to many, for he was generous with his joy. Through the conduit of his wit the delight that brimmed in his life flowed into even the most melancholy of hearts and caused them to beat briefly with vicarious pleasure.

For fear of fainting, I was forced to grip the edges of the specimen table. My voice trembled a little as I replied: 'I believe Mr Darwin is preparing a paper on the subject of insectivorous plants. He is said to be impressed by the fact that plant cells possess the same capacity for irritability response as animal cells.'

'It depresses me tremendously to think I'll never read it!' cried Oscar, apparently unaware of the upheaval in my breast. 'I am far too superficial a person, concerned as I am only with how things look and feel, rather than how they work. I like to pretend to myself that beauty is effortless. Oh, how very differently you and I consider the lily!' and with a theatrical flourish he produced from behind his back a wilting specimen of *Liliaceae anmintionis*. My heart still warm with its new emotion, I hovered in the greenery like the Handmaid of the Lord before the Angel Gabriel, while Oscar considered the lily for several minutes in language I can only describe as unscientific.

'So who cares about your Origins or your Fertilisations,' he finished, by now on one knee, ' "for you are one of the most beautiful and most useless things in the world", according to my mentor Ruskin – who I believe returns from Italy at the end of the month. I wonder if you have met his gardener, a Mr Downes?' He staggered to his feet, knocked a tray of seedlings off a shelf, and fell to his knees again to repair the damage.

'Mr Downes is up on the Hinksey Road, laying stone with the Balliol men,' I replied.

'Dear Mr Ruskin! I am so very interested in his road-building project!' He removed a glove to scoop soil and seedlings back into their tray, willy-nilly, then rose to wave his lily at me once again. 'Which reminds me of why I have brought this useless object into your greenhouse. In obedience to my mentor's injunction that beauty should be accompanied by toil, a concept horribly foreign to my own instincts, I have decided to grow my lilies myself, needing a constant supply – and I require some information about how to go about this act of gardening.'

With a great deal of anxiety about fragile species near the edges of shelves, I led my visitor past the spectacular Bird of Paradise (*Strelitzia reginae*) in the Succulent Room, and through the blaze of bougainvillaea in the Temperate Corridor. Here I nearly lost him as he gazed longingly at the riotous Mediterranean blooms. 'I could make an exquisite buttonhole of these,' he mourned (for picking the specimens was, of course, forbidden). 'A miniature work of art, so underestimated by the general public.' We made our way out into the evolutionary beds where species were arranged according to their botanical families. His voice lilted on, effortless and melodious, nourishing the tender shoots of pleasure in my heart. 'I am convinced that a really well-made buttonhole is the only link between Art and Nature. This is my sole, though vital, contribution to the world of scientific thought!' A couple of butterflies shot out of the chrysanthemum bed and hovered over the yellow checks of his jacket.

I cleared my throat. 'We have reached the Liliaceae bed,'

I announced, and proceeded to deliver a brief lecture on the genus Lilium with its six-segmented flowers, three-chambered capsular fruits, and scaly bulbs, and to offer advice about pot culture, which I felt sure would never be put to use. At the end of my speech, Oscar clapped me on the back and beamed at me, exposing those somewhat protruding front teeth which would one day be blackened by sulphuric treatment for syphilis.

'What a fountainhead of information you are! I shall have to recommend you to the chief gardener. Pray tell me your name.'

'My name is Francis Wills, and I must inform you that I am a student of the Natural Sciences, at present working on the classification of rare and exotic flora, and that I have rooms in 2 pair Right in Chaplain's.'

'I say, that's only a door or two away from mine!' cried Oscar ingenuously. 'And did you say your name was Wills? Can we by any chance be related? My name is Wills Wilde – Oscar Wills Wilde – Oscar Fingal O'Flahertie Wills Wilde' (by now his voice had thickened into a deliberate Irish brogue) 'and I must ask ye if ye're related to the great Irish playwright W.G. Wills, after whom I am named.'

'I am his second cousin,' replied I, and this seemed good enough reason for Oscar to sweep me to his rapturous breast and call me cousin – a kinship that would certainly not have been recognised by the Linnaean rules of nomenclature. Nevertheless, our chance mutual ownership of family name was to bind us with a loyalty as strong as any found among siblings: he is the only man who could make me laugh. And love.

CAPE TOWN 1899

After my interview with the Colossus, some distraction was necessary.

I switched on the red light of the dark-room, closed the door, and prepared the chemical solutions for the printing process. There is something all-absorbing in this activity, perhaps because one is sealed off from the rest of the world in a delightfully claustrophobic atmosphere of dim redness and potent chemical. The dark-room is indeed a sanctuary for hermits. I placed each negative in the developing and fixing dishes, marvelling, as ever, at the gradual emergence of ghostly outlines that slowly intensified into a dense black and white representation of recognisable objects. One can think of nothing else but the removal of the print from the dish at precisely the right moment so that the result is neither too pale nor too dark, at which point one pegs it upon the line and examines the near-finished product. Most of the sugar bird prints were highly satisfactory, partly due to the sharp African sunlight which gave the images an almost three-dimensional quality. Unfortunately my attempts to capture the curious movements of the bird's wings and tail on celluloid were less than successful: though the protea head itself was clearly etched against the backdrop of pines, the bird's streaming tail and fluttering wings were something of a blur. Nevertheless, a creditable sequence of wet photographs now hung upon the line. In the red glow of the electric bulb I studied the fruits of my labours more closely.

The recently purchased lens of my camera had picked out the bird's habitat in quite astounding detail. Not only was every feather of the bird and every petal of the flower reproduced down to the last particular, the pine plantation in the background was also revealed as clearly as if I had trained my lens upon the rows of trees as well as my little feathered friend. Yet even as I admired the pleasing symmetry of the plantation I became aware that in among the tree trunks hovered a human being. The powerful lens had reproduced exactly the agitated expression on the woman's face as she leaned against a pine tree and stared into the garden, all unaware that a man was photographing her from his hide of jute. I recognised her at once as the woman on the bench: short, stout, imperious, with a troubled look in her dark eyes. Perhaps she was gazing at the happy family on the back verandah, but whatever she was doing there, she was spoiling my photograph. Fortunately it is simple to remove unwanted images: a few movements of my fingers under the light would cause the intruder to fade into the darkness of the interior forest when I redeveloped the negatives.

A quick glance at my fob-watch informed me that an hour had sped past and that it was time for my next meeting. I gathered together my equipment, hurried down the stairs (bumping my free hand against Phoenician hawks all the way) and entered the vestibule.

Great gusts of cigar smoke assailed my nostrils as I passed the open library door, and an animated male dialogue made me pause, in a sudden desire to eavesdrop. I recognised one of the voices as that which had risen from the hydrangeas the day before, no longer mellow with child-love, but sharpened with outrage. The other voice I did not know, but could guess at its owner.

'And this frontispiece photograph!' cried Kipling. 'Three niggers hanging from a tree with the pioneers standing around. Pretending to be an illustration to her piece of propaganda! I thought the woman had more sense!'

His companion spoke in rapid, emphatic tones. 'The only niggers I ever saw hanged were nigger spies, I can tell you that.'

'She calls him "death on niggers" when we all know the natives fairly worship him! I've seen for myself how they follow him round like dogs, longing for him just to throw them a smile or a glance. *Life* on niggers, more like. Jobs for niggers. And possibly, one day, civilisation for niggers.'

His companion snorted. 'She's one of these New Women who feel it is their duty to shriek about male domination, sexual inequality, and all that rubbish. In my book, she's nothing more than a female hysteric who isn't able to reproduce herself. Lost her child recently after a series of miscarriages. It's unbalanced her mind. But you know of course the real reason for this outburst?'

'Well?'

The unseen speaker sniggered. 'The truth of the matter is she's been in love with our host for the last ten years. Fancied herself as his missus, you might say. When it was clear there were to be no wedding bells, she turned nasty. Don't know how her husband puts up with her antics.'

I caught a glimpse of my face distorted in a bronze Netherlandish spittoon probably once owned by the first Dutch gardener Jan van Riebeeck himself, and decided it was time to move. I had not long left the house and made my way down the avenue when I heard fast, firm footsteps pound after me.

'Professor Wills, sir!'

I lowered my equipment to the ground and turned to confront the young man I recognised as the Colossus' blond secretary who had caused my teacup to fly out of my hands the day before. He alone of the gaggle of young men constantly in attendance upon their master had not succumbed to the unfortunate after-effects of too much food and drink. The whites of his eyes were devoid of the network of red veins that bulged from those of his colleagues; the blue irises were equally clear. In a tornado of dust and gravel he skidded to a halt beside me and waved a telegram under my nose.

'I'm very sorry to disturb you, sir, but I saw you walking down the avenue and I thought I'd catch you. I've brought you another message. He says he meant to ask you when you met him this morning but he forgot!' The young man who had collided with Huxley yesterday morning now turned the full beam of his engaging smile on to me.

I glanced at the scribbled message. *'Please dine with us tonight, Dr Jameson would like to meet you.'*

'I thought I had made it clear that I was not to attend evening meals,' I sighed, resisting a throb of curiosity. 'Will there be many people?'

He smiled encouragingly. 'Only very interesting and unusual people, sir. You could even say very famous people!'

'I have no interest in famous people,' I muttered; then, as disappointment blanched his exuberant features, I added, by way of an excuse, 'I'm afraid I'm a bit of a recluse, you see. I haven't been well.' He raised his eyebrows politely, inviting me to continue. 'I partly agreed to come here so that I could recuperate in a healthy climate. Instead of which . . .'

The young man's face lit up. His white teeth flashed within the virile growth of his moustaches. 'Then you must go to the seaside, sir!' he exclaimed. 'That is where all invalids go to convalesce. You can walk for miles around a perfectly unspoiled coast, or even swim in the waters of False Bay, which are quite warm, I assure you. Mr Kipling likes nothing more than a morning stroll along Muizenberg beach.'

The innocence of his enthusiasm amused me. 'I should like nothing better!' I lied, though on that beautiful autumn morning, with the sun filtering down through the crisp oak leaves and all the tropical plants tumbling in violent hues out of their display beds, the preposterous idea of swimming in an Ocean did not sound quite as alien as it might otherwise have done. 'But unfortunately I have to prepare my birds for their release in three days' time. Much is expected of me, I'm afraid.'

'Perhaps you will visit the seaside after the Release. He' – and here the young man waved his hand in the direction of the Great Granary – 'has a cottage in Muizenberg which you could easily reach by train. It has a most magnificent outlook, right across the bay.'

'Well, we'll see.' I felt I could not tell this enthusiastic young person that I was booked to leave for England on the *Windsor Castle* the following Monday, this time up the west coast of Africa. In order to divert his mind from the seaside I changed tack.

'May I ask you your name, young man, as you seem to know mine?'

'James Joubert, sir,' replied he proudly, pushing his chest out a little. 'Directly descended from the Huguenot refugees. And I can't speak a word of French!'

'And now you are a secretary here?'

'Yes, sir. He made me learn shorthand. I have been very fortunate.'

'Well, thank you, Joubert. I must be on my way. I've no doubt we shall meet again.'

His grin radiated health. 'Oh, no doubt, sir. You'll be getting more of these telegrams, I expect!'

We bade each other farewell, the poor man colliding with

the flirtatious daughter on his way back up the avenue, she fluttering all about him as he tried to stride along, clearly indifferent to her overtures. I proceeded on my way, marvelling at the picaresque turn my life had taken. It seemed that every hour of the waking day I was destined to meet complete strangers or unrelated figures from my past, one after the other, and become involved in some small adventure with them. How very different from the predictable pattern of my Oxford existence!

I could now hear the rumbling of a carriage which drew up not far from where I stood with my camera and equipment. The horses tossed their heads in the air while Alfred's long legs unfolded from the open carriage, segment by segment. The object of our photographic session was lifted down from the back of the vehicle and Alfred murmured words of thanks and instruction to the coachman. As the carriage clattered off, he turned to greet me with a condescending smile.

'I have exactly eighteen minutes.'

The bicycle was brand new, as far as I could tell, and of the most recent design.

Sir Alfred Milner had metamorphosed from the stiff-collared senior statesman of yesterday into a sporty gent in full cycling regalia. I suppressed a thin smile: he might just as well have appeared in a clown's outfit or a woman's skirt, so incongruously did his present accoutrement sit upon those long, spidery limbs. Or so it seemed at first. He was holding the bicycle close against him as if he knew not what to do with it, but suddenly extended his multi-jointed right leg and mounted the saddle with easy confidence.

Now boyish Sir Alfred Milner opened his mouth and laughed outright as he cycled round and round me, ringing the bell and waving his hat as if performing in a circus. 'Do you cycle? Wonderful release! Everyone should try it!'

I shook my head impatiently and began to set up my tripod

without comment. In a cloud of dust he skidded to a halt beside me, his heels grinding through the gravel and acting as brakes.

'Surprised you, eh, Wills? This is my one relaxation – in England, that is.' A shifty look gleamed in those gimlet eyes and I wondered what was coming. 'She and I chose this together. I promised I'd ride it every day here, for the exercise. She thinks I spend too much time shut up round negotiating tables and the like.'

'She?' Would everyone in the Southern hemisphere feel compelled to pour out their private lives to me?

'Mmmm.' He began pedalling down the drive in a leisurely fashion, even humming a little tune from *Patience*. 'I think here would be best.' He had dismounted in order to position himself with the Great Granary in the far background. 'Bit of a wedding cake, isn't it!' He pulled a face in the direction of the house. 'That whitewash looks exactly like icing-sugar in this sunlight, wouldn't you say? Still, she'd like it. I promised her I'd send her photographs of all the grand houses I went to. As well as photographs of myself upon the bicycle. She didn't believe I'd ride it. She was right.' He consulted his watch, hidden in a striped breast pocket. 'Twelve minutes. Sorry about this, old chap. It's the life I lead.'

'Right, now, if you put your foot actually on the pedal – that's perfect . . .' And the next five minutes or so were spent with my head under a piece of black cloth while Sir Alfred Milner froze into different shapes and attitudes illustrating leisure, both on and off the saddle. In the easy atmosphere he felt inclined to chatter.

'Kipling tells me he rode round Rhodesia on a bicycle recently – or was it just Bulawayo?' (*Freeze.*) 'Interesting chap, Kipling. Got a lot of time for him.' (*Freeze.*) 'Can laugh at himself. Apparently he hired his machine from the only cycle shop in the town. The proprietor thought him such a scruffy little fellow that he demanded a guarantor.' (*Freeze*.) 'Kipling brought along none other than he from whom the Colony takes its name. Acute embarrassment on behalf of one cycle proprietor!' (*Freeze*.)

'Will you now cycle along the avenue very slowly, backwards and forwards, while I attempt to improve on my exposure technique for objects in motion?'

He began to speak again, his foot safely on the pedal. His voice was perhaps a semitone higher.

'I'll never understand why Oscar didn't jump bail. He had every opportunity. There was even a steam yacht at the ready, I'm told. I was in Egypt at the time. He didn't have to go to prison.' Backwards and forwards Milner pedalled, back very erect, knees rising far higher than the average man's. I followed his movements, ghost-like and upside down on each glass plate. 'At Oxford his favourite painting was St Sebastian studded with arrows, the Reni, in Genoa. There was always the martyr element in Oscar. The slings and arrows of outrageous fortune. So unnecessary. I believe six hundred gentlemen crossed the Channel on the night the warrant for his arrest was issued.'

I withdrew my head from under the cloth. 'Thank you,' I said. 'I think that's enough. Would you mind riding to the curve in the avenue and I'll try a long-distance shot.'

'Only too happy, dear chap. I see I have four minutes left.'

I readjusted the tripod, added a lens, buried my head in the cloth and watched Alfred Milner float off into the distance, the wrong way up. I always enjoy this moment, when the world is shaped by the boundaries I impose, and my brain is required to interpret the primitive message of the plate-glass retina. It does not take long to adjust to the inverted world of the camera, so when I observed a shape begin to extrude downwards from the near end of the pendulous avenue along which Sir Alfred cycled, I did not have to reorientate my eyes in order to recognise what I was seeing. The figure hovered upside down under one of the great oaks, her reticule clutched tightly in her hands, looking as if she might dash out at any minute and throw herself before my aerial subject and his bicycle. I withdrew my head sharply from beneath the black cloth, with the intention of frowning her away. Her feet now on the ground and her head in the air, she smiled brightly – even brazenly – at me, and vanished across the lawn, towards a cluster of palm trees.

Alfred was now on his return journey, quite unaware of the intruder. My head returned beneath the cloth. He called out to me: 'Her name is Cecile. You could say that we have cycled many miles together. But I have had to say goodbye. A mistress in Brixton is too dangerous for a man of my status. One has to make sacrifices for the Empire, for the greater good.' He had reached me now. Though I had no further pictures to take I remained with my head covered. 'She understood completely, of course. But she has been part of my life for nearly ten years. Do you have a woman tucked away somewhere, Wills?'

The question made me jump. I felt my cheeks flame. I emerged. 'I too have dedicated my energies to my life's work,' I stammered. 'I am not a man for domesticity.'

He sighed. 'There is nothing so sweet as to have a woman's head upon your knee, her hair all undone and flowing through your hands.' He paused, then laughed through his nose, a habit of his I remember finding distasteful twenty-five years ago. 'Especially if one has just dined with the Queen. Or the Duke of Marlborough. From Blenheim to Brixton. I have to say that the risk of exposure added considerable spice to the affair. Fortunately my Teutonic upbringing has trained me to know where to draw the line – unlike some of my colleagues. And *un*fortunately, the line has had to be drawn through Cecile's dear heart. Nevertheless, these photographs will console her. I could not entirely abandon her.' His moustache-fangs twitched.

'I shall have them ready by tomorrow,' I said briskly. 'There is a dark-room at my disposal, with every facility.'

The wheels of a carriage clattered towards us. 'He has arrived half a minute early. Ah well, better that way round. Thank you, Wills. This has been a pleasant break. Will I see you tonight?'

'I am expected.'

'I shall naturally remunerate you for your services.'

'I wouldn't hear of it,' said I mechanically.

And the coachman, whose face too bore the mark of tribal etchings, gravely relieved the Viceroy of his vehicle.

'Well, then – *merci beaucoup! À bientôt!*'

CHILDHOOD

I had lied to Huxley about brothers in the Church and Army. It was necessary for me to invent another family, another childhood.

My real childhood was spent in bed. I had not been expected to survive long after my birth, which had been difficult, my foetal self resisting with all its might an ejection from my mother's body. My first six months were passed in my sisters' shared christening shawl: I showed no interest in playing with my toes, or waving my hands before my eyes, or exhibiting the usual infantile behaviour designed by nature to stimulate the senses and awaken the mind. Indeed, for almost a year it was considered that I might be suffering from some form of cortical blindness, as I refused to track a moving light or blink at an advancing hand. For, from the very beginning, I placed more trust in my supernaturally sharp ears than my eyes. The stillness of the body required for intent listening was quite misinterpreted by my family and the physicians, who supposed me to be the victim of some genteel paralysis. But within each ear the chain of ossicle, nerve, muscle and fibre worked with a furious intensity quite invisible to those who study only the orbs of vision for signs of health or intelligence. Thus it was that long before I began to speak myself, I could understand the secret murmurings that accrete in the corners of any large household. More than that: I could interpret an abnormal breathing pattern, a fleeting suspension of breath, a sigh or gasp so infinitesimal that its perpetrator was unaware of the clues he breathed out into the passage of air between his lips and my busy, but externally motionless, ears. In fact, so sharp was my hearing during those first few years of my life that I could even hear the pounding of a heart half-way across the room as fear or joy caused its volume to increase. This remarkable ability was achieved through absolute control over every muscle of my body, a control which enabled me to lie in a state of suspended, though eavesdropping, animation.

My mother, a vigorous woman more interested in horses than humans, kept out of my way, perhaps in preparation for my early exit from this life (I believe enquiries were made about infant coffins). After a year or so it became apparent that, in spite of my stiffness and pallor, I was a perfectly normal child, with full powers of vision but too feeble to move from his cot. As the years passed and nothing changed in this respect, my parents therefore resigned themselves to keeping me permanently in bed, an arrangement which I found much to my taste.

By contrast, seven rosy-cheeked older sisters spun about the Vicarage, always singing with excitement about the toad-stools that had sprung up overnight in the middle of the lawn, or the fledgling that had fallen out of its nest into the wheelbarrow. From birth, they had been in the grip of some natural history craze, whether it be bugs, birds, frogs or baby alligators, and could recite the names of dozens of different species of fern or fungus with considerably more zest than they recited their Latin verbs. The fruits of their enthusiasms were crowded into the drawing-room: miniature Tintern Abbeys and Crystal Palaces housed mighty jungles of glossy fern upon bookshelves, bureaux and occasional tables; sea anemones waved their tentacles amidst forests of algae in glass tanks and crystal vases; while above them, on marble and mahogany stands, kingfishers, humming-birds and a barn owl displayed their wings in frozen flight. Pride of place was taken by a glass case on the grand piano containing a red squirrels' tea party (the squirrels drank from tiny cups and ate even tinier slices of china cake). No wonder my childish mind perceived this museum as an intermediary stage between life and death where my lifeless body would eventually be displayed, pinned down like Gulliver, inside a glass fern-case.

My oldest sisters had, in addition, other more obscure interests which nevertheless required much shrieking and mimicry of each other and a great deal of prancing about in front of the full-length mirror stationed near the end of my bed, into which I chose to gaze soulfully for much of the day. For several years I was unable to distinguish between these older sisters and my mother, who spent most of her time galloping about the countryside on a dappled stallion and digging up rare ferns, instead of attending to my father's parishioners. Indeed, my only means of maternal identification was the vicious snarl emitted by her coal-black lap-dog whenever he entered my bedroom ahead of his mistress: Kaffir would have nothing to do with my sisters and loathed me in particular, detecting a maleness about me that my family seemed to have overlooked. I think my mother occasionally confused me with her dog, absently addressing me as 'good boy' and rubbing my pale halo of hair as if it were animal fur.

My sisters regarded me as a favourite doll, fashioned out of fragile and opaque white china. They liked to trace the blue veins in my neck, legs and arms with their pink fingers. As I lay propped up on seven precisely arranged cushions, they would recreate for me, in blasts of cold air which always followed them into my bedroom, the world called 'Outdoors', which seemed to consist entirely of objects to be collected. Through my bedroom window I observed a confusion of trees, flowers and grass, all of which came to an abrupt halt at the wall which bounded the outer edge of the garden, together with a row of small tombstones inscribed with the names of deceased dogs, and grinning at me like a row of unevenly spaced bottom teeth. No wonder I preferred to recline in the soft confines of my bed.

Into this paradise occasionally strayed private tutors who attempted to direct my sisters' attention to other branches of learning, such as Latin and Arithmetic. These young men, whose interests were not robust, began to wander into my bedroom and, no doubt mistaking me for yet another sister, began listlessly teaching me declensions and logarithms. I had mastered the entire Latin language in a month, and was racing through Catullus and Ovid, when an unsuspecting tutor introduced me to the delights of Linnaeus' *Systema Naturae* in order to give my new-found skill some practical application. The veils fell from my eyes; I left Icarus flying towards the sun with his wings of wax and feather; I had discovered taxonomy and the Great Chain of Being. My sisters might Collect, but my role was to Classify – in secret, as the family physician had assured my parents that any mental activity on my behalf would undoubtedly lead to Brain Fever followed by madness and even more premature extinction than was predicted. (I was not even allowed the Bible, the opening chapter of Genesis being regarded as far too rousing for a boy whose heart beat as feebly as mine.) I felt a curious contentment in this immaculately classified universe; and a certainty that this was the correct order of things, as opposed to the terrifying tangle of animal and vegetable life that seethed beyond the Vicarage walls.

Sadly, the tutor concerned soon after moved on to another

post, but not before smuggling into my room *Species Plantarum* (from which I learnt the delights of binomial nomenclature) and *Philosophia Botanica* (in which I learned the delights of sexual organs). My imagination was inflamed by Linnaeus' descriptions of plant reproduction: '*The actual petals of a flower contribute nothing to generation, serving only as the bridal bed which the great Creator has so gloriously prepared, adorned with such precious bed-curtains, and perfumed with so many sweet scents in order that the bridegroom and bride may therein celebrate their nuptials with the greater solemnity. When the bed has thus been made ready, then is the time for the bridegroom to embrace his beloved bride and surrender himself to her.*' Naturally I had no idea as to what this surrender involved but the erotic nature of the language led me to examine my own organs of procreation with some interest.

I hid my books under my bed and bade my nursemaid Elspeth cut me great bunches of every flower in the garden, that I might observe these nuptial delights for myself. Thus did my bed become even more like a coffin prepared for its final journey, and my angelic head, protruding above a cloud of flowers, required only a glass dome from the drawing room for the image of child-death to be complete.

But Elspeth was determined to prevent me from dying. Elspeth did not believe I was suffering from some wasting disease, boldly attributing my unnatural pallor and apathy to a lack of fresh air and exercise, and a misunderstanding by my parents as to how to bring up Boys. On occasions, when the whole family, my father excepted, was out riding furiously across the hills, she would whisk me out from under the bedclothes, turn me upside down and thump my back while I screeched for mercy. A prolonged, indignant coughing fit would follow, after which my cheeks glowed and my eyes sparkled unwillingly for the rest of the morning.

'What wouldn't I give to take you home with me and mix you up with other lads of your age,' she would mutter. 'All stuff and nonsense, this bed business.' The fact that I knew she was right only fuelled my determination to be terminally ill.

To begin with, the only member of my family whose presence I could tolerate was my father. A gentleman naturalist of the first order, he collected rare species of moths with beautiful nets specially woven for him by one of his parishioners who, like himself, believed that capturing, killing and displaying the variety of God's creation was the most Christian thing a person could do. He was certainly at his most content as he sorted out his booty in the privacy of his study lined with dark cabinets containing exhibits of every known species. Boxes of exotic moths from all over the world, usually in the cocoon stage of their metamorphosis, would frequently be sent to him by explorers and globetrotters who knew of his passion. Sometimes, as he opened these boxes, a cloud of winged creatures would tumble out and alight upon his spectacles, his pink lips, his neat grey beard, mistaking him for a multi-sensory, exotic tree. I allowed him to carry me into his room occasionally, where he would remove for my inspection select trays of moths which he had pinned and labelled in microscopic italics.

Attached to his sanctuary was a conservatory filled with moths and plants from every continent. (My sisters begged him to install within it an aquarium balanced upon a sheaf of bronze barley heads and surmounted by a triple fountain in the shape of conch-blowing Cupids, as advertised in Mrs Hibberd's *Rustic Adornments for Homes of Taste*: for once he refused them.) He attempted to interest me in the winged creatures that fluttered inside the rustically unadorned conservatory, bringing to my bedside live specimens like the Noctuid moth with brilliant cat's-eye markings on its wings, or, more daringly, a Death's Head Hawk moth, *Acherontia atropos*, that squeaked like a mouse when stroked. He was particularly interested in the camouflage tactics of certain species and would occasionally journey to the outskirts of our nearest industrial city to capture moths that had adjusted the colour of their wings to merge with their new sooty environment. Once in the salubrious atmosphere of his conservatory, the offspring of these moths would slowly return to the colour God had intended, as my father saw it. I think that cleaning up the moths was his way of fighting the adverse effects of the great Industrial Revolution sweeping England, outside the Vicarage.

One day, when all the female members of the family were out riding or collecting, my father invited me into his study with a solemnity that suggested something out-of-the-ordinary was about to happen. By this stage it had been ascertained that I could walk unaided – I must have been about seven years old at the time – so, still swathed in my sisters' christening shawl (my own christening had been a hasty affair, performed by my father the day after I was born), a woollen night-dress and fur-lined slippers, I tottered into his darkened sanctuary. My father was clearly excited by the visit. I was made to sit in a leather armchair while he proceeded across the room to a small table covered in red chenille cloth, upon which stood a giant aspidistra. First he lifted the aspidistra, placing it, to my surprise, upon the floor; then he removed the cloth, which he folded meticulously, to reveal that the table was in fact not a table but a large metal safe.

'Now, my boy,' said he, 'while the ladies are out of the house I want to show you my most prized possession. Not even your mother knows of its existence. Your sisters I consider to be altogether too rough to be allowed near treasures of this nature. This is to be secret business between father and son, wouldn't you say?'

And my father smiled at me, revealing a set of large white teeth that always took me by surprise (I too now have the same impressive dental structure which probably helps me to produce my bird whistles with such clarity). Throughout his little speech to me he had indulged in his nervous habit of beard-tugging, whereby, while he spoke, he would locate a particularly thick and springy representative of his facial hair, and rub it between his forefinger and thumb, pulling at it gently, as if about to pluck it from its fellows. He seemed quite unaware of this private activity which he performed regularly in public, much to the distraction of his companions. (Strangely, this is a habit which I seem to have inherited from my father, though I hope I keep it more secret than he. Even as I write, I find a friendly coil of hair between the first and second fingers of my left hand.) I believe the only time he desisted from this habit was during the delivery of his sermons, when he clung with both hands to the pulpit to steady his nerves.

'Listen!' he continued, as I sat propped and shrouded, a tiny ghost in the depths of a large armchair. 'This is the safe inside which my treasure lies. And this is a combination lock.' He pointed to the round dial surrounded by numbers. 'I twist it forward . . .' – click click – 'I twist it backward . . .' – click click click click – 'I twist it forward again . . .' – click click – 'And – *voilà*!' The heavy metal door leapt open, as if it had been straining to do so all day.

I felt no particular curiosity about the impending revelation. If anything, I felt only mild irritation, as I had been looking forward to spending the morning with Linnaeus without fear of noisy interruption. I watched my father extend his unsteady hands into the safe, slowly, slowly, as if what he was about to grasp might fall apart at the merest touch. In careful triumph he turned to me.

'Do you know what this is?'

Charles Dodgson had not yet published *Alice*, or I might have been able to guess. What I saw was a large bluish oval shape inside a velvet-lined box.

'It's a negg,' I replied dully.

'Ah, but *what* an egg!' exclaimed my father. 'This is the last unfertilised egg of the Dodo *Raphus cucullatus*, a miserable species of bird who lived on an island in the Indian Ocean and forgot to grow wings!'

'A creature without wings cannot be a bird,' I piped, mindful of Linnaeus.

My father's red lips stretched apart in delighted laughter at my pomposity. '*Ergo*, a creature *with* wings must be a bird, is that so?' he exclaimed. 'And yet I can tell you of frogs and squirrels and monkeys that fly, and fish whose fins are busier in the air than in the water!'

I frowned impatiently. 'I am speaking of the feathered wings common to the species Avis. Frogs and fish do not grow feathers.'

My father's good humour was inextinguishable, even by the cold wash of my contempt. 'Thank you for that information, my son. But look carefully.' He held the box under my face. 'This egg is over two hundred years old – probably the only one of its kind in the world. When the great gardener Tradescant brought over the last remaining head and foot of that bird to Oxford together with his collection of rarities, he brought with him this egg. It never reached the Ashmole, together with the other rarities, because Tradescant did not know he had it. The egg had been discovered by our great-great-great-great-grandfather, then a young apprentice gardener collecting specimens, unhatched and cold under a bush of oleander – almost as if the Dodo foetus saw no reason to leave the shell only to be slaughtered. Our ancestor never revealed his find: instead the egg has passed from father to son over the generations. I feared that this practice might end – because of your ill-health – but now I see I have a son who will love the objects created by God so that we might know and love Him in return.'

'But that egg represents the failure of the bird to adapt to its changing environment,' I replied (for Mr Darwin's theory already simmered below the surface of Victorian doctrine, and was soon to come to the boil). 'An inept species cannot expect to survive.'

My father's laugh was a little nervous this time. 'It is the fate of all species, however fit, to become extinct – in the fullness of time. But we have had enough excitement for one morning. Let me return you to your bed.'

I might have faded away according to plan had the household cat not one day caught a young blackbird which one of my sisters nursed back to health. Instead of releasing it back into the wild she had the idea of procuring a cage, placing the bird inside it, and depositing the cage on the table beside my bed. As it was springtime the bird burst into ear-splitting song at an early hour of the morning, and continued to serenade me at intervals through the day until the room was finally darkened, at which time a most mournful but piercing lullaby issued from the bird's inexhaustible throat. My initial impulse was to order the creature's instant removal, for its music drowned every other sound in the house, but I found myself listening with a purely scientific interest to the ever-changing patterns of the liquid trills, whistles and melodic phrases that now poured into my solemn bedroom. When no one was about, I imitated this bountiful song with my own lips, and found I had a talent for whistling. Naturally, I kept this discovery to myself.

It so happened that the spring of that year was a particularly warm one, with the result that the persistent Elspeth threw open with her strong arms all the stiff windows to allow in the warm sweet odours of lilac and honeysuckle, and the brilliant shafts of sunshine unrefracted by panes of glass. While complaining bitterly of the delicate drifts of air which I considered to be dangerous draughts, I was obliged to observe that the songs of my bird were undergoing a subtle change. For not only fresh air, garden perfumes and sunshine now penetrated the gloom of my room through the open windows, but also the torrential music of a hundred different species of bird. A family of blackbirds had nested in a hedge near my window (my room was on the ground floor), and the father and husband announced his territorial boundaries with strident and penetrating song, almost as if trilling into a megaphone. The offspring soon began to try out their own voices, and I was interested to note that their song was similar in structure to my own bird's efforts, a mere template without the ornate embellishments and flourishes which tripped so easily off the tongue of their progenitor. Almost immediately, the question occurred to me: what would happen if they were deprived of adult song? And then: if they couldn't hear their own song? I longed to experiment then and there.

It was at this point that two crucial events occurred which set the seal on my future development.

At the age of eight I had begun to notice my mother. It had become apparent to me that she held some special power over my sisters, as if they all wore invisible bridles, the seven reins of which led to my mother's strong hand. In some mysterious way, I began to understand, she held the rein attached to my own very different bridle. I felt caught up in her current: I began to long for her rough goodnight kiss, always remembered by her at the last minute; indeed, often forgotten. And with the tentative emergence of my new feelings, a kind of abrupt fondness for her only son stirred in my mother's unmaternal breast. A mutual interest started to develop between us, an osmosis of kindred feeling rather than a release of love. She spent a little more time at my bedside, proportionately less of which was spent in shouting commands at her lap-dog, who now stared at me with pure hatred as her interest appeared to shift from dog to son. (My mother had owned several dogs – though always one at a time – during her twenty-year marriage to my father. Their portraits were displayed along with those of favourite ponies and stallions in a less formal drawing-room, where the family could move about freely without fear of knocking over aquaria, fern houses or domes of stuffed animals.)

On the day in question – 22 November 1859 – my mother had suggested to me that I might like to go Outdoors. It was now evident to her that if I was strong enough to walk about the house I could venture out into the bracing world of Nature, a world in which I had by now some considerable academic interest. A pony would wait by the door (the idea of being Outdoors without a horse was inconceivable to her): I could even sit upon its back for a while and begin to understand the joys of horseriding, in which the imperfect human body flows into that of the most noble of beasts, and is transfigured.

'But, Mama, I have never seen you ride.'

This was probably the most intimate line I ever addressed to my mother.

She looked at me in astonishment, then rose decisively from my bedside. Prodding with her foot the ever-vigilant Kaffir, she gathered up her skirts and announced: 'I'm going straight to the stables where I'll get Lewis to saddle up Blenheim. Watch the wall at the end of the garden, Francis, and not only will you see your mother ride, you will see her fly!'

I can see her flying now, she and Blenheim together, a Valkyrie in the grey English sky, all power and noise and joy. They are frozen in mid-air above the Vicarage wall because I do not want to see Blenheim's hoof entangle with wistaria, nor hear the jolt of flesh and bone as my mother tumbled down the wall and struck her unprotected head against a dog's tombstone.

My father, who had that day made a special journey to Birmingham to buy his copy of *The Origin of Species by Means of Natural Selection or The Preservation of Favoured Races in the Struggle for Life* hot off the press, arrived home to find the body of his wife laid out in the drawing room, her dog curled between her icy breasts.

The next day a new tutor took up his duties.

In the months following her death, I perceived that it had been my mother's will-power and physicality that had energised my seven sisters, who slowly began to wilt and grow pale without her sustaining radiance. One after another they succumbed to diseases reminiscent of that mysterious malady experienced by Mrs Robert Browning before she married the well-known poet who has done so much to mislead the public about the crowd behaviour of vermin. As they faded, one room after the other grew dark and silent; they lay stretched out on sofas or chaises-longues, too weak to walk across the room. Some coughed and spat blood; others stopped eating altogether; others went mad and had to be put into strait-jackets. Within a year, two had died and the rest had become phantoms, reminiscent of my youthful self. Today only one sister survives; I pay for her to be looked after in a home for female opium-addicts. Such is the fate of women who have happy, carefree childhoods thrust upon them by mothers who die suddenly.

While my sisters shrivelled, a strange new energy entered my pale body. The day after my mother's death I climbed out of my bed unaided and strolled across the frosty lawn in my bedclothes. The new tutor, Mr James, followed me in his wheelchair, respecting my silence. I stood bright-eyed among the tombstones. After a while Mr James began to whistle. He knew the song of every bird known to man. In an enormous bag slung over the back of his chair he carried his cameras. He pulled one out and showed it to me. I stared into its round eye and wondered.

My new tutor, who resided in our picturesque Oxfordshire village, was not a gentleman. A specimen hunter-gatherer by profession, he had once travelled to obscure corners of Africa, South America and the Far East in order to satisfy the English craze for ever more exotic beetles, bird skins and butterflies. He had sent regular moth specimens to my father which sometimes had to travel across two or three oceans and continents before arriving safely at the Vicarage. Mr James also took photographs of his specimens in their original habitat, in so far as this was possible. Intrepidly, he had carried his heavy load of photographic equipment, including a portable dark-room, to the most inhospitable of environments. One stormy day, while angled upon a cliff in Patagonia with his head in a black bag in order to photograph the nest of a rare type of albatross, he plunged downward, breaking both legs and his back as a result. By some miracle, the handcart remained perched on the cliff, and was rescued by the sailor who found his crushed but living body.

On returning to England James found himself confined to a wheelchair. His means of livelihood no longer available to him, he was obliged to seek an income from his wits, which were not inconsiderable. When he heard of this unfortunate man's accident, my father, in true Christian spirit, offered him a teaching position in our household, even though there was no vacancy, my sisters being regarded as ineducable. In fact, the two men spent a great deal of time together examining specimens and arguing about the origin of species, my father with his marble-white face and thin grey beard looking for all the world as if it were he who should be in the wheelchair, and not the bewhiskered, sunburnt Mr James, whose eyes twinkled with secrets my father would never know.

James taught me how to take photographs of the specimens we caught in the garden. I was only eight years old, but I much enjoyed preparing the collodion and applying it to the glass plates which would shortly after be developed in his light-proof tent: this activity has continued to be a source of interest to me, even though I no longer use wet collodion.

To all intents and purposes I forgot about my mother. I had quickly learned the dangers of close attachment, and in some unstated way felt responsible for her death simply because I had weakened her by loving her. To the outside world at least, it seemed as if Kaffir, her lap-dog, pined over her demise more than I did, and in doing so increased his loathing of me to a state nearing ecstasy. (He would have nothing to do with my unhealthy sisters, who patted their laps, but were rejected.) I suspect his plan was to tear out my throat jugulars, and to this end he developed a capacity to leap from surfaces high into the air, like a winged creature, my frail neck his object. On one failed attempt to terminate my life with his teeth, he at least succeeded in biting the hand I flung out to protect myself, and for two weeks I had to submit to the inconvenience of bandages.

He was severely beaten and his own life might have been terminated had my sisters not wailed for mercy on his behalf. But I knew Kaffir was waiting.

One day, upon discovering a handkerchief belonging to my mother under my mattress, I made the mistake of holding it to my face for a while, inhaling her brisk perfume and resurrecting sudden memories that in turn released an unexpected moisture from my eyes. I was unaware at that time of the dog's almost supernatural powers of smell, and was therefore quite unprepared for Kaffir's sudden charge from the kitchen to my bedroom, and his extraordinary flight from the dressing-table to my exposed throat, which he missed as I hunched my shoulders in self-defence. Instead, his sharp little canines embedded themselves in my left cheek, where he hung, tearing at my flesh like some crazed vampire, until Elspeth heard my screams and saved my life. I bear the scars of his attack to this day, and dread all dogs, understandably.

For reasons pertaining to the sacredness of my mother's memory Kaffir was not shot, but was soon after found torn to shreds apparently by a fox, near the tombstone responsible for his mistress's death.

A few months later my father, whose calm life seemed not to have been much disturbed after my mother's untimely exit from this life, except for the inconvenience of my sisters' unexpected decline, took James in his carriage to nearby Oxford to a meeting of the British Association for the Advancement of Science to be held in the brand new University Museum. An American professor was to talk on Darwin and social progress in this glass-roofed cathedral to science, in which God manifested himself free of charge in the shape of dinosaur-skeleton moulds and trays of beetles. Soapy Sam, the Bishop of Oxford, who, through his influential disapproval, had prevented Darwin from being awarded a knighthood, would speak as well. Mr James was magnanimously excited: he claimed to have discovered the theory of Natural Selection himself while capturing Amazonian parrots, and noting their individual variations, but had not thought to put pen to paper on the topic. My father had him lifted into the carriage by a gardener who was obliged to accompany them to Oxford in order to lift him out again, my father being quite unable to bear heavy weights. For the first time I felt the desire to move beyond the confines of my home and to enter the sacred city of Oxford to bear witness to what promised to be an historic occasion. There was, of course, no question of my attending the lecture.

My interest in Mr Darwin's theories had been greatly increased by my tutor's enthusiasms and I awaited their return impatiently. When it became apparent that neither man was returning home in time for dinner, and that I would be obliged to spend the evening with my gloomy sisters who took no interest whatever in descent by modification, my chagrin was considerable. The redoubtable Elspeth would have nothing of my sulks, however, and I was made to retire to my bed at the usual early hour.

The next morning I found my father and tutor in a state of high excitement at the breakfast table. It was clear from the feverish nature of their talk that neither had slept but had instead spent the whole night discussing the events of the debate, as it had turned out to be. Soapy Sam had apparently expressed his views on the theory of evolution by enquiring of T.H. Huxley (could he be related to my host's manservant, I wonder?) whether it was on his grandfather's or grandmother's side that he was descended from an ape. In the uproar that followed an elderly admiral waved a large Bible over his head and implored the excited audience to believe God's word rather than man's: the admiral turned out to be Fitzroy, the captain of the *Beagle* during its fateful voyage round the earth, visiting even this colonial outpost where I now find myself. An arch-Creationist, Fitzroy, in spite of the evidence of his eyes, accepted unquestioningly that the hills and valleys of South America had been formed by Noah's forty-day flood. Now, as a result of his unwitting invitation to that young gentleman naturalist, Mr C. Darwin, to accompany him on the *Beagle* during his lonely five-year voyage, he had unleashed upon the world the most revolutionary scientific discovery of the century, which turned men into brutes, and undermined the legitimacy of Genesis itself. (Did this dreadful responsibility compel Fitzroy to slit his own throat a few years after the Oxford debate?)

I listened spellbound to the arguments that now raged between my gentle father and my fierce-browed tutor. My father, though an evolutionist, still believed that the creation of species was miraculous proof of God's omnipotence, and that man was the noblest species on whom God had conferred the gift of intelligence contained in the frontal lobes of the brain: Natural Selection alone could not account for the human mind. Mr James, on the other hand, claimed that in every way man was at one with the rest of the organic world, there was no line of demarcation between instinct and reason, and that there was more difference between a baboon and a chimpanzee than there was between a chimpanzee and man. Mr James was fond of baboons. He had spent a year living among them while collecting baby crocodiles from the Limpopo (on one occasion actually extracting them from the mother's mouth as she carried them, newly hatched, to the river), and had written a paper (unpublished) on the ability of the chakra baboon's ability to ferment alcohol by adding berries to warm rockpools, and getting deliriously drunk on the resulting brew, thereby proving beyond question that the baboon is the first cousin of man.

In the doorway Elspeth beckoned. Her apple cheeks were blanched; her motherly eyes had a wildness about them I had not before observed. The two men did not notice my exit. Elspeth could not bring herself to speak, but propelled me towards my father's greenhouse. As ever, the warm tropical fragrances that billowed from the exotic flora took me by surprise. Lush creepers sagging with brilliant blooms blocked out much of the morning sunshine, creating a density of green shadow that suggested creatures hiding.

The stone floor was adrift with petals. Not the blood-red of bougainvillaea nor the yellow of mimosa but pale soft triangles of gauze that fluttered helplessly as our feet crushed the living creatures among them.

'Only one wing off!' breathed Elspeth. 'What kind of mind would do a thing like that? It's evil, that's what it is. Off your father's prize specimens. It'll break his heart, it will.'

Was she accusing me? I stared unblinking up at the glass panes of the greenhouse ceiling, where a few surviving moths clustered. 'My sisters,' I uttered in a clear voice.

'It'll break his heart,' she whispered into my ear.

CAPE TOWN 1899

I now had a third rendezvous to keep. First, with a sinking heart, I visited the aviaries.

In every cage the birds still clustered together in silence, occasionally fluttering feebly from one side to the other. At least there were no corpses today, but my examination of the nightingales presented me with a new anxiety: the males had shuffled to one end of the cage, while the females gathered together in the branches of an aromatic bush. This was indeed extraordinary behaviour on the part of birds who mixed freely in the wild, and who had formed sexual partnerships in earlier seasons. It seemed impossible that they would feel impelled to burst into song within the next three days: neither courtship nor territory seemed to hold the slightest interest for them.

I did the only thing possible: dug my sharp shoe into the backsides of Salisbury and Chamberlain, threatened to halve their pay, instructed them to redouble their efforts with the nightingales, and stalked off, closing my ears to their sleepy giggles.

A garland of bougainvillaea descended on to my shoulders as I strode up the mountain path. I brushed it away impatiently. Would the child be there? What had I to say to her after I had taught her to whistle? Surely she would not expect me to romp with her in the manner of Kipling and his daughter? Perhaps I could recall the Alice Liddell story, if she did not already know it. It would mean nothing to the child that I had known its author. (Dodgson and I had often strolled to the University Museum to view once more the scant remains of *Dodo ineptus*, Dodgson imploring me to g-g-guess at the song made by the extinct and ugly bird. (His stammer disappears in the presence of children.) Because he identifies so much with this wretched creature, I had to answer carefully. Something between the gobble of a turkey and the croon of a pigeon, I suggested, resisting the croak of the vulture; a pleasant sound, like water boiling for tea, or gurgling out of a bath. We debated over whether the bird would have had a syrinx, Dodgson's delicate mouth curling.) Perhaps she might enjoy a recitation of 'Jabberwocky'.

I plunged on up the mountain path, reciting out loud the ridiculous lines which somehow seemed appropriate to this illogical spot, yet knowing they would have even less meaning for the child than Lear's verses. But they gave me courage:

> '*One, two! One, two! And through and through*
> *The vorpal blade went snicker-snack!*'

Even as the nonsense babbled out of my mouth, I felt my auditory nerves pass a message to my brain which caused me to stop short in my recital. Freezing like a primitive animal who hears a twig snap and knows that only a certain species of predatory paw could release that particular timbre of soft disintegration, I listened to the remains of the snigger. A wave of unpleasant heat flushed through my body: it is not often I make a fool of myself, and never have I witnessed mockery of my behaviour. For this was not an amused and friendly response to my foolishness, but more a contemptuous sort of neigh, of the kind I have sometimes heard snorting from the noses of foreign women, untrained in the British art of stifling untoward utterances.

And as I remained frozen I heard too a delicate clink of metal reverberating from the same spot: the sound of draped jewellery swinging against itself – and then the furtive footsteps picking their way along what must have been an upper path for the public. A waft of sugary perfume filtered through the smell of pine.

I had no sooner allowed myself to move forward again than yet another unexpected sound assaulted my ears, though this time the auditory message settled, not in my temporal cortex, but in my heart, which began to throb with a sensation I can only describe as pity. I can quite definitely say that I have never heard a man weep (it is true that my father howled all night on the discovery of his de-winged moths, but that was a form of madness, as his subsequent actions would show); now, the uninhibited flood of male sobs which were flowing from the direction of the teak bench aroused in me a strange desire to investigate rather than flee! Against my better judgement I continued along the path, my thoughts of Maria by now somewhat distracted.

Upon a bench sat a tall, well-dressed young man, his face buried in his hands, his body shaking with grief. Even though I could not see his features I recognised him at once to be one of the secretaries, and his blond locks suggested he might be Joubert. As I stood uncertain as to whether I should tiptoe past him or announce my presence by a clearing of the throat, the young man withdrew his hands in a rush and stared straight at me with reddened eyes. Those orbs, swollen and bloodshot as they were through excessive weeping, shone more brilliantly blue than I had imagined possible. I began to tremble. Should I comment on the pleasantness of the weather or the beauty of the lilies that sprang around his feet? Should I offer him a handkerchief with which to relieve his clogged nostrils? Instead, I uttered his name: '*Joubert!*' Thus did the surge of sympathy which swelled my throat translate into a smooth, neutral greeting.

I expect I anticipated some display of embarrassment in his response; a manly attempt to disguise his tears in a flurry of coughs – instead he opened his mouth in a great round O, like a small boy who has broken his favourite toy, and bawled: 'Oh Professor, I am so unhappy!'

I slipped on to the bench beside him and placed a restraining hand on his sleeve.

'Tell me why,' I said.

For a moment Joubert was too overcome with misery to use his breath for speech and I found myself patting his back and murmuring clichés like: 'It can't be as bad as all that, old chap,' in an undertone which I hoped he wouldn't hear, but finally he regained sufficient control of himself to sob out four doom-laden words before collapsing back into his stricken state:

'*He has dismissed me!*'

'Good heavens!' I felt a slight shock. 'Why?'

Much trumpeting of nose in handkerchief before the revelation: '*Because I have become engaged – to Miss Pennyfeather!*'

I had no idea who Miss Pennyfeather was but I seized upon her as the saviour of the situation.

'But surely that is an event to celebrate?'

Joubert stopped sniffing and stared into the distance. 'He always warned us that he wanted only single men to work for him. That marriage gets in the way of work. That wives get in the way of Great Ideas.' He fell silent for a while. A plumbago petal drifted on to his knee. 'Even his loyalest servants . . .'

'Come on, man,' I said in a bright voice, 'he'll write you a good reference. You'll easily find other work.'

Joubert gazed at me uncomprehendingly. 'You don't understand, do you? *I worship him like a god!* We all do. I loved and served him as I cannot possibly serve another man again.'

His voice began to disintegrate so I said firmly: 'But now you will love and serve Miss Pennyfeather.'

Joubert ignored this. 'No father could have reposed greater confidence in his son than he placed in me. He hid nothing from me. Not even the whole Raid episode.' He shook his head and groaned as he remembered. 'Just think, Professor, I was there when the telegrams came through. He was frantic. But he still didn't blame JimJam for going in without permission. I think he actually admired him for his foolhardiness! I made him coffee the whole night through. He wouldn't touch his whisky. Then he resigned as Prime Minister the next morning. Do you know what, Professor?' He turned his beautiful tear-stained face to me. 'At five o'clock in the morning he put his head on my chest and groaned, "It's all over for me now, Joubert." We clung together for hours, it seemed. Schreiner left the room. We never saw him again.'

'Schreiner?'

'He was our Attorney-General then. Now he's our Prime Minister. And we're his Opposition. The Raid split us apart. That night Schreiner understood for the first time that we were all in it up to the neck, not just JimJam. He felt betrayed.' Joubert's eyes were drying as he recollected this historic night. 'It didn't bother me. I think if he had asked me to walk through the gates of Hell I would have done so. The greatness of the man! Do you know, Professor, that the morning after that terrible night, when he saw his whole career collapse in smoking ruins, he entertained an entire cricket team for lunch! You'd have thought he hadn't a care in the world! And he'd just that morning resigned!' Joubert's amazement, though four years old, had lost none of its freshness. He extended his arms towards the rustling forest. 'But it was the mountain that saved him. He spent the next five days and nights up here – alone most of the time, though he once asked me to accompany him. He had just heard that JimJam and the raiders had been captured and put into a Boer prison. His whole face had collapsed, I can't describe it any other way. His voice shook as he said, "*Well, it is a little history being made, that is all.*" We sat on this very bench and once again he laid his head on my breast as if the warmth of my body was his only consolation. Within a few days his hair had turned completely grey. I placed my hand on his brow and stroked it.' Joubert's eyes became dreamy. 'As we sat together on this bench, my arm round his shoulders in an attempt to comfort him in his appalling tragedy, I thought back to the time when I was a mere Clerk of the Papers in the House of Assembly. I was only twenty when I first met him.'

This could only mean a new wave of confession about to break, so I consulted my fob-watch somewhat ostentatiously. Joubert took the hint.

'I'm sorry to go on like this, Professor. I won't keep you any longer.' He tried to suppress a slight tremble in his voice.

'No, no, not at all, this is very interesting,' I murmured, in spite of myself. I could tell that the fellow was gaining some relief by his outpouring, and envied his ability to bare his heart so spontaneously.

'It was shortly before he became Prime Minister. He noticed me in my office off the Assembly Chamber and after that he always had a kind word for me,' Joubert continued as if he had never been interrupted. 'He asked if I could speak Dutch and whether I had a knowledge of shorthand. I replied I could not write shorthand. He said to me – very emphatically – "*You must learn shorthand!*" and went into the House. It was then that the most uncontrollable desire took hold of me to become his secretary!' Joubert clasped his hands together and nearly jumped off the bench in his excitement. 'I developed the strongest imaginable hero-worship for him. Just the thought that he was present in the House made me the happiest man on earth. I loved to see his face if I left the door that led from my room into the Chamber slightly ajar and sometimes I fancied he caught my eye. I would lie awake at night in a state of almost delirious joy thinking of the pleasure that would be mine when I became his secretary and would always be with him! That was all I wanted! Sorry, Professor, to take up your time like this but I want you to understand how the greatest man in South Africa can change the lives of the most ordinary men on earth, like me, as well as the most rich and famous – like Mr Chamberlain and Sir Alfred.' As he seemed to be subsiding I rose from the bench but he held my arm. 'Then one day in March 1894 I received a private letter saying he wanted to appoint me as his chief clerk! I will never forget that day – the most important day of my whole life, Professor! I wrote back joyfully, accepting the appointment. Two weeks later I assumed duty in the Prime Minister's department. The Prime Minister of the Cape Colony, as he was by then, called me into his private office. He said to me: "I suppose you thought I had forgotten all about you. Now let me ask you something: "*Do you know shorthand*?"'

And the irrepressible Joubert burst out laughing at the wonder of this scene, allowing me to smile back at him, and, with some relief, take my leave. I heard him whistle as he descended the path back to the Great Granary.

Maria was waiting for me at the same rocky spot of our encounter the day before. While I groped in my mind for the appropriate greeting and appellation, she waved her hand in the air, positively jumping up and down with excitement, and cried out: 'Look!'

I had yet to learn that young untrained children do not see the point in hellos, howd'ye-do's or good afternoons, these verbal rituals being entirely foreign to their spontaneity. But

I was an avid and quick pupil, and instantly swallowed whatever unnecessary greetings were forming on my lips.

She held something between her thumb and index finger, which she thrust before me, while performing a little dance of triumph on the uneven rocks.

'Hold still,' I said gently, and put my own hand on her wrist to prevent it from waving about. She seemed quite happy about a stranger's touch, even as I marvelled at the silken texture of the child's skin. It was then that I realised, with a sudden grief-stricken surge, that I had only once before held a small child's hand. Still grasping her by the wrist I drew her hand close to my eyes, and observed between her fingers not the trapped firefly I had expected but a tiny whiteish cube, which I could not immediately identify.

'Look!' she exclaimed again, this time waggling the tip of her tongue in a gap which had opened up in the very centre of her front teeth.

'You've lost a tooth!' I cried, and instinctively felt with my own tongue for the gaps in the back of my ageing mouth.

'I'm gonna hide it for the tooth fairy,' she announced in her strange colonial accents, clambering off the rock and obliging me to relinquish my hold. 'My mommy said I must hide it under the pillow, but I'm not going to.' She pattered down to the stream. 'There's l-l-lots of nice places down here and this is where the fairies live so now they won't have to come all the way to my h-h-house to find it.'

The delightful child had not so much a stutter as a shimmering delay round certain words, not dissimilar to Dodgson's. In my panic the day before I had not noticed her charming defect.

'That's very considerate of you,' I murmured. 'The fairies will be very grateful.' My head began to spin (rustily) with plans to visit this place later that night and leave behind – what? 'What do you think they'll leave you?'

'A tickey,' said the child promptly. 'Then they can t-take my t-tooth and use it like a brick to build they own house. Where shall I hide it?'

We poked about the pebbles and shelves of moss and starry flowers, I the ass to her Titania. I have to confess that, entranced as I was, I nevertheless managed to catch and trap in my specimen bottle several unusual species of flying insect, some gleaming with phosphorescence, some equipped with poisonous stings, some with abnormally large antennae. Since Mr Darwin's voyage to the Galapagos it has become difficult for the scientist to view mossy banks with the serenity of Shakespeare. What was once an emblem of permanence and harmony is now a battleground for survival and reproduction: thank heavens for fairies, a species for whose continued existence the evolutionary process holds no threat!

Finally we settled on a perfectly round pebble in a cluster of wild violets which seemed a likely enough home for Maria's benefactors-to-be. It was also positioned directly in line with a fallen pine, which would make discovery in the dark easier. I had no idea what a tickey was – no doubt some form of remuneration for loss of tooth – and would have to make immediate enquiries.

The child chattered on in the disconnected way of young children, apparently not requiring the stimulus of questioning. However there was one piece of information I urgently required from her, and when we had finished burying the tooth I said, as casually as I could: 'And is your daddy at home now?'

'I only got a mommy not a daddy.' She pushed some fallen hair back into a band round her head and momentarily became interested in me. 'And where is your children, can I please play with them?'

'I'm afraid I don't have any children, Maria,' I said. 'And do you have brothers and sisters?'

'No, it's only me.' For a few moments she lapsed into some private world, then widened her eyes, contracted her lips, and began to whistle.

For the next ten minutes or so I tried to impart to her my secret techniques for reproducing birdsong, even demonstrating how the two hands can augment and manipulate the sound chamber of the mouth by clenching and fluttering, thus providing improbable passages in which to convert breath into music. The child did not have the quick facility of Salisbury and Chamberlain, and soon grew frustrated when her repeated attempts at trilling and warbling continued to fail. Finally she flung her plump little hands from her mouth and, to my inexpressible alarm, burst into piteous tears.

Tears would seem to flow more easily in the Southern hemisphere. This situation was unique: what do I do to staunch this flow, my second of the morning? My twin impulse was both to run away fast and to gather her in my comforting arms. As neither response would be appropriate, I opened my mouth and hoped my vocal cords would be inspired.

'Oh dear!' I cried in a loud voice that gained her immediate tear-stained attention. 'Look what's happened to my ears!'

Pointing ostentatiously at my left ear, I observed her gaze settle in astonishment upon the antics of that well-trained auricle. (Never before had anyone save my own reflection been permitted to observe the rotations, flaps and quivers that each of my ears could perform independently. This unusual skill had been privately acquired during my early years in bed, before the mirror.)

Her tears vanished in a trice. After a minute or so's admiration of my left ear, her gaze shifted to the right one, which instantly obliged with even more outrageous stunts.

'Do them both together!' she begged.

Could I really enjoy playing with children? Certainly I

seemed to be an endless source of entertainment to this young creature. And I myself was experiencing something very like pleasure: I suppose peals of happy laughter after each new antic do have an uplifting, even regenerating, effect on the meanest of spirits. Like Oscar's Selfish Giant, hope began to blossom in my selfish old heart.

By the end of my performance Maria's face had that look of wide-eyed astonishment and awe that is so conspicuously absent from the faces of my students of ornithology. For a few minutes she was tentatively struck dumb as she considered the expertise of my ears and the wonder of my whistles. Taking advantage of her silence, I embarked on a short biology lesson, thinly disguised as an anthropomorphic story.

'Once there were three friends who also had ears,' said I. 'Friend number one was the cicada.' I waved my hand as if to point to the invisible creatures responsible for the shrilling that never ceases in Africa. 'He wanted to waggle his ears too, but he couldn't 'cause the cicada's ears are on his tummy!' (My listener's hands stole to her own firm abdominal region to check for growths.) 'Friend number two was the cricket.' (At present creaking a semitone below the cicada.) 'He couldn't waggle his ears either because they were on his legs!'

'All of them?' Alert.

'The first walking legs. Friend number three was the mosquito. He couldn't waggle his ears either because his ears were on his feelers!' (I waggled a forefinger on either side of my forehead, astonished at how easily so unaccustomed an activity came to me.)

'A mosquito bit me last night,' said the child, rejecting my educational story for the more immediate gratifications of personal experience. 'Look!' She rolled up her sleeve and exposed the most delightful rosy bump just below her elbow. My finger itched to stroke it and feel the silk again. I tutted in sympathy. 'And guess where the blood is now.'

'The blood?'

'From my arm, you silly. That the m-mosquito sucked out.'

'In his – tummy, perhaps?'

The child burst out into sudden fiendish laughter. 'It's splatted up against the wall – splosh! Like that!' And she smacked her two hands together with some violence. 'My mommy killed it.' She paused. 'My mommy says I mustn't come here.'

I understood at once. 'Perhaps if I came to visit your mother . . . ?'

'OK.' She shrugged off the idea, with liquid, narrow shoulders. 'I have to go now. B-but I'll come tomorrow for my tickey, hey?'

'Even though Mother says you're not to?'

She cocked her head on one side as if deliberating a reply, but I could see her eyes resting on my ear. I gave it a quick jiggle and she rewarded me with a missing-tooth smile.

'Where do you live?' I called as she flew off. No kiss today.

She shouted out some guttural Afrikaans name and fluttered away. From the depths of the forest three words floated up. 'Down – the – avenue!'

'Shall I come and see you?' I cupped my hands round my mouth to make a loudhailer. 'I want to ask your mother something.'

No response, only the patter of little feet in pine needles.

I followed her slowly; then collapsed on to the teak bench half-way down the mountain path, yielding to a wave of joyous exhaustion.

*　　*　　*

'You are old, Father William,' the young man said,
  'And your hair has become very white:
And yet you incessantly stand on your head –
  Do you think, at your age, it is right?'

HINKSEY 1874

Ruskin's road was a challenge to rail. It was also an art school project: in wanting to demonstrate to his drawing class an understanding of a perfect country road, he proposed that they should build one. He had already found the spot.

The village of Hinksey just outside Oxford suffered from a surfeit of water in its surrounding fields, with the result that it had become impossible to walk across the water-logged green in ordinary shoes. Thus it was that the Slade Professor of Art arranged for his drawing class to level and drain the ground, and sow the banks with the wild flowers that ought to be growing on them. This Human Pathway, rightly made, would be an example to Britain of the superiority of Road over Rail (following the natural curves of the country rather than jackknifing through them), as well as an opportunity for the upper classes to demonstrate their ability to use their muscles, serviceably, for once. The project appealed to a number of high-thinking undergraduates who felt some dim need to be useful to the lower classes.

I was astonished to find Oscar rising before midday in order to lay stone.

'To push a wheelbarrow upon Ruskin's road is the equivalent of helping to build a medieval cathedral on the Hinksey village green, my dear Wills,' he explained. 'Can you understand that here Useful Muscular Work joyously unites with Art and Beauty, in the best Gothic tradition? Besides, Ruskin sometimes rewards us with sensational breakfast parties in his rooms at Corpus.'

In fact, Oscar was less enchanted by useful muscular work than by the spectacle of toffs breaking stone with their lily-white hands, and once he had discovered my ability with a camera he persuaded me that a photographic record of this historic enterprise was necessary. It was over four years since I had attended Ruskin's inaugural lecture: rumours were rife about his eccentric lifestyle, his bouts of madness, his reported dependence upon opium and sherry, his inflamed and destructive love for a girl over thirty years his junior. Yet in spite of his erratic behaviour and his oft-declared contempt for Oxford, he still exerted an extraordinary influence over the entire University: crowds (including university professors) flocked to his lectures, and burst into spontaneous applause as he entered the cramped confines of his dark lecture hall (a request for a more spacious auditorium having been refused by the authorities). Unkind critics claimed that many of his lectures were pure drivel, though he was still able to entertain his audiences with unpredictable verbal – and physical – pyrotechnics.

Thus it was that I was ferried to Hinksey one autumnal afternoon, burdened with Mr James's camera, dark-room, chemicals and handcart. It was Oscar's job to transport barrows-ful of prepared stone to the undergraduates who were actually laying the road, but it has to be said that his trundling lacked the purposefulness of the common labourer. Indeed, the entire focus of his attention was directed towards the melancholy figure of Ruskin himself, chiselling at slabs of stone in his customary frock-coat, from the upper limits of which protruded his tall collar and bright-blue neckcloth. At first it seemed to me that Oscar wanted merely to bask in the proximity of his mentor and occasionally gain his attention with witticisms considerably better chiselled than Ruskin's stone, but as I watched (no one had yet perceived my arrival) it slowly dawned on me that Oscar, already cognisant of his own fund of comic genius, was engaged in the impossible task of trying to entice a smile from Ruskin's thin and somewhat asymmetric lips.

For misery had indeed hunched the shoulders of the Slade Professor, and shortened his height; his nose was more beak-like than I remembered it, while his facial skin was covered in a web of fine wrinkles. A tall hat was pushed at an angle upon his head. He was serenely indifferent to an audience of Scoffers that had gathered upon the grassy verges, some of them having travelled from as far afield as London. These self-appointed critics, who included several dons among their number, even took to picnicking among the yarrow and the wild autumnal roses (planted by the undergraduates during the spring), shouting and catcalling at the comical spectacle of lords labouring like navvies. One of them leapt to his feet soon after I had arrived and, exactly imitating Ruskin's fulsome cadences, cried out a piece of doggerel that had recently appeared in *Punch* magazine:

> '*My disciples, alack, are not strong in the back,*
> *And their arms than their biceps are bigger.*
> *Yet they ply pick and spade, and thus glorify Slade:*
> *So to Hinksey go down as a digger!*'

Though this performance elicited cheers and whistles from the picnickers, Ruskin continued to utter long, perfectly-formed sentences in his wistful tenor voice, as if there had been no interruption. He seemed able to chisel and speak simultaneously, and was concerned to show the diggers how to break stone without losing the heads of their hammers, a skill he had learned from a professional stone-breaker in an iron mask.

Oscar laughed delightedly at the performing Scoffer; then noticed me.

'Coz!' he exclaimed, clearly pleased to see me. 'You have come to immortalise this historic venture! Allow me to introduce you to these noble navvies whose images you will soon magically convey on to your plate glass.' And he grabbed at the nearest noble navvie, whose copious moustaches and spidery legs put me in mind of my newly-acquired pet from Mexico. Alfred Milner allowed a wintry smile to flicker momentarily across his face, and then continued to heave stone out of Oscar's barrow, his long arms twisting at curious angles. Undeterred by this cool response, Oscar led me to the Master himself, who was comparing, in a seamless flow of prose, the stones of Hinksey with those of Venice. His gaze settled upon my handcart with some anxiety, and he paused for a moment to raise his enquiring blue eyes to meet those of my friend.

'You know that I cannot admire the camera.' But he withheld the chisel from the stone for a few minutes in deference to my presence. 'Better your cousin were to draw or paint this busy scene and thereby convert a work of Labour into a work of Art.'

I managed a watery laugh. 'I have come merely to record the image of your project for posterity. My inept drawing would scarcely do justice to the scene.'

A peevish expression flitted across Ruskin's face. 'You bring a wagonload of equipment to synthesise a picture that would be more beautifully produced by a simple pencil on a plain sheet of paper. But go ahead. I have only one request: pray do not include me in your collodion composition!'

It was true that my equipment was disproportionately

cumbersome, and as I unpacked my box camera, lenses, tripod, chemicals, glass plates, scales, weights, trays, dishes, funnels and pails (at least there was no need for me to carry water to Hinksey), I reflected that the advent of dry collodion would indeed save me a great deal of labour. Rumours were rife that within a few years it would no longer be necessary to prepare the plate first with wet collodion and then with silver nitrate, taking care that no dust particles settled on the wet plate, which must at all cost *remain* wet throughout every stage of the process.

Oscar had decided in favour of informal pictures of the diggers in various attitudes portraying hard labour within the picturesque framework of crooked cottages and hedgerows laden with crimson berries. I was therefore obliged to explain to these young aristocrats that it was necessary for them to turn to stone themselves for some thirty seconds while I buried my head under a cloth. So relentless was the intellectual activity of my photographic subjects that neither they nor their mentor could desist from a torrent of discourse, even as they somewhat self-consciously, under Oscar's directions, arranged themselves into a useful muscular tableau.

The topic now under discussion was the University itself. Ruskin was complaining once again about the inadequacy of his accommodation at the University Museum. 'But the provision of amenities for the enhancement of intellectual and artistic thought is of no interest to a university that values Oars above Art – to a university that has become a mere Cockney watering-place for learning to row!' exclaimed he in a voice sharpened with anger.

'I certainly see no point in going backwards down to Iffley every evening,' agreed Oscar, motionless in an attitude of hard labour behind his barrow.

'But rowing, rightly done, can be an art in itself.' Alfred

Milner, lean, spidery and dangerous, held a stone above Oscar's barrow.

This challenge caused Ruskin to lay down his chisel and orate for several minutes in a great flow of indignant words. 'Even digging, rightly done, is at least as much an art as the mere muscular act of rowing; it is only inferior in harmony and time.' His hands flew about. 'On the other hand, the various stroke and lift is as different in a good labourer from a tyro as any stroke of oar. But all that is of no moment!' cried the Professor, rising suddenly. 'The real, final, unanswerable superiority is in the serviceableness and duty and the *avoidance* (this is quite an immense gain in my mind) of strain or rivalry! Do wheel your barrow round that Rosebay Willow Herb, Arnold, and not over it!'

I suppose it is a tribute to Ruskin that I found myself listening to his talk even as I rushed, wet plate in hand, into my portable dark-room to develop and fix it immediately in a variety of chemical solutions in order to produce a successful negative. This procedure was necessary for each photograph, and by the end of the session, as ever, I found my clothes and hands stained black with chemicals.

After an hour or two my task was completed, or rather, the first part of my task was completed, for I had now to varnish the negatives in order to make positive prints. At least this could be done at a more leisurely pace at my rooms at Magdalen, and was a process I enjoyed perhaps more than actually taking the photographs. As I painstakingly packed my handcart and prepared to leave the novel scene, I became aware of a tall, golden-haired youth in a blue spotted bow-tie and creased tweed trousers who stood upon the grassy mound, somewhat detached from the Scoffers. He was staring, as if mesmerised, at the Professor's attempts at stonebreaking: his expressive mouth knew not whether to curl in derision or to fall open in astonishment. Something stirred in my memory, and I recognised the young man as the member of the public who was hoping to discover his Destiny at Ruskin's inaugural lecture. Four years had matured his bearing and endowed him with a glow of confidence that he had earlier lacked. Where once his figure had been almost girlishly slender, it was now apparent that the upper part of his body was grown muscular, and his face burnt by a stronger sun than that which hides behind English clouds. It struck me that his eyes were no longer those of an immature young man (he was not much over twenty), but had become infused with a shrewdness one might expect from a man in his middle age. I was considering going over to him to ask him about whither his destiny had led him when Oscar tapped my shoulder.

'That man rattles loose diamonds in his pockets and believes everyone can be bought,' he whispered, pointing to the very youth. I had heard of the undergraduate who had made his fortune in diamond speculation in the Cape Colony, but had not yet seen him. 'He used to dig with a pickaxe once as well, but for rather different motives,' Oscar continued. 'He is a bore upon the subject of diamond claims. I know, for he belongs to my club.'

I watched the young man with his weatherbeaten features and thatch of untidy hair make his way uncertainly over to the Professor of Art. I thought he might fall upon his knees before the Master, so reverent was his bearing. But at that moment Ruskin moved on to the topic of Rail (in both senses of the word!), and his admirer hesitated.

'Amputation! Penetration! Pollution!' shrieked the Professor. 'Where the landscape is round and female, the railway slashes like a knife through its delicate tissues, leaving scars on park and copse, and mounds vaster than the walls of Babylon!' In this state, it was quite possible to believe that Ruskin was mad. 'Those tracks of steel cannot curve round hillocks or caress their slopes; instead they slice through the landscape in their abominable straight lines, throwing up huge embankments for crossing the valleys! And the greatest sin of all is that now the road builders emulate the rail builders, knocking down ancient hills or cutting them in two that their road may be the shortest distance between two points!'

My young man, whose mouth had already opened to identify himself to his hero, now began to retreat, a confused look in his eyes. I abandoned plans to reintroduce myself, and bade farewell to Oscar and his colleagues, who looked as if they were ready to return to their colleges soon in order to soak in hot baths. A gloom, caused not so much by the imminent setting of the sun as by the exhalation of grey vapours from the watermeadows, had imposed itself upon the entire project. The Scoffers had disappeared without a sound.

The clock of Carfax Tower was chiming four as I rested a moment with my heavy barrow. Other photographers, I knew, could push their handcarts across fifty miles of rough terrain in all extremes of climate, but I lacked their energy: my journey up the Botley Road and past the station had tired me considerably. Though I had merely the length of The High to complete before reaching Magdalen, I needed to regain my strength, and sat upon one of the benches erected at the crossroads beneath the ancient tower.

The late afternoon was now damp and cheerless. The fog which had seeped up from the Hinksey fields now uncoiled from the rivers and canals that both penetrate and surround Oxford, dissolving the edges of venerable buildings, and reducing the city to a uniform greyness. I shivered, and thought with pleasure of the hot water, bright lights, tea and muffins that awaited me at Magdalen. This reflection was enough to make me rise to my aching feet – when a lean clerical figure (whom I instantly recognised) emerged from the mists and hobbled towards me. His movements, though jerky, were brisk and purposeful; but almost *too* purposeful, as if he planned to climb into my cart and order me to drive him to his college. Instead, he stopped a few inches short of my barrow, and gazed at it with a rapture its humble appearance scarcely merited. His sparkling eyes met mine; he opened his mouth to speak; his upper lip trembled; no sound emerged.

Charles Dodgson closed his mouth and curled it into a wistful smile. I too seemed to have lost my powers of speech, so startled was I to be in the presence of this famous writer, mathematician, photographer and stammerer. Whereas the gigantic egoism of Ruskin made speaking by anyone redundant, Dodgson's interest in my cart and even myself seemed unnervingly sincere. I looked anxiously at his sensitive, clean-shaven face, as if we might perhaps communicate through our eyes rather than our voices, and found the corners of my mouth sliding about. For a moment I felt I might, in his eyes, be some curious dream-like creature that inhabited the pages of *Alice*, stranded at the crossroads of Carfax, my pale face disintegrating into the mists; and for that moment, perhaps the only moment in my life, I felt as odd and eccentric as the White Rabbit or the Mad Hatter or the Cheshire Cat.

When at last he spoke, his voice was light, quick, amused. 'Do-do-Dod-son, Fellow of Christ Church. Th-this is indeed an impressive handcart.'

'Francis Wills. Under-g-graduate, Magdalen,' I stammered back.

'It is so good to see a fellow photographer prepared to push a barrow through the streets of Oxford. Let me guess: have you been taking pictures upon the Hinksey Road?' His body could not keep still, even though his feet did not move; a shoulder clenched briefly beneath an ear; an elbow jerked;

his chin angled first to one side, then the other, so that his gaze tended sideways.

I admitted that he was correct in his surmise.

'How very fascinating!' He paused and placed a black-gloved finger on his chin. 'I should be so interested to see your photographs ... how you have arranged the men, positioned their hands – that sort of thing. I wonder ...' He looked politely apprehensive. 'Might you be prepared to come to my rooms and print your plates in my dark-room? I b-believe I make an excellent pot of tea!'

It was clear that Charles Dodgson was a man quite untouched by his fame. His natural shyness, which infused both his speech and his movements, gave him a vulnerable charm that was strangely irresistible. I became like one of the Pied Piper's children – or rats – as I scampered down St Aldates with my barrow; past the Christ Church corner turrets bedecked with Cardinal Wolsey's mitre; beneath Wren's gracious Tom Tower; and into the most opulent quadrangle in Oxford. There was no time to admire the fountains, the archways, the stained-glass windows of the Great Hall, or the noble lawns, all designed by the doomed Cardinal for his own pleasure as Dodgson, the upper half of his body held stiff as a tin soldier, led me to his home. We abandoned my handcart to the care of a sullen scout and ran up staircase 7 to burst into Dodgson's suite of ten rooms at the top of the stairs.

I felt I had entered a children's paradise. Every room we passed through was packed with toys, games and gadgets displayed in orderly fashion upon every available surface. But Dodgson raced past the printing press, the dumbbells, the Ammoniaphone, the skeletons, the mechanical toys, the music boxes, the calculating machine ('It adds up to one million pounds,' he mentioned as I lingered a while over the latter), the travelling inkpots and the machine for turning over pages. He called to his scout to heat up water for tea – and then we entered his dark-room.

Humbly, I handed my prepared wet plates to the most celebrated photographer in England. With intense concentration he rocked them to and fro in his acid baths, exclaiming in delight as the images gradually emerged from their dark cells . . . there was Oscar with his wheelbarrow; Milner with his shovel; Toynbee with his pickaxe. Dodgson began to make prints immediately, speaking at top speed as he did so. (I marvelled at his fastidious organisation, his ruthless powers of logic which he imposed upon the potential chaos of his own imagination.) How Mr James would have loved to have partaken in our animated debate on the wonders of collodion; how he would have enjoyed discussing the crucial importance of lighting; how he would have envied Dodgson his glass house erected upon the roof above his chambers, where he could place his young sitters *outdoors*, even upon the wettest and coldest and foggiest of days.

An hour must have passed before we left the distraction-free confines of the dark-room for the distraction-filled space of the drawing-room. The scout fussed about with heated water, and Dodgson, having complimented me upon the composition of my pictures, now offered to show me his albums. While he strode up and down, swaying a teapot between his hands ('It needs to brew for precisely *ten minutes*, and this technique *entices* the full flavour from the leaves!'), I, gawky but deeply flattered, turned over the pages of his meticulously indexed albums.

By now the chill I had experienced at Carfax had quite thawed: if anything, the temperature in the room was a little too warm for my complete comfort. I noticed that rugs had been rolled up and placed against cracks between the four doors and the thickly carpeted floor, apparently to exclude any suggestion of draught. On my lap lay precise landscapes, perfectly lit: chains of logical hills and valleys, luminous with their photographer's aesthetic sensibility. A few seascapes followed; a growing number of portraits of well-known faces – Tennyson, Rossetti, Ruskin; groups of Oxford dons gathered round archways, or examining skeletons . . .

And the next album was devoted to little girls. They leaned, one at a time, against trees, staircases, walls, each other; they lay sprawled among cushions, pillows, sheets. They played violins, climbed ladders, held kittens, read books. Group pictures represented the stories of Little Red Riding Hood, St George and the Dragon, *Twelfth Night*, all in fancy dress. In the 'Cherry Group', one little girl dangled a cherry over another's lips. Yet how *knowing* those young females looked! Their average age must have been six or seven, yet each child had a world-weary glint in her eye, an ambiguous smile on her lips. They were the loveliest portraits I had ever seen.

'Tea's ready!' cried Dodgson. The buttered muffins were hot. I murmured words of praise while sipping the lukewarm liquid. My inarticulate compliments released a wave of new energy from my host. His stammer had vanished.

'At all costs, the children must be absolutely themselves; I must take them unawares – even if it means producing a tea-cup from my ear . . .' (and indeed a teacup identical to those from which we were sipping materialised in Dodgson's hand as he brushed it against his head) 'or spending half an hour climbing up ladders or sliding down snakes. Or playing with them in the dressing-up box.' His gentle eyes grew dreamy. 'The clouds of glory. The state of innocence. Excuse me.'

He darted across the room to read a thermometer placed near an oil stove. The reading caused him to adjust the heat of the stove; then, to my surprise, he moved on to another thermometer and another stove, which was also adjusted; then two further thermometers and stoves, which this time he left untouched.

'My theory,' he said as he hurried back to the teapot, 'is that all d-draughts will die if the temperature is the same throughout the room. Another muffin? More tea? No?'

As I stood up, as if to leave, he cried out: 'Please stay a little longer, Mr Wills! It is not often that I am visited by a fellow-photographer and a zoologist all rolled into one! We must visit the University Museum together and you must tell me about the poor old Dodo, with whom I do so identify!'

And so began a ten-year friendship, of sorts.

CAPE TOWN 1899

'Professor Wills?'

A nervous hand tugged at my arm.

I awoke in a state of panic, quite unable to locate myself: had I fallen asleep in the Fellows' Garden grown suddenly wild . . . ?

'I'm so sorry to waken you, but this is my only chance.'

I turned my head to look down at the speaker, who was now sitting on the bench with me.

She returned my gaze with steady brown eyes, though her lips could not keep still, as if a barrage of words was waiting to burst through them. Upon her head she wore a concoction of straw and lace and battered silk roses, from beneath which escaped several wild black curls. Even I could recognise that here was a woman to whom clothes were of no importance whatsoever: her bottle-green jacket was ill-matched with her yellowish complexion, and she had made no effort to contain her thickening girth within the incarceration of the female stay. She must have been one of the shortest women I have ever seen – her head scarcely reached my shoulder – but the extreme straightness of her back gave her a dignity that far outweighed any failure to conform to the ideal female figure. She wore no jewellery.

I recognised her at once as the woman in my photograph.

'Madam, why do you follow me?'

Her eyes began to swim with some unimaginable emotion, and her low voice trembled.

'*I am relying on you, Professor, to help me save this country from total catastrophe!*'

If she had not spoken so solemnly I would have burst into embarrassed laughter; the woman was clearly deranged. Instead of laughing, however, I rounded my eyes as if speaking to Maria and said, to humour her: 'Madam, I'm afraid I have had no experience of saving countries from catastrophe. I think you have the wrong man.'

On hearing my words her face froze for a moment as if she realised she did indeed have the wrong man; then a somewhat haughty expression came over her features as she said: 'Please do not patronise me, Professor. I am quite serious, as you will hear.'

Immediately adjusting the tone of my voice so as not to incur her anger, I asked: 'Why me? You don't even know me.'

'Oh, but I do!' she at once exclaimed. 'I have watched you most carefully these past few days and I can see you are a kind, dear Englishman who loves his birds and will do anything to ensure their survival. But more than that – I can see you have the ear of the most powerful man in the Cape!'

At this point everything in me rose up and told me to turn my back on this woman, to run away from her as fast as my thin legs would carry me, to escape her mesmerising eyes and passionate speech – but my body would not listen to the wisdom of my brain. Like a hopeless insect I was trapped in the web of her strong, mad will.

'What is it you wish me to do?' I delivered this line of monosyllables without emotion, though my heart was pounding with anxiety – and a form of unwilling gratitude as well, for no one has ever called me a kind, dear Englishman, though as for the survival of my birds – I would rather not think about that.

At this point a shout of childish laughter rose from the lawns below. The entire Kipling family, nurse and all, had tumbled into the garden and were romping around with what appeared to be a small lion cub. My companion rose at once. 'Please follow me, Professor. I must not be seen.'

As there seemed to be no question of my refusing her anything, I leapt to my feet and plunged after her, up the very path I had so recently descended. We rushed upwards at a pace that was too fast for me; nevertheless I called out to the rear of her extraordinary hat: 'May I ask your name and who you are?'

'My name is Olive,' she called back. 'I write books.'

This reply did not altogether surprise me. In fact, the thought that I might be in the presence of Miss Olive Schreiner had crossed my mind almost at once. Now a dozen questions sprang to my lips, but I thought to save my breath till we sat down.

She was leading me to Titania's grove. Her progress through the trees was slowing down inexplicably, but she was nevertheless driven to continue speaking.

'I have written a pamphlet.' Her voice rang out clear and confident, a voice practised in oratory before large audiences, I could tell. 'It is an English person's view of the situation. In it I try to open the eyes of the people of England to the fact that they are being duped by a man who thinks he is Napoleon. I explain that everything must be done to prevent – this – country from – slipping into an abyss of – hatred – from which it will – take – generations – to – crawl – out!' Her voice began to lose its clarity, as if her vocal cords had been punctured by a spiky growth in her throat. Nevertheless it still rose imperiously above her hat as she called to me in cadences as emphatic as those of a Beethoven symphony:

'Professor Wills – I – am – talking about – *war!* A war – which – you – can – help me – *prevent!*'

By now she was having to stop every few yards to gasp for air. My own breathing was by no means regular, as a result of the uphill gradient, but I certainly did not yet find it necessary to pant. By the time she had reached the grove, she was no longer able to speak, and collapsed upon a rock by the stream, her shoulders heaving.

I waited for her breathing to regulate itself, becoming aware that it was not so much the inhalation she found problematic as the process of expelling the air that had found its way into her lungs, which she managed to do only with a great deal of shallow coughing.

'Forgive me,' she wheezed, in between coughs. Somehow she was able to fumble at her hat pins and remove her great load of millinery, which she tossed carelessly on to the ground.

'Can I be of any help to you?' I was obliged by good manners to ask.

'If only you could.' Her breathing had settled enough now for her to be able to infuse these words with bitterness. 'We asthmatics await the miracle cure!'

This demonstration of physical frailty had created a sudden bond of sympathy between us, and I considered regaling her with a description of my own recent bronchial attack, which had left its mark in a persistent dry cough, not unlike hers. However, before I had time to embark upon this interesting topic, she had begun to speak again, her hands pressed down hard against her knees so that her back was arched and her chest hollowed, a posture that evidently facilitated her inhalations – or exhalations, I could not be sure. She was looking at me out of the corner of her eyes, with an expression on her face which I could only call coy.

'Do you know why I trust you, Professor?'

'I cannot even begin to think.' I cast my eye around for somewhere remotely comfortable to sit.

'I trust you because the Child trusts you.'

'You know little Maria, then,' I asked cautiously.

She was too busy dividing her breath between speech and exhalations to listen to me, though, as I was to learn, listening was not something that came easily to her. 'I've seen you playing games with her. I've heard your beautiful whistling. What further recommendation do I need as to your good character?'

'I am a humble Oxford don,' I said, 'whose expertise is in the field of ornithology. I cannot see this as a suitable qualification for averting wars.'

'But that's just what you aren't!' she cried in a stronger voice, her asthma attack evidently abating. 'At least, you may be humble in your own eyes. But remember that He –' and here she flicked her fingers in the direction of the Great Granary, an expression of distaste upon her face – 'has the greatest possible reverence for Oxford. You must know that He took time from the diamond fields to gain an Oxford degree in order to qualify as a superior human being.' The bitterness in her voice did not escape me.

She stopped short and sank into a deep reverie, quite as intense as her passionate words. After a full minute of silence I asked her cautiously: 'Have you known him long?'

She raised her head. In her dark eyes I could see luminous memories brimming, like water lifted from the deepest well, and her voice, when she at last spoke, quavered a little.

'Professor Wills, may I tell you something that no one else, not even my husband, has heard before?'

Abandoning all thoughts of a prolonged afternoon rest, I attempted to smile benignly, settled myself on a fallen tree trunk and prepared myself for yet another set of confessions.

OLIVE REVEALS A SECRET

'Some say that the diamond mine at New Rush in the early seventies was a chasm of the damned, the inner circle of an inferno, where Satan himself reigned among a hundred thousand tormented souls. Have you ever see Gustave Doré's engravings which illustrate Dante's journey through the rings of hell? Gaze at them, and you will at once see a close representation of life inside the yawning pit which only two years earlier had been a little hill upon which scrawny sheep nosed for green shoots among the thorn bushes. Can you, an Oxford don, even begin to imagine the stench, the dust, the squalor, the drunkenness of the camps that surrounded this hell-hole? Yet it was upon this most unlikely site that I experienced a revelation so intense that it was to change utterly the life of this obscure missionary's daughter. I was a mere seventeen years when I arrived at the New Rush mining camp – the name was changed to Kimberley during the ten months I spent there with my sister and brother.'

Miss Schreiner appeared to be serenely confident that her story would be of irresistible interest to me. Her eyes did not leave my face for a second. 'Theo was what they called a Digger. He worked fourteen hours a day on his claim with a gang of Kaffirs. The natives picked, shovelled, hauled and sifted, while Theo sat under an awning outside his tent and sorted through the red gravel they had mined. Ettie did what she could to provide him with some home comforts within their tent. Through their despair at the excesses of gambling and drinking that dominated life on the fields – for both belonged to various Temperance organisations – the hope that Theo would find a large diamond glittered in their dismal lives quite as brightly as the precious stones themselves.' She sighed deeply and shook her head.

'Although there was more than enough Cape Brandy there was never enough water; we suffered from scurvy because of a lack of fresh vegetables, and from dysentery because of primitive sanitation, and the *flies*! The canvas walls were black with flies: they dropped into your tea and coffee and cooking food; they buzzed in your ears and settled on plates and crawled over your dry lips, hoping to find a moist crack into which they could insert their busy probosces – I'm sorry if I disgust you, Professor – you have turned quite pale!' And indeed I felt quite faint at the image she had just conjured. Although as a child I had pulled the wings off flies, and, as a student, dissected them under microscopes, I have never allowed an insect to crawl across my face. (Alfred was not an insect.)

'But more terrifying than the flies, Professor, were the dust-storms.' And here she gave an involuntary shudder, though I thought I might prefer dust to flies.

'We would always know when one was about to break: for an hour or so a strange, almost tangible silence would fall upon the camps. Then a faint breeze would flutter among the huts and chase bits of paper into the air. Within minutes corrugated-iron roofs began to rattle, tent ropes creaked and strained, and you could see a dense brown wall blustering towards you from a distance. The closer it got to the camp the thicker it became: then tents were ripped out of the ground, shacks and shanties collapsed like houses of cards, pots and pans rolled across the veld, and vast clouds of dust engulfed the whole settlement. For hours afterwards we became diggers of a different kind as we struggled to spade out the layers of dust and grit that had accumulated in our tent – and which now coated our eyes, mouths, food, clothes and bedding. I remember breathing in clouds of dust and breathing it out again in clouds, like steam from a kettle.

'Afterwards, deep rumbles of thunder would promise refreshing rain – but sometimes the thunderstorms were as terrifying as the dust-storms. Tents would be flooded in the downpour, the ground became sodden, everything was unbearably wet and filthy; often we had to choose between sleeping in a pool of water or upon the table.' She scrutinised my face even more closely, to see if I appreciated the horror of what she was saying. 'Needless to say, as a woman I was expected to perform women's tasks, well away from the masculine preserve of the diamond fields: I helped Ettie tidy our tent, fetched water from the river and wells (two buckets a day was all we were allowed), picked flowers and taught in the night schools. Occasionally I helped at the sorting table, sieving and washing the diamondiferous pebbles. Around us seethed thousands of natives who kicked up the red sand in clouds above their heads; some stark-naked savages from the interior, some half-dressed colonial blacks, but all with one thought in their heads: the guns they would buy with the money they earned. It was a rough, raw environment, Professor.' She paused for a moment, her eyes and mouth twitching with the emotions awoken by ghastly memories – then set off again.

'Some Diggers who had struck it rich had clubbed together into "messes": they shared food, expenses and servants. To signal that they had no shortage of food, they had commandeered large trees from which they hung legs of mutton like Christmas decorations. These young bachelors were on the whole a better class of person, not the drunkards and desperadoes who spent all their free time reeling from bars to gambling houses to back-street brothels. I, of course, took no interest in these young men who altogether lacked the spiritual dimension which is of the first importance to me in any man or woman. What little spare time I had was spent reading – John Stuart Mill, Charles Darwin, Herbert Spencer, John Ruskin – or writing. I had started work on various stories and novels, but could not bring myself to believe my writing was of any value . . . However, I could not help noticing a tall, fair-haired youth, not much older than myself, whose individual behaviour distinguished him from his companions –'

At that moment the sound of a disturbance caused us to raise our heads in alarm. A group of treetops began to thrash and sway until out of the foliage exploded a couple of black eagles, their powerful wings whirring like machines. Higher and higher they tumbled into the mountain air, emitting shrieks and howls so piercing that the rest of the forest held its breath. Were they mating or were they marauding? They wheeled in ever larger circles, one apparently chasing the other. My companion, too, was silenced by this outburst, which ceased as suddenly as it had started, as both birds glided back to the very spot from which they had burst.

'Oh look!' She darted from the bench to pick up a gigantic black feather that had drifted down and landed on the very rim of her discarded hat. Now, as she jabbed the feather into the jumble of lace and roses, it struck me that the Colossus, too, cared little for his appearance because he, like her, was *not quite right in the head*! You could see it at once in their eyes: a certain madness that goes with obsession on a grand scale, obsessions and dreams that focus not on people or objects, but on whole countries, races, Empires. I peered at her eyes more closely, and fancied I saw in them the great diamond mine of which she spoke with such passion, and more besides that made me uneasy.

Her hat now reset upon her black curls, she resumed her monologue as if nothing had happened. 'This young man first came to my attention when I carried a lunch pail to Theo, at work on his claim. My brother was supervising his labourers as they hauled up leather buckets of ore from the bottom of the pit on aerial tramwires, and dumped the flame-coloured gravel into waiting mule carts. All around him the perpetual hum of manual labour rose from the chasm itself: the thud of pick and shovel against the soil, the clank of rope and bucket, the shouted commands between pit and roadway, the breathy songs of native gangs as they worked deep in the crater that was once a kopje. The white supervisors bustled about, sometimes scrambling down the ladderworks into the pit to stand over their gangs to prevent them from hiding – and swallowing – the diamonds their spades had exposed. Let me not talk of the curse of illicit diamond buying, the greatest of all the plagues of the fields, to which every ruined Digger attributed his failure . . .'

Here she once again paused and allowed herself to remember unspeakable tragedies. Then the expression on her face softened as she continued.

'Amidst all this confusion of male comradeship, I became aware of a separate figure sitting on an upturned bucket, an opened book in his hand. He was staring dreamily into space, his mind a thousand miles away from the gangs of Diggers he was supposed to be supervising and, as I watched, he withdrew a pencil from his pocket and began to underline some of the text. The incongruity between his studiousness and the brutish environment quite enchanted me, and I stood among the mules and buckets with a sudden feeling that I beheld before me a kindred spirit, a soulmate, a fellow-being who thought as I did. Finally I asked my brother who the dreamy young man might be. Theo snorted. "He may dream, but he has the sharpest head for finance of all of us. In just a couple of years he has trebled his earnings through clever enterprises, and he is not yet twenty."

'From that moment onwards I began to notice this angular youth, often dressed in white flannels stained red by the earth, leaning moodily against a street wall with his hands in his pockets. Though I stared at him with an intensity that amounted to insolence, not once did he raise his eyes to meet mine. I believe that if a flock of beautiful women passed before him he would be unaware of their presence, so much more urgent were his own thoughts and dreams.'

Olive pursed her lips briefly and reflected on this opinion. She sighed before continuing.

'One evening, when the noise and stir in the camp pressed upon me like a great weight, I escaped to the solitude of the Big Hole in the bright moonlight. It was like entering the city of the dead in the land of the living, so quiet it was, so well did the high-piled gravel heaps keep out all sound of the seething noisy world around. Not a sound, not a movement. I walked to the edge of the reef and looked down into the crater. The thousand wires that crossed it glistened in the moonlight, forming a weird, sheeny, mist-like veil over the black depths beneath. Very dark, very deep it lay all round the edge, but high towering into the bright moonlight rose the unworked centre. In the magic of the moonlight it was a golden castle of the olden knightly days; you might swear, as you gazed down at it, that you saw the shadows of its castellated battlements, and the endless turrets that overcrowned it; a giant castle, lulled to sleep and bound in silence for a thousand years by the word of some enchanter.'

Miss Schreiner seemed to have entered some kind of trance, and indeed I myself felt swept away to this magical scene where hell-hole becomes fairy castle. Her voice had sunk very low, while her eyes stared sightlessly through the forest trees.

'I thought I was alone, but a slight movement in the periphery of my vision told me that some other living creature lingered nearby, drawn to the silence of the place as I was. It scarcely surprised me when a woman's voice floated towards me.

'"It is utterly transformed at moonlight, is it not? It becomes a thing of sublime beauty and mystery – like a Gothic cathedral dug up out of the earth," said she.

'"I doubt the diggers would find it so," said I sharply, for I preferred my own image of a crumbling castle (and perhaps, if the truth be known, myself as the sleeping princess waiting to be awakened by a prince). "But no doubt Mr Ruskin would admire the beauty that moonlight confers upon manual labour."

'"You know Mr Ruskin's works then?" The figure stirred with evident interest and moved slightly towards me.

'"I am interested in his dreams and how they shape the dreams of others," I replied – and then my very heart turned over. That fierce African moonlight not only throws a silken veil over man's monstrosities but also reveals what the darkness of night would otherwise have hidden. I could now see that my companion was no woman.

'His pale eyes blazed like two African moons, full of cold passion. But do not think this passion was directed at me. He was pointing down into the crater. "This is where *my* dreams begin. I can think of nothing else."

'"Then you are a mere fortune-hunter like all the rest?" I did not attempt to hide the scorn in my voice.

'He laughed with equal contempt. "I am not interested in personal fortune. My dream concerns the entire Anglo-Saxon race, and for that I need all the riches this earth will yield."

'This unexpected reply silenced me for a while, which was

just as well, for the young man proceeded to break into a perfect rhapsody of plans to fill the entire African continent with British settlers, and to acquire for Her Majesty the Queen vast tracts of land which she might call her Empire. His aspirations were not restricted to Africa: the American colonies must be restored to British rule, for the British race is the finest, and each tract of land becomes a finer place for its presence.

'The young man's speech rushed out in fits and starts, and his voice soared upwards as his excitement grew. I felt my heart beat more quickly as his vision grew to encompass the whole world – when he stopped almost in midstream and turned his burning gaze on me.

'"And you – what is your dream?"

'"My dream?" I was startled that he could have any interest in a young South African woman's hopes for her future, and for a moment I could not answer him. Then, as I began to speak, I felt that my life's decision was being made, endorsed even, by his grave attention.

'"My dream is to write of Africa, of its desolate landscapes and bigoted, God-fearing, idle people. And I will explore Woman and her sexuality, her identity, isolated in the lonely expanses of the Karoo, about which no English-speaking person has yet written." Now it was my turn for language to tumble from my mouth as I told this utter stranger of all my wild imaginings that had haunted me day and night. I could see his eyes catch fire as I spoke of the empty interiors with their ancient histories and seething insect life, none of which was known to the civilised world who avoided this barbaric hinterland because it was neither picturesque, nor was it sublime. Even when I spoke of women's role in society and the absolute necessity for a man and woman to be equal, he listened with an alert interest which stimulated me to explore these ideas further.

'When I had had my say, he waited to see if there was yet more. My old doubts rose up and I murmured: "But of course all this is only a dream. I do not yet believe in my abilities."

'"But you have no choice," he said at once. "You contain within yourself a rich gift, a gift of space. It is a space which those people crushed together in the claustrophobic terraced houses of England long to inhabit. They long to meet human beings uncrushed by civilisation, who are at one with indigenous animal and plant life but who love and hate, cheat and suffer just as much as they do. It is your duty."

'And I knew it must be so. I told him that soon I would be leaving the diamond fields for my sister's farm, some three hundred miles away, in the heart of the Karoo. He, for his part, was about to depart for Oxford, in order to carry out the next stage of his grand plan. We had both come to bid farewell to this gigantic and mysterious crater in the earth, which was to influence both our lives so profoundly.'

Miss Schreiner paused for at least a minute while she reflected on this potent episode. I shifted on my tree trunk, fearing a chill (I suspected it was damp, though the surface seemed dry enough), or, worse, anal haemorrhoids. Such physical discomforts clearly were not occupying her thoughts, for she took up her story with renewed energy, the only indication of her recent asthma attack being a slight hunching of the shoulders.

'We went our separate ways. The young man was right: ordinary suburban people *did* want to enter the lives of simple Boer farmers and rebellious young women trapped in those wild and lonely plains. My book about life on an African farm sold in hundreds of thousands and was translated into many languages. I spent many years in England, mixing with progressive thinkers, achieving some kind of unwanted fame. Ten years ago I returned to live in South Africa, a country now torn apart by racial antagonisms on every level. I had heard much about a man of genius, a Colossus of the Colony, who would pull this country of diverse races and needs into one glorious union, using his great wealth for higher purposes. I began to feel an almost painful interest in this man and his career. It became a necessity for me to meet him.'

She stared at me with passionate eyes, and I was unwillingly stirred by the intensity of this little woman's emotional life.

'I had chosen to return to my beloved Karoo, so kind to asthmatics with its clear unadulterated air. The little hamlet where I lived had become a stopping-place on the railway line from Cape Town to Kimberley, where passengers on the through-train might take meals at the station café. It happened that this man travelled frequently to Kimberley, where he had made his fortune; and I happened to know that he greatly admired my novel about life on a Boer farm. My brother, who worked for his diamond syndicate, arranged for us to meet on the station one morning, and partake of a meal together in the café.

'As I waited for the steam engine to draw in at the station, my excitement at the prospective meeting was almost unbearable. By now my feelings for him were positive and mysterious, feelings which I had never experienced towards anyone else – the deliberate knowledge: *"That man belongs to me!"* I must have paced that small platform a hundred times.

'The train was not late that morning. He had offered me a choice between breakfast or evening meal, as the train runs twice a day: I felt I should like to combine our meeting with dawn rather than dusk. At last the great engine panted into the station cloaked in the white steam which always reminds me of the swirling feathers of the ostriches on the Karoo farms. A door opened almost immediately – he has his own private carriage – and in the midst of the steamy plumes the gigantic figure of a man became discernible. I moved towards him as if in a dream.

'Oh, how the years had altered my young man of the diamond rush! Where once his face had been almost anaemic in its pallor, now the cheeks were swollen and flushed. His vast body, which now towered over me as he bent low to shake my hand, was crammed into crumpled white trousers and a tight jacket, while a spotted bow-tie looked as if it might shortly strangle him, so red and thick was the bulging neck. Yet for all that, he had retained that curious far-off look, and an almost childlike quality in his speech and movements. I could see at once that he did not recognise me – even then I was no longer the slender creature I had been at seventeen – and that the episode beside the Big Hole which had changed my life so powerfully had vanished from his memory. I did not remind him, though the disappointment caught at my throat.

'Over a cooked breakfast, which I scarcely tasted, marvelling how he wolfed it down and called for more, I found him to be even higher and nobler than I expected. He did not speak with the quick-witted fluency of my English friends, and his fluty tones entirely lacked the gravitas we expect from great men, but the vastness of his ideas more than made up for his vocal peculiarities. His plans to extend his railway right through the heart of Africa, to reconcile Boer and British in a unified South Africa, the dreams for his mighty Chartered Company, all utterly enthralled me, and as I sat in that remote railway café, my bacon congealing on my plate, I knew I faced a man of genius. Once again he did not confine his discourse to his own achievements and hopes, but spoke more lovingly and sympathetically of my African Farm than anyone else has done. I longed to remind him of our meeting of twenty years earlier, but in a flash, as it seemed, the train was ready to move on, and we bade each other goodbye, each conscious of the other's energy and intellect, each longing for another such meeting . . .'

I pulled out my fob-watch. 'I hate to interrupt you, Miss Schreiner, but –'

Miss Schreiner appeared not to have heard me. 'We met many times after that – on the humble railway platform, in my own small house, and for days on end at his great mansion down there, before it was destroyed by fire. Society hostesses fell over each other to have us both present at their dinner parties, and he gave me precedence over all other women at his own dinners.'

'Speaking of dinners . . .' How frail and feeble my voice sounded next to her ringing tones.

Miss Schreiner fumbled in her reticule and withdrew a box of cigarettes without a shade of embarrassment. Lighting one, she inhaled deep into her asthmatic lungs. 'So close did we become –' she blew out a stream of smoke which appeared to be having no ill effect on her bronchial tubes – 'that the rumour was spread that we were about to marry!' She gave a short, smoky laugh. 'I would lay my head on the block that he never loved a woman. Men, certainly. But he has a horror of being left alone with a woman, unless she has a formidable intellect!'

I rose from my tree trunk. 'I'm afraid I really have to go now. It has been most interesting to hear –'

She was opening her reticule again with nervous fingers. Inside it I could see a confusion of papers, one of which she passed to me. Sensing my reluctance to accept it, she raised her wild, tragic eyes.

'This is the Appeal of which I spoke. I have put all my energies into it. It is my last hope.'

'But really . . . I'm sorry . . .'

To my consternation Miss Schreiner grabbed both my hands in hers.

'Professor Wills, we are on the brink of a bloody war in this country, a war which will stir inextinguishable hatred in the breast of the Boer, and inextinguishable guilt in the heart of the Englishman. This beloved country will be rent apart to make way for an evil so great that it will become a pariah even in this world of evil. And you, Professor, have a *vital* role to play in preventing this calamity.'

I was conscious of the dampness of my palms, pressed into her warm dry hands.

'Madam, I am an ornithologist. I have no influence with your Colossus.'

She looked at me in astonishment and allowed my trapped hands to fall. With scorn in her proud eye she cried out: 'I am not asking you to present my Appeal to a man whose heart is entirely eaten away by corruption! I am asking you to present this Appeal to the High Commissioner, Sir Alfred Milner, and to request him to meet me – here – tomorrow. Ten minutes of his time will suffice. I will wait at this spot all tomorrow.'

'But why on earth should he listen to me? I hardly know him.'

Miss Schreiner's features hardened. 'I have observed that you have his ear.'

'I've taken photographs of him on a bicycle, if that's what you mean.'

'Professor Wills.' Her chest was heaving. 'In moments of extreme desperation I am prepared to resort to blackmail. I think the mention of the name "Cecile" may act as a gentle stimulus in this case. A woman in Brixton, you may remember. He loved to feel her hair flow into his lap. After dining with the Queen.'

Needless to say the cages were quiet as I passed them.

'You've got less than three days!' I hissed at a bleary-eyed nightingale.

Chamberlain and Salisbury were sliding their pebbles about on the gravel patterns, uttering a combination of low-pitched chants and sudden shrieks.

'You should be whistling to the birds, never mind the mumbo-jumbo!' I yelled, though I privately considered that their primitive magic was more likely to succeed than my avian music classes.

But I hurried on, by now thinking only of my delayed afternoon nap, especially necessary on this busiest of days, with an evening's socialising ahead.

Part Two

GREAT GRANARY 1899

Mr Joubert was giving me a lecture on blue china. It seemed he had fully recovered from the afternoon's tragedy. Or was putting on a good show, though I would not have thought him capable. In any case his master had just slipped him a cheque for one thousand pounds, and had already found him a post, with house attached, on one of his fruit farms outside Cape Town. 'But I may stay for the release of your birds, Professor, isn't that good?'

In order to keep my back turned upon the assembled guests in the Great Granary drawing-room, I attempted to assume an expression of high interest in the items of rare crockery collected by my host and exhibited behind glass in multiple teak cabinets. In any case, I was enjoying Joubert's company. It is not often that a charming, vigorous youth chooses to spend time with me: I cannot include the undergraduates with whom I work at Oxford, for they all, to a man, become respectfully subdued in my presence, though animated enough among their peers. Yet somehow it seems that the people of the Southern hemisphere disregard my Arctic nature and speak to me as if I were a child of the tropics.

Joubert's passion for porcelain took me by surprise. On the two previous occasions of our meeting, the unreassuring

179

phrase 'bull in a china shop' had flickered through my mind, so, in spite of his evident enthusiasm and fund of knowledge, I was relieved that the precious vases we were surveying were safely locked behind glass doors. In fact, Joubert's interest seemed to reside chiefly in *broken* blue china, of which there was a display upon a set of shelves. He pointed to some incomplete plates which had been partially re-cemented, and continued his lecture.

'The porcelain you see there was rescued from a wreck off the East Coast a couple of hundred miles away from here and glued together by someone with a lot of patience!' He laughed heartily at this idea, swallowing the entire contents of his sherry glass between chuckles. 'But do you know, Professor, there is nothing I love more than to spend a few days on that wild coast where hundreds of East India vessels must have sunk over two centuries ago on their journey back to Holland. I roll up my trousers and scour the shores for the bits of priceless pottery that are washed up from the wrecks every day. Sometimes you can find shards from the same pot – my ambition is to piece together an entire plate from the K'ang Hsi dynasty!'

As Joubert attempted to explain the features of K'ang Hsi to me, his eyes vivid blue in their clear whites, I had a curiously energising vision of the young man dancing bare-footed upon a far-off shore, where monkeys swung on mango trees and flamingos strutted through the waves, a perfect Ming vase in his upraised, exultant hand. Indeed, such was the energy pulsing from his restless body that I feared he might at any minute feel obliged to cartwheel across the floor.

'Do let me join you, Wills,' murmured a voice behind me. Milner edged his way between us, as if hoping that we might conceal him completely. 'I have spent the last twenty minutes discussing the infallibility of the Pope with the Jesuit chief of Central Africa. Have you seen the tea and coffee service he has given our host? – entirely covered in dead gold by a process known only in his monastery, giving it the appearance of solid metal. No doubt each is squaring the other for reasons we shall understand only when it is too late. I'm so sorry to interrupt your animated conversation.'

'Have you met Mr Joubert?' I enquired, feeling for the envelope in my breast pocket and wondering how to get rid of the young man who had become awed into sudden silence by the august presence which had descended upon him. But he remained solidly put, his half-open mouth revealing his faultless teeth.

'I recently spent the weekend at Petworth, where the Duchess of Somerset has a most extraordinary closet of china,' gabbled Milner, after nodding at Joubert. 'Seven vast blue-and-white vases from the K'ang Hsi period – I don't see anything here on the same scale. I remember as a child in Germany hearing how Augustus the Strong of Saxony exchanged a whole regiment of dragoons with the King of Prussia for six such vases!'

'Joubert was about to test me on which is Delft and which from China or Japan,' I heard myself improvising. 'He is quite the expert.'

'Ah, now, let me see.' Milner drew on his cigarette and directed his hooded gaze at the blue-and-white crockery. 'Now, that I would say is early K'ang Hsi, because the blue still has overtones of grey, whereas . . .' And for a full five minutes he held forth on the precise origins of every jug and jar, dismissing the Delft (some of which, to my eyes, seemed very fine) and causing Joubert's jaw to drop even further. Finally he angled his head kindly towards the young man. 'Am I right?'

Joubert's tanned face flooded with admiration. 'Oh, yes,

sir. You obviously know far more about china than I ever shall.'

'We once had a friend, did we not, Wills, who famously aspired to the condition of his Sèvres china. I suppose you could say that he fulfilled his ambition too well, and became a broken man as a consequence.'

'Someone you know wanted to become a piece of china?' Joubert's voice was full of good-humoured disbelief. I noticed his Dutch colonial inflections for the first time.

'The pernicious influence of Pater, I'm afraid.' Milner turned to smile at the innocent young secretary. 'Something which I'm glad to say you appear to have entirely evaded, Mr Joubert.'

Our host's voice arched like a rocket through the silence that followed this observation. 'Wills! You are hiding! There is someone I want you to meet!'

The Colossus was looking rather distinguished, having made the effort to change into a formal dinner jacket and tie, which, together with a pair of well-cut trousers, had a decidedly slimming effect on his great bulk. Even his hair was combed and oiled flat upon his head. His mood was ebullient as he thumped his enormous hand on to my shoulder and withdrew me, as if I were a book upon a shelf. Milner at once slid away, while Joubert rushed to join a gaggle of inebriated secretaries.

'Or should I say,' continued the Colossus in his excited, soprano voice, 'there's someone who wants to meet you. Don't try to escape, there's a good man!' – as I followed Milner with my eyes.

We were approaching a group of men and women who had gathered in a circle around a slight, vivacious man. The women, who included among their number the breakfast mother and daughter, twisted their necks and corseted bodies in an attempt to gain the little man's attention, while the men spoke to him in respectful tones, their eyes gleaming. My host ploughed through this company as if it were froth or foam, and laid his other hand on the small man's shoulder. 'This is my friend, Dr Jameson,' he said to me proudly. 'Dr Jameson – Professor Wills.'

Jameson's eyes were large pools of transparent hazel. His face appeared to be absolutely symmetrical, the right side the mirror image of the left, as if fashioned in a machine. So frank and open were his facial features that the onlooker was left without a purchase on which to settle: no irregularity of any sort offered itself for inspection. I found my gaze sliding about the broad dome of his forehead and his wide cheeks, avoiding those limpid eyes that, for some reason, were examining my person with undisguised interest. For a moment he did not respond to his friend's introduction, but allowed his stare – for by now the interest in his eyes had reached an uncomfortable intensity – to travel to my shoes and back to my own eyes. Then his lips split apart beneath his moustache into a brilliant, triangular smile, the reckless smile of the devil-may-care, irresistible to men and women alike.

'How d'ye do, Wills,' he said. 'You must be relieved there are no dogs in this house.'

Even as my brain tried to make sense of this curious remark, I felt my heart perform a somersault at the mere mention of my private phobia. How did this neat little man know that I have only to see a pampered lap-dog upon his mistress's knee for the perspiration to burst from my brow in fat, wet buds?

My knees began to buckle; the blood to drain from my face. I was aware that Jameson's circle of admirers had melted away and that the Colossus loomed over me, genial but expectant. In the absence of a rejoinder from me (it was all I could do to remain upright), he gave a kind of preliminary whine and exclaimed: 'Extraordinary! How on earth do you do it, my dear Jameson?'

I could now detect a certain patness in this response and realised I was their plaything.

'Elementary, my dear Watson,' replied the doctor. 'A glance at Professor Wills' right hand told me that in his youth he had been savaged by a small dog: the scars are almost imperceptible, but visible, none the less, to a physician's eye. A closer look at his face revealed further small scars beneath his beard, which I assume the Professor has grown to hide these minute blemishes. To be bitten on the cheeks by a dog of whatever size will inevitably induce a fear of further attacks that in the end will become unreasonable – though understandable.'

My face flooded with colour and I felt able to speak. 'Your deductions are absolutely accurate,' I admitted. 'For the reasons you have given, it is indeed a relief to me that I do not have to encounter dogs in this household.' In fact, my physician had made full enquiries into this possibility before I would agree to undertake the songbird project.

'I think we have enough animals on the estate as it is,' smiled the Colossus, visibly delighted by his friend's astuteness. 'I like to see my pets in their original, wild state, roaming free and unspoilt by the hand of man. But now I shall leave you two gentlemen as I see I am wanted by Father McVlellan.' He withdrew, and I felt suddenly exposed, as if a great tree had vanished from beside me. Jameson, a mere sapling, was reluctant to relinquish the topic of his deductive prowess. He puffed on a rather large cigar.

'I'm simply using the techniques of Conan Doyle's tutor, Dr Bell, at Edinburgh; my tutor as well, as it happens. His method was simply to make the medical students study their patients in silence before enquiring about their ailments, so that the students could recognise this one as a left-handed tailor or that one as a retired guardsman who had served in Barbados. As a result, I pride myself that my powers of accurate observation are almost as good as Sherlock Holmes's!' He took another puff of his cigar, undeterred by my silence. 'I go so far as to say that I am able to read precisely the train of thoughts that pass through my good friend's brain simply by watching his features work while he is seated in a state of reverie.' He blew out an immense stream of blue smoke that he had somehow retained in his lungs during this last utterance. 'You have no doubt read *The Adventure of the Cardboard Box*, one of Doyle's best. In this story Holmes amazes Watson by his ability to read the good doctor's thoughts, simply by observing the movements of his eyes from the newspaper to the pictures on the wall, and the changes of expression that took place during those movements. I can honestly say that I have only to look at my friend's eyes, and then follow his gaze, to know almost exactly what he is thinking.' Jameson laughed briefly. 'Ironically, he likes to think that he is Holmes to my Watson. For a man of his state of ill-health, it is essential to humour him. He loves to play his little games, to guess where I have just been, or the occupations and predilections of unfamiliar guests who arrive in this house.'

I was watching Jameson as carefully as he was watching me. As the words spilled from his neat mouth I found myself beginning to vibrate with the restlessness, the nervous energy, that lay beneath his air of garrulous *bonhomie*, and that caused him – and me – to startle with every sudden noise, to flex unseen leg and arm muscles, to glance at both clock and human faces even as he tried to fix me with his own powerful gaze. And within those brilliant eyes, that vigorous frame, at last drifted upwards, intangible as fragrance, a fatal exhaustion, a morbidity, an aura of failure which permeated even the brightest smile.

I nodded, and even ventured some mild congratulation.

He continued: 'My friend believes your nightingales will restore to him the gift of youth – or immortality. As a medical doctor, I cannot of course support this view.'

I replied as calmly as I could: 'I am merely a supervisor of songbirds. Their song has no medicinal – or magical – property known to me.'

His eyes were following the arrival of a woman who had caused some considerable stir. I recognised her at once as the woman who had helped me find my way through the corridors that morning.

Mrs Kipling was by far the plainest woman in the room, and made no attempt to erase the hard vertical line between her brows with the kind of false smile that stretched the lips of the other female guests. Instead she bustled straight up to her husband and, after a brief nod at the other gentlemen, began murmuring to him in low, urgent tones.

'That woman can't stand the sight of me,' said Jameson, unexpectedly. 'One of her children is ill, and will she call me in? Not on your life. Now Daddy will have to go up and tell stories instead.'

Sure enough Kipling immediately left the room, while his wife remained with our host, who seemed relaxed enough in her company. (I had watched him twitch horribly while conversing with the flirtatious women.) Jameson's eyes were cold as he watched her smile calmly at the great man's sallies. 'He's building a house nearby for them to stay in during the summer. A writer's residence.'

'Ah.' When would he get to the point? I made my restlessness visible by rotating first one, then the other, shoulder.

He cleared his throat briskly. 'I don't know if you happen to know that a few years ago I spent a short period in Holloway prison – detained at Her Majesty's pleasure, if you like. An interesting experience, curtailed by gallstones.' He cleared his throat again.

I raised my eyebrows. Jameson's cigar had become a cylinder of ash.

'I stayed in a common criminal's cell. Graffiti covered the walls. I read it avidly. In among the illiterate scrawl, a chain of initials stood out, clearly written by a person of letters. O.F.O.F.W.W. The initials were followed by four lines of verse. I later learned that Mr Wilde had occupied my cell between his trials, less than a year before.' Jameson placed the dead cigar between his lips and struck a match. 'Our host tells me he is your friend.'

'Do you remember the lines?' I asked carefully.

Jameson laughed amidst plumes of smoke. 'Remember them! Why, they kept me going in my darkest days. I learned them off by heart.'

'Could you repeat them to me?'

Jameson cast his eyes about to ensure that no one was eavesdropping; then, in a low voice, uttered these lines:

> *'Who never ate his bread in sorrow,*
> *Who never spent the midnight hours*
> *Weeping and waiting for the morrow –*
> *He knows you not, ye heavenly powers.'*

'Goethe,' I said. 'Oscar repeated those very lines in his *De Profundis*.'

'I too could have written a *De Profundis*,' said Jameson rapidly. 'Do not for one moment think that the so-called hero-worship I now receive in any way compensates for the catastrophe of my life. Kipling simply got it wrong – I've long ago lost my heart, nerve and sinew, though perhaps I haven't yet lost the common touch!'

Gusts of laughter rose from a nearby group. Orpheus swirled a silver tray of sherry between Jameson and me. He continued: 'It's a relief to talk about this. In England, people walked out of the room if you mentioned your friend's name. Did you know the man who prosecuted him – ruined him, more like – was my defence?'

'Ah, Carson, the Irishman. He was at Trinity with Oscar before he went up to Oxford. At first we thought this might be an advantage.'

Jameson was overcome. He looked downwards and agitated his head, as if trying to shake loose a thought. Finally he raised his face, his eyes full of confusion. 'You know what I think, Wills? I think: *it's a bloody small world!*'

In response to which observation (or so it seemed to my overtaxed imagination) Huxley struck one of the Javanese gongs and announced that dinner was served. The flirtatious mother became clamped to my unwilling arm, but she had no eyes for me. A sleek little man escorted her daughter and was engaged in the energetic task of twisting his moustache suggestively at both women, and ravishing them with his fiery eyes.

'Good heavens!' I exclaimed as the doors closed behind us. 'It's Frank Harris!'

LONDON 1885

Only once did Oscar attempt to intrude upon the asceticism which has been so distinctive a feature of my life: it was upon this occasion that I met Frank Harris for the first time.

I had been invited to dinner at the Wildes' House Beautiful in Chelsea, and accepted the invitation on condition that no one other than his wife, Constance, should be there. The visit was not to be a success.

On arriving, I could tell at once that my friend's extravagant décor would upset my digestion: the Moorish flamboyance of the library with its blue and gold walls, heavily adorned ottomans, Aladdin lamps and exotic hangings made my stomach palpitate with fear of foreign cuisine. A reproduction of Oscar's favourite martyr, Saint Sebastian, pierced with arrows, his head twisted improbably to expose his manly neck, hung in the hallway, surrounded by candles, while the dining-room, with its endless swathes of white curtains embroidered in white silk, had the curious effect of resurrecting my bed-ridden childhood.

On top of this, Constance was heavily pregnant, and Oscar could not bring himself to look at her. Indeed, her boyish, sprightly figure, hidden though it was within brilliant fabrics which hung, Grecian-style, from her shoulders, seemed forever lost. Yet ironically, Oscar's girth was greater than hers: his jowls flabby; his cheeks puffy through physical sloth. But the incandescent fancies and paradoxes which permeated his conversation overrode these physical considerations so that I sat torn between enchantment and revulsion throughout the meal.

However, it was plain that Oscar had another appointment later in the evening which interested him more than dining at home (thankfully, on plain boiled food, as I had requested) with his wife and old friend. His eyes kept straying to the Louis-Quinze clock surrounded by his blue china of Oxford fame, and he grew tetchy as Constance, apparently a founder member of the Anti-Tight Lacing League, embarked on a lecture concerning the curse of the corset. She informed us that even after her pregnancy she would continue to wear loose, hanging garments without bustles and the like. Her remarks were directed very largely at her husband, who had strong views on this topic, having once edited a women's magazine, but who refused to meet her pleading eye, gazing at me instead, with sardonic humour. Finally she turned to me.

'Do you know, Francis, there is a general belief that women breathe only from the chest, so it doesn't matter if their abdomens are held in a vice?'

Never in my life had I heard a series of words uttered with such sudden fervour, as if their meaning was something quite other. Oscar spread his purple lips into a polite smile, his fingers fluttering across his mouth to hide the blackened teeth, and drawled, while examining the variety of rings on his fingers: 'Well, my dear, not even a vice could hold in your abdomen at the moment. Besides, fashion has decreed that the waist is not a delicate curve but an abrupt right angle in the middle of the body. But we can take heart from the fact that fashion is merely a form of ugliness so unbearable that we are compelled to alter it every six months.'

I believe we rose from the table there and then, leaving Constance to run her hands across the mound beneath her Grecian robe, rocking her torso as if the babe were already in her arms.

In fact I was spending the weekend with Mr James and Elspeth in their Battersea home, and now looked forward to the sanctuary of 147 Lavender Hill, where Elspeth was no doubt at that very moment placing an earthenware hot-water bottle between my sheets. But, having thrown myself with some relief into the Wilde carriage, I was alarmed to note that the route we were taking to Battersea – which should have been a simple trip over Chelsea Bridge – had become absurdly circuitous. The bright lights and bustling crowds of Piccadilly, even at that late hour, were far removed from the quiet environs of my foster-parents' house; somewhat sharply I enquired of Oscar the reason for this diversion.

He pushed his face close to mine and smiled reassuringly: 'I have your education at heart, my dear Francis. I am taking you to my club, where you will meet men of Empire, soldiers and explorers, hunters and traders, who have lived for years in colonial outposts. They meet to exchange experiences, you could say. I feel their stories of native habits and customs, to say nothing of the local flora and fauna, would be of interest to you.'

It is an indication of my naïveté that I was prepared to believe that it was towards some form of Geographical Society or Travellers' Club that we were heading, even though I was fully aware that Oscar had never expressed an interest in this area of human endeavour; indeed, I expressed regret that he had not thought to include Mr James in this expedition, whose knowledge of the wildlife of colonial outposts far exceeded mine.

A thick fog had settled upon the centre of London, but this

murky weather in no way deterred the crowds who thronged the streets at that late hour, their faces scarcely visible in the dim gas-light. In Piccadilly, a woman shoved her head at the window of our carriage to bare her broken teeth at us in a suggestive manner, while a number of half-grown youths lolling on the steps of Eros watched her performance with a sneering interest. With some difficulty our vehicle struggled through swarms of high-hatted men and sumptuously dressed women released from the Piccadilly theatres, and clattered up the curve of Regent Street, past the Café Royale, until we suddenly turned into a narrow, ill-lit side street.

Before long we stopped outside a door which was clearly well-known to the coach-driver, and Oscar nudged me out. 'We'll find our own way home!' he called to the driver, a message that to me did not augur well: I felt in my pockets for money with which to pay for a cab later on, should this expedient become necessary.

Oscar knocked upon the door with the ivory handle of his cane. His tapping seemed to be some sort of code, as the door flew open almost immediately to reveal a gigantic doorman in full black-up, wearing no more than a leopardskin loincloth and a silver earring.

'Good evening, Lizzie, how are you?' enquired Oscar.

If I had been disturbed by the decorations of Oscar's house, I was thrown into a panic by the wholesale disregard for culture, country or era exhibited upon the walls of the foyer in which I now found myself. African masks hung side by side with Indian tapestries, while whips, spears, assegais and shields clustered round golden Buddhas, Islamic mosaics, Amazonian stuffed parrots and other foreign booty designed, no doubt, to make the visitor feel he had been magically spirited away from the familiar ambience of London into an environment where unusual codes of behaviour would be tolerated.

'Evening, Your Highness!' cried Lizzie (for this indeed seemed to be the name of this *ersatz* Zulu warrior) in cheerful Cockney tones. 'Sign the visitors' book here, please, sir.' He addressed me with a total disregard for the incongruity of his appearance (or name). As I bent over to do as he requested he lowered his lips to my ear and murmured: 'All virgins tonight, sir, every one of 'em!'

This piece of information was followed by a brisk beating of his hands upon a primitive African drum, in response to which a small person appeared from behind a curtain. The small person bowed deeply, though with a satirical air.

It was impossible to ascertain the gender of this child, who could not have been more than ten years old. He or she wore a flaming red fabric twisted around its narrow belly, and his or her hair was curled into wild black ringlets, obviously dyed for the occasion. Some attempt had been made to paint the child's body chestnut brown, but woeful streaks of pale liquid revealed the underlying racial tendency. The child in turn led us to a set of double doors which he (I see him for the moment as a male personage) flung open with considerable expertise. A great billow of smoke – mostly tobacco – at once enveloped us; my eyes began to water. I thought of running out, but Oscar had taken my arm and steered me into a room which was lit by one feeble candle upon a table in the middle of the floor. A man with a short dark beard sat by this table. He was addressing a group of some thirty or forty other men who sat or stood round tables in almost complete darkness. A tray bearing champagne in an ice-bucket had materialised in the hands of our youthful guide, who now pranced through the dark to a table occupied by two gentlemen. Not one word did this child utter, but threw us what seemed to me a girlish look as she left the table.

'Good evening, Harris!' cried Oscar, with no thought to

the disturbance he was causing. 'May I introduce you to my cousin Francis?'

Harris and I shook hands briefly and, my eyes having adapted to the gloom, I recognised his companion to be an elderly Lord of the Realm. We were not introduced, but Oscar murmured to me, as we somewhat ostentatiously settled, 'He loves first editions, especially of women; little girls are his passion.' I was glad of my champagne. Even in the darkness, Harris's eyes sparkled with a light that reflected not so much the flickering candle in the centre of the room, as an inner brightness suggesting immense energy and intellect. He motioned to Oscar to be quiet so that we could hear the words of the man at the table. I took the liberty of enquiring (in an undertone) the speaker's identity.

'Frederick Selous, the hunter,' whispered Harris.

My heart somersaulted.

But it was not the name of the famous explorer, rumoured to be the model for Rider Haggard's Allan Quatermain, that set my blood racing through my veins at a danger-ous speed. I realised I was in the presence of the elder brother of the world's leading ornithologist, *Edmund* Selous, whose observational diaries on the behaviour of field birds had recently appeared in the *Zoologist* – notes of such extraordinary insight and meticulousness that I had been obliged to revise my own records of birdsong, which seemed irresponsible by comparison. Selous the younger was of an even more reclusive disposition than myself – 'monkish' was the word most often used to describe him, a word which, strangely enough, is applicable to many who have chosen the discipline of ornithology.

In the meantime, Selous the elder was delivering a blood-thirsty résumé of his hunting life in Africa. 'So – in the space of six months I shot twenty-four elephants, nineteen buffalo, two zebra, five black rhino, four white rhino, four warthog, two giraffe, one hippo, one lion and fifteen assorted antelope,' he informed us in a voice devoid of emotion; but I found it difficult to concentrate on his big-game anecdotes as I privately formulated a request to meet his elusive brother. The talk was drawing to a close, in any case, and Selous drank deeply from a beaker of wine. At once Harris leapt to his feet.

'It would seem to me that in the world of big-game hunting, enough is clearly nothing like enough,' he declared, with all the confidence of a man used to speaking to the rich and famous. 'Am I right in supposing that this is your addiction – and we all have our addictions' (a chorus of catcalls greeted this remark, for Harris's addictions were scandalous) '. . . that, in fact, there can never be satisfaction: that even as you shoot the zebra you want to be shooting the giraffe, and as you shoot the giraffe you long to be toppling the elephant?'

'In much the same way as you go about your conquests, Mr Harris,' replied Selous suavely. 'Except in my case, I also send home rare specimens to museums and universities. I don't believe your own excesses contribute to the higher studies of animal behaviour.'

Shouts of laughter followed this remark, which seemed mightily to amuse Harris as well. 'One day I shall document my own insights into the animal behaviour I know and understand,' he announced, tilting his body at an extraordinary angle, 'but for the moment I worry about your elephants. To slaughter these marvellous creatures merely for their tusks seems to me a criminal act of wastage. May I ask what you do with their carcasses?'

'I agree the wastage is excessive,' said Selous, with a hint of regret in his voice. 'If there are no natives about, the carcasses have to be abandoned to the predators. Ivory is the only thing obtainable in this country with which to defray the heavy expenses of hunting; and if you depend on the gun for a living it behoves to do your best when you get a chance.'

'Exactly what I do, sir!' exclaimed Harris, straightening up. 'I always do my best when I get a chance!'

I sensed a restlessness at the tables. Respect for the explorer and hilarity at Harris's badinage was giving way to anticipation of something else: Selous felt it himself and vacated his chair to join a group of companions in the gloom. Two of these men were young and playful, judging by their impatient, but vigorous, movements, as if the constrictions of sitting in one place for a long time were proving too arduous for their high energies. The other gentleman, his face buried in shadow, was a giant of a man who, by contrast, sat slumped in his chair; he rose mountainously to congratulate the returning explorer and the two men at once became engaged in deep conversation. Now the conversation swelled, and laughter broke in waves from each of the tables, almost in turn, as if a wonderful joke was being passed from one table to the next. Our little personage – of whom there were several, all equally genderless with naked torsos and dusky ringlets – plied us with more champagne and smiles. Oscar seemed peculiarly excited: his hands shook as he raised his glass, and the epigrams flowed at an alarming rate.

I had just summoned up enough courage to approach Selous's table, when a tall, military-looking gentleman strode across to the vacated chair and grinned at us suggestively. He held in his hand a few sheaves of paper. His presence caused the audience, as I suppose we were, to burst into enthusiastic shouts of encouragement.

'Thank you, Mr Selous, for that interesting account of your experiences in Africa. I would now like to read a poem I have written about some of my experiences in India. I believe some of you might have heard it before.'

Wild cheers followed these words, and once the audience

had calmed down a little, the military gentleman, a handsome enough young officer with an erect bearing, began to read. His poem, written in the Byronic style, attempting to encapsulate a witty thought in each rhyming couplet, began harmlessly enough as he described the different parts of India to which he had been posted. My thoughts were still with Selous the younger, and my dark-adapted eyes rested longingly on the other side of the room.

But as my mind dwelt on the new methods of field-bird classification developed by the reclusive young ornithologist, I became aware of a quickening of excitement in the audience, an intensity of concentration upon the lines delivered by the young officer that seemed to me unusual even for poetry readings. I began to listen.

> *'And now the scene shifted and I passed*
> *From sensuous Bengal to fierce Peshawar*
> *An Asiatic stronghold where each flower*
> *Of boyhood planted in its restless soil*
> *Is* ipso facto *ready to despoil*
> *(Or be despoiled by) someone else: the yarn*
> *Indeed so has it that the young Pathan*
> *Thinks it peculiar if you would pass*
> *Him by without some reference to his arse . . .'*

I was startled by the celerity – even the violence – with which my body responded to the gross words which then began to flow from the young man's lips, as he described every lewd detail of his intercourse with young Pathans. Yet at this stage of the evening I was still able to observe my physiological reactions through the cool prism of science, and marvelled that a sequence of verbal images could so potently stimulate that part of the brain designed to control only the basic bodily functions which one would have considered to be impervious to poetry. Had someone written a paper on this interesting topic? I wondered, even as I felt my bland body transform into an inferno of powerful sensations.

When the young man had finished reciting his catalogue, which in terms of number was not unlike Selous's, except that it had rhyme, the entire audience groaned in appreciation. Our little person refilled our glasses. And I heard Oscar breathe to Harris: *'No, no, Frank, enough can never be enough!'*

My fingers dug into my pockets and found the coins which I reckoned would pay a cabby to drive me back to Battersea. But as I rose from my seat – somewhat unsteadily – I discovered that a new drink had been set before me, which Oscar urged me to raise to my lips. Frank and the Lord of the Realm had already lifted their glasses, which contained the same milky-looking liquid, so good manners (and a certain mellowing of my normal social anxieties) compelled me to raise mine as well.

I had not tasted absinthe before. I can only suppose that its effect upon my nervous system must have been similar to the *grand mal* convulsion experienced by the epileptic. As I felt the liquorice-flavoured drink roll down my throat, my body actually lurched into uncontrollable spasms (my brain now abandoning all attempts at scientific investigation), after which I began to hallucinate wildly. Whether these hallucinations were due to the effects of the absinthe or a possible epileptic seizure not even my physician is able to say, but the bizarre memories I have of the remainder of that evening can have no connection with reality, of that I am certain.

For could it be possible that I then saw the Lord of the Realm straddled across that very table, his buttocks exposed to the air, while Lizzie whirled above these pale mounds a rod of twigs which he proceeded to whip downwards, causing the noble Lord to call out in pain, as rod audibly met soft flesh. The howl was misinterpreted by Lizzie as a demand for further flogging, which he administered with great energy and no pity. As further proof of the illusory nature of this experience, my companions seemed to be enjoying their friend's discomfiture, and made no attempt to run to his assistance. 'Stolen from Winchester School,' laughed Harris (or so I seem to remember). 'They boil their rods in grease there and leave them up the chimney to grow hard!'

Further hallucinations of an equally perverse nature hover yet in my memory. The little persons were making great shows of affection towards certain gentlemen, even going so far as to perch on certain knees and fiddle with certain moustaches. These gentlemen tolerated this impertinence with smiling faces, clearly much entertained by such childish games.

In the midst of these observations, much was my astonishment to find our table's small servant suddenly cuddled into my lap and extending a slender arm round my neck. So light and insubstantial was this creature, more like a cat than a human, that I felt its movements rather than its weight; there was a pleasing delicacy in the texture of the experience, if I can put it that way. And could its teeth be nibbling at my earlobe, its tongue darting about like a kitten at a bowl of milk? Overwhelmed by curiosity, I allowed my hand to slide beneath the flaming fabric, to determine the virgin sex of the little urchin, as one might of a rat or a puppy.

GREAT GRANARY 1899

I was surprised to find myself included among the favoured half-dozen at the top of the table, placed between Milner and Mrs Kipling, with the Jesuit priest opposite. Jameson, Kipling and an empty seat made up our number, with the Colossus presiding at the head of the table. Harris sat a little further down, mother and daughter on either side; he had acknowledged my presence with a suave, unsurprised bow, murmuring that we should meet afterwards. It seemed extraordinary to me that this notorious *bon viveur*, womaniser and friend of Oscar Wilde should be an acquaintance of the Colossus; on the other hand, I was aware, through Oscar, that Harris, a brilliant fellow who spoke twelve languages fluently and edited several journals, was privy to the confidences of virtually everyone who counted in government, society and the arts. As to the identity of the missing person, we were given no clue, and, accordingly, made no comment. No one seemed curious, and I wondered briefly if our host had some prank in mind.

I have attended many a sumptuously laid high table at various Oxford college halls, but I have to say that the table glass on this occasion must have been worth a small fortune. Accustomed as I am to the brilliant glitter of Waterford crystal goblets of various shapes and sizes, geometrically arranged on the right-hand side of every plate, I was at first perturbed to note that the display of glass at the Colossus' dinner lacked the precision of identical place settings upon the vast swathe of lace tablecloth. I soon appreciated that this was because each set of golden cutlery was accompanied by a unique combination of eighteenth-century Dutch or English wine glasses: some with intricate patterns cut into their cups; some with elaborate engravings; some with spiral air twists in their stems; some with gilded brims; and, at each plate, an engraved German beaker mounted in silver. The plainer glassware, bearing only my host's monogram, was nowhere to be seen.

And the wine that filled these glasses was like no other wine I had tasted in this house. With each sip, a sensation of well-being flooded through my fragile veins, accompanied by a growing belief that each sip rendered my presence ever less corporeal, and that eventually I would become utterly invisible and impervious to small-talk.

I was wrong. Mrs Kipling leaned towards me. 'You found your way, then?'

Mrs Kipling reminded me of someone. As I framed a polite reply to her polite question, I felt her matronly energy warm my blood. Something in my stomach began to relax for a moment, even as I watched Milner out of the corner of my eye, and patted my inner breast-pocket, inside which lay Miss Schreiner's Petition. But Milner, who, on sitting, had given me no more than a perfunctory nod, afraid, perhaps, that I might bring up the topic of bicycles, was deeply engrossed in talk with Mr Kipling on his left.

'I wonder if he will bring out the *pokaals* with the dessert,' said Mrs Kipling.

I looked at her in astonishment. For out of her no-nonsense brown eyes, from the very depths of her sensible, kindly being, stared my long-dead mother. It is not often that I speak to women; even less often do I meet with women who do not repel me.

'*P-pokaals?*' I stammered.

'Loving-cups. From Holland. He brings them out for special occasions. They're priceless. At least two hundred and fifty years old. They should be in a museum.' Even the New World drawl had my mother's brisk intonations.

'I should be too terrified to drink from one,' said I, swallowing the contents of my slightly less valuable glass and casting a furtive glance at the still-preoccupied Milner. 'So let us hope that he *won't* do any such thing.' My heart was pounding, but pleasurably for once. I allowed Huxley to refill my glass almost as it left my lips.

At this point the first course arrived and was laid before each one of us by white-gloved Negroes: a bowl of brilliant green soup, utterly tasteless, but with overtones of spirogyra and moss, once swallowed. I laid down my spoon after two mouthfuls and blotted my lips. The wine allowed a surge of interesting emotions to beat in my breast, like uninvited humming-birds. Indeed, Mrs Kipling appeared to be humming an amused little song to herself as she sipped at her soup, the very song my mother crooned to me on the odd occasions when she remembered to bid me goodnight. Just as an extremely painful lump began to develop in my throat, a movement on my left suggested the men's conversation was at an end, and I turned abruptly to confront Milner with Miss Schreiner's blackmail offer, my hand in my breast-pocket. But I had no sooner opened my mouth to address him, even gaining his half-amused attention, when our host rose to his feet and banged a golden spoon against a crystal beaker.

It seemed that the topic of conversation to dominate the dinner table, with its miraculous display of porcelain and glass, was to be the compulsory washing of scab-infected sheep.

'Tonight we have much to celebrate!' His soprano voice rang out clearly, but I could see he was having difficulties with inhaling. 'First I want to propose a toast to a group of men who attended a luncheon I held in this house exactly three years ago. Ladies and gentlemen, will you drink to the two hundred back-veld farmers who refused to dip their sheep in disinfectant! To the back-veld Boers!'

The company repeated this absurd toast with a great deal of merriment, and begged him to recall for them the visit to which he had referred.

It appeared that during his Premiership the entire sheep population of the Colony had become infested with highly contagious scab mite. The more sophisticated farmers who lived closer to British civilisation had immediately eliminated this pest through disinfectant dipping, but the backward Trekboers, who had effectively sealed themselves off from British influence by living hundreds of miles inland upon a lunar landscape, steadfastly refused to contradict what they saw as an act of Divine Will. The Lord had his own reasons for infesting their sheep with parasite: who were they to contradict the wishes of their creator? As a result the sheep industry collapsed, and overseas buyers got their wool from disinfected Australia.

Parliament hurriedly proposed a so-called Scab Bill which would make sheep-dipping compulsory, and two hundred Bible-thumping Boers trekked out of their disease-ridden, drought-stricken homeland into the decadent hothouse of the capital city to oppose it.

'And what could I do,' shrilled the Colossus, 'but invite them all to lunch?'

Throughout these reminiscences, Mrs Kipling sat very straight, inclining her head and her frown now to our host, who dominated the talk in his blundering way; now to Milner, who somehow, out of the immensity of his education, was able to make trenchant and wittily delivered contributions to this unpromising topic; now to Jameson, who appeared to be drunk, and who shouted his opinions of the Boer with a vivacity which infected the whole male company, my stern self excepted; now to the secretaries, who quipped and quaffed and quizzed (I caught the radiant eye of the messenger-god Joubert) with wondrous displays of fine teeth beneath pliant moustaches; now to her husband, who gazed through his thick round spectacles with nothing short of devotion at both Colossus and Jameson, and said little.

By this time, the glassware upon the table had done its work and everyone was inebriated to some extent, except for Mrs K. I say this bluntly, for I myself, who, at the best of times drink only a little Hock mixed with spring water, had succumbed to the miraculous wines which filled the miraculous glasses. Each sip had transported me back to the Mediterranean with its heavy scent of lemons and olives, an olfactory combination able to flood even the most reluctant nervous system with sensations of well-being and irresponsibility. Thus it was that I found myself shouting back to our host, along with the rest of the table, words of mirthful encouragement which, had I been sober, I would have regarded as sycophantic and crude in the extreme. The Colossus, for his part, radiated a huge delight in the reception of his story and, for all he was a dying man, enmeshed us in his jovial power.

'And Huxley would have had me put out my less costly wines for the Boers!' He shook his head at the solemn major-domo who happened to be filling my glass at the time. 'I ask you, just because a man has drunk only cheap brandy – that poisonous stuff they call Cape Smoke – does this mean his palate is to be forbidden the bouquet of fine French wines?'

Some sort of fish dish, lying in a bed of curry and onions,

had appeared before me. I made a pretence of prodding it with my fork.

Seamlessly, Jameson continued the story. 'The meal was such a success that one old farmer, creaking in his unaccustomed three-piece suit, stooped down to pick a handful of gravel from the paths upon which he and his companions strolled in leisure after their six-course meal – and pocketed it!' Sleek and groomed, the Doctor grimaced in mockery of his own smile.

'What a strange thing to do!' cried a lady from the far end of the table. 'Why did he do that, do you think?'

'He did it to remind him of his great and wondrous host, why else!' chortled the Doctor. He turned to the Colossus, who had devoured the entire fish dish in the time that it took me to chew and swallow one mouthful. 'What was it you sent him when you heard – one of your best silver snuff boxes, was it? A cheap price to pay for your Scab Bill, I'd say!'

With a sudden change of mood that sent a subdued shudder down the table, the great man cried out: 'But I ask you this! Did they refuse to dip their sheep because of their sacred beliefs or because they were *loafers*? Some of those Boers up in the Karoo are as lazy and as unwashed as any Kaffir, sitting on their stoeps drinking coffee all day while their sheep wander for miles into other men's property, spreading disease. Is this the will of God, or is it sloth?' A look of revulsion contorted his face as he uttered the last word, while the secretaries stirred anxiously, mouthing a chorus of echoes . . . 'Sloth undoubtedly, never seen a bar of soap in their lives, did you see their fingernails, they had their price . . .'

Slabs of red meat, apparently cut from the thighs of the buck or the kangaroos grazing on the mountain slopes, now replaced the fish. Sweet potatoes and cabbage, an unhappy combination, filled up the rest of my plate. As I tried to find a soft pathway among the tough sinews of the venison, I became aware that Milner was making a speech. Everyone else had stopped eating, and gazed at the softly-spoken Proconsul as if he alone had the key to their futures, indeed to the Colony's future.

'The Trekboer knows nothing of the ideals of Liberty, Equality and Fraternity, nor of the revolution that threw up these ideals. He knows nothing of the revolutionary theories of Mr Marx nor the evolutionary theories of Mr Darwin. He lives only for his piece of land and the memories of ancestors who were slaughtered by Zulus. To him, the insect dwelling within the wool of his scraggy sheep is an essential part of his *Weltanschauung*. Nature is not there to be tamed or undermined, but to be lived with in partnership, for better or for worse. The Englishman, the Uitlander, is the devil in disguise, trying to catapult him into what will very soon be the twentieth century.' Milner lifted his knife and fork and sliced his venison effortlessly. 'His world view is as foreign to us as that of the savages in loincloths who outnumber us – is it four to one?' He stabbed at the meat with his fork. 'There is a solution.'

'And what is that?' demanded the Colossus.

Milner licked his lips. 'Make 'em speak English,' he said softly. 'I believe absolutely in the civilising powers of a civilised language.' And swallowed his forkful, quick as a snake.

The Colossus had collapsed into a posture of exhaustion, one hand fiddling with a porcelain salt cellar, the other propping up his large and heavy head as if it might slump forward in sleep were it not so supported. When Milner had indicated that he had done with speaking by blotting his Bismarck-moustache with his table napkin, my host heaved himself into an upright position. The earlier exuberance had disappeared. His eyes were now bleary, his face crumpled and his hair ruffled (he looked, in fact, as if he had just that moment crawled unwillingly out of bed), but before our eyes he summoned a new, miraculous energy that eradicated the fatigue of his physical appearance.

'To that, I have only one reply.' His moon eyes blazed. The company fell utterly silent and laid down their golden cutlery. 'I have made this reply many hundreds of times in my lifetime, ever since I was a mere boy in my teens, raw among the diamond diggings of what was then the hill of Colesburg Kopje.' He paused, inhaled as deeply as his clogged lungs would allow, and continued. 'Look around this table. What do we all have in common?' The company dared not look. 'Fine, Anglo-Saxon minds, that's what we have in common. And none of us loafers! Here is my reply: *I contend that we are the first race in the world, and that the more world we inhabit the better it is for the human race!*'

'Hear hear!' chimed the entire table, thrillingly.

Our host turned his exhausted head towards Milner and addressed him directly. 'Every acre added to our territory means the birth of more of the English race who otherwise would not be brought into existence.' Out of the corner of my eye I could see Milner nodding. Now our host relaxed into a ruminative smile. 'I remember, when I was that young Digger, living in filthy tents among the stampede of English . . . Dutch . . . German . . . American . . . Australian . . . fortune hunters – all of us digging, sifting, sorting from morning till night, day after day, month after month . . . Now and then I would walk out into the immense brown – completely flat – plain that surrounded our circle of tents, to get away from the noise and turmoil and drunkenness . . . And as I walked, I looked up at the sky and down at the earth and I said to myself: *This should be British!* And it came to me in that fine, exhilarating air that the British were the best race to rule the world!'

'Hear hear!' we chorused again.

His voice sank to a whisper as he fastened a startled Kipling with his bloodshot eyes:

'*Take up the white man's burden . . .*'

A look of anguish crossed Kipling's face.

'Yes, Mr Kipling, I have spent a considerable time this afternoon learning the first verse of your new poem, and with your permission I should like to repeat it to the good people at this table, all of whom are admirers of your poetry and your stories.'

Kipling blushed. The company fell to begging his permission.

'Just one verse, dear!' sang out his wife, leaning across the table and smiling. 'It is so very appropriate.'

'Well – I – I don't know that . . .'

The Colossus beat his glass with his spoon again. He leaned forward, his hands spread out on the table, bearing his weight. He began to declaim in his falsetto voice, his gaze moving from one member of the company to the next after every few words, as if he were issuing us with our instructions:

> '*Take up the White Man's burden –*
> *Send forth the best ye breed –*
> *Go, bind your sons to exile*
> *To serve your captives' need;*
> *To wait in heavy harness*
> *On fluttered folk and wild –*
> *Your new-caught, sullen peoples,*
> *Half-devil and half-child.*'

The company remained immobile in a silence of the kind that occurs after an extraordinary performance of a Beethoven piano sonata or a Bach cantata. Perhaps our hearts beat in unison. The Colossus continued to stare round the table at individuals, as if mesmerising them, one by one, into submission. Indeed, no one dared return to their plates, where the already unpalatable food was congealing with cold, until Jameson broke the spell by clapping his hands together and shouting 'Hoorah!' At which point everyone clapped, shouted, swallowed wine and tried to finish their food. The Colossus seemed to be trying to cajole Kipling into reciting the rest of the poem, but the little man dimpled under his mountainous moustache, and declined.

This seemed the moment to mention Miss Schreiner's request to Milner who was staring at a particularly fine goblet, lost in thought. I had got as far as withdrawing her Appeal from my pocket and uttering the first words of a carefully structured sentence with no mention of blackmail: 'I wonder if I could . . .' when I realised that Milner was, in fact, preparing an impromptu speech in response to the verse we had just heard. He rose to his august feet and waited for the company's full attention.

'As we have just heard, our responsibilities for being "the best race in the world" are indeed onerous.' He paused, and seemed to grow in height and shrink in breadth. 'For there can be little doubt that the British race stands for something distinctive and priceless in the onward march of humanity.' He looked around the table. 'We are indeed tied together by the primordial bond of common blood. And if, as Mr Darwin tells us – or is it Herbert Spencer? – the struggle for existence leads to the survival of the fittest, then we may soon have to engage in a struggle that will select a race fit to govern the whole of Southern Africa. I can have little doubt as to the outcome of such a struggle.' He sat down.

The high seriousness with which he spoke engulfed the table in sudden gloom. Everyone stared at Milner in awe – with one notable exception. Harris's dark eyes, too, were fastened upon the High Comissioner, but they altogether lacked the almost frightened respect that flickered in the collective gaze. Throughout Milner's speech – indeed, throughout Kipling's poem – an expression of deep cynicism, even dislike, was etched upon Harris's mobile features, but his voice was languid as he addressed the Colossus.

'You know, it's a strange thing. I can understand God in his youth falling in love with the Jews, an extremely attractive race.' Harris was completely at ease. 'But in his old age to fall in love with the Anglo-Saxon is proof of a senility that I find unforgivable!'

The ladies on either side of him tittered, while the rest of the table stirred with surprise. Our host cried out: 'You say things, Harris, that hurt!'

'I would like to shock this idolatry of the English!' smiled Harris. 'Fancy the race that loves commerce and wealth more than any other, yet refuses to adopt the metric system in weights and measures and coinage!'

'The Masters of the World, Harris!' yelled the Colossus.

'Nonsense – the Americans are already far stronger and more reasonable,' mocked the little man.

Now Milner spoke. 'Are you suggesting that the Americans are further up the evolutionary tree than the British?' He sounded genuinely astonished.

Harris looked at him with contempt. 'Evolution has nothing to do with it. Xenophobia has everything to do with it.'

Milner smiled thinly. 'You don't believe in evolution?'

'Not in the sense that you do.'

The Colossus had had enough of this exchange. To my inexpressible horror, he fixed me with an exuberant stare, invisible as I felt myself to be.

'You believe in evolution, don't you, Wills?' he yelped. 'Fish . . . birds . . . apes . . . man . . . the Anglo-Saxon race? Isn't that how it goes?'

The whole company smiled at me with relief. It was clear

that I was expected to lift the mood, to parry the thrust with academic elegance. I caught the bright encouraging eye of Mr Joubert, and coloured, anticipating my humiliation.

I cleared my throat of the anxious phlegm that had gathered.

'It is true,' I said in my strangled voice, 'that the fish, the birds, the apes, man, have all so far struggled successfully, in terms of species survival. On the "Anglo-Saxon race", as you put it, I cannot comment, as this group is not a species. As for the hierarchy you mention, not all species of each of those orders have been equally successful in adapting themselves to a changing environment. Those that still survive are the most highly evolved. No one species, let alone race, is better than another. It is therefore pure fallacy to identify evolution with the onward march of progress. Man is no better evolved than a bird or a fish, and there is no evolutionary difference between a naked savage and the Queen of England.'

'I couldn't agree more!' laughed Harris provocatively.

'Oh come now, man!' responded the Doctor. 'I'm a man of science myself. And practising my science in the real world rather than the laboratory, I can call myself an empiricist, however unfashionable that term may be today in the upper echelons of scientific thought.' He puffed himself out a little. 'And I can tell you that I have met the full range of humanity, from that naked savage in loincloth to Her Majesty the Queen, God bless her! I've fought hand to hand with that savage, you see. I've stared at him eyeball to eyeball. Good God, man, I've even doctored him and cured his gout! Surely ye'll not deny we're the superior race, evolved over the millennia!' A witty thought occurred to him, and he looked at me mischievously. 'If what you say is true, we might as well prepare ourselves for a Kaffir to run this country, live in this house, sit at this table, drink out of this remarkable flask!' And with a flourish he tipped his head back and swallowed the remains of his wine, while the company turned their lips down at this somewhat tasteless fantasy.

It so happened that Orpheus was removing my largely untouched plate as Jameson spoke. An involuntary muscle spasm flickered between his lips and his nostrils, and under his breath he uttered a line of tribal dialect which only my ears could hear.

I said, with all the calmness I could muster: 'I think that is an event which is altogether possible.'

'Half-devil and half-child, Wills!' yelped our host. 'I'm afraid you haven't been in Africa long enough to understand the black man's mind.' He drank hurriedly from his silver beaker. 'It all boils down to power in the end: the race that can rule and control other races, that is the best race, the fittest race! Natural selection, the best race wins; that's what Darwin says: the race that can exploit natural raw materials can stimulate industry!'

'But look at the massive influence even the smallest species can have on its environment – and on the mightiest of human races at that!' I was emboldened to interrupt. 'Look at that scab mite *Astigmata psoroptidae* – an organism so microscopic that it does not even have to breathe to survive – which has ruined your colony's wool production. It will almost certainly develop a resistance to your disinfectant which you will then have to modify in response. Look at the malaria parasite – an animal organism consisting of precisely one cell, only a step away from the vegetable kingdom. Yet the presence of that protozoan parasite has determined the fate, the history, of whole geographical areas. How very different a continent Africa might be if *Equus equus* had been able to withstand the bite of the anopheles mosquito – to say nothing of your settlers up north, who, I gather, succumb almost immediately to the fever.'

As I droned on, mistaking, I fear, the dinner guests for

undergraduates at a seminar, I noticed our host nod meaning-
fully at Huxley, who in turn nodded his own bullet head with
the utmost seriousness at a line of Negro manservants who
seemed to have been waiting in anticipation of this signal,
for even as my closing pronouncement on the mosquito left
my mouth, they surged over to the dinner table and, with a
silent dexterity that was awesome, removed everything from
it, including the gigantic lace tablecloth, by now somewhat
stained by the various liquids and gravies that had attended
the earlier courses. Within seconds the glassware and cutlery
had been returned to the bare boards of the table, together
with a set of rare and exquisitely fragile loving-cups, their
stems twisting into a double spiral. Exclamations of polite
appreciation sounded across the table.

'Ah!' sighed Mrs K, 'the *pokaals*. I see you and I are to
share one, Professor.'

At this point a heavenly vision floated towards me. So
light, so aerial was the apparition that I could have thought
it a cloud dropped from the skies and trailing a cinnamon
fragrance, had not a white-gloved hand descended along
with it. I have a weakness for sweet milky puddings, and
this one was closer to heaven-spun manna than anything I
have ever eaten. Helplessly, I succumbed to the seduction of
pastry made by angels with an inner froth of egg, cream and
sugar. Argument about mosquitoes and sheep-scab raged all
around me, but no words could tempt me from the paradise
in my mouth.

At last, as I scraped at the last magical traces of this
confection, I became aware that Mrs Kipling had leaned over
to me. 'You seem to have enjoyed your *melktert*, Professor!'
exclaimed she in tones of maternal interest. 'That is the first
course you have not pushed to one side.'

'*Melktert*?' I enquired, licking my lips in an abandoned
fashion.

'A very popular Boer recipe. I believe you have to make the pastry late at night and hang it up in a damp muslin cloth in a draught. It has to be baked before sunrise for the light flakes to be formed. I shall try it as soon as we arrive in England.'

'Ah,' said I, unused to discourse of this nature, but fascinated by the details none the less.

'And speaking of evolution,' continued Mrs Kipling in the pleasant American drawl which curled up the edges of her words and made them light as Boer pastry, 'have you noticed how the great chain of being is represented in this evening's meal? Primeval soup – fish – flesh – manna? Even to the point of imitating the textures of the soul? But look, he is about to speak again. That poor man does not look well. He needs to spend a month at a spa, in my opinion. I believe there are many hot springs further north.'

The Colossus was indeed struggling to his feet with some difficulty. So massive, so weighty, so purple, did the hulk of his flesh now appear that any physical effort seemed likely to bring on heart failure. But in the end he reared himself upright, and, swaying slightly (he had refilled his silver beaker many times with a curious mixture of champagne and stout), he begged the company's attention.

'I have an announcement to make, ladies and gentlemen. The distinguished scientist in our midst' – and here his gaze rested almost respectfully on my startled visage – 'has been prised out of his Oxford college and brought across the high seas to this faraway city for a purpose. He has brought with him some two hundred songbirds – nightingales, blackbirds, thrushes – from the mother country. In two days' time these songsters are to be released from their cages into the forests surrounding this house, and there they will fill the air with the glorious sounds of the English countryside which we all know and love.' His voice trembled briefly. 'I am now inviting the present company to attend that grand opening of the cages which will be held on my lawns – along with suitable celebrations – on Saturday at midday. Ladies – gentlemen . . . let us raise our loving-cups – in honour of nightingales!'

Mrs K slipped her arm through mine and together we held the slim spiral of glass and sipped from the ancient cuplets, now brimming with finely-bubbled champagne. The intimacy of this ritual, to say nothing of the reason for it, would normally have caused my blood to acidify; instead I found myself hoping she would lay her hand upon mine. Indeed, I believe our fingers did touch as we drank, by accident, and I did not instantly withdraw my hand.

In the midst of these warm sensations, I felt Milner's eye turn upon me. 'What a shame I'll be locked up in a railway carriage in Bloemfontein with the old Boer President and his Bible at the very moment your birds fly into the forests. I shall allow my thoughts to fly with them for a few seconds.'

The moment had arrived. I cleared my head of all other thoughts, as a lifetime of discipline has enabled me to do, within reason. The hand that had held the *pokaal* stem now dived into my breast pocket and I began to deliver my well-rehearsed sentence in confidential tones. 'I wonder if I might deliver to you an urgent message from someone who has the highest opinion of your ability to prevent war.' I produced Miss Schreiner's envelope with a discreet flourish.

Good wines had relaxed the vulture gleam in his eyes. He glanced at the missive in my hand and opened his mouth to reply.

At that precise moment the brass gong thundered to the uncarpeted floor, causing the entire company to freeze in their poses of inter-prandial discourse.

'Hands up, and shut up, the lot of you!'

In the doorway, a fiendish grin contorting his ravaged features, stood a familiar figure, his Holland and Holland double-barrelled eight-bore rifle balanced on his shoulder and aimed at the upper end of the dinner table. His poodle barked prettily at his feet.

'I assure you it's loaded.' He moved the barrel up and down, as if unsure who to select as his victim.

'Oh, good evening, Challenger,' exclaimed the Colossus. 'I was wondering when you would arrive!'

As I sat at that colonial dinner table, strangely indifferent as to whether Challenger blew my brains out or not, my hands nevertheless held high above my head, one of them bearing Miss Schreiner's Appeal, I thought of Mr James.

After the massacre of the moths, my father had sunk into a deep depression, spending his days slumped in his shuttered bedroom, unable to shoulder his responsibilities to the Church.

Two weeks later, he hanged himself in the conservatory. I had found his body, with its purple, protruding tongue, as I tiptoed about the house on my early morning tour of inspection, which had become a feature of my new-found mobility. The bodies of his treasures still carpeted the flagstones: he had not allowed them to be swept away. Elspeth immediately sent for Mr James and locked me in my bedroom. She had discovered the door of my father's safe flung open: inside it lay all the missing single wings from the dead moths, piled over the Dodo egg like a mound of dried petals.

Mr James propelled himself post-haste in his wheelchair from his cottage in the village. Elspeth and he arranged the funeral, a subdued and hasty affair, because of the suicide. The Anglican Church allowed us orphans to remain in the house while they looked for a new vicar.

Full summer was upon us. Birdsong still flooded the gardens, and every day several new species of flora burst into life in the flower beds. James and I grew inseparable. Every day we would tour the vicarage gardens and surrounding woods, both of us equipped with the compulsory paraphernalia of the serious natural-history collector: net, game bag with multiple pockets, box with cork damped in chloroform for the insects, pincushion with six sizes of pins. Between us we netted every variety of butterfly and moth around the vicarage. No beetle escaped our rapacious fingers, James even placing one in his mouth (like Darwin) when both hands were filled with booty.

His photographic equipment always came with us, solemnly pushed by either James or me in the handcart. By the end of the summer I was able to prepare the wet plates as well as develop and print them in the portable dark-room immediately after taking the photographs. My first formal portrait was taken at the age of nine on the occasion of Mr James's marriage to Elspeth; it still resides upon her mantelpiece, next to a portrait of my father (which their visitors often mistake for a portrait of myself).

When a new vicar was eventually appointed and it became necessary for the couple to move, they chose to live in Battersea, South London, where Mr James could push himself to the local Working Men's Club and teach the workers about natural history across the world. He always carried a shrivelled human head around in his wheelchair having discovered a whole basketful of them under his bed while sojourning in one of the islands of New Guinea. It resembled nothing so much as a withered old pomander, with the cloves mostly fallen out. I begged that we should slice it open with a bread knife to see what lay within, but some sort of superstitious fear he had picked up from the natives prevented him from agreeing to my request, which otherwise would have interested him greatly.

My father had left a substantial sum of money to Elspeth, with the result that she was able to buy a house large enough to hold my sisters and myself as well, our relations in Ireland having declined to adopt so unpromising a set of offspring. I was happy enough in Battersea, attending a preparatory school along the Thames during the week, and listening to Mr James's adventures during the weekends. Elspeth developed a fanatical interest in cookery, more particularly in recipes from far-flung spots of the Empire. Guided by her husband's culinary experiences, she was able to produce exotic meals like *Nasi Goreng* and obscure curries requiring ingredients from Asian chefs in Soho or the East India Docks. The decline of my sisters was rapid: they did not care for Battersea even though they had not availed themselves of the Oxfordshire countryside after my mother's death. Eventually it was considered kinder to allow them to fade away in a sanatorium in Kent which specialised in distressed gentry. I did not miss them.

Mr James had many bird stories to tell. (Although all natural history was of interest to me, it seemed I had a particular feeling for ornithology, and I filled the house with cages of live birds whose behaviour I carefully recorded from an early age.)

James informed me that in parts of the remote bushveld of Southern Africa birds proclaim their joint territory by singing in the same key. He knew when he was moving out of one territory and into another because all the birds, whether singers or squawkers, sang a semi-tone higher or lower than their neighbours. Thus hornbill, stork and toucan would rumble in the key of, say, B flat, while lilac-breasted rollers, white-fronted bee-eaters and the ubiquitous red-winged starlings chorused out the harmonic series of the home key. A hundred yards further on, the same species of bird, but different individual members, would shrill out the same sounds in B major. And so on. James was an excellent musician, with perfect pitch, and an uncanny ability to play the piano with his back to the keyboard, especially after his fall, when he had more time for activities of this sort.

He added that in the desert-land even further north, a German missionary taught his pet starlings to sing the opening phrases of Mozart's G minor Symphony (*dadadum dadadum dadadahdi*). After a local massacre, during which the starling cages were smashed open, the birds escaped, and proceeded to produce wild offspring – each of which sang Mozart in preference to its inborn high-pitched whistle. James swore that if you sat motionless for a whole day, you would hear the whole of the first subject of the first movement of this symphony, reproduced in perfect sequential order; more astounding still was the birds' ability to improvise a second subject of their own, in the required dominant key, with a typically embellished coda.

James had been taught how to whistle in New Guinea by the owner of the human heads. The bird whistling was amplified by cupping the hands over the mouth and flapping combinations of fingers open and shut. However, a tribe of Indians in the Amazon Basin had showed him how to produce similar effects using only the cavities of his cheeks as resonators.

This was the technique that he had passed on to me.

GREAT GRANARY 1899

Challenger did not know where the birdsong was coming from. Years of discipline had enabled him to keep his blood-shot eyes on the target even when a chaffinch shrilled just behind his ear and a blackbird called above the dining-room door. But when the nightingale burst into liquid song from the tapestry at the other end of the room he allowed his irises to flicker in recognition of a supreme artist, rather than out of curiosity or surprise. It was in the split second of that saccadic shift that Huxley (who had been pouring a stream of champagne into a loving-cup when Challenger's command rang out) was able to smash the heavy bottle, already held obediently aloft, over the head of the armed (and armless) guest, thereby rendering him instantly unconscious upon the floor. At once a knot of manservants gathered about this prone form and carried him, one to each limb, into the multiplicity of corridors in the Great Granary.

'You were saying?' Not a muscle appeared to have moved in Milner's face during this interruption, as if he had been inconveniently petrified for a few minutes.

'This message.' I slid the envelope along the tablecloth among the wine glasses. Milner swept it on to his knee and opened it without moving his arms.

Challenger's name bubbled down the table, but the Colossus helped himself to more *melktert.*

'Saved by the song of the nightingale!' exclaimed Mrs K. 'What a fortunate coincidence that a flock of invisible birds should happen to pass through this dining-room at the very moment Mr Challenger was threatening to pull his trigger!'

'Oh, there was never any danger,' smirked Jameson. He opened his fist to display a small pistol with mother-of-pearl inlay. 'This pretty little lady has saved the day on many an occasion, I can assure you.'

'I'd rather be saved by birds, thank you,' replied Mrs K smartly, and her husband lifted his head from a plate of pudding to reveal his massive moustache laden with cream. Without bothering to blot his lips he enquired: 'Where did those birds come from? And where are they now?' His gaze fastened on me in friendly fashion through his round glasses, as if I alone must have the answer.

At this the whole table became extremely animated, each face (with the exception of Jameson, who appeared to be lost in thought) turned towards me at a different angle of curiosity mingled with incipient gratitude, evidenced in the display of bared teeth and elevated eyebrows, in some ludicrous way reminiscent of Leonardo's *Last Supper*. I lowered my eyes modestly, for once not appalled to be the centre of attention.

'Well now!' squealed the Colossus, with his mouth full. 'It seems we have a hero in our midst! A man of many talents, I'd say! A true Oxford man, in fact!'

'Three cheers for Professor Wills!' cried Mrs K, and for the first time in my life I became the object of a resounding roar of appreciation. This experience, to my surprise, released a slender flow of pleasure into the pool of anxieties which made up my usual emotional state, and, with a shy smile, I lifted my head to acknowledge the accolade.

'I say, Wills, let's have an encore!' Jameson's boyish face was defiant.

With a shrug I made a sparrow cheep so loud upon his shoulder that he jumped, then laughed in his embarrassment. Rallying, he cried: 'I don't know why you've brought those damned birds in the cages out there with you: you're a good deal more tuneful yourself, old chap!'

In the midst of all this frivolity Milner had been casting his cold eye over Miss Schreiner's Appeal, which he held on his lap among the folds of the tablecloth, at the same time appearing to take part in the table's activity along with everyone else. Once the conversation had become general again, he leaned towards me and murmured: 'Not my style, Wills, not my style at all. I have already received some hysterical communication from the lady which I have chosen to ignore.'

'The lady is very determined. Ten minutes is all she asks.'

'Impossible. I don't have ten minutes. If only someone would give *me* ten minutes . . .'

I drank deep from my silver beaker. 'Miss Schreiner happened to overhear you tell me about the – female – personage from Brixton earlier today.'

The glance that flickered over me could have been the lash of a whip. He snorted. 'A complete waste of my time. But I'll do it for your sake – she'll not leave you in peace otherwise. I make one condition, however: you must accompany me. I do not want to be compromised. The woman's a man-eater, I believe.' He swung his shoulder away from me to engage in conversation with bright-eyed Kipling. At the same time Mrs K leaned towards me. 'I should be much obliged if you would whistle for my children,' she smiled. 'I know they'd be enchanted.'

'I am already training a small girl to whistle,' I replied, and to my surprise found myself describing to her in some detail my encounters with Maria-of-the-Mountain, including my plan to replace the tooth under the stone with a silver tickey which Huxley had obligingly given me.

'Oh, what fun!' she cried. 'I must say, Professor, when I met you in the corridor this morning I thought you were a typically austere English academic, but now I see you in a quite different light!'

'I assure you I am very austere,' I said hurriedly. 'Women and children are usually repelled by my presence. I cannot understand why things have changed since I arrived in this hemisphere.'

'So there is no Mrs Wills?' she smiled mischievously.

I confirmed that there was indeed no Mrs Wills. She cut herself a slice of hard cheese and then said: 'To pick up on an earlier – but related – theme –' I awaited a return to the language of food, but instead she said: 'Doesn't it occur to you that if the company at our table considers the breeding of British babies on British territory to be one of the finest things we can do, then they themselves aren't doing very much – again, in evolutionary terms, of course – to ensure the continued survival of the Anglo-Saxon race. I know for a fact that my husband is the only man of the company at the head of the table to have brought forth Anglo-Saxon offspring – with a little help from me, of course!'

I looked about me in some alarm at these indiscretions, and then replied: 'I believe the feeling is that children get in the way of Great Men. The sound of childish romps disturbs Great Thoughts.'

She looked sceptical. 'I am sure there's a lot more to it than that. However, as our meal is drawing to a close, I have another question to ask you. Would you care for a companion on your journey up the gorge later tonight? I know all about milk-teeth, should you need an expert. But there is a different reason why I should love to accompany you.'

'Which is?' I shook my head at the proffered cheese.

'I wonder if you've heard of the Nocturnal Thumbed Ghost Frog, which I'm told lives in the fast-flowing streams of the mountain slopes. Its habits are so silent and secretive that very few specimens have been located. In the whole world.' She paused. 'I would be most interested to look for the Ghost Frog before we set sail for England, but my husband shows no interest in accompanying me on a midnight expedition. And I'm not quite bold enough to go by myself.'

'I'd be delighted to have your company.' As I uttered these words I was surprised to note that I meant them. Perhaps for the first time in my life I attempted a little joke. 'I'm not quite bold enough to set out into the wilds of Africa in the middle of the night without the protection of a strong woman!'

She laughed delightedly at my joke, which had issued from my lips without censure from my brain, enmeshed, as it seemed, in a golden cloud of mellow wine fumes.

The men at the table were discussing Challenger's entourage of monkeys and cockatoos which had evidently accompanied the intrepid game hunter to his sedate hotel in Cape Town. Unknown to me, he had disembarked at the Mother City at the same time as I had, when it became apparent that his stump grew gangrenous and was in immediate need of hospital attention. No one seemed to hold his behaviour against him: a man who has shot seventy-two elephants in one year is entitled to a little fun with his gun.

The men adjourned for coffee and port. I excused myself, pleading exhaustion; then slipped outside to meet Mrs K near the dead hydrangeas.

To find a milk-tooth beneath a pebble in the middle of the night is no easy task and I might have given up very soon (feeling somewhat uneasy in the dark forestation) were it not for Mrs K's bright chatter and womanly optimism. It was plain that both she and her husband were accustomed to excursions such as these and considered the magical world of childhood to be every bit as important as the largely mundane world of adulthood. I could not remember that my own mother had ever introduced an element of magic into my childhood, yet the brilliance of her outdoor passions was similar in quality to Mrs K's enthusiasms. Perhaps what both women had in common was a refreshing lack of ambivalence about the way they conducted their lives: they moved swiftly from A to B in a slip-stream of certainty, while their more talented husbands wavered in mires of self-doubt.

I began to long for my bed. To my plea that we might spend the whole night lifting up round pebbles surrounded by violets, and swinging a lantern over the insect life that crouched beneath, she replied that each failure to discover the elusive pearl would wonderfully enhance the final discovery. The fallen pine with which the treacherous pebble was aligned now seemed to have realigned itself with a thousand other such pebbles, and I cursed myself for not making a clear mark on the hiding place with my fountain pen, or leaving my handkerchief nearby. In addition to her relentless optimism, the woman appeared to have nerves of steel. As we were crossing the moonlit lawns and were about to embark upon the forest path, a shadow slid from the trees and advanced towards us. I have to confess that my first instinct was to drop the lantern and run back to the house, but Mrs K broke into peals of laughter: 'Why, Kenneth, you are a naughty fellow! You'll be getting a dose of shot in your stern if you go on doing this!' The apparition glared at us, a loaded branch of green bananas twined around his horns, which he devoured with a jerk, one by one, unselfconsciously, as we watched. A bull-kudu of some eighteen hands, he must have jumped the seven-foot fence which separated the vast gardens from the mountain fields above, wherein grew no banana trees.

Mrs K reminded herself to report this invasion to the head gardener, and opened the forest gate for me to enter.

While this good woman helped me lift stones, she also kept an eye out for her frog, darting off every now and then to the turbulent waters of the stream, over which she waved her own lantern (obligingly supplied by Huxley) to see if she could find this silent creature gripped to a rock. For an amateur she had an impressive understanding of the mountain flora and fauna. The forest shrilled with the voices of a thousand insects and frogs, many of which she could identify by the correct generic name. Even the dark woodland odours released by our footfalls were recognised by her as drifting from this mushroom or that leaf mould. Yet at no stage did she make me feel she was in competition with me: her observations were made with a gentle humility that I felt would have much improved Miss Schreiner's delivery and general womanliness.

We had been searching for perhaps an hour when my ever-vigilant ears detected the crunch of feet upon pine needles further up the forest. I could tell at once from the rapid regularity of the sounds that this was not another Kenneth, but a light-footed biped, probably female. The footsteps were too far away for their owner to be able to see our lanterns held low over stream and pebbles, and were soon absorbed among all the other night sounds chorusing in the forest. The sound made me uneasy, but was clearly unrelated to our presence.

I suppose I must have lifted the stone, found the tooth and smelt the smoke at the same moment. I had forgotten just how tiny a milk-tooth is; probably I had picked up the same stone several times only to find the tooth rendered invisible by a beetle or an earthworm. Such was the intensity of my delight – as if I had discovered an extinct species of beetle under a pebble – that the wisp of smoke which passed under my nose seemed merely to be a physical manifestation of my triumph, and I allowed myself to ignore it. 'Hooray!' I sang out, and Mrs K came running from her position by the stream where she had just encountered twelve small Ghost Frog tadpoles clinging with all their might to the pebbles in the fast-running water.

'A priceless pearl!' she breathed as I held up my trophy. 'Far more valuable than any one of his precious stones!' Then her nostrils twitched.

'Professor Wills, do you smell what I smell?'

Only then did I realise that a multitude of odours had been entering my nostrils all the while: the forest became at once a giant pot-pourri in which a thousand fragrances were blended into an integrated whole. But even as I sniffed with widened nostrils, a half-visible plume of smoke drifted by and jolted my heartbeats momentarily.

'It's coming from up there! Quick!' There was no time for further panic, and I am pleased to say that I remembered to put the little tickey in place before straightening my stiff knees.

We pushed our way up through the closely packed conifers (my treasure safely tucked in my fob-pocket), and further up into the tangle of jacaranda and eucalyptus, releasing wave after wave of powerful odour. Yet even as my nostrils sustained this olfactory assault, my ears sharpened to the faint tinkle of jewellery swinging against itself. And was I being fanciful, or did I for a few seconds inhale the faint aroma of the morning's over-sweet perfume as well? But before I could confirm this with further active sniffs, we arrived at a scene requiring our immediate attention.

No breeze fanned the little plume of smoke that coiled lazily from the mound of leaves and twigs that had been piled together, but it was clearly a matter of moments before the crackle inside it flared into fire. 'Hurry!' shouted Mrs K, even as I fumbled with my fly buttons, all thoughts of modesty abandoned. I felt excited as a naughty child: my hand shook as I directed my nervous waters at the smouldering heap and aimed at a flame. Then, with a thunderous sizzle quite out of proportion to my thin stream, water triumphed over fire, and I found the foreign sound of laughter rising in my throat.

'You're not taking this very seriously, Professor!' Mrs K was giggling herself. Acrid clouds of smoke shot out of the destroyed fire and our eyes watered horribly as we kicked at the remains of the arson attempt and stamped on glowing embers, our lanterns high above our heads, causing the upper reaches of the trees and creepers to bulge with light.

'I suppose it must have been some Boer,' sighed my companion as we began our somewhat precipitous descent through the smoke-scented forest. 'Someone full of resent-ment – perhaps still holding a grudge after the Raid!' She was plunging downward rather more quickly than I would have liked, her lantern swerving violently among the night foliage.

'Hmmm,' replied I. 'Rather a half-hearted attempt, don't you think? Why set the forest alight? Why not the house?'

'After the last blaze, I believe there is some kind of infor-mal patrol round the house every night. But of course the strange thing is that our host doesn't really care if all his possessions go up in flames – I suppose you know what he said when they told him his beloved house had burnt down: "*Is that all? I thought you were going to say Jameson had died.*" Extraordinary response.' She turned round suddenly to face me, just as I was negotiating a rather complicated tangle of roots. 'Can I confess a dreadful secret to you, Professor Wills?'

I cleared my throat. 'Please do.' My head had brushed her bosom as I lifted it, and the sensation had revived a rush of nursery memories.

'I don't think I like Dr Jameson very much.' A frond of

plumbago became entangled in her hair, and she swept it away impatiently. 'My husband worships him, of course. I think he'd like to have the Doctor as the hero of his next novel – if he could somehow transport him to India. But to me . . . I must say . . . he's just a . . . *filibuster*!' She held up her lantern to my face to measure the degree of my shock. On finding a gleam of sympathy in my normally impassive visage, she continued more briskly: 'If only you knew the damage he's done with his dratted Raid! In the first place he's caused the greatest man in South Africa to have to resign his premiership. And in the second place he's pushed this country much closer to a war that Britain is by no means ready for. Can you imagine the national humiliation if Britain were to be conquered by a barbarous tribe of unshaven Boers? It would be the beginning of the end of the Empire, for a start.' Mrs K seemed to have forgotten that we were standing on a damp mountain slope at half past two in the morning.

'According to the newspapers I read, our host was not altogether guiltless in this affair,' I volunteered, edging down closer to her in the hope of moving her on, for I was more than ready for my bed by this time. But Mrs K wanted to continue her lecture.

'Certainly he appreciated the fact that that monstrous old Boer was oppressing British men, women and children – not giving the vote, and that kind of thing – and he sincerely wished to come to their aid – but that Doctor Jameson! He saw himself as some kind of knight in shining armour rescuing damsels in distress, and meanwhile the damsels had no need to be rescued. I swear he just wanted to ride in front of a troop of soldiers and wave his sword, pretending to be Sir Lancelot in pursuit of the Holy Grail!'

'I believe he ended up waving a Hottentot maid's apron.'

'He was lucky to escape with his life,' replied she. 'And only because that cunning old Boer didn't want him turned into a martyr. And to see him strutting about now . . .' To my relief she turned and made her way down the remainder of the path. I was now quite overwhelmed with tiredness and longed for my bed.

The gables of the Great Granary shone silver in the moonlight, their elongated shadows staining the terraced lawns. We slipped like conspirators between the columns and across the chequerboard tiles of the back verandah, silent at last. Mrs K produced a large key with which to open the back door.

'I'll report the fire, if you like,' she whispered, as if reading my thoughts. 'Not much point in doing it now. Good night, Professor. I've very much enjoyed hunting the tooth with you.'

An almost intolerable exhaustion had overcome me by the time I began to mount the stairs, and I found myself pausing every four or five steps to relieve the ache in my thighs caused by my unwonted midnight exercise. I longed for nothing more than to find myself in bed, and with heartfelt relief flung myself upon the embossed handle of my bedroom door. Just as I was about to enter, the door of the room belonging to the flirtatious mother slid open. Flushing with embarrassment at the idea of meeting female company of any kind in a corridor at nearly 3 a.m. I was about to slip silently into my room when a sharp whisper met my ears.

'*Wills!*'

Frank Harris crept down the corridor, grasping his shoes in his right hand, smoothing his hair with his left. He smiled brilliantly at me in the dim electric light.

'I say, old chap, I've a bottle of excellent brandy in my room. Come and join me for a night-cap, won't you? Then you can tell me what on earth you are doing here!'

OXFORD 1891

It was upon Frank Harris's lips that I first heard the word c—t. The occasion had been a visit to my college rooms by Oscar, who had come to see Walter Pater at Brasenose, accompanied by Harris. Their visit to Oxford caused a considerable stir, for Oscar's short novel, *The Picture of Dorian Gray*, had just been published, to howls of opprobrium from that rather large section of society who did not agree that the act of lounging upon a sofa could be an art form.

I suspect he and Harris had an hour to kill, in between invitations to the great houses. Over a bottle of my finest wine (Perrier Jouët 1875 – served by a disapproving Saunders) Oscar encouraged his friend to talk about John Ruskin, whom Harris had known well in the eighties, and whose face he claimed was sadder than Lear's. Oscar was aware that my feelings about Ruskin were mixed, for I had been partly responsible for the Slade Professor's abrupt resignation when the university authorities had elected to support our new vivisection laboratories, rather than extend his overcrowded lecture theatre next door. He had departed on the grounds that Oxford preferred the screams of agonising, dumb animals to his lectures in praise of beauty and goodness – a response which I considered to be highly emotional, but which nevertheless caused my heart to contract, briefly, with regret. That his mind was unhinged is amply proved by the sad fact that the greatest art critic of the century now writes nothing but his name, over and over, in his house beside Lake Coniston.

I do not care to dwell on the topics raised by Harris in connection with Ruskin's private habits: suffice it to say that phrases such as '*glorious silken triangle*' and '*Venus mound*' flew thick and fast through my chaste bachelor quarters and I was left in no doubt that Ruskin and Harris had very differing attitudes towards these features of a woman's anatomy.

'But the Turners, Frank,' urged Oscar. (Why is it that only paintings and sculptures have achieved metonymic equality with their creators? One does not speak of the Mozarts or the Shakespeares: words and music have less reality than pictures.)

Frank Harris had a tale to tell about the Turners.

'Of course, it is as an art critic and defender of Turner that Ruskin is chiefly known, in spite of his efforts to reform the ills of British society,' he began, clearly relishing the opportunity to tell a good story. 'When Turner died and left his paintings to the nation, the nation was not interested. Ruskin found these great works of art in boxes in the cellars of the National Gallery, unappreciated and uncared for. He wrote to Lord Palmerston and asked to be allowed to put Turner's works in order. He then spent a year and a half mounting and classifying the pictures. To him, the good, the pure and the beautiful were one, perfectly manifested in Turner's sublime pictures, with their exquisite and subtle interplay of light and water and colour. Ruskin adored colour, associating the beauty of colour in paintings with the holiness of life.'

'I couldn't agree more,' interrupted Oscar. In spite of the insouciance of his pose and the flabbiness of his face, his eyes gleamed with youthful intelligence. 'I have always held that a good colour-sense is more important than a sense of right and wrong. But pray continue, now that we have at last reached the point to the story.'

'Turner was his hero, his god. Because Turner created beauty without blemish his life too must be blemishless.' Harris raised his eyebrows knowingly and drew upon his cheroot. 'One fateful day in '57 Ruskin came upon a portfolio filled with painting after painting not only of the pudenda of women, but of women twisted into erotic positions in the ecstasy of love. He was filled with revulsion. It seemed to him utterly incomprehensible that the man who had produced *Rain, Steam and Speed* could also paint a woman's c—t. But worse was to come. He learnt that his hero, far from leading the pure and virtuous life that Ruskin himself lived, would go down to Wapping on Friday afternoons and live there till Monday morning with the sailors' women, painting them in every posture of abandonment.' Harris paused, his eyes asparkle, as if envisaging these postures with some relish, and tempted by a diversion into his own scandalous adventures.

'But where *are* these pictures?' I enquired, partly to forestall any confessions of this sort, but also out of natural curiosity.

Like a politician Harris avoided answering my question directly, the better to construct his story. 'For weeks Ruskin was in a state of torture, wondering what to do with these shameful likenesses. He could not frame them; he refused to classify them for fear of staining his hero's reputation, as he saw it. Finally it came to him in a flash: he took the hundreds of scrofulous sketches and paintings and burnt them, burnt *all* of them. When he told me this, he insisted he was proud of what he had done. "*Proud?*" I cried. "I think it dreadful to kill a man's work!" I was deeply shocked; in fact, I could not bear to see him again; and soon after he left London for his home in Cumberland.'

Oscar was nodding and rounding his eyes; a playful smile twitched at his mouth, but I could sense his sadness at this destruction. 'So you see, Ruskin is a villain after all,' he said. 'Far better to kill an animal than a painting, wouldn't you say?'

My head seemed suddenly afloat with champagne and I found myself speaking aloud the thoughts that passed secretly through my brain. 'I have to say my sympathies are with Ruskin,' I said in a voice that was thicker and stronger than usual. 'The public visits the National Gallery to gaze at landscapes, portraits and still-lifes, not the private parts of a sailor's whore, indecently exposed.'

This response excited Harris very much. 'But my dear Professor Wills, surely you will agree that there is nothing more beautiful on this earth than a woman's c—t. Even more exciting than the sexual act itself is that moment when, having undressed the – preferably – young girl, and admired her little breasts, her tiny waist, her swelling hips, you plunge your head between her thighs and gaze upon those secret lips which often grow crimson with excitement in their nest of silken hair. And as I place my own lips against her bud of joy I feel an incomparable surge of ecstasy overwhelm my entire body: my tongue thirsts for the love-juices that pour from those rosy lips and – I say, old chap, are you all right?'

I had sprung to my feet as a wave of nausea overcame me. Trembling, I ran to the window and pushed it open: the sweet fresh air and the orderly Fellows' Garden revived me in an instant and I was able to turn to my guests and smile reassuringly.

'I have no head for champagne, particularly in the afternoon.' My firm voice did not betray the upheaval in my breast. 'Now, Oscar, tell me about your book. I believe there are undergraduates here who have read it a dozen times. They now speak only in aphorisms. Some say you have single-handedly become responsible for the moral decline of the nation. Can this be true?'

Oscar smiled, hiding his blackened teeth with his hand. 'Dear Francis, I hope that you will agree with me that aesthetics are higher than ethics – they belong to a more spiritual sphere. I am simply teaching the nation how to live in style. I am teaching individuals how to become works of art.'

'Style is something that seems to bypass the scientist. Perhaps it is because scientific research can never become a work of art, as science will not allow that fatal ambiguity which is the essence of artistic creation,' I suggested.

A lively debate followed, in which no mention of women's pudenda was made, and Harris and I parted on the best of terms, though two men more different than ourselves would be difficult to find.

GREAT GRANARY 1899

Now I found myself not tucked up under the longed-for coverlets but perched on the edge of Frank Harris's bed in a room further down the corridor, drinking his very fine Napoleon brandy.

'And what on earth are *you* doing here, Frank?' It was easy to address him by his first name although I hardly knew him.

'Well, Francis, there are a variety of answers to that question. In the first place, I have come here in my capacity as editor and journalist to cover the imminent outbreak of war in this country. In the second place I plan to make my way up to the Zambezi and shoot a few crocodiles, if I have the time. My last expedition failed miserably, and I can't tolerate failure.' Harris busied himself with a large cigar. I waited patiently for it to take light. When finally the pungent odour of Havana filled the room he continued as if he had never stopped. 'And in the third and most immediate place, I arrived from Durban late yesterday afternoon only to find every hotel full: I telephoned our host knowing he had many spare rooms – I know him well, fortunately – and he at once invited me to come and join the party for dinner. I hurried over in a Cape cart, met a number of acquaintances, enjoyed our host's excellent wines (how *does* he get hold of them, I wonder?). I was less pleased to discover that Milner would be here as well.'

'Oh, what do you have against Milner?' I asked casually.

'Well, in the first place, he is a perfect example of the modern German: he trusts only reason and what he has learned. The best type of Englishman, on the other hand, has an unconscious belief that there are instincts higher than reason, and though these immature spiritual antennae are what makes the Englishman the tragic creature he often is in practical life, they also make him lovable. Their absence makes the German supreme in the present but forecasts their failure in the future. More Cognac?'

'And in the second place?' I allowed him to pour an inch of brandy into a tumbler meant for water.

'In the second place, and probably as a result of his complete absence of imagination, Milner will antagonise the Boers when it is essential to win them over by treating them fairly. If he quarrels with them, as he surely will, he is going to have a war on his hands that will tragically retard the development not only of South Africa but also of Great Britain. It will cost hundreds of millions and improve nothing, mark my words.'

Little did Harris know that the unworldly ornithologist sitting on his bed had been entrusted by Miss Schreiner with the awesome task of averting this imperial calamity! I was fleetingly tempted to tell him of my assignation the next day: how he would enjoy such a meeting! Instead I took a deep breath and said: 'I have another question.' From the serious look in his eye, he knew what it was to be before I had asked it. 'Have you seen anything of Oscar in France? I regret to say that I have lost all contact with him.'

'Let's say there is no beggar like an Irish beggar.' Harris paused. 'You know, I used to believe that Oscar was innocent of the crimes and perversions we heard about during his first trial. It was only when I visited him in Holloway that he broke the news to me himself that he – indulged in perverted sexual activities. I have to confess to total astonishment when he

237

told me – I thought I had known and understood him so intimately.'

'And did this knowledge make any difference to your friendship?'

Harris blew out a stream of lazy smoke. 'Not a scrap. I can never understand how anyone can prefer the hard straight lines of boys to the fleshy curves of the female, but each to his own.' For a moment he studied my eyes briefly as if to discover my own preferences, then continued. 'If only Oscar had agreed to cross the Channel in my friend's yacht after the first trial . . . I was frantic, I knew two years' hard labour lay in store for him . . . but he would not hear of it. Now he lives off hand-outs from his friends, and endures appalling humiliations at the hands of those who once would have wept with joy to have him at their dinner table.'

'It is indeed extraordinary that he refused to accept your escape route. Perhaps – in some way – he *wanted* punishment – hell-fire, even – for the excesses of his life. He has dallied with Catholicism for years, of course.'

Harris pursed his lips. 'In all confidence – I have another theory that explains everything – his excessive behaviour and lack of control . . .' He paused.

'Well?'

'He's mad.'

'Mad?'

'Constance always said he'd been quite mad for at least three years before his trial.'

'On what do you base your theory?' I frowned.

By way of reply, Harris bared his front teeth and tapped one of them significantly. 'The syphilis he caught at Oxford eventually affected his brain. You should know – you're the scientist.'

'I know nothing about venereal diseases,' I said stiffly. 'Oscar never seemed mad to me.'

'Don't take offence, old chap. It would explain a great deal of bizarre behaviour. Of course, he has long periods of lucidity.'

'Has he –' I hesitated. 'Has he mentioned my name?'

'Funny you should mention that. I last saw him about three months ago. He was in love with a little soldier who wanted nothing more than a nickel-plated bicycle out of life. Oscar, penniless of course, was determined he should have it. In the midst of trying to borrow a hundred francs from me for the purposes of pleasing his new young friend, he suddenly asked if I'd seen his cousin. I couldn't think who he meant, until he reminded me of our visit to your rooms in Oxford: I had forgotten you were related. Oscar said, in a voice that was genuinely mournful: "I fear he has dropped me, Frank, like all the rest."'

'*No, no, no!*' I shouted. 'I wrote to him in prison. I sent him money, through Constance, after his release. I want nothing more than to see him again and receive his forgiveness.'

'Forgiveness?' enquired Frank Harris in astonishment. 'Good Lord, Francis, you're weeping! Let me fill your glass. Now why don't you tell me what you mean?'

GREAT GRANARY 1899

I was awoken the next morning by cacophony. My head raged with brandy; the sounds I was hearing seemed designed to torture a man suffering from overindulgence; and yet I felt strangely uplifted; almost, dare I say it, *happy*.

I had not registered the presence of a pianoforte in the drawing-room, though it was hard to believe that the flatulent, dislocated sounds I was hearing could thunder from strings designed to vibrate with the inspiration of Mozart, Beethoven, Liszt. This music, if music I must call it, was utterly disobedient, straining like a dog at its leash: the left hand pounding out a relentless rhythm while the right hand took horrible liberties, the treble seeming to dislocate itself quite deliberately from the bass. As if this wasn't extreme enough, a clarinet began to wail in blatant collusion with the hammering on the keyboard, followed by the impudent rattle of the banjo, the twanging of whose strings reminds me of a cat vigorously scratching itself for fleas. Could this be the Cakewalk, at present taking London and the Americas by storm?

It has to be said that not even the dons and fellows of the Oxford colleges are safe from the pernicious influence of this so-called music. Well do I remember how my sacred evening hour in the company of the Senior Common Room was recently shattered by the triumphant entrance of a young history tutor bearing aloft a most hideously decorated cake, his prize for an unseemly display of leg-kicking and bodily contortions, produced with the energetic co-operation of a female partner. These antics are performed every Wednesday afternoon in a local dance house from whose windows issue the sort of sounds presently disturbing my fortifying slumbers; with what gusto did that young cake prize-winner proceed to demonstrate to his startled audience those very gyrations which had won him his honours.

I lay in my bed, the image of the dancing don suddenly vivid in my memory, resurrected, it seemed, to strut again to the raucous noise from below. My own neat legs lay outstretched beneath a monogrammed blanket, while the upper part of my body sloped upward at forty-five degrees, with the support of four large pillows, still necessary after my bronchial attack.

Reluctant to move from my warm bed in spite of the dissonance, I found my mind drifting back to the events of the night before. In the haze of alcohol that still made ordered thinking impossible, I remembered little of my conversation with Frank Harris, though the earlier part of the evening was vivid enough. Nevertheless, I was aware of a feeling of warmth towards Harris, a feeling that began to arrange itself into an urge to see him again, though for ill-defined reasons.

Then I noticed something very peculiar happening to my nether anatomy.

I could scarcely believe the evidence of my astonished eyes. The entire length of my left foot, from the ankle to the tips of my toes, was twitching under the blanket with a violent, rhythmic movement, as if it belonged not to my precise body but to the unseen players in the room below. I watched its gyrations, dumbfounded, as if betrayed by the insolence of an outer limb – but even as I watched, the realisation dawned that another part of my feeble frame had succumbed to the influence of the music: my head, the very seat of my accumulated wisdom and discipline, was nodding in an equally compulsive fashion, in frank collusion with my foot.

And then, strangest of all, my entire body rose from its bed, as if pulled by the dancing don himself, and proceeded to wriggle and writhe in a most unseemly fashion, my legs even kicking out and upwards in an abandoned manner. (It occurred to me that I might have been bitten by a tarantula, apocryphal as the stories of its dance-inducing venom might be.) The ludicrousness of the situation was exaggerated by the fact that my jittering legs were entirely naked under my night-dress! Unwillingly, I observed the extreme pallor of my skin, and the veritable forest of black hair, sprouting to no purpose from the knees down.

I am a man unacquainted with his body. I do not admire the exposed flesh of Michelangelo's sculptures or Rubens' overfed women. In particular – like Ruskin – I am repelled by bodily hair. I do not see the need for it. The late Mr Darwin could undoubtedly have explained to me how the unnecessary coils around my genitalia fit into the evolutionary process, but I doubt if such an explanation would lessen my disgust. I avert my eyes when bathing. I forget I am related to the ape. Now the sight of my pale hairy legs prancing about so absurdly filled me with acute embarrassment. I wrapped my dressing-gown about my limbs, and looked for warm water.

The music stopped for a moment. Voices chattered and laughed. The players were speaking in their clicking tribal languages. I could recognise the throaty inflections of my valet . . . Which instrument did he play? Was it possible to perform upon the pianoforte with a missing little finger?

Then a chill icicle of thought needled its way into the conflicting emotions stirred by the cakewalk. They are rehearsing for the day of the Release, less than two days away now! The day when my soundless birds will soar into pine forests, already fully occupied by winged predators. Something like pity stirred in my cold heart, whether for myself or my small charges I could not say.

A gentle rap on the door interrupted these wretched thoughts. Impatiently I swung the door open, and was confronted by the radiant messenger, Joubert.

'Good morning, sir. Another telegram for you, I'm afraid. He says he'll discuss the contents with you this evening.'

'Thank you, Mr Joubert. I am glad to see your spirits are fully recovered.'

'Thanks to you, Professor!' the young man cried. 'If I hadn't met you on the bench yesterday . . . I might even have broken my engagement to Miss Pennyfeather!' He cocked his head, listening to the sounds from below with obvious pleasure.

'I can see you enjoy this music.'

'Oh yes, sir!' he cried. 'It makes me want to dance!'

'There will be plenty of opportunity for that when the birds are released, I should imagine.'

'Miss Pennyfeather is looking forward to meeting you then, Professor.' The irrepressible young man bade me good morning and withdrew. I moved across to the bedside table to fetch my reading glasses. As before, only a few words were scrawled on the back of the telegram.

'Thanks, Wills. You're a good chap. But when are you going to get those damned birds to sing? Come and have a drink with me on the back verandah tonight 6 p.m.'

After my late start, the hot water which Orpheus brought me had become lukewarm but strangely invigorating. I certainly had no thoughts of breakfast as I paid special attention to my toilet, even going so far as to extract certain facial hairs which detracted from the symmetry of my beard. Then it was time to embark on my quest.

Down the avenue of monstrous stone pines – quite the

wrong sort of tree to have planted to line a road, in my opinion, with a top-heavy canopy of needles one hundred feet above and nothing but angular tree trunks at eye level – I strolled, in search of Maria's house. A multitude of grey squirrels raced up and down these trees, undeterred by the total lack of branches from which to leap. The avenue led from the Great Granary down on to a kind of High Street which ran through the village of Rondebosch, yet to be visited by me. I have felt no impulse to move outside the perimeter of the Great Granary estate, though I am assured that a tour of the peninsula on which it is situated would be of great interest.

A narrow-faced peasant of a man pushed his sharpening-stone up the road, flickered his eyes at me with intense dislike, and disappeared into one of the cottages which lined the lower end of the avenue. The redness of his skin and the blueness of his eyes suggested he was a recently arrived immigrant.

I fingered the tiny tooth I had procured in the early hours of the morning. Its sharp edges bit pleasantly into my fingertips, a pleasure enhanced by the memory of the little mouth in which it had once lodged.

Each of the cottages was provided with a large shady verandah surrounding the front door. Strong pillars held aloft the red-and-white-striped corrugated-iron verandah roofs which gave the otherwise gloomy houses a somewhat skittish appearance. One verandah wall was adorned with antlers, horns and stuffed animals' heads with glassy eyes; another with dried *fynbos* bouquets hanging upside-down from the beams of the roof.

In which did my Maria dwell? I hovered uncertainly before each front gate, feeling self-conscious; then spotted a large triangle hanging among the dried bouquets. At the same moment the child herself slipped out from behind a hedge of blue plumbago and chanted gleefully: 'The fairies took my tooth! The fairies took my tooth!' She was holding a small cardboard box.

I felt my face suffuse with colour as a feeling of most exquisite pleasure rose through my body. 'Y-your tooth?' I stammered, and then, controlling the swooning sensation, I said sternly, 'Good morning, Maria.'

'Mornin',' she droned. Her large brown eyes shone with a lustrousness I felt I could dive into. 'They l-left me a tickey, that's nice of them, hey?'

'Oh I am pleased!' I exclaimed in a jolly voice I could scarcely recognise as my own. 'And what do you think they'll do with your tooth?'

'They'll b-build they houses with it,' she said. 'They houses are built out of t-tooths, you see.'

'How beautiful they must be! Have you ever seen one, Maria!' (I found myself shamelessly imitating Dodgson's whimsical cadences.)

She contracted her nostrils in disbelief at my stupidity, a gesture which raised the curtain of her top lip and revealed the delightful gap in her top row of teeth. 'You can't see fairies' houses!'

'What's that you've got, Maria?' Out of my depth, I changed the subject.

'Look.' She proffered me the cardboard box she had been clasping. Its lid was punctured with a number of slashes. I paused, conscious that a woman's face was at the window of the house next to which we were standing. The child seemed quite unperturbed about this, her little mind now thoroughly engrossed in her new interest.

Hesitantly, I lifted the lid. Inside the box were a number of mulberry leaves which were being audibly munched by hordes of pale, naked caterpillars. Cocoons of yellow silk had already attached themselves to the corners of the box.

'They my silkworms. They turn into silk.' Her curious

colonial inflections made the word sound more like 'sulk' than rhyme with 'milk'.

'And what will you do with the silk, Maria?' Once I would have given the ignorant child a lesson on metamorphosis. But this was the wrong question.

'I'll keep it.' She was beginning to have doubts about my powers of reasoning, I could see that, and extended her hands for the return of the box. I wished the woman in the window would move away. Maria showed no inclination to take me inside the house.

Studying my face with great intensity, she enquired with her usual suddenness: 'What's your bir-bir-birds' names?'

'My birds' names? Do you mean their Latin names or their common names?' (Alice Liddell would certainly have been able to answer this question.)

A small frown appeared between her dark brows. 'What they called?' she said patiently.

'Well, I have some nightingales, some blackbirds, some chaffinches.' I decided against the Latin names.

The frown did not disappear. She became helpful. 'I got a canary called Cecil,' she explained. 'And a pussy cat called Chaka Zulu. What's the birds' names?'

'Oh my goodness me!' I exclaimed as understanding dawned. 'Do you know how many birds I have, Maria?'

She stared down at her shoes.

'I have – well, I did have – two hundred birds in my cages. That's a lot of names to have to make up, don't you think?'

'Duzzen matter.' (Only later did I realise the child had no concept of tens, let alone hundreds.) 'Poor birds.'

'Well then –' I paused, as a delightful thought occurred. 'Would you like to come up to the cages and name them for me?'

'I been to the cages.' She pouted. 'The Kaffir boys chased

me away. They shouted at me. I'm a bit scared of those boys.'

'Are you indeed?' I said. 'I don't think you need be any more.'

At this moment the woman threw open the window and called out angrily, in strong Dutch accents: 'Maria, come in now! I've told you not to talk to strange men!'

Though I bridled at the deliberate rudeness, I realised action had to be taken at once. Stretching my pink lips into the most charming smile I could muster, I turned to the woman who challenged me thus at the window, and bowed with frigid politeness. 'Professor Francis Wills, madam, from Oxford University.'

Thank goodness my face never registered my true emotions, for my eyes would have widened with surprise when they settled on the woman's face. Without doubt this was Maria's mother: the bright brown eyes, the pouting lips, the small round chin, the robust beauty. But the colour of her skin: Maria's mother's skin was nearly as dark as that of my Negro servant (at present thumping his way through minstrel music in preparation for my downfall), though her features were as European as my own. In the full glare of the morning sun which had escaped the feathery grasp of the pine trees, I now realised that Maria's skin was a glorious golden-brown colour, not unlike that of a Spaniard who has been through a harsh Mediterranean summer.

The mother was unaffected by my charm. 'What's an old man like you doing with my little girl?'

Oh dear, these colonials and indigenes do speak their minds. Language here has clearly never developed beyond an unfiltered expression of simple needs and opinions. I cleared my throat in order to stimulate my vocal cords into mellifluous action.

'I beg your pardon, madam, I fear there is some mistake. I

was merely discussing with Maria the possibility of her giving names to the songbirds I have brought with me from England.' Surely to God there's no harm in that?

The frown on the woman's face did not melt away. 'Maria says you meet her up the Glen.' Outright hostility was evident in the quick flare of nostril that accompanied this rejoinder.

I became even more magnanimous, more ingenuous. 'We've been teaching each other to whistle. I work with birds, you see, at the University of Oxford.' Clearly the implications of this hallowed name were quite lost on this harridan.

'I don't want my child meeting strange old men up the mountain.' Though the hostility still flickered round the nostril, her eyes, previously weapons of destruction, now began a wary search of mine.

'I quite agree,' I said affably, storing up her unflattering description of me for later analysis. 'Which is why I've come to pay my respects to you – and also to ask you about Maria's magnificent bird-whistle. She tells me you made it yourself. May I offer you my congratulations? It is a superb instrument.'

My unctuous flattery seemed to be working. Drawing herself away from the window the woman said in resigned tones: 'You better come in.'

Maria, who had been playing inside the laurel hedge during this exchange, now emerged looking dusty, her clothes and hair covered in leaves and twigs. Though I found her even more enchanting in this state – a leafy nymph escaped from some sprawling Renaissance canvas – her mother burst into a fit of scolding in kitchen-Dutch, which sent the child scuttling into the depths of the house, much to my disappointment.

The house was cool and dark inside, and sparsely furnished. Accustomed to the clutter of English homes, I found the bare walls and uncarpeted floors somewhat startling, though no doubt conducive to clear thinking. I could tell at once that the plain furniture was of the best: the favoured yellow-and-dark-wood combination in the table, bureau and chairs. The occasional stool and bench featured that curious leather-thong loose weave I have noted in the Great Granary. In fact, the interior of the house was a humble microcosm of that of the larger house, and more successful for its lack of pretension. The Great Granary was, in effect, not much more than a great hotel, while this simple house had the welcoming properties of a home.

My general astonishment was compounded by the full appearance of the woman herself. Whilst leaning in the window frame she had presented herself as a person of normal healthy physical proportions, but great indeed was my surprise to discover that from the ribcage downwards her girth expanded suddenly outwards, so much so that as she moved, her hindquarters, clad in fashionable European silks but clearly not encased in the usual stays or corsets, rose and fell in gigantic waves to the rhythms of her movements.

My final surprise awaited me in the room into which she then led me. It was not so much the pretty Broadwood piano and musical instruments – ranging from violin to penny whistles of the type I remember seeing on a visit paid by my father and myself to our relations in Ireland – that made me stop short in the doorway. Over the fireplace, before whose empty grate stood a large, deep, indigo high-glaze pot filled with brilliant sea-blue dried hydrangeas, hung a formal portrait of the Colossus – a photograph upon which had been superimposed the original tints and hues of my host's benevolent-looking visage; a photograph, I may add, taken some years back, to judge by the firm smoothness of the facial skin, the youthful glow in the grey-blue eyes, the golden streaks in the curly hair. Maria's mother made no attempt to explain the presence of the portrait; nor indeed would she even have attempted polite conversation with me, had I not myself initiated a vestigial verbal exchange through formal questioning. Nor did she volunteer her own name, and I found myself lacking the courage to ask it.

It seemed that the invitation into her house automatically included refreshments. While she made a pot of tea, I ruminated over her position in the Great Granary hierarchy of servants: probably a cook in the hidden kitchens, as I had certainly never seen her cleaning or serving in the house itself, but then I had seen no female servant in the house. As I waited for her return, and, indeed, for Maria's reappearance, I took care to preserve a gentle smile on my lips in order to counteract my habitually stern expression. This effort imposed considerable strain on the muscles of my mouth, with the result that a slippery sort of twitch affecting first one then the other corner of my mouth came into effect just as the mother re-entered the room bearing a large tea tray, of which burden I hastily relieved her. Once we were settled I re-introduced the topic of her bird-whistle as she poured me a very pleasant cup of China tea, which quickly subdued the nervous tic in my lips. There was still no sign of Maria.

'I am a musician, you see,' said the mother with undisguised pride. 'I play all those instruments you see over there. Those instruments come from overseas, and cost a lot of money, but it is also possible to make your own musical instruments – that is what I learnt when I was a child.' She leaned over the table and removed a beaded net cover from a bowl of confectionery. 'Help yourself. There's a serviette. As a child I made bird-whistles out of the clay we dug up from under the hill, but those whistles imitated the birds of Africa – the hoopoe bird, the hadeda, the bee-eaters, the laughing doves. Go on, eat.'

I stared helplessly at the little plaited cakes soaked in syrup and sprinkled with desiccated coconut. It appeared I was to pick one up in my fingers, holding the table napkin beneath it to catch any dripping syrup.

I do not like getting my fingers sticky. Now I felt myself break out in a cold sweat at the thought of handling this messy food.

My fear communicated itself to her. She said, less harshly, 'Pick one up with your serviette if you don't want to dirty your fingers. It's *koeksusters*, a local food. You can't go back to England without eating *koeksusters*.'

Wrapping my table napkin carefully round my hand I did as I was bidden. She could see my hand shaking as I reached for the syrupy cake.

'You English are a funny lot,' she remarked, filling my empty cup with tea. 'Wash, wash, wash, all the time.' She looked briefly up at the portrait and nodded her head. 'He's exactly the same. Even in the middle of the veld, miles away from anywhere, he's got to be spotlessly clean and shaven. Yet for all that, he never brushes his hair.'

I nibbled at the *koeksuster*. It was too sweet for my liking and I did not care for the rather soggy texture, but good manners made me chew through it to the end. The woman's familiarity with the private habits of the Colossus did not surprise me; by now I had decided she must be the widow of some deceased valet. I swallowed the last glutinous crumb with a sip of tea, and felt the moment had arrived for me to reveal the true reason for my visit. 'Mrs van den Bergh,' I began, but she interrupted me. 'Fun!' she exclaimed with a contemptuous smile. 'Not "van"!'

My brain, so carefully prepared for the request I was about to make, swivelled on its axis. She began to explain: 'In our language a "v" is pronounced like an "f".'

'Mrs fun den Bergh,' I continued: 'I have a favour to ask of you.'

All fun vanished as she tightened her mouth and prepared for refusal.

'I am an amateur photographer. I have brought my cameras

here in order to take pictures of the local environment and birds in particular. It would give me great pleasure to take Maria's photograph – and yours, of course – to bring back to England, to show the colonial people in their natural habitat. I have had some considerable success with portrait taking.' This was a complete lie, but nevertheless Dodgson's famous portraits – Alice as beggarmaid et cetera – sailed before my mind's eye as if I myself was responsible for their existence.

'You want to take Maria's photograph?'

'Yes. And yours, if you were willing.'

At this moment Maria herself, now clad in a clean pinafore, sidled into the room and headed for the *koeksusters*.

'I should be delighted to present you with such a portrait before I leave for England next week,' I continued. 'There are excellent dark-room facilities available to me in the big house.'

To my surprise, the woman addressed her daughter. 'Would you like the Professor to take your photograph, Maria? She's not looking her best, you know, she's just recovering from measles, she lost a lot of weight.'

'The Professor says I can go up to the cages,' Maria replied.

'Where would you take these pictures?' continued the mother. 'In this house?'

'Well, ideally I'd like to take them outside – on the mountain slopes – among the wild flowers – that sort of thing.'

'I tell you where's nice,' said Mrs van den Bergh. 'There's an old summerhouse up the mountain, with a rose garden and a fountain. That's a very pretty place, isn't it, Maria?'

It seemed that the mother was content with this arrangement. We agreed to meet at ten o'clock the next morning; I was given elaborate directions; and finally got away, feeling triumphant. Maria ran after me.

'M-my mommy says I can come with. To the cages.'

And to my indescribable joy, she placed her small trusting hand inside my own contaminated one.

OXFORD 1895

To rear in total isolation; this is the only way to corner Mother Nature. Only then will she unwillingly reveal those secret mechanisms which our forefathers attributed to Divine Planning: *how*, *why*, *when*, *where* do birds sing? The human race deserves an answer.

A young German half-wit, standing entranced in a village square, caused a sensation in both the scientific and literary worlds earlier in this century. The boy, deathly pale and hideously unwashed, appeared not to register his whereabouts; he held one hand over his eyes to protect them from the pale winter sunshine. In the other was a letter. On being approached, it was discovered that he could neither speak nor understand any human language, but merely used his larynx to grunt, howl, whine. It became apparent that Kaspar Hauser had grown up in absolute isolation from the human race: never having heard speech, he could not produce speech, although fitted with the organ which most immediately distinguishes man from all other species.

I had no need to vivisect. Nevertheless, posters bearing the image of a dog, the left side of whose brain had been sliced away, began to appear on college walls and noticeboards. Looming over the dog with a bloodstained knife was the silhouette of a scientist, the outline of whom was remarkably similar to my own.

Unfortunately the Poet, too, has a more potent weapon than the Scientist.

> *'A Robin Redbreast in a cage*
> *Puts all Heaven in a Rage.'*

Self-righteous twaddle! But a convenient emotionally-charged slogan seized upon by my opponents.

My experiments: The isolates, enclosed in miraculously soundproof boxes made by a carpenter friend of dear old Saunders for a very reasonable price, had produced predictably abnormal song. If only I had stopped at this point of the initial experiment: a clear result, elegant in its simplicity, uncontaminated by the scientist's ruinous need to eliminate variables. Wild nightingales learn to sing their songs by imitating one another; isolated nightingales produce only a song template, in which features of the wild song are only partially present. Nothing for Keats to swoon over, I'm afraid. But then, of course, we must ask the question: what of the nightingale who has been allowed to remain in the wild for nine months, and is then placed in the soundproof chamber. Removed before it starts to sing or after? Hear its own song or not? One can go on indefinitely, and one does. On behalf of the human race we scientists probe and dissect reality till we come up with a single, often ugly but unquestionable truth, unlike our literary counterparts who consider truth is beautiful only when it adorns a Grecian Urn.

I mentioned to Saunders that my further experiments into the song of the nightingale required me to employ young energetic persons who were able to perform protracted repetitive actions that would influence the behaviour of my trapped birds. It would be advantageous if at least one of them could play the whistle or flute. It is possible that Saunders, normally the most discreet of servants, was not quite discreet enough in his advertisement of my needs. There is, after all, no law against caging animals, nor subjecting them to experiments that will lead to a deeper understanding of the contradictory behaviour of the human race. I believe he discussed the matter with the landlord of a public house in the insalubrious east part of Oxford, where men and youths are used to factory work of numbing repetitiveness, and are glad to be paid a pittance to turn themselves into machines for ten hours at a time. As a result, a steady stream of illiterate males of all ages, and even one or two women of the franchise disposition (Saunders had asked specifically for men), trailed up my stairs to be interviewed by me.

I would have nothing to do with the females, of course, whose contempt for me and my experiments (and, I suspect, my comfortable bachelor's den) was expressed through their folded arms and pursed lips. The boys – some of whom had pretty, slithering faces under the grime – I deleted from my list at once, knowing that high spirits would soon overcome the disciplined approach that was required. In the end I appointed a rota of six young men, none of whom appeared to be otherwise employed. My criteria for employment were two: rude health and some musical ability. My six young men were perfect specimens of manhood, with biceps and callused hands that would have shamed the Hinksey diggers. Five of them asked no questions, their faces frighteningly impassive as I outlined to them their unusual duties. I should have been warned by the momentary flicker of sharp interest in the otherwise cool eyes of Desmond Philips when I mentioned the cymbals.

For what my dear Saunders had neglected to take into account, when choosing for his recruiting ground that indigent area of Oxford (to the outsider, a contradiction in terms), is that where the proletariat are dehumanised by their own labour, the revolutionary will flourish. I do not merely refer to those followers of the late Herr Karl Marx who dedicate themselves to the overthrow of the bourgeoisie, and who utter phrases like 'class struggle' and 'means of production', as if somehow embedded in these words is the very secret of human life. It has to be said that these revolutionaries have the whole species in mind, and their actions are unlikely to affect the individual directly, except in the instance of civil uprising. More insidious are the sub-revolutionaries they have spawned, who take on 'causes' rather than mankind as a whole. The fanaticism of these groups is only too well illustrated by those 'new women' who feel that their demented protests will convince everyone that the franchise should be extended to females! To an ordered mind like my own, it is incomprehensible that this kind of wild behaviour can be considered proof that women are men's intellectual equal, and able to elect parliamentary representatives. But wild behaviour, I was to learn, is the hallmark of these minority groups, and when Mr Philips' eyebrows twitched during our interview, this minuscule facial movement was to prove the first flexing of a much larger set of muscles.

'Cymbals, sir?' he queried, in his rustic Oxfordshire voice. Later I was to recognise satire in those melodious tones, but in my early ignorance, I attributed his question to stupidity.

'The idea being,' I explained, as if to a child, 'that the bird must be prevented from hearing its own song.'

'And the cymbals must be clashed for a full twelvemonth?'

'I have different birds in different parts of my laboratory, each providing a control to its pair. Some of the birds will be subjected to daily cymbal clashing, some will not; some will hear only the sound of your whistle playing Irish jigs and ditties, some will not.'

'I'm told that a certain farmer in China, wishing to prevent the birds from eating his crops, instructed his serfs to strike a series of gongs continuously, night and day, till the birds fell exhausted from the sky, and died. A year later, no bird visited his fields.' Desmond Philips permitted himself a short, sour laugh which, again, should have put me on my guard. 'But his crops were worse than ever. Of course.'

What did he mean, 'of course'. My brain worked furiously. Mistaking my silence for encouragement he continued: 'Every insect known to man moved in, didn't they? No predators. But you'll know this story, sir.'

'Pure folklore.' The words came too quickly. I said, with authority: 'Besides, it is not the diet of the nightingale that I am investigating: it is his song. You and your companions will be required to play up to sixty different phrases on your whistle every day, as well as clashing cymbals.'

My severity appeared to have the required effect. 'I'm glad to have the work, sir.' And he doffed his peaked cap.

Glad to be able to find his way to the other cages and chambers, he meant. Glad to infiltrate the laboratory and find the birds attended to by Professor Mitsubishi's deft fingers.

Ten years earlier I had attended the meeting between the university authorities and Ruskin which had terminated with the Art Professor, now bearded and white-haired, crying out: '*I can no longer remain at a university which descends to such depths of human cruelty. I cannot lecture in the next room to a shrieking cat, nor address myself to the men who have been – there's no word for it!*'

I found it unsettling that Ruskin could find no word to describe what my colleagues and I planned to do in our laboratories. In my darkest moments I wonder how that innocent promoter of beauty and goodness, particularly as manifested in the natural world, would have responded to my more recent experiments. Perhaps it is as well he has gone mad.

*　　*　　*

Ten years earlier also saw the termination of my friendship with Dodgson.

Since our Carfax meeting in the early seventies, the creator of Alice had allowed me to use his dark-room – an extraordinary privilege, which even now overwhelms me with its generosity. The reason was simple: he admired my photographs of the natural world (his own camera work was restricted to portraits and landscapes), and wanted the prints to be of the finest quality. Consequently he put at my disposal a range of dark-room gadgetry, some of it designed by himself, that was uniquely fitted to its task. Being a perfectionist in everything he did, he was satisfied only with a perfect print, no matter how onerous the process. In fact, he very much enjoyed the fiddly process of working with wet collodion, time-consuming as it was, particularly when his little girl subjects 'helped' him develop the large glass plates. On several occasions I arrived at his Christ Church rooms to find the dark-room had been metamorphosed into a thrilling theatre full of mystery and adventure in which Charles played the part of cunning magician, excitedly assisted by a small female, still in fancy dress, who stood upon a box, open-mouthed, watching the image of herself gradually appear in a shallow acid bath, upon a negative plate.

Though he loved to adorn his young subjects with theatrical finery or national dress, and to arrange them into artful poses with ingenious props, his favourite costume was no clothes at all. 'Naked children are so perfectly pure and lovely, but Mrs Grundy would be furious – it would never do,' he said to me as we paged through an album of half-clad young girls climbing across rocks or flitting through fields – all labelled and classified in his accompanying notebooks with compulsive orderliness.

He instructed his scout to let me into his rooms, should he not be at home when I wished to use his equipment – and instructed me on how to ensure the consistency of temperature and elimination of draughts in his drawing-room.

One evening he shows me tiny photographs, the negatives of which he claims to have destroyed. He places a miniature ivory telescope viewer in my hand. 'You will see that an artist has painted in some highly ingenious backdrops!' He has changed into a clean pair of grey cotton gloves.

The little naked girls overwhelm me with their blatant physicality. They lie stretched out upon imaginary fields and rocks, as if waiting to be ravished by a passing Greek god. They stare at me with their insolent eyes. I see no innocence there.

But Dodgson's gaze is reverent. 'Such purity,' he whispers. 'Theirs is a sacred presence, preserved forever.' His face twists briefly with pain. 'Who could see anything other than beauty in these pictures? The children come with their mothers. Yet I have heard vile rumours . . .'

And now Charles Dodgson's eyes are filled with a simple, hopeless sweetness that is altogether absent from those of his sitters. I feel a stab of envy. For in those eyes dwell not only innocence and goodness, but an emotion which is new to me: unreserved love; a love which demands of itself no mirror image.

Dodgson was thoroughly involved in university and college affairs, being Common Room Curator, Sub-Librarian, Mathematical Lecturer and Curate, among other things. But I began to feel somewhat alarmed when he took a passionate interest in the issue of vivisection, both within and beyond the university walls. Although I was still an undergraduate when he first embarked on his anti-vivisectionist crusade, I had long ago acknowledged that the killing or maiming of animals was necessary for a scientific understanding of their behaviour, particularly within an evolutionary framework. Like any other scientist I recognised that man's superiority over animals gave him the right to use less intelligent creatures in any way that might further human progress or even alleviate human suffering. During our occasional walks round Oxford, usually culminating in a museum visit, I fell silent as Dodgson held forth, in his gentle, stammering voice, on the question of whether experiments with animals might not well eventually lead to experiments with human beings: he predicted that scientists might become tempted to cut open the live bodies of incurables and lunatics in the interests of research, informing the unfortunate victims that they should be thankful to have been spared by natural selection for so long.

In 1880 the art of photography was revolutionised by the dry-plate process. Though tempted by the speed with which prints could now be developed, my friend considered the end result to be inferior to that achieved through the endless timings and delicacy of control of wet collodion. He shut down both his dark-room and the glass house above his chambers, and never took another photograph.

A few years later, when I received Dodgson's note informing me that he could no longer sustain friendship with '*a man who vivisects*', his decision cut as sharply into my heart as any vivisector's knife; but I fear my heart cannot compete with the imploring eyes of a lobotomised dog.

GREAT GRANARY 1899

As we waltzed up the avenue, hand-in-hand, I allowed Maria's shrill chatter to pour over my ears and into my central nervous system like warm balm. I did not on the whole listen to the content of her monologue: the unexpected cadences, the rising and falling pitch, the stammering staccatos and syncopated silences were to me of far greater interest than what she was actually saying. Thank heaven the stream of words required no more than grunts and expressions of astonishment by way of reply, for even when I tried I could make neither head nor tail of her discourse. Quite apart from the fact that her accent was quite foreign (though charming) to my ears, the rapid, fragmented topics which she covered were equally alien to me. These topics seemed mainly to concern local characters, all called only Auntie or Uncle, with whom she expected me to be as familiar as she was, an assumption which somehow gave an air of pleasing intimacy to our system of communication (I cannot call it 'conversation'). I felt curiously at peace with myself.

There was something about the atmosphere on that long, shadowy avenue that reminded me of Oxford, though I knew perfectly well that no such conifer-lined road existed in that city of parks and gardens. Perhaps it was merely the pleasure of being in the company of an adorable chatterbox that soothed me and allowed me to surrender my defences, making me feel for once at home with both myself and my immediate environment.

But all at once I knew exactly why I felt I was in Oxford.

From the direction of the aviaries floated a familiar sound. At first one could be forgiven for thinking someone was sliding his lips up and down a flute or pipes of some kind, testing out the instrument with rapid scales. This precarious solo was followed by a chorus of whistles and chirps, and within minutes the blissful music of the English countryside was flooding through the palm trees and bougainvillaea as every blackbird, nightingale, thrush and chaffinch that I had brought with me across the sea burst inexplicably into song. It seemed scarcely believable. I was now in the ridiculous position of wanting to rush to my cages to ascertain the cause of this sudden phenomenon but having to drag my feet unbearably in order to keep pace with the dear little creature beside me. I longed to pick her up, to swing her on to my shoulders so that I could break into a run – what vestigial parental instinct yet lurked? – but knew such behaviour was doomed to failure because my inexperience with such matters would be only too evident: oh for the gift of spontaneity!

Our progress across the lawns beside the horseshoe of hydrangeas was made even slower as Maria bent down to gather acorns dropped by squirrels, or stiffened into statues of arrested excitement when the squirrels themselves darted across the lawn. An earthworm abandoned by a sparrow caused her to drop to her knees with a cry of pity, whereupon she proceeded to dig a hole in the lawn as a safe haven for this fortunate Annelid, which she tucked beneath the soil with all the concern of a mother putting her infant to bed.

At last we reached the aviaries, submerged, as usual, in purple shadow while the rest of the garden glowed in the sun. There was no sign of Salisbury and Chamberlain leaping in exultation, as one might expect. I could see in a flash that no nightingale sang, nor any thrush in the cage next door. The chaffinches and blackbirds too were songless as ever, hunched accusingly in the dark. The entire clamour tumbled from the cage of starlings who had, to the last bird, given up their vow of silence and were simultaneously exercising their syrinxes not so much in song as in unadulterated mimicry! The singing lessons they had received daily from their absent tutors now repeated themselves endlessly in the liquid trills, warbles and flutings of their silent co-species, and I cursed myself for having been so entirely deceived by their well-known imitative powers.

But what had triggered off this chorus of plagiarised birdsong from a species that, till the morning, was struck dumb as the rest of them? Even as the question formed itself in my mind, a jaunty whistle from a starling by my ear gave me the answer. The bright-eyed little mimic was reproducing, with syncopated expertise, exactly the rhythmic melodies that had disturbed me in my morning slumbers. It seemed that the dissonances of the cakewalk were having precisely the effect upon the starling syrinx as they had had on my naked legs: neither song nor dance could resist its call.

'The b-birds are singing nicely, hey?'

Maria's little face was alight with pleasure. I could not bring myself to speak of my own disappointment, so I said, consciously imitating the sing-song way Kipling spoke to the very young: 'Well, Maria, would you like to give names to the birds who are singing or to the ones who aren't singing?'

She placed her chubby index finger over her chin, its tip poking into her mouth and arousing the interest of her gleaming red tongue.

'I think . . .' Clearly she had no idea what she thought, but much enjoyed this pose of deep seriousness. 'I think I'll name the singing b-birds ... no, the birds who aren't singing ... no ...' Then: 'The singing ones mustn't sing too much or they'll get sore throats, hey?'

I took her by the arm and led her to the silent cages. 'Perhaps if you give these ones names they'll begin to sing,' I suggested.

'Then will they come when I call them?'

'We'll have to wait and see.'

Maria's system of nomenclature was unrelated to the methods of taxonomy I had hitherto encountered. I did not try to influence her decisions other than to point out that female birds might not logically be given names such as Eric, Cyril or George, and after making several such mistakes the clever child moved on to genderless names like Sunshine, Whistle or Treetops. Certainly the naming of birds was a passionate affair for her and an object of considerable interest to me, as I perceived the absolute necessity in the child for bestowing individual identities upon each of these creatures. Salisbury and Chamberlain, who had materialised from nowhere, pretending they had never been absent, sulked on the other side of the aviaries and grumbled loudly in their own tongue: it struck me that they had already named the birds according to some primitive classification system of their tribe.

'Say good morning to the Professor, dear.' Mrs Kipling's soft voice curled up from behind my back. A conflict of emotions instantly erupted in my breast: displeasure at the interruption of my intimacy *à deux*, and pleasure at the sound of Mrs K's motherly voice. However, fixing my features into a rictus of indifference, I turned to confront the smiling woman, who pushed forward the little girl of yesterday's hydrangeas. This young person curtsied briefly and uttered the required greeting in a leaden voice (quite unlike the sugary chirrups provoked by her papa), her eyes resting with lively interest upon Maria's pointing finger as the child continued to reel out her list of imaginative names.

'I see we are interrupting a christening!' exclaimed Mrs K gaily. 'Run along and help, dear. Isn't it interesting, Professor Wills, how children's first concern is always to give everything a name – whether it's a toy bear or a tortoise. Oh dear! I mustn't speak too loudly or my husband will instantly compose a story upon the topic. Did you know he was writing a little book of children's stories – how the leopard got his spots, that sort of thing. Not quite the explanation Mr Darwin would have provided, I daresay . . .' Her plain face darted with mischief.

'Mr Darwin has certainly incited a mania in the literary world for inventing origins,' I remarked dryly. 'I only hope that the confusions created in the children's minds will not create havoc in their later lives.'

This attack on her husband's work seemed to amuse her further. 'Oh, these stories will certainly ruin any sense of Geography, I assure you – rhinoceroses by the Red Sea, hedgehogs on the Amazon – but does it matter, as long as they delight the imaginations of children?'

'I am the wrong person to ask. I deal in facts, not imaginative fictions. Invention plays no part in my drab life.'

'Are you then opposed to delight, Professor Wills?' she enquired, a smile twitching in just one corner of her mouth.

'It is perfectly possible to obtain delight from the natural world just as it is. Darwin's *Beagle* journals are full of rapture at the infinite variation and diversity of nature, as indeed is his *Origin of Species*. For myself, I consider imagination to be much overrated.'

'Well, you must be delighted to have your birds singing at last! What a relief!' She seemed so pleased for my sake that I found it almost painful to have to inform her of the true state of affairs.

'Oh, no one will know the difference!' she exclaimed, then turned, still smiling, to the little girls at the aviaries, each outdoing the other in choosing bird-names. 'Listen!'

The names had drifted into the category of the absurd.

'Umbrella!'

'Cough-drops!'

'Suitcase!'

'Moustache!'

'Frog!'

Mrs K was clearly enchanted. For a woman who had scientific aspirations, her enthusiasm for nonsense seemed excessive. By the end of their performance she was nearly bent double with laughter, and I must say I envied her sense of humour: to me the children's game dwelt in the impenetrable category of *play*, an area of human behaviour about which I know little. Finally, wiping a tear from her eye, she controlled her laughter and gasped: 'Oh what fun! I assume – by the gap in her mouth – that the little one is responsible for our adventure last night. She's gorgeous, Professor. Where did you find her?'

I never know whether questions like this are meant to be taken literally, and was about to reply to this one with complete geographical references when a jovial greeting saved me the effort.

'Hail to thee, blithe spirits!' called out Kipling, skipping down the flight of stone steps that led to the aviaries. 'Or am I in the wrong poem? Good to hear your birds singing, Wills. And how are you, O best beloved? Your Mummy tells me you are quite, quite better.' And he swung his daughter into the air with a lack of self-consciousness that I could only envy.

'Can I smoke your chimbling, Daddy?' The little girl whipped his smoking pipe from the depths of his moustache and placed it between her tiny lips.

'Yes, darling child. Why not wear my hat as well!' With

high seriousness he drowned her in his drooping Panama and placed her back on the ground. The child shrieked with glee, evidently enjoying the sensation of being plunged into utter darkness.

'Look, Mummy! Now I'm Daddy!' The effort of speaking with a large pipe in her mouth proved too much, and a violent coughing fit followed. Papa retrieved his belongings, while Mama thumped the child on her back till normal breathing was resumed: 'Really, dear, you do over-excite the child! You know she was poorly last night.'

'I'm a terrible man,' agreed Kipling, packing his pipe bowl with fresh tobacco and inhaling sharply in the way smoking men do. He directed his boyish, dimpled smile at me. 'We owe you a debt of gratitude, Professor Wills. I must say, I'm having to revise my opinion of Oxford dons. I can make precisely one bird sound –' and he proceeded to emit a harsh rasping noise, flapping his arms and bending his neck forward as he did so, much to the delight of the little girls. (Chamberlain and Salisbury choked back giggles from behind their hands.)

'The vulture?' I suggested.

'Ah, now the vulture is the bird to bring back my earliest childhood memories.' He puffed on his pipe, his eyes dancing behind his thick spectacles, while the children gathered round. 'The vultures of Bombay, these are the birds responsible for my very first memory.'

'Not in front of the children, dear,' murmured Mrs K, but he continued as if he had not heard her.

'We lived by the sea in the shadow of palm groves, but I did not know that our little house on the Bombay esplanade was near the Towers of Silence, where the Hindoos expose their dead to the waiting vultures. One day something dropped from the sky into our garden. I was playing in the open, near the palms. The something fell almost at my feet. My nanya rushed across and picked it up before I could see the something.' He sucked hard on his pipe, which appeared to have died on him again. 'She thought I hadn't seen what fell out of the sky. But even now I often think of that little brown *hand*, dropping from the vulture's beak – or would it have been talons, Professor?'

'As I remember, the vultures of the Old World have feet like eagles, designed to grasp their prey,' I murmured. 'Unlike New World vultures.'

But Kipling's attention had been diverted by the arrival of another guest who now limped down the stone steps, his face still a brilliant yellow above his none-too-clean collar.

'Vultures?' yelled Challenger. 'Stupid bloody birds, if you'll pardon my language, Madam. They can be standing right next to rotting flesh in the grass, and unless they can see the thing, they won't know it's there. Not like the black-and-white carrion crow that can smell a carcass from miles off. Good morning, Madam.' He bowed at Mrs K, releasing wafts of brandy and tobacco as he did so. 'Good morning, all. Morning, Wills. Good to see you again.'

It fell to me to introduce Challenger to the Kiplings, a task I rather enjoyed doing with heavy formality.

'I trust you have had a good night's sleep?' said Mrs K, perhaps in the hope of an apology for the previous night's events, but it was plain that Challenger had no recollection whatever of any irregular behaviour.

'Top of the world, thank you,' he replied. 'Mind you, once you've slept under a cloud of malaria-carrying mosquitoes in a leech-infested swamp, anywhere is comfortable.'

'Ah, Challenger.' Kipling interrupted the wild cackle that followed this piece of information. 'I was hoping to get a chance to speak to you. You're a famous ivory hunter and dealer. Your African elephant is a very different creature from my Indian one, and I need some information for a story I'm writing. May I pick your brains?'

'By all means. What's left of them. Africa addles the frontal lobes, I'm afraid.'

'My story goes like this: An African tribesman kills an elephant with poisoned arrows. Tusk number one is exchanged with a slave trader for a Snider rifle and a hundred cartridges; the slave trader exchanges the tusk for neck yokes and brass collars; eventually it reaches the West Coast of Africa from whence it is transported to Europe. Meantime the original hunter's village is raided by Arabs and his wife taken prisoner and ransomed for ivory in the form of tusk number two. This tusk finds its way to the East Coast and on to Zanzibar and on to the salesrooms of the London docks where it is reunited with tusk number one. Tusk number one is converted into piano keys while tusk number two is less gloriously metamorphosed into billiard balls and umbrella handles. Now, what I need to know is details about the weight of tusks, their length, their quality. Are both the tusks the same size, for instance? Can you help me?' He gave an amiable puff on his pipe.

'Ah, elephants! What couldn't I tell you about elephants!' And for the next twenty minutes Challenger regaled us with one elephantine anecdote after another (Mrs K and the two girls stole away half-way through as much of it was bloodthirsty). And once elephants were dealt with, he lectured us on the most appropriate guns for shooting different types of big game; this led him to reminisce about his childhood and his ability with guns even in his early youth; this in turn reminded him of Winchester, whose playing fields he had transformed into the cradle of Africa; now he remembered his burning childhood ambition to discover the true source of the Nile and his bitter disappointment when Speke proved that that mighty river sprang from Lake Albert and not the Four Mystical Fountains of Herodotus, as Livingstone had so passionately believed; this led him to regret the intrusion of the missionary . . .

How is it possible to be a bore when the content of your discourse is extraordinary? Perhaps if we had been sitting in a lecture hall we might have listened with awe to this frenzied monologue but, instead, both Kipling and I found ourselves shifting from one foot to another, glancing at each other helplessly as either he or I attempted to interrupt the relentless torrent of words. Yet, even in the rigidity of my boredom, I felt soothed. I could spend hours, days, weeks, in the company of this madman, thought I, as I tugged at my beard and found the most coiled spring of hair in it; there is something about his craziness that allays my fears. Perhaps I will one day capture the Dodo with him, and become ravaged by Africa, that I may ravage her in return . . .

'Even twenty years ago Africa was still the *terra incognita* where we Europeans might at last come to know ourselves,' cried Challenger, revived by the deep draught he had taken from his flask. 'But now, with all due respect to Dr Livingstone, whom I admire more than any man, living or dead, we have missionaries by the hundred trying to introduce that very civilisation from which men like myself are trying to escape. In their innocence, those missionaries do untold damage to the tribal structures they seek to uplift through Christianity –'

At this point Kipling removed his spectacles and began to clean them with exaggerated vigour. 'I would have thought,' said he, his face owlish and round-cheeked without the protection of his glasses, 'that the arrival of the *gun* had more impact on African social structures than any missionary. Surely –'

'*Bunduki sultani ya bara bara*!' thundered Challenger in a terrible voice. 'The gun is the Sultan of Africa, as Mr Stanley's *wangwana* so succinctly expressed it. Why do you think Robert Moffat, the most successful missionary in Southern Africa, had the Matabele flocking to his sermons? Not to be converted, I assure you. Twenty-four is a generous estimate of the number of Matabeles Moffat succeeded in converting. No, Moffat had two attributes the Matabeles wanted and needed: he could cure their ailments with his medicine box and, more importantly, he was prepared to mend their guns!'

'And would you not say that a man like yourself has done untold damage to the indigenous wildlife of Africa, to say nothing of its social structures?' asked Kipling politely, though continuing to polish the lenses of his spectacles till I feared they might fall apart. 'My tusk story will have the sister of the slaughtered elephant finding herself safe in the sanctuary set up in the north by the old Boer president.'

Challenger's eyes roved wildly. He seemed to be addressing the top of a distant palm tree when he next spoke. 'The truth of it is not so much that I possess the gun, but that the gun possesses me. I cannot live without it. When I have my new arm measured in England, I might just as well have a rifle fitted permanently to my shoulder instead. When in Africa, shoot. It's the only language that everyone understands at once. Give me a light, old chap.' From some other pocket he produced a silver case of heavily scented cigarillos, which he offered me with his shaking hand. Kipling sprang forward to oblige. 'I keep a tally of what I have shot: most hunters do. Last year in the space of six months I had shot a hundred and seven big-game animals: thirty-two –'

An abrupt movement at the top of the flight of stone steps made him pause. Frank Harris leaned on his cane, raised his hat, and grinned. 'Ah, Wills! I was told you'd be down here!' Spruce and gleaming, he could have been on the way to his club, or the opera, a dandy on the Strand. It struck me that this man was always in remarkably good health. His eyes bore no trace of our late-night drinking; his body was lean and supple; the flush in his cheek was due to good circulation rather than over-indulgence. Again, I felt an unaccountable surge of affection upon hearing his voice.

Challenger was gazing at the intruder with an incredulity that I at first attributed to outrage at this interruption. But as he knitted his brows together and gazed upon Harris with a fervour that altogether lacked resentment, I saw in his eyes the stirrings of delighted recognition. Harris, for his part, bounded down the steps, swinging his cane and greeting Kipling with a breezy confidence that made me realise they already knew each other. Challenger watched his every move; then a hideous smile cracked open his face, and he staggered towards the swarthy little fellow before him.

'*Inundi! My brother!*' he cried hoarsely.

Harris looked up at him in surprise, no doubt taking him for some beggar we had stumbled upon in the gardens. Then surprise was overtaken by horror as the beggar threw his remaining arm round Harris's neck and implanted a resonant kiss upon his closely-shaved, perfumed cheek. The little dandy leapt back, wiping his face with the handkerchief that peeped from his pocket: for a moment I thought he had lost his famous self-assurance.

'I fear you are – mistaken!' he exclaimed, but even as he uttered the last word, doubt entered his flashing eyes, and exactly the same emotion I had observed upon Challenger's face now began to transform his gaze. In a changed voice he whispered:

'*It is you!*'

'Zambezi rapids '96!' blurted Challenger. 'Treacherous carriers; malaria; high fever; no quinine; imminent death – then you appeared like a mirage with your line of porters and your medicine chest: you saved my life, no less – and I never even learnt your name!'

By now Harris had recovered his composure and was

puffing out his chest with ill-disguised pleasure as Challenger catalogued his gratitude. 'Think nothing of it, my dear chap,' he purred. 'We were ships that passed in the night. You'd have done the same for me, no question of that. But that excursion of mine along the Zambezi was soon to become a nightmare of intolerable proportions. I can quite honestly say I nearly died.' He shuddered theatrically, and continued: 'My charming porters deserted me and smashed my medicine chest when I was in a state of delirium brought on by blackwater fever. I was left with three tins of sardines to live on. By the time I arrived in Portuguese East Africa, I weighed eighty pounds, literally skin and bone. The Negroes fled from me in the streets, thinking I was a zombie or suchlike.' His glance suddenly descended to Challenger's empty sleeve. 'I say, lost an arm, have you?'

'Perhaps you two need to be introduced,' interposed Kipling. 'Frank Harris, editor, adviser to the rich and famous, *bon viveur*. G. B. Challenger, ivory hunter and explorer.'

Harris's editorial eye lit up. 'You don't mean *the* Challenger – whose exploits the nation reads about in the broadsheets? The man I have longed to meet and interview?'

Challenger took a swig from his flask and bared his yellow teeth. 'The very same!' he leered. 'At your service!'

'But where is Mary?' cried Frank. 'Where is your little poodle? Of course! How could I have been so stupid? You and she were already inseparable when I met you in '96 – but in '96 you were not a household name!'

'Mary!' called out Challenger, and the little creature flew out of a pot of tumbling geraniums and scampered up to her master on her hind legs. I began to back away, my whole body at once throbbing with high anxiety – when Mary turned round and daintily, daintily, dropped her front paws to the ground and trotted up to me. I felt the sweat gush from my forehead and armpits, and by a supreme act of self-discipline restrained myself from shrieking out aloud.

'Go on, old boy, give her a pat. Not often she comes up to a stranger!'

Mary sat on her haunches before me and smiled. Whether this was a circus trick she had learnt from Challenger I could not say, but her black lips stretched back into her white curls in what was unmistakably a gesture of friendliness. She raised one tiny paw.

'She wants it shaken. She'll never forgive you if you don't!'

The dog's laughing eyes egged me on. I could see the pleasure of grasping her paw momentarily with my fingertips – but what if those sharp little teeth sank into my scarred hand?

Kipling and Harris had joined Challenger with cries of encouragement, somehow sensing the seriousness of this moment. I forced a shrill, quivering voice out of my throat:

'Sure she doesn't b-b-bite?'

'Not if she likes you – which she does! Clear as day!'

I bent my knees. A drop of moisture fell from my face on to the dog's head. Her tail began to wag. Inch by inch, as it seemed, I extended my hand.

And touched her little paw with my finger. She lowered her jaws, but before I could whip my hand away, her pink tongue protruded into my palm. It was extremely wet and extremely warm.

'There you are!' cried Challenger. 'She's giving you a kiss!'

Her job done, Mary began to sniff at the shoes of all the gentlemen, and might have offered them her paw (I found myself hoping she would not) when an unfamiliar noise drifted up from the far end of the avenue.

At this point, Chamberlain and Salisbury disentangled themselves from the shadows beyond the cages and ran forward joyously, chanting out a word at first incomprehensible to me: *'ah-tah-mah-beeleh! ah-tah-mah-beeleh!'*

And from the curve of the driveway emerged the object of their excitement, all brass and leather and heat and dust, with the Colossus himself behind the wheel, surrounded by three laughing female faces.

Jove in his chariot could not have looked more exultant than our sweating host, most of whose face was obscured by a pair of grotesque, rubber-rimmed spectacles, surmounted by a well-worn slouch hat. Beneath this headgear hung an ecstatic smile that nevertheless suggested to me a hint of mental derangement, in the style of Dodgson's Cheshire Cat. And clustered around him, like laughing cherubs upon grubby clouds, were the two little girls and Mrs K, her stern visage relaxed into the same beaming smile.

'Well, what do you think?'

Our host levered himself out of the driver's seat and removed his ridiculous rubber spectacles. Miraculously absolved of our father-confessor roles, Kipling, Harris and I hurried to the top of the stairs, while Challenger appeared not to have heard the summons. Mrs K and the two girls waved feverishly.

The Colossus had by now pulled off his hat so that the crumpled thatch of his hair stood on end. His eyes were bloodshot once again, but full of blue animation. Words began to erupt from his mouth. 'The country's first horseless carriage – sprung and braked, single cylinder, belt-driven, fixed-ignition, twelve miles an hour: shall I buy her?'

At once Kipling, Harris, Salisbury and Chamberlain sprang into action. It was as if an invisible key had been turned to ignite some area of their consciousness and set their motors throbbing. The two boys danced in adoration around the automobile, touching the tyres, the brass trimmings, the folded Victoria hood, with a reverence they had certainly never accorded my birds, while the three men entered into a contest concerning the superior features of the French horseless carriage as compared with German and American rival makes. I had the feeling that unless someone turned their engines off they would run forever.

It seemed that Kipling already had a steam-car called a Locomobile, and had test-driven the very first Lanchester, whose springing he pronounced to be perfect. Harris, needless to say, had bought a motor-car three years earlier in Monte Carlo: a Georges Richard, seven horsepower, driven by belts. He was the first person in the world to have seen the four great cathedrals of France in one day, driving his motor from Amiens to Paris to Chartres to Rheims before the sun set.

'Of course, aeroplanes will eventually supersede motor-cars,' he declared in his confident way. 'Last year I went up for three hundred yards in an American machine – not far I know, but you can see that as far as flying's concerned, not even the sky's the limit!'

Mrs K was growing restless, even in her position of driver's consort. When the men paused to draw breath in preparation for excited debate on this topic, she cut in swiftly with a revived smile and said, her voice sharp as a sword: 'I'm sorry to interrupt you two gentleman, but I have a suggestion to make.'

The men gazed at her vaguely, as if trying to remember who she was. Then good manners forced the Colossus to stammer: 'A–a suggestion?'

'What I would like to suggest,' Mrs K's smile was charming, 'is a visit to the seaside. In this very vehicle. I have recently discovered that Professor Wills here has spent several days on this estate without once setting foot outside it! In my opinion he needs to roll up his trousers and paddle, and I'm sure the girls would be only too delighted to assist him!'

I felt myself grow scarlet at her words. The notion of visiting the seaside was to me almost as foreign as that of visiting the Bangweolo Swamps, and my initial reaction was to reject the idea outright. But the little girls had immediately broken into cheers, and both the Colossus and Kipling stroked their moustaches to hide their smiles, while the excitement of my two young assistants grew to fever pitch. I could see that the suggestion had kindled the interest of our host, who, one would think, should have had more important things to do than paddle in the sea.

'My dear Mrs Kipling, what a delightful idea,' said he. 'I should like nothing more than to visit my little cottage in Muizenberg. And I can think of nothing more pleasant than rolling up my trousers and refreshing my feet in the Atlantic Ocean. It will take us an hour to get there by automobile. We can paddle for an hour or two and be back in time for supper.'

'Hooray!' cried Kipling and threw his hat into the air.

'Please, *baas*!' whimpered Chamberlain and Salisbury, their eyes brimming with incipient gratitude.

'It will be an entirely new ornithological experience for you,' said Mrs Kipling as I shrank away from the vehicle into which her husband, wreathed in smiles, was now climbing. 'There are some quite remarkable waders for you to observe, I can assure you.'

Fortunately I remembered to look at my fob-watch at this point and was able to exclaim in quite genuine surprise: 'Oh dear! I'd quite lost track of the time. I'm afraid I have an appointment to keep!'

'And I should like to take this opportunity of interviewing Challenger,' said Harris, though I don't believe he had been invited on the trip.

'Oh, Professor, what a shame!' Mrs K's face puckered. She looked as if she wanted to query the nature of my appointment, but the Colossus had already started the engine by some mysterious means. With wild cries of delight the boys jumped on to the running board (they would be allowed to remain there as far as the gates).

Somewhat thankfully, I left Harris and Challenger to each other.

'Ten minutes.' Milner looked even grimmer than usual. The Cape cart waited outside the front entrance of the Great Granary, the two horses pawing the ground, their reins still in the driver's hand. 'In two hours I catch a train to Bloemfontein to meet the Flat Earth disciples. Where is the lady?' He turned to mount the short flight of steps to the front door.

He reminded me of a fully wound clockwork toy, let loose to march around in circles. Clearly it would be fatal for him to stop moving.

'Um, if you remember, the arrangement is that we'll meet her on the mountain. As you'll appreciate, she can't very well come to this house.'

'Stupid of me.' He wheeled round to face me, suddenly half-smiling. 'I suppose I'm quite intrigued to meet her. Not a beauty, though, is she?' He was fiddling with his moustaches, nevertheless. 'Come on, man, I've wasted two minutes already.'

'This way.' I led him across the lawn to the gate and we walked up the path rather more quickly than I might have wished. He was dressed very formally in pin-striped trousers and frock-coat, and carried his top hat under his arm. His head was bent forward in intense thought: he seemed oblivious of the banana trees and oleander that brushed his shoulder – an elephant or tiger would have crossed his path unnoticed.

Into the dark pine forest we marched, and I hoped that Miss Schreiner had kept her word and was waiting for us in Titania's grove. The possibility that she might not be there began to stir considerable anxiety in my breast, as I did not feel strong enough to endure Milner's displeasure.

'How much further?' he snapped as a mossy log caused him

to slip and trip (his highly polished spats were quite unsuitable for this mountainous ascent) straight into the arms of Olive, who was standing ready for his entrance.

'Sir Alfred!' she cried, and then she too toppled over in a flurry of petticoats and hat-pins, his long body proving too heavy for her. As the two of them struggled on the ground I felt a spasm of regret that my Kodak did not hang around my neck.

'You may laugh, Wills!' Milner was all elbows and knees, trying to revert to the vertical on the slippery pine needles, while Olive was a dumpy pincushion with her legs splayed out. Her reticule had burst open, discharging its contents all around. Milner's hat had landed upside down on a rock, as if begging for coins while the concoction on Olive's head hung at an angle that released a torrent of dark unruly hair. I extended a helping hand.

'Five minutes!' shouted Milner, a gigantic segmented spider on his knees and hands, one of which held the fob-watch he had removed from his waistcoat pocket.

Miss Schreiner had a speech of exactly five minutes prepared. Summoning all her energies, and oblivious of the chunks of plant life that now clung to her bottle-green coat, she began to declaim:

'Sir Alfred, I have to ask you to consider a very simple question. It is this: *Who gains by war*? What is it for? Not England! She has a great young nation's heart to lose! She has treaties to violate ... Not Africa! The great young nation, quickening today to its first consciousness of life, to be torn and rent ... Not the brave English soldier. There are no laurels for him here. The dying lads with hands fresh from the plough; the old man tottering to the grave, who seizes the gun to die with it ... Who gains by war? Not we the Africans whose hearts are knit to England. We love all. Each hired soldier's bullet that strikes down a South African does more; it finds a bullet here in our hearts!'

And she struck her own breast thrice in her tremulous passion. Milner's facial expression was deadpan. He had finally seated himself on the same fallen log that I had used the day before, and recovered his hat, which he placed upon his precariously crossed knees. Olive continued addressing her audience of one in the same ringing tones:

'It may be said: but what has England to fear in a campaign with a country like Africa? ... she can sweep it by mere numbers. We answer yes – she might do it – there is no doubt that England might send out sixty or a hundred thousand hired soldiers to South Africa, and they could bombard our towns and destroy our villages; they could shoot down men in the prime of life, and old men and boys, till there was hardly a kopje in the country without its stain of blood. When the war was over the imported soldier might leave the land – but not all. Some must be left to keep the remaining people down. There would be quiet in the land. South Africa would rise up silently, and count her dead and bury them. Have the dead no voices? In a thousand farmhouses black-robed women would hold memory of the country. There would be silence, but no peace!' Miss Schreiner paused for dramatic effect.

'There would be peace if all fighting men in arms had been shot or taken prisoner,' remarked Milner.

Olive's eyes lit up. 'Yes, but what of the women? If there were left but five thousand pregnant South African-born women and all the rest of their people destroyed, these women would breed up again a race like the first!'

She had finished, and gazed fiercely down at Milner, whose expression had not changed. Then a fleeting contraction of his lower eyelid muscles indicated he was about to speak.

'You have a high opinion of the Boer.' His voice was distant.

Miss Schreiner took a deep breath and began again. 'As a child I was brought up to despise the Boer. I remember being given a handful of sugar by a Boer child and throwing it away when I thought no one was looking because I thought I would have been contaminated if I'd eaten it. But later, when I lived among them for five years as a teacher on their farms, watching them in all the vicissitudes of life from birth to death, I learnt to love the Boer; but more, I learnt to admire him. I learnt that in the African Boer we have one of the most intellectually virile and dominant races the world has seen; a people who beneath a calm and almost stolid surface hide the most intense passions and the most indomitable resolution. Sir Alfred, the British race cannot afford to make an enemy of these people! There is a spiritual depth in the Boer entirely lacking in the treasure hunters and goldbugs who leech off the mines in the North and pretend they have come to Africa for some greater purpose. The Boer loves Africa for her own sake, and curses the day that gold was found in the rocks of their simple Republic!'

Milner hooded his eyes. 'So you do not believe in economic progress? You think the world should remain in its primitive state?'

For a moment Olive wavered. She recognised that this cool man, who respected only restraint and shrewd logic, had opened up a trap into which she must not fall. But her fiery nature could not contain itself, and she broke into inflammatory prose:

'But what does all this vast accumulation of material goods lead to? Does the human creature who craves more and more material possessions become a better creature? I say that the human spirit and even the human body are being crushed under this vast accumulation of material things, this ceaseless thirst for more and more; that the living creature is building up about itself a tomb in which it will finally dwindle and d–'

Milner stood up, an elaborate unfolding of a multi-jointed gentleman. I heard his knees crack several times.

'Miss Schreiner,' he declared, 'I'm afraid my time has run out. These people you describe may be decadent and degenerate in your opinion, but you forget one thing. They are British. And I cannot tolerate the spectacle of thousands of British subjects kept permanently in the position of helots, calling vainly to Her Majesty's Government for redress. I bid you good afternoon.'

I detected a click of highly polished heels among the pine needles. Olive looked as if she might fling herself at these very heels: instead, she straightened her stricken hat and said, in an altered voice: 'You do not see the larger issue. Thank you for your time.' Her face was grey.

Milner began his descent and I started to follow him, feeling I did not have the strength to remain with Olive in her state of mind. But even as I timidly moved into the shadow of the august High Commissioner of South Africa, Olive grabbed my arm with frightening strength, and pulled me back.

'Stay!' she hissed. Her eyes were wilder than I had ever seen them. 'I have another card to play. But I need your help. Together we can still save this country from the catastrophe of war!'

Alfred the tarantula lasted two years in a glass box contained in a larger box of straw in my bedroom. I gained a certain notoriety through being his owner. He was the only pet I have ever had. He allowed me to stroke his furry back. One day I found him dead in the straw, his legs neatly folded. I grieved, but made no effort to replace him.

Violins appeared to be playing in Miss Schreiner's chest.

Brushing a frond of fern from her skirt, she informed me, in a voice which sliced through this delicate string accompaniment: 'You may be interested to hear that my brother Will is Prime Minister of this colony!'

Her hand was still on my arm. We could hear Milner beating his retreat down the mountain path. I pulled my elbow free.

'Miss Schreiner, I have business to attend to.'

How is it that some people can command by the timbre of their voice alone? Miss Schreiner looked absurd: her hat was askew and her clothes covered in foliage, but her speech, wild as it was, brimmed with an absolute assurance which cannot be ignored: like an obedient dog I stayed and heard her out, though longing to escape to some ill-defined freedom. (I once heard an old woman calmly require a street urchin to return the purse he had just picked from her pocket: as if mesmerised, he complied with her request, even muttering a few words of apology. I have absolutely no doubt that had I attempted to address him in the same way I would have had mud or worse slung in my eye, accompanied by a barrage of impudent imitations and verbal assaults.)

Olive began to speak.

MISS SCHREINER TELLS
ANOTHER STORY

Once, like herself, Miss Schreiner's brother Will had been among the Colossus' most ardent disciples. In his mind there was no question but that this man of genius would unite the Colony's disparate elements and open up all of Africa to the benevolent influence of Great Britain.

'But below the fascinating surface the worms of falsehood and corruption were creeping,' hissed Miss Schreiner. 'He thought nothing of betraying his loyalest supporters in order to become the most powerful man in South Africa!' On the night of Jameson's fiasco, as the gallant raiders galloped across the Transvaal border to their own destruction and that of the entire country, Will, by then the Colony's Attorney General, had visited the Colossus in his library. He had found a broken man, in the company of a sycophantic secretary.

Miss Schreiner, wheezing horribly, said to me: 'You must know the sonnet *Ozymandias* by Shelley. The traveller from an antique land finds a shattered visage of stone, half sunk in the desert sands, its wrinkled lip and sneer of cold command still intact, though the mighty statue is wrecked. That is the image that instantly occurred to Will as he entered the library and saw his Prime Minister hunched in his chair, his eyes red, his face unshaven. He had aged ten years. He did not greet my brother, but lifted his mighty head and exclaimed at once –' (and here Miss Schreiner placed the back of her hand against her brow and rolled her eyes, in a satire of despair) ' "*Yes yes, it's true! Old Jameson has upset my apple-cart: he has ridden in!*" Will grew frantic, understanding at once the implications of this act of rashness, and begged his master to think of some way of stopping the madcap doctor from his dash to disaster. Even at this stage a telegram could have halted the futile incursion. But Ozymandias knew he was already ruined.

' "I thought I'd stopped him! I sent messages to stop him! Twenty years we've been friends, and now he goes in and ruins me! I can't hinder him. I can't go and destroy him!"

'Attempting to assume a mantle of calm, Will asked: "How far are you implicated?"

'Ozymandias replied in his strange, soprano voice: "It had my backing, Will – the whole thing, from first to last. Johannesburg, Jameson, everything."

'Will stared at the man whom he had loved and trusted with all the purity of his simple heart. It was almost impossible for him to believe what he was hearing: he longed to awaken and find that this was but a terrifying nightmare. But there was to be no such solace. After a long silence Will asked: "Will you resign?" And Ozymandias replied: "I have done so already! I am finished!" He did not disguise his bitterness.

'Even though he was aghast at these revelations, my brother stayed with his master for four hours that dreadful night. During this time, Ozymandias cried out repeatedly that he was finished, that it was Jameson's fault for going in when he knew there was to be no uprising in Johannesburg, no frantic women or children to save, that it was his own fault for setting Jameson up. Every now and then he would stagger up from his desk and begin to pace back and forth in the library, scarcely touching the whisky and soda at his elbow, so great was his agitation. Tobacco was his only solace: Will says the smog of London was nothing compared to the fog of guilty smoke that filled the library that night. And in these surges of impotent energy he would call out the name of our Colonial Secretary: *"Chamberlain! He's in it up to the neck!"* Then a grimace that was intended to be a smile would distort his mouth. Even in his anguish he could be cunning. *"If he denies it, I've got him by the short hairs!"*

'My poor brother enquired as to the meaning of this assertion. Ozymandias pointed to a pile of telegrams and letters dating back some years which now lay in a heap on his desk. Will glanced through them. His heart sank even lower. The telegrams indicated beyond doubt that Chamberlain had long been in favour of the Raid as a means of ousting the Afrikaners who stood in the way of his imperial designs! He had supported it in the usual convoluted, ambiguous way of politicians: at the very least he knew it was going to happen and that Great Britain would benefit immeasurably. Yet at that very minute Chamberlain was publicly condemning the Raid as a flagrant piece of filibustering, and sending off apologies to the old Boer President himself!'

Miss Schreiner fixed her fierce dark eyes on me, and I returned her gaze meekly. 'During the Committee of Inquiry, set up to discover exactly who the guilty parties were in this bungled affair, we expected these telegrams to be produced and Chamberlain's involvement revealed to the world. But the telegrams – eight of them – went mysteriously missing!' Miss Schreiner's indignation caused her bronchial string-trio to multiply into a veritable orchestra, and her shoulders heaved painfully at the effort of speaking. Ignoring these obstacles, she continued with her scornful denunciation. 'Needless to say, everyone was squared to keep quiet: Ozymandias and Chamberlain were intent on saving their own bacon, and the Lying in State at Westminster achieved nothing. Professor

Wills, I have failed to convince Milner that war will utterly destroy this land. There is only one other course of action left to me. I must have those telegrams! And only you can get them for me!'

'Good God, woman!' I exploded, my meekness evaporating in a trice. 'Have I not done enough for you? You are asking me to commit a crime not only against the State but against my host! I can scarcely believe what I am hearing!'

Miss Schreiner was unmoved by my outburst. 'I can assure you you would be doing your host the greatest favour by revealing the contents of the telegrams. He would have liked nothing more than to drag the Colonial Secretary down into the mire with which he was now so thoroughly coated!'

'So why didn't he release the telegrams at the time?' I enquired irritably.

'There is no simple answer to that question,' replied Miss Schreiner. 'But judging by the outcome of the Inquiry, I would guess that Chamberlain had promised the survival of Ozymandias' beloved Chartered Company and railway plans in return for the withholding of the telegrams. By rights the Charter should have been withdrawn and Ozymandias should have found himself in gaol.'

I tried to be patient. 'But surely all this is buried in the past now? The Inquiry was heard over two years ago – what benefit is there in producing telegrams that everyone's forgotten about? Who would be interested?'

I realised as I spoke that I was allowing myself to be ensnared in her grotesque plans simply by discussing them. Perhaps something in me wanted to find out just how far she was prepared to go, and what her crazed expectations were of this unlikely burglar.

'Don't you understand? I've failed with the High Commissioner, so now I must go a step higher. If I can prove to the British public that their wonderful Brummagem Joe,

Pushful Joe, was *lying* to save his career, their sympathies will shift to the Boer cause – where there is considerable sympathy already! If the telegrams are published, Chamberlain will have to resign! The British government won't be able to survive his fall, and in the confusion war will become impossible!' Her eyes blazed with furious triumph, but I could hear that her breathing had become a battle which she could not win.

'Miss Schreiner, calm yourself. You will have another attack. Let us drop this fruitless subject. I cannot hunt for missing telegrams.' I kept my speech plain, in the vain hope that she would listen to me.

Once again she seized my arm. I could feel her fingertips burn into my flesh and was certain there would be bruise marks by evening. Her face had assumed a new seriousness.

'Professor Wills, people think this war is a straightforward conflict between the British and the Boers. Let me tell you, something far larger is at stake. Six million people stand to lose their freedom, their land, their social organisation, for the greater advantage of gold-greedy ghouls! The indigenous peoples of this country will be cast into the position of near-slaves; they will be utterly deprived of the franchise; and the ghouls, whether English or Afrikaner, will be assured of an endless source of cheap labour which they need if their deep-cast mines are to be profitable. Though the white men may do battle, it is the black men, women and children who will be vanquished, whoever wins the war! And then, God help us all, such a gulf will open between the races, and this country will be cursed by every nation that believes in justice to all men. Believe me, Professor, the catastrophe will endure from one generation to the next – but we can prevent it yet!'

If Miss Schreiner expected this argument to cause me to change my mind, she was indeed mistaken. 'I'm afraid I am not much interested in the fate of the natives of this land – they mean nothing to me,' I said coldly. 'They are an alien race. And now I must return to attend to my birds. That is my responsibility.'

At this Miss Schreiner fell upon her knees and flung her arms about my legs. I was utterly trapped as she spoke in a low, sobbing voice, quite unlike anything I had yet heard from her.

'Professor Wills, I will do anything to help you in return for the telegrams. You will find them somewhere in his bedroom, where he keeps everything of any value to him. I have considerable influence in Great Britain: there must be some way I can be of assistance to you in return.'

For a few moments I considered her wild offer. Then I disentangled my legs and stepped backwards.

'In fact, there is something you could do for me.'

She stared up at me from her kneeling position, her grief-stained face suddenly transformed by joy.

'Professor, I will do anything! *Anything!*'

And so did we square each other that fateful afternoon.

Back at the aviaries, Salisbury and Chamberlain were play-ing their games in the gravel, and moving their mysterious pebbles into new positions. As usual they leapt up and began whistling and chirruping in an attempt to convince me of their dedication to the task for which they were being generously paid.

I looked down at the weaving patterns in the gravel, and in an inspired flash I guessed their meaning.

'*Ah-toh-mah-beel*?' I pointed at the motor-car pebbles and road-grooves.

'Beep-beep!' giggled Chamberlain. 'Vroom-vroom!' cried Salisbury. I heard myself chuckle rustily. Was I growing fond of them? Could it be true that I was a dear, good Englishman who loved children and birds? A sinew in my heart gave a pleasant flicker.

Six corpses were laid out by the cages, two of them nightingales. The remaining birds drooped. All except, of course, the European starlings, who seemed relaxed and confident, singing with gusto and imitating the sounds they heard around them – including the ring of the Colossus' telephone. The boys continued to whistle to the non-singers. I could see they thought it was pointless.

My fob-watch told me it was already four o'clock. My stomach had not reminded me about lunch – perhaps because the *koeksuster* still sat undigested upon my sensitive duodenal lining. In fact, I felt an overwhelming desire to sleep after my crowded day, and soon made my way to the front steps of the Great Granary, deliberately avoiding the back verandah where I saw the Kiplings' family nursemaid playing with the two children who had not gone on the seaside trip.

A profound and dreamless sleep was granted to me almost as soon as I entered my bedroom.

OXFORD 1898

With the delicate precision that only Japan can offer, Mitsubishi removed the cochleas from the ears of newborn nightingales in 1895. He performed the same operation on five-week-old and four-month-old birds. Half had been exposed to their parents' song: a control group had not. The deafened nightingales were minutely observed, and their songs – mere sketches for songs – were notated by a professional musician who could be trusted not to gossip. After three years the all-important questions could be answered: to what extent would the crucial length of time for which they had been allowed to hear normally influence their song pattern? Would all song patterns of birds deafened at birth be exactly the same? How would their subsongs differ from those who had heard only cymbals clashing during their lifetimes?

The answers to these questions are to be found in my book: *On the Song of the Nightingale*. The real song, utterly unaffected by family, is revealed in this book, which, in my opinion, has the poetry of truth, if not rhyme, about it.

The publication of the book was the result of twenty years of investigation. My chief experiments could be performed only during the months of April and May, the short-lived period of nightingale song in England, though the subsequent behaviour of the deafened birds was closely observed throughout their lives. They could not, of course, be released into the wild.

I do not know how Desmond Philips discovered the existence of Mitsubishi's birds. The Anti-Vivisectionist League, of which I learnt he was a leading member, had kept up their resistance to the physiology laboratories, distributing pamphlets and posters in which my name continued to be unflatteringly mentioned. Although the removal of the nightingale cochleas was as nothing compared with the scale upon which vivisection was being practised on the Continent, I recognised that deliberate sensory deprivation as an experimental technique would be regarded by these fanatics as the worst form of torture, such as practised by notorious authoritarian regimes across the world. Accordingly the deafened birds were housed in a room in the laboratories to which I alone had the key: I can only assume that the laboratory caretaker with his master key was bribed.

My book was well received by the scientific community, elevating me to the world's foremost expert on nightingale song. Letters of commendation poured into my college, where my position of Fellow was elevated to Professor: I received requests to deliver speeches at conferences on the Continent, and in America and Japan. I could ask for no higher accolades.

It is my practice in Oxford to start my day at the full-length Queen Anne windows of my study, once Saunders has drawn the curtains. From this vantage point I can gaze down into the geometrically arranged Fellows' Garden which at once imposes a pleasing sense of order upon the thought patterns of my brain, all too often recovering from nightmares of the most vicious nature. I stare down into the Jacobean symmetries, the miniature topiaries, the white blooms (no other colour is admitted). In the very centre of the garden stands an ancient monkey-puzzle tree, the branches of which are arranged with mathematical precision. I sip my cup of China tea, and begin to feel in control. I can hear Saunders preparing my ablutions: the pleasant smell of soap and steam wafts past.

A few weeks after the publication of my book I awoke to find Saunders in an uncharacteristically agitated state of mind. To my astonishment he tried to divert me from my ritual, and suggested, in a shaking voice, that he bring me my cup of tea in bed that morning. Noticing his deathly pallor and haggard eyes I enquired after his well-being, to which he replied that it was not *his* well-being with which he was concerned, but my own. This response made me leap out of bed to prove to him that, though I might complain to him every day about the state of my bowels, the aches in my head, the pains in my chest and so on, the sum of health is larger than its parts, and I was very well, thank you. Poor Saunders, not given to improvisation, had tried to prevent me from striding across to the study windows by the simple expedient of not opening the curtains. The unaccustomed darkness of my study at once alerted me to the fact that something unusual had happened, and with a violent gesture I flung back my damask hangings and gazed truculently into the Fellows' Garden.

The monkey-puzzle tree is an intellectual challenge. Its branches fork out from its trunk much like the passages of a maze: the philosopher may run his eye over its angular and unexpected progressions, and feel some answering call in his own thought processes. The branches are covered in the sharpest of needles, designed, according to the inhabitants of its native Chile, to prevent monkeys from reaching the tasty nuts at the branch tips (a further puzzle as there are no monkeys in the tree's native forests).

On this morning a circle of gardeners, scouts and one or two dons, including the Master of the college, were gazing up into the maze of branches, shaking their heads, even *scratching* their heads. Some underling hastened through the topiary, a full-length ladder upon his shoulder.

Whoever had scaled the tree that night had been undeterred by needles.

The effigy which had been suspended from the highest branch bore a representation of my own facial features, though the body bulged grossly, unlike my own trim lines. Twisted beneath the instantly identifiable grey beard was an exaggerated hangman's knot: a gigantic tongue, livid purple, had been made to protrude from my pink lips.

'I must tell you, sir,' murmured Saunders, passing me my cup of tea with quivering fingers, 'they have released all your birds. They have destroyed your papers, sir, in a bonfire in the cages. It is a miracle that the laboratory did not burn down.'

'Saunders,' I enquired, 'why does my father hang from the tree?'

Saunders placed his hand under my elbow and steered me away from the window. I allowed him to lead me into the adjoining room which looked out over a cobbled street.

'Drink this, sir,' he urged. I sipped obediently, my olfactory nerves recognising good malt whisky in the fumes.

'He hangs, he hangs,' I said, wondering if I was about to break out into song. 'Elspeth thinks I kept to my room, but I can climb out of mouseholes. He hangs among the moths. His tongue is black. Yet he grins, does he not?'

'That was a long time ago, sir,' replied poor Saunders. 'It does not do to dwell upon the past.'

'He hangs because I have left half-winged messages in his safe place.' It was a relief for me to explain to Saunders. For the first time in all the years I had known him I gazed directly into his eyes, and held my gaze.

His rheumy old eyes filled with tears. 'They are wicked

men!' he exclaimed. 'And women. They will be arrested and sent to prison. All your files. Quite, quite destroyed.' He blew his nose loudly into a very large handkerchief.

A knock sounded on the door. While Saunders scurried to attend to this summons, I sipped thoughtfully at my tea. With each swallow I felt myself change shape, grow smaller, until, with the last swallow, I observed myself disappear altogether.

'So that is why we drink tea!' I exclaimed as I faded from view just as Saunders rushed into the room in the company of the distraught college Master.

GREAT GRANARY 1899

He was slumped in a large wicker chair, his long legs crossed, a glass of something dark and frothy in one hand, a Turkish cigarette in the other. His massive head sagged. Beside him stood a trolley of crystal decanters and glasses. The long verandah had been cleared of children and nurse-maids, though I saw Huxley vanish through a far door as I approached.

Yes, I suppose there is a look of Napoleon, even Caesar, in that florid face. The big nose, hooked and slightly askew. The meaty cheeks. The working mouth. The glaring eyes. Which were turned upon the darkening mountain-face but which I knew had registered my arrival by their slight tremor.

'Pull up a chair, Wills.' His falsetto voice soared. 'No, not that way – look what you're missing, man. And pour yourself a drink. I've got something to say to you.'

Though I did not normally drink alcohol at that early hour, I felt that a strong whisky would give me the courage I would probably need during the exchanges to come. I turned a wicker chair to face the mountain so that we sat side by side, sipping our drinks. I could not bring myself to lift my eyes, and focused instead on the formal Dutch garden immediately before me. A cicada began to shrill from under one of the great wooden chests behind us.

'Great things are done when men and mountains meet, Which are not – which are not what, Wills?'

'Which are not done by jostling in the street.' I swallowed the entire contents of my glass and wished I had poured more into it.

'I've never heard a truer word. I'm not what you call a practising Christian, Wills, but the church I'd like to meet is up there, made of cliffs and ravines and waterfalls and trees. I have some of my best Thoughts in some mountain kloof, when I'm alone with the Alone.' (He had forgotten that I'd already heard all this mystical claptrap.) After a melancholy pause: 'What time is it, Wills?'

I informed him that it was a quarter past six.

'You'll have noticed that the sun has already set on this side of the mountain. People told me I was crazy to build my house in the mountain's shadow, but I like the shade, Wills, I like the shade.' He shifted his great mass in the chair. 'If we were in Cape Town itself we'd be sitting in bright sunlight, watching the sun still quite high above the ocean's horizon. Magnificent sunsets you get there. Pinks, oranges. All reflected in the sea. Pity you haven't got time to see them.'

'This is indeed a land of extraordinary beauty,' I murmured.

'And all the more beautiful for being British, Wills. And the whole of Southern Africa could be beautified in the same way: a united South Africa under the Crown, through peace and gold. Now I fear it will be federation through *blood* and gold.'

I remembered Milner's words and said: 'Once you have Africa, what of other continents?'

He was ready enough to reply, though his voice slurred a little. 'I would recover America if I could – just think, if we had retained America there would be millions more English living. Yes, I would procure the Holy Land – China – Japan

. . .' He threw out his arms at the darkening sky. 'Why, man, I would annex the planets if I could!'

He flung his head backwards so that it rested on the upper rim of the chair, and fell silent. A cricket in the garden struck up a dissonant counterpoint with the cicada. I myself had no inclination to speak. Minutes must have passed. When he spoke again his voice was calm.

'See that pine up there, Wills? The solitary one. Apart from all the others.'

A very fine, exceptionally tall specimen of Corsican Pine stood alone behind the Dutch-styled gardens, separated from the forest that darkened the lower slopes. 'I wonder how that happened,' I mused politely. 'Was it a gardener's decision, or a careless act of nature?'

He ignored this contribution and drew on his foul-smelling cigarette. 'A few years back a Dutch Member of Parliament and I were sitting on that old Chesterfield back there, admiring the view. In those days I had many Dutch friends, strange as it might seem now.' His voice quavered in the upper registers, but a gulp at his glass steadied him. 'Suddenly the Dutchman turned to me and said, "Do you know, *Meneer*, who that tree reminds me of?" I replied in the negative. He laughed and said, "*Meneer*, it reminds me of you!" It was my turn to laugh. "I don't follow. Why do you compare me to a tree?" He then said: "Because it stands out by itself; and do you not stand out by yourself in comparison with other men?"'

Privately, I wondered what the Dutchman wanted from my host – free scab disinfectant for his constituents' sheep, or something like – but I allowed my vocal cords to release a non-committal grunt which could have been interpreted as admiring agreement. However, he was not interested in my response and continued with his somewhat immodest ruminations.

'I could have met an ocean, if I'd wanted to.' His voice floated up softly between the columns. 'Many men of my stature like to gaze upon a vast sweep of ocean. I could have built a seaside mansion like the others. But I prefer to pour my money back into Africa, into my railway. My railway is like a spine, a backbone, pushing its way up through the African hinterland right now, through the swamps, round the great lakes, soon to reach the deserts. Yes, I like that image – I'm giving the continent backbone, Wills. But what were we speaking of? Houses by the sea. Today we visited the little hut I've bought in Muizenberg. I can breathe there. The sea air clears my lungs. Sometimes I fancy I might die there, Wills, on the rim of the Atlantic Ocean.'

'Let us not speak of death,' said I, for want of any other reply.

'Do you know how long they gave me to live when I was twenty?' he demanded.

'I've no idea.'

'Six months. Six months, would you believe. And that was – how long? – nearly thirty years ago.' He snorted derisively. 'But the big question is: how long d'ye think they'll remember me after I've died? Ten years? Fifty? A hundred? A thousand? I would reckon a thousand. That's the only thing that makes the thought of early death endurable – that what I've done will live on long after me.'

'Your achievements must make you very happy,' I said uncomfortably.

He pulled his gaze from the mountain to turn the full force of his ravaged face upon me. 'Happy? I, happy? When there is still so much to be done?' He lifted an arm as if it were made of lead. 'Look at this pulse of mine, Wills.'

He rolled back his cuff and thrust his inside wrist beneath my nose. 'Just look at it jumping!' And indeed I could see a great blue knot in his wrist throbbing at a highly irregular

rate. I fingered my own pulse and began counting in private
while he said: 'That's my heart, Wills. It's letting me down.
So I'm relying on your nightingales. The day after tomorrow
they'll be released. A great flock of British birds, ready to
breed on an African mountain. It does me good just to think
about it.' He inhaled deeply on the stub of his cigarette.
'But leave that aside for the moment. I've called you here
to thank you personally for your quick thinking last night.
Don't suppose Challenger really meant to shoot anyone – a
little the worse for Cognac, and felt he had to make a show,
you know, since losing the arm. I expect those psychology
chappies from Vienna think they could explain it all to us –
lot of nonsense, really. Anyway, thanks, old chap!' He raised
his glass and presented me with one of those elastic smiles
which contract into melancholy a moment later.

He fell silent as he attended to the lighting and inhaling
of his tobacco. A light breeze had sprung up, making such
tasks more difficult. I sipped my whisky and enjoyed the
warm glow in my head. The entire garden was humming
with cicadas.

'Your friend. His case interests me a great deal.'

'My friend? Oh, you mean Oscar?'

Oscar. The word flew out of the back of my throat and
hung like a bat between the colonnade columns, stretching
and folding its wings. Stretch and fold. *Oscar.* It occurred to
me that no other English word filled the mouth so completely.
My own name was a mere twitch of the lips by comparison.

He exhaled a dense cloud of tobacco smoke. 'Above all,
one must stand by one's friends, Wills. That is my first rule
in life. I think I said this to you yesterday.' The silence that
followed was so lengthy I thought he had finished with this
topic. Just as I was searching for an excuse to take my leave,
he heaved a great sigh and started again. 'I am a man to whom
friendship means a great deal. Almost as much as my railway.

I've seen pictures of Lord Alfred Douglas, Wilde's – friend . . . He bears an uncanny resemblance to a close friend of mine – who died many years ago now. When he died I thought I would never recover. I suppose you could say I still grieve for him. Another drink, Wills?'

'No thank you. Well, perhaps, yes. May I recharge your glass?'

We resettled. I could feel every muscle in my body slacken and grow warm. Never had I drunk so much whisky in one sitting – and on an empty stomach at that.

'He was a sunny-tempered kind of chap. Charming. Gregarious. Everyone loved him, including the ladies. He made me laugh. He had cheek. Do you know what he gave me, Wills? He gave me *youth*! I made him my chief clerk of the mining company. I lived with him in a shack in Kimberley not much bigger than a native's hut. And not much better equipped. Material things have never meant much to me. Friendship means far, far more.' These observations caused him to ruminate privately once again, with many a sigh and grunt. I felt compelled to remind him of my presence.

'Would this have been before you came to Oxford, or after?'

Without moving his head to acknowledge my question, he appeared to address the mountain, or a star which flashed above it before the sun had fully set. 'After. I'd made my fortune, after a fashion, in diamonds. Then gold was discovered up on the Witwatersrand. Beginning of all the trouble. I was up there inspecting the prospects, about to buy a block of claims, when news came that he was dying. I dropped everything to be at his side. I've often thought, if I hadn't done that, I could have been the richest man in the world. But all I could think of was, *how am I going to go on living when he's gone?*'

The rocky texture of the mountain had softened in the

evening gloom. A purple mist melted the sharp edges where grey cliff plummeted into green ravine. The breeze was persistent. Dead leaves scuttled about. I might have grown cold had not my body been hot with whisky.

'His death was so unnecessary. He'd fallen off a horse and landed on a thorn bush two years earlier. Those damned thorns had poisoned his system, his bones, in some way, and eventually they killed him. At his funeral I wept like a woman. I wanted to die myself – jump into his grave, that sort of thing. It was a bad time.'

The violet sky was suddenly pierced with alien stars. I found myself searching for the Southern Cross.

'Jameson saved me,' said the Colossus. 'He pulled me up from the abyss. He gave me back my life. Wonderful doctor, actually. Wonderful friend too. Everyone loves him. We call him JimJam. Silly name, I know, but it's a mark of our affection.' His queer soprano voice trembled. 'I like to think now, in these troubled days, that I have given him back his life.'

'He has much to be grateful for,' I said guardedly.

'Friendship, Wills, friendship and loyalty. These are the chief emotions, in my book. And gratitude. He went in without my authority, Wills, but I'd placed him on the Transvaal border in readiness.'

'He meant well.'

'Some show of strength was necessary. It still is, God help us all. There are more Britons in Johannesburg than there are Boer men and women in the whole of the Boer Republic; they're responsible for nine-tenths of the wealth in the land – but they're not allowed to vote. Pity you don't play bridge, Wills.'

'I need an early night. I wish I had your energy.'

'Your friend. Where is he now?'

'He's somewhere in the north of France.'

'I hear he is a bankrupt.'

'His financial state is not good. He has become dependent on hand-outs.'

'That so?' I could see a light kindling in the Colossus' damp eyes. 'I have a certain sympathy with the chap, though in many ways he is a loafer of the very worst kind. Tell you what, Wills.'

'Yes?' I could almost hear the thought processes whirring in that great, untidy head.

'I'd be happy to send him a few hundred – anonymously, of course. Would he accept it, d'ye think?'

'There would be no question of that,' I smiled.

At this point Huxley appeared, looking animated. 'Mr Selous is here, sir,' he announced, not even trying to keep the awe out of his voice.

'Selous!' I exclaimed, for a foolish moment thinking he meant the ornithologist.

My host smiled. 'Yes, he works for me now – has done for the last ten years or so – up in what used to be called Mashonaland. He helped me gain the land for Her Majesty's Empire. Come to think of it, I nearly employed his brother to bring the songbirds out. But the brother wouldn't hear of it. Bit of a hermit by all accounts. You bird people are a funny, nervous lot . . . ah, Selous! Good to see you!'

The man who strode down the verandah had not changed much from the personage I had seen in that candle-lit club nearly fifteen years ago. A slightly receding hairline and a grey beard were all that pointed to the passing of time, but his step had retained its spring and his figure was that of a young man's. He showed little interest in me when introduced, until I said, perhaps in a spirit of pique, and strengthened by whisky: 'I once attended a talk you gave many years ago.'

'And where would that have been?' His teeth flashed ivory against his sunburnt skin.

'A little club off Regent Street. Doorkeeper by the name of Lizzie. You were telling a group of gentlemen about your exploits.'

Selous glanced at the Colossus, who was stubbing out a difficult cigarette.

'My dear chap, I fear you've made a mistake. I've never spoken in a little club off Regent Street – you're confusing me with someone else.' He turned away.

I smiled. 'Perhaps.'

After bidding good evening to the two gentlemen I finally rose from my chair. My knees were weakened by alcohol: I felt I was stepping into dark, open pits as I made my way across the chequered floor of the verandah. But as I opened the door which led back into the house, my host turned his head and called out: 'See one of my secretaries about writing a cheque for that charity we were talking about. Make it five hundred.'

'It will be much appreciated.'

If it is not too late.

GREAT GRANARY 1899

At night, the mountain withdraws its power over this house. During the day the hybrid architecture, the settler furniture cheek by rough jowl with Louis-Quinze, the gloomy panelling, flags, maps and Zimbabwe birds are somehow yoked together by the great sandstone mass that heaves itself out of the Great Granary gardens: when the sun sets, the house loses impetus. It becomes a museum, a collection of items and styles. It is a house on show.

I remember seeing one of those Perspective Boxes made by the Dutchman van Hoogstraten which were all the rage a couple of centuries ago: one peered through a peephole into a model of a typical Dutch house and saw within it all manner of three-dimensional objects: coats hanging from hooks, cat before fire, corridors leading off to other rooms. But when one gazed with both eyes through a glass window at the back of the box, one saw that all these signs of habitation existed only in two dimensions, being painted with cunning perspective half on to the walls, half on to the floor, and at carefully calculated angles. So does everything in this Great Granary present itself as authentic, but in truth lacks a vital dimension.

Nowhere is this more true than in the bedroom of the Colossus. The great bay window now opens out on to nothing but darkness. The photographs and flags on the walls could be hanging in a schoolroom or a museum. Gone is his private church with its cliffs and kloofs. It occurs to me that my host was at his happiest living in a shack in Kimberley with his beloved. I stare at the before-and-after pictures of Colesburg Kopje and think of Miss Schreiner, who has sent me hither. Downstairs the Colossus entertains a miscellany of people: I hear the shrill mew of his laugh rise above the babble of conversation and the clatter of dishes. It seems safe to have turned on the electric lights.

As I stretch my hand out to touch the frame of the paired pictures, I realise I am still slightly drunk after my earlier interview with my host. The euphoria attendant upon alcohol still hovers in my head and makes me fearless. I flick open the frame. There is the safe, with its combination lock encircled with numbers. I close my eyes and open up that part of my memory which holds sounds. Outside, the insects are screaming out a torrent of sound which interferes with the rhythm I am trying to revive in my head. Click clickety click click. It is the sound of my father's safety lock which I hear first, a succession of minute clicks which returns to me now and then in my dreams and causes me to awaken drenched in icy sweat and retching horribly.

I feel the chill of my father's presence in this room and even look around.

My hand holds the lock with infinite tenderness. My wrist seems scarcely to move as I turn it clockwise: *click click*. It does not matter what the numbers are: it is the pitch and spacing of the sounds which I need to recreate. And then anti-clockwise: *cleck cleck cleck*.

I feel yet the presence of my father in this room. I cannot banish him, for he now exists outside my thought processes.

Before making the final infinitesimal clockwise rotation of my wrist, I hold my breath and listen for sounds in the corridor. I have of course taken the precaution of closing the Colossus' door, in the unlikely event that someone will come upstairs during the meal. Nothing stirs outside the bedroom door, though outside the window the air is thick with the groans and ululations of insects, frogs and night-birds.

With the final click of the safety lock, the door swings open as I know it will. The egg, the pistol and the nightingale are lined up at the front of the safe. Behind, as before, the shapes of the Zimbabwe phallic memorabilia and four bundles of papers, tied with thin ribbon, are dimly discernible.

I feel a sudden interest in the contents of these bundles. (My father is watching over my shoulder, equally interested.) I extend my hand into the jaws of the safe and withdraw the first packet.

It contains love letters of a somewhat florid nature. At first I think they might be from Miss Schreiner herself, improbable as it is that the Colossus would hoard such missives, but a glance at the diminutised name at the end of the letters soon gives me reason to believe that they were written a long time ago by a male hand. My curiosity having been satisfied on this account, I feel no interest as to the contents of the letters, not being of a voyeuristic disposition – as far as other men's affairs are concerned, at any rate.

The second, thicker, bundle contains yellowing letters that date back some thirty years. The Colossus' mother appears to have written to him every week after his departure for South Africa in 1870, to join one of his brothers on a cotton farm in Natal. I read quickly through the first letter, full of maternal solicitude for his poor health, and outrage that his brother had not been at the quayside to meet him. 'Herbert has no right to go diamond hunting when his young brother (you may think that seventeen years is an advanced age, but a loving mother knows better) arrives alone in a wild and foreign land. No matter that a neighbour welcomes you in his stead: I have written to Herbert to express my displeasure.' And so on. 'I do not like the sound of your Kaffirs. Can it really be true that they carry their snuff boxes in a hole bored through their ears? You complain about their smell: has no one introduced them to the expedient of soap and hot water?'

The mother's letters continue for some three years, responding in anxious detail to her son's move from cotton to diamonds, and describing the minutiae of life at the vicarage: my own mother could have learnt much from her exemplary behaviour towards the poor and needy among the parishioners (I hear a sigh from the dead vicar at my shoulder). The last letter, written in a weaker hand, implores him not to return to England on her account: 'My attack was nothing like as bad as you have been told. You are in the middle of your ice-making and water-pumping schemes: pray do not abandon these for your mother who has many years of health in her yet.' The ink is a little smudged, whether by a false move of the hand or a small spillage of liquid, it is impossible to tell.

Having flicked through this bundle, I pause again to take stock of the sounds outside the bedroom door. The murmur from below has not changed in volume or intensity; I hear no servants creeping about. I am now curiously relaxed, even though my father's presence lingers on: it is a benign presence; perhaps it will melt away before long. In any case, I now feel resigned to the flow of fate, as I recognise that logical sequence plays no part in this inverted world.

The third bundle consists of a series of wills. The Colossus wrote his first will at the age of nineteen, to judge by the date at the foot of the document. In it he left all his worldly goods to the British Secretary of State for the Colonies, to be used for no less grand a project than the recivilisation of the earth through the extension of the Empire. I find my eyebrows – and my father's – have risen a little.

The second will, written in Oxford a few years later, had even loftier ambitions and included a Confession of Faith. The young Colossus proposed the formation of a secret society to bring the whole uncivilised world under British rule: 'Africa is still lying ready for us it is our duty to take it.' (His Oxford education seems to have failed in the matter of colons or full stops.) He wished the United States to be recovered and filled with proud Englishmen instead of low-class Irish and German emigrants. In fact, most of the world was to be conquered by this secret society: the Holy Land, the valley of the Euphrates, the islands of Cyprus and Crete, the whole of South America, the islands of the Pacific, the whole of the Malay Archipelago, the seaboard of China and Japan. (His ambitions clearly have not diminished with time.)

In the next will, drawn up some ten years later, the plans for the secret society are spelt out in greater detail. The Colossus' entire fortune is to be used to establish this secret group which must be organised along the lines of the Jesuit constitution. The purpose of the society is the same as before: to extend the British Empire across the length and breadth of the entire planet, with great men working in high places, bonded together by their clandestine membership.

I can hear footsteps mounting the stairs that lead to the landing. The footsteps are buoyant, and trip up the stairs two at a time. The Colossus' bedroom is some distance from the landing: there are corridors and fire doors that have to be negotiated. I turn off the bedroom light and use my torch to examine the remainder of the bundle.

There are four more wills. They concern the education of young male colonials and the establishment of a scholarship scheme whereby these young men would be sent to the

University of Oxford 'for the instilling into their minds the advantages to the colonies as well as to England of the retention of the Unity of Empire'. The successful young colonists must be moderately fond of manly field-sports like cricket or football. Under no circumstances are they to be 'bookworms'. The proportions attained by the ideal candidate should be four-tenths scholarship, two-tenths athletics, two-tenths chivalry, manhood et cetera, two-tenths leadership. These young men will be groomed at Oxford in order to rule the earth. My father expresses surprise by whistling through his teeth.

The footsteps, light as a gazelle's, have not faded into the corridor as I thought they would, but patter purposefully towards the room in which I stand. I withdraw the final bundle, glance at its contents (which are brief but unambiguous), close the safe door, replace Colesburg Kopje, and move over to the bay window just as the door opens and electric light floods the room.

Enter Dr Jameson, chortling. My father's ghost flees.

Dr Jim does not at first appear to notice me. He bounds into the room, like a young secretary, and heads straight for the Colossus' bed. Still chuckling, he scrabbles for a minute among the bottles of pills and phials of medicine – I begin to wonder if the Colossus has suffered some form of heart attack which the Doctor can arrest with medication – but it is a book he finally snatches from the bedside paraphernalia. He turns over pages rapidly, finds what he is looking for, laughs aloud, and snaps the book shut. 'Good evening, Wills,' he says, without bothering to establish eye contact. 'I'm pleased to tell you I have just won five pounds. Thanks to my friend, Conan Doyle.'

'He has joined the party?' I am sufficiently curious to condescend to a response, and regret it immediately.

'Oh no, old chap, Sir Arthur's scribbling away in Southsea at this very minute, I should imagine. No, no – the company at table have been arguing about a detail from *The Adventures of the Noble Bachelor*.' Dr Jim is enjoying himself, and not only at my discomfiture. 'Do you know it?'

I shake my head: an impatient quiver, such as I give visitors to Oxford who ask me for directions.

In return, Dr Jim favours me with his brilliant triangular smile. 'We were trying to remember the name of the hotel Holmes visits, you know, when he comes upon the bill that had been settled at one of the most select London hotels – eight shillings for a bed, eightpence for a glass of sherry, that sort of thing. Because these prices tally exactly with the ones Our Host knows, he was – is – convinced the hotel was the *Burlington*. He always stays there when he's in London. Always. I felt fairly certain the name of the hotel was never mentioned in Conan Doyle's story. I find I was right. I am now five pounds the richer!' He withdraws his silver cigarette case from a pocket and lights a slender cigarillo. 'I seem to remember you do not smoke?'

'My congratulations on both scores.'

The Doctor blows out a series of impressive smoke rings, then regards me with an amused light in his eye. 'Well now, Professor,' he smiles, 'this is an interesting challenge for me, is it not? I wonder if I can use the skills taught by Dr Bell and performed so miraculously by Mr Holmes. In other words, can I deduce what brings you to my friend's bedroom? I would not be so brash as to suspect you have come here simply to steal money or precious objects, as I understand you have little interest in acquisitions. I would wager you have come here to pry: there is a prying air about you. Now what can it be that you are hoping to find?'

He is walking towards me, smoke trailing from the cigarillo clamped between his lips. I breathe in its spicy aroma, and am transported to the Senior Common Room. I feel no nostalgia, only a sudden yearning for good Madeira.

I am not afraid of the Doctor. He is not a malevolent man. He is a man of action, without guile. To look into his clear brown eyes, tainted as they are by suffering, is to see a man anxious to shorten the distance between cause and effect; in other words, a simple, impatient man. When I make contact with the moist orbs of the Colossus I feel I slither through spirals of cunning that no man, except perhaps the one before me now, can ever truly penetrate.

I am nearly a head taller than Dr Jameson. I look down at his upturned face and say quietly: 'Evidence.'

'Evidence.' He repeats the word exactly as I have said it. Then frowns. 'Evidence of what?'

I decide to be playful. 'Evidence of Britain's guilty conscience, what else?'

Something is happening to the perfect symmetry of Jameson's face. His left cheek begins to sag, as if made of hot, melting wax. The lid of his left eye inexplicably droops, while the right eye and brow now seem to be slanting upwards. His moustache is at an angle. His teeth bite into his lower lip. I am watching a face disintegrate before my very eyes, as they say.

I wait.

Now his stricken features gather themselves together as an explanation dawns. There is even a glint of admiration in his eyes as he speaks.

'Are you some kind of agent then? I might have guessed.'

The idea is so preposterous that I give a wan smile. His face reddens.

'Guilty conscience!' he blurts out, then slumps on to an upright mahogany chair laced with leather thongs. 'I could tell you a thing or two about guilty conscience!' He is biting the nail of his left thumb. 'And betrayal,' he adds, his thumb still in his mouth.

I realise, from the strong waft of alcohol that is released by these movements, that he is probably very drunk. I sit in the Colossus' great chair behind his desk, and prepare myself.

Jameson is chewing his thumb, his face haggard once again. He is a man of honour, fighting temptation. I help him.

'It is not always possible to be consistent in friendship,' I say, fiddling with a paper-knife.

'You can say that again!' Jameson mumbles. 'One minute he's the closest friend a man ever had, the next –'

This room has become the centre of the universe. A multitude of sounds vibrate around it: the febrile cries of insects, the hum of post-prandial discourse, and a new sound: the wind. The breeze which played among the columns of the back verandah earlier today has, even while I have been in this room, gained in momentum. Now it gusts against the window panes, whistles under the door. The pine trees sing like musical instruments. The mountain, riddled with caves, gives forth a booming sound.

But in here it is as still as the cramped confessional box inside a vast Gothic cathedral where the hurricane of human life roars and clanks, waiting to relieve itself of sin.

'Do you know,' says Jameson, 'that the day I landed in Pretoria gaol he sent Joubert up to tell me to shoulder the blame for the whole fiasco.' He looks at me with imploring eyes. 'He was going to abandon me utterly. Only when he conceded there was no way of disguising the full extent of his own involvement did he change his tune.' He pauses. 'I told him I never wanted to see him again. Simple as that.'

'But there was no rising in Johannesburg,' I murmur. 'No women and children for you to rescue.'

'*Judasburg*, you mean!' The anger in his voice makes him jump out of his chair. His cigarillo, now a mere stump, is still planted between his lips as he hurries across the room.

He bends over the amputated elephant's foot next to the Colossus' bed. The foot has opened to reveal a range of monogrammed glasses and decanters. 'Cognac?'

'Is there Madeira?'

'There's anything you like.'

His hand shakes as he pours first amber and then golden liquid into the crystal glasses. He hands me the golden glass, and stands before me, holding the amber goblet. Something of the devil-may-care flits across his face as he proposes: 'To all guilty consciences, everywhere!' I smile and nod and sip my Madeira.

'Cowards, the lot of them.' He has returned to his leather-thonged chair, and lights another cigarillo. He perches half on, half off the chair: I fear he may fall off its well-polished edge. For a few moments he chews at the upper joint of his thumb. Then the words pour from him, as if they have been memorised. 'I had written evidence they would rise: my band of men was to rescue the women and children. Good God, man, their appeal for help was published in *The Times*, what further proof do people want?' He drinks sharply from his glass and flings his legs out. 'Then they go and change their minds. Two men on bicycles ride up as we approach Judasburg and say the Reform Committee's compromised with the Boers – but they're looking forward to having a drink with my men and myself!' He snorts. 'An expensive way of sharing a glass, you might say!' He stares at his feet, his features twitching and sliding about as a range of emotions takes over. Without raising his gaze to meet mine, he murmurs: 'Of course, there is one person to whom I feel nothing but gratitude. Without his intervention I'd most likely still be in Holloway, or hanging from some primitive Boer gallows . . .' He heaves a mighty sigh and falls silent. After waiting a sufficient length of time, I enquire as to the identity of his saviour.

In a rush he lifts his face, which is distorted by a smile of the deepest cynicism. 'None less than our good Queen's grandson, Kaiser Willie! His telegram to the old Boer congratulating him on the preservation of his independence did the trick for me all right. The idea of Germany staking a claim in the Golden City and indirectly offering military aid to the beastly Boers was too much for British pride. National shame became national outrage. Suddenly I became St George, shining armour and all, defending British honour against the Hun. I owe much to Kaiser Wilhelm!' He leaps to his feet, clicks his heels, and lifts his glass: 'To the Kaiser!'

I smile tolerantly. 'There is no doubt you are regarded as a great hero in England.'

'I don't give a fig how I'm regarded. I've told you – the whole affair's an embarrassment to me. You may find that difficult to believe – I can see you think I'm a cocky little chap, and in an honest moment I'd admit the truth of that – but to be a hero because of a Kaiser's telegram is no hero at all, I can assure you.' He flings himself back into his chair, crosses his legs daintily, calms down.

And puffs out his chest. 'Yet the strange thing is, even our Boer captors treated us like heroes – challenged us to a shooting competition en route for Pretoria – the best Boer marksmen against the best British shots. The Boers won. Spent their lives shooting from horseback, you see, got a different concept of war altogether, no formal marching, uniforms, all that sort of thing. We were fighting against puffs of smoke. Nice chaps, really. Considerate. Considering . . .' He swallows the remains of his Cognac. 'We never had a chance. There's a line of poetry could have been written for us: '*Into the valley of death rode the six hundred.*' That was us. If you count the Coloured boys who looked after the spare horses. A regiment of six hundred against the entire Boer army! Ah, well, there it is!' He looks into his empty glass, puzzled.

Now darker thoughts cross his mind. He has not noticed that his cigarillo has died. 'Chamberlain himself came to see me in Holloway. Incognito. All very hush-hush. Didn't even wear his monocle. Told me to keep my mouth well and truly shut about who knew what, and to go along with whatever came out in the Inquiry. In a bit of a funk, you might say. Tried to suggest that I had ruined his career, so I'd better make up for it by toeing the line. I could tell he both knew and didn't know the Raid was going to happen. Left hand didn't know what right hand was doing. We think these politicians consider everything with perfect clarity, know all the facts, remember everything that's said to them. Absolute bunkum! They're as muddle-headed as the rest of us!' He grunts, and sips at his drink. 'I was too ill to argue – gallstones, y'know – they released me early.' He lapses into silence. The wind hurls its shoulder against the window panes. A tile flies off the roof and shatters on the ground. The insects have ceased their song.

'And do you know, in all the months I was in Holloway, the man who calls himself my closest friend never visited me once. I languished in gaol while he stayed at the Burlington and played his games in Westminster.' Jameson's thumb has returned to his mouth. He gnaws at it as he continues: 'Yet the strange thing is, I forgave him. I'd thrown my whole life away for him, what's the point in stopping now, that's how I thought. Greater love hath no man, and all that.'

He wrenches his hand away and stares at me full in the face. His eyes have doubled in size. He blinks away the liquid which fills them: the tears slide wetly down his cheeks into his moustache. He withdraws a handkerchief from a trouser pocket and blows his nose. 'Sorry about the outburst, old chap,' he snuffles, his nose still in the handkerchief. 'I don't know why I'm telling you all this. Not like me to blubber.'

I can hear someone coming up the stairs. Jameson can as

well. He gives a final trumpet into his horribly crumpled kerchief, and stuffs it into a pocket. He cannot stop talking. 'The worst of it is that history will blame me for single-handedly precipitating an unnecessary war, right at the end of the century, at that.' He shakes his head in astonishment. 'I don't want Britain to go to war, Wills. The Raid was meant to prevent war, not cause it. Simple as that.'

He stands up, walks unsteadily, but neatly, towards me. 'Come on, old boy, hand it over.'

I am staring into the barrel of his mother-of-pearl pistol. Jameson does not apologise.

I have led a sheltered life. I live in the most sheltered spot on earth. My skin is pale and soft, almost like a woman's.

Yet I find it exhilarating to have a gun pointed at my brains for the second time in twenty-four hours. I am not afraid. My knees do not tremble. Instead I experience a kind of joy as my smothered life, oxygenated by the prospect of death, bursts into wild blooms.

'And don't start whistling like a bird, either,' says Jameson, misreading my radiant smile. 'Or I'll pull the trigger.'

The footsteps have stopped outside the door. Three raps upon it remind me inexplicably of the opening bars of *The Magic Flute* and all the Freemasonry that permeates both that opera and this house. I say, in an undertone: 'In my breast pocket I have the eight missing telegrams which were not produced at the Inquiry. They indisputably prove Joseph Chamberlain's support and encouragement of your Incursion. If they are published now, the Colonial Secretary will be reviled as a blatant liar and your name will be forever cleared. More than that. If Britain's guilty secrets are bared to the public, an Anglo-Boer war would become impossible. You would not have to live with the knowledge that your reckless ride across the border had directly caused a catastrophic war.'

Jameson slowly returns his pistol to the handkerchief in his pocket. His eyes bulge. 'Come in!' he calls out cheerfully.

ENGLAND 1895

Mr James had died suddenly: Elspeth telephoned to my college with the news, and a few days later I made my way to Battersea to attend the funeral. Having important work in the laboratory to see to in the morning, I caught the 1 p.m. train from Oxford, and, after changing at Reading, found myself on a platform of Clapham Junction.

My thoughts were melancholy. I had loved my guardian, perhaps not quite as boys should love their fathers, but with an amused admiration. His devotion to Ruskinian ideals had increased with time: as a member of the Utopian St George's Guild he argued for the redistribution of wealth, the establishment of smokeless zones, and an end to modern warfare, among other things. Elspeth had supported him in these endeavours, becoming ever more buxom as her interest in cookery grew (she made cakes for Ruskin's teashop in Marylebone, which sold tea in small packets for the poorest customers): she planned to write a revolutionary vegetarian recipe book as a direct challenge to Mrs Beeton's tome which encouraged the daily consumption of red meat and food cooked in lard. That she could not have children was her greatest regret, but this meant that both Mr James and I received from her ever more solicitous attention. I felt apprehensive of her state of mind, now that she was deprived of her invalid husband.

The day was exceptionally bleak. February is the most dismal month in Britain, and as I gazed out of the carriage window at the frozen fields between Oxford and Reading, I could see nothing of beauty which might lighten the gloom. It occurred to me that my guardian had died exactly twenty-five years to the day after the inaugural lecture at the Sheldonian Theatre, which he considered to have exerted such a profound influence over his life. To my shame, this had been the last time we had gone out together to a public function, for once I had gone up to Oxford to read Ornithology I had found myself increasingly absorbed, if not ingested, by the University, and thus reluctant to leave its safe environs. Because I visited their Battersea home so seldom, Mr James and Elspeth (I never could think of her as Mrs James) had made monthly visits by train to see me in my rooms, Elspeth always bringing some delicious edible item which at the same time contrived to be conducive to my health. Over the twenty-five years, as I grew more reclusive, their visits had been almost my only contact with a society that was not directly connected with my experimental work.

I say 'almost' as there was one other person whom I allowed into my rooms, with great joy, whenever he visited his Alma Mater. Though his life lay in London, Oscar regularly returned to his circle of friends in Oxford – more especially after his fateful meeting with Lord Alfred Douglas. (This beautiful and unmanageable creature spent four fruitless years at Magdalen.) Oscar made it his business – I will not say 'duty' – to spend no less than half an hour with me at some stage of his visits, crammed as they were with exotic dinner parties and social events of a demanding nature. In the safe and shadowy confines of my bachelor rooms he would collapse into my most comfortable armchair and rest. With me alone was he able to speak simply, without recourse to the glittering aphorisms that were endlessly expected of him, and in plain language, all the more moving for its lack of ornament, would he express to me the very depths of his feelings and heights of his aspirations. This was not the Oscar Wilde known to the rest of the world: the secrets of his heart which he shared with me were imparted to no other man or woman, and they will go with me to the grave. For I was his 'cousin', by however devious a route, and into the vessel of his cousin's heart could he pour his pain, knowing that no word of what he said would ever escape from that fail-safe receptacle. In his presence I too was able to express the anxieties of academic life which I so assiduously hid from my colleagues, who believed I had succeeded in excising the entire range of emotions experienced by all other human beings.

The last time I saw Oscar before his arrest, he had found it impossible to remain seated in the comfortable chair, so great was his agitation. I knew only too well of the details of his sublime love for Alfred Douglas, a love which had long ago transcended the physical, but I recognised also the symptoms of self-surrender, where a man has handed over his life entirely to the loved one, as if in a hypnotic trance. Why else would he pursue this pointless libel case, other than to obey the loved one's wishes: to collude with the son's ravenous craving to destroy his father? I knew of Oscar's illegal meetings with boys in hotel bedrooms: his '*feasting with panthers*'. I feared that these episodes would be revealed at the trial: Oscar declared there was no means of establishing they had happened. I remember him so clearly now, standing at my study window, staring into the geometry of white roses and yew hedges of the Fellows' Garden, and remarking: 'Do you remember, Francis, that morning twenty years ago when we strolled round Magdalen's narrow bird-haunted walks, do you remember I told you that I wanted to eat of the fruit of all the world and that I was going out into the world with that passion in my soul?'

I replied that I did, and that the walk in question had occurred during the week that the meadow was purple with snake's head fritillary.

Oscar looked at me affectionately. His face had indeed grown unpleasantly fleshy ('a great white caterpillar', a mutual friend of ours had fondly called him), but his smile was as sweet and as heart-warming as ever, in spite of the blackened, protruding teeth. 'Ah, the fritillaries, coz: we never did resolve our argument. I declared that they were native to Magdalen, but you insisted that some incumbent from Ducklington had transplanted the bulbs a mere hundred years ago. I cannot bring myself to believe that the fritillaries of Magdalen Meadow have not waved their purple shawls for as long as Magdalen itself has stood: surely they cannot be colonists from a village near Witney!' His smile suffused his teasing words.

'I can still only say that the Ducklington fritillaries are entirely indigenous. I cannot say that with certainty about the Magdalen colony.'

Oscar grew nostalgic. 'I once made a buttonhole of lilac and mulberry fritillary bells in the spring – the only flower I know which Nature has imbued with checks. I considered ordering an entire suit of the fritillary pattern to be woven in tweed, to go with it. Instead I wore it with that very loud yellow-and-black chequered jacket, do you remember?'

'You were wearing it when I first met you. In the Botanic Gardens' greenhouse. You attracted the butterflies.'

'And you were dropping insects into the green jaws of carnivorous plants. I watched them writhe in the plants' transparent stomachs. You told me that the Venus's flytrap could count to three. Or was it two?'

'What are you going to do about this trial, Oscar? I fear you have been ill-advised.'

He turned back to the window. 'At first I confined myself exclusively to the trees of what seemed to me the sunlit side of the garden, and shunned the other side for its shadow and its gloom. I was determined to know nothing of failure, disgrace, sorrow, despair; remorse that makes one walk on thorns, anguish that chooses sackcloth for its raiment. And now I am forced to taste each of them in turn.'

'Do I detect the influence of Rome? You would not suit sackcloth, Oscar.'

He ignored my feeble jibe. His voice was caterpillar soft. 'You know that I have deliberately gone to the very depths in the search for new sensation. Will you ever understand how desire can become a malady, or a madness, or both? I grew careless of the lives of others. I took pleasure where it pleased me, and passed on. I forgot that every little action of the common day makes or unmakes character, and that therefore what one has done in the secret chamber one has some day to cry aloud on the housetop.'

'No, no, you are wrong!' I interrupted. 'We would not hear ourselves speak if everyone shouted their secret sins from the housetops! Think again, Oscar, for all our sakes!'

He gathered his hat, stick, coat. 'Goodbye, dear coz. I will keep you informed of my sojourn in the outer rings of hell.'

I was to see him only once more.

GREAT GRANARY 1899

Huxley's face is hewn from concrete, but tonight it has assumed the elasticity of animal flesh. He cannot prevent himself from smiling, the demand upon unused muscles causing the layers of brick and cement in his cheeks to crumble dangerously.

'The Princess!' he cries out in a voice distorted by repressed hysteria. 'They've caught her at it!'

'At what?' Jameson frowns, and cocks his head.

'Lighting the fires, sir! In the forests. The master thought you'd best know. She's downstairs, sir, in a sorry mess.'

'That woman!' exclaims Jameson angrily. 'She's been hounding him for years. He's obviously not going to marry her – so this is her revenge. Hell hath no fury, and all that!'

'Does she wear a great deal of jewellery and perfume?' I enquire.

Jameson pulls a face. 'I should think so! Some of these foreign women dress up no better than gypsies, if you ask me. But I'd better go down. Perhaps we can continue our discussion some other time. Goodnight, Wills.'

CLAPHAM JUNCTION 1895

On alighting from the train at Clapham I became aware that a disturbance of some kind was causing a crowd to gather on the opposite platform. This communicated itself to the passengers on my train who were continuing to Waterloo: they pulled down the windows and, hanging out of them, some two or three to a window, became extremely animated, whistling and catcalling and shouting out terms of Cockney abuse. My curiosity thus aroused, I waited for the train to pull out from the platform in order to see for myself the cause of this merriment. So densely packed had the Waterloo–Reading platform become that it was at first quite impossible to discover what irresistible incident or personage lay within the ranks of the onlookers. My dignity, of course, would not permit me to cross the railway bridge in order to jostle with the multitude, and finally I concluded that some sort of side-show from a visiting fair must be delivering an impromptu performance for the diversion of fellow travellers. A number of passengers who had disembarked at Clapham with me now also lingered, tantalised by the spectacle across the railway lines. I was about to leave my platform and locate my connection for Battersea when the crowds on the opposite platform suddenly parted, revealing the source of their entertainment.

Whoever has decreed that a few seconds is a short space of time has not stood in the rain on a railway platform and discovered upon it his closest friend in handcuffs.

At first I thought I saw only an unkempt man in prison dress, his exhaustion and sorrow almost tangible. But as my brain cells began to fire with such violence it was as if an electric storm had broken out in my head, I could see that Oscar was trembling. His great body was so much reduced in size it seemed impossible that this gaunt frame could belong to the man I had seen in my rooms not six months earlier. A short scrubby beard bristled from his chin; his head of curls had been cropped by a clumsy knife and was partially covered by a prisoner's cap, marked with arrows. These arrows descended in a trail all over his drab uniform, already several sizes too big for him. A downcast Sebastian, he stood linked by metal cuffs to a prison warder's arm. So pale was he, I thought he might faint, or vomit.

The crowd had discovered his identity, and were shouting out his name: 'Mr Hoscar Wilde, hauthor and poof in 'andcuffs!' Not all of the men (for there were few women) were of the uneducated classes, but their jibes were of the coarsest nature. One man stepped forward and spat full in Oscar's face: I could see the saliva trickle, untouched, down my friend's cheek.

The group of passengers around me began to snigger. One well-dressed gentleman stepped forward and called across the railway lines in a penetrating voice: '*To lose one trial, Mr Wilde, may be regarded as a misfortune; to lose all three looks like carelessness*!' Howls of appreciation from the scoffers.

Oscar raised his eyes. The crowd held its breath. Was he preparing an epigram that would forever transform Clapham Junction into a gathering place for wits; a piece of repartee that men could repeat in pubs, and grow glorious?

Instead, Oscar's exhausted gaze shifted from face to face

until it settled upon my own. The flesh around his eyes was swollen from weeping.

Perhaps three seconds had passed.

Out of the depths of his suffering, a smile of recognition and of love surfaced timidly in his eyes. He bit his lip with his black tooth.

For how many seconds did our gaze thus lock? These incidents cannot be measured in the language of time. My gaze will ever be locked into that moment on Clapham Junction when the accumulation of my life's experience was called upon to be judged.

Oscar was waiting for me to raise my hat.

I turned my back and hurried to catch my connection.

CAPE TOWN 1899

So this is where the Colossus comes to be alone with the Alone; to think his Great Thoughts, to have his Big Ideas; to gaze across the scrubby land to the pale frill of ocean with blue ripple of mountains beyond. *Your hinterland is there!*

This is the settler summerhouse on the foothills where he sits and stares out. Evidently those stolid Dutch gardeners had a feel for views as well as vegetables. Oleander and plumbago tumble out of the nearby ravine, from the depths of which rattle forth the relentless semiquavers of a mountain stream. A simple fountain stands in the rose garden.

Now my Maria flits among the white roses. Her movements are different from those of the English children I know. She has a quick agility which suggests imminent flight in any direction. She has never been trained to sit still or curtsy: she has made a contract with the sun and the earth, a contract unknown to children of the North. She somersaults unashamedly down a grassy slope and crawls back on her hands and knees. She cartwheels in perfect circles among the rosebushes. She is getting dirty already.

Her mother has not come with her after all. When I arrived at the appointed hour, panting with the exertion of lugging my heavy equipment up the long mountain track, I found

Maria paddling in the fountain, her boots and stockings thrown anywhere.

'Where's your mommy?' I smiled brightly (no pointless greeting today).

'My mommy says she can't come. Mr du Toit came so my mommy must stay.' The child scratched at a scab on her knee.

My grey heart burst into colour. 'And who is Mr du Toit?'

Maria became aware of my camera, which I was erecting upon its tripod. 'What's that?'

'Have you never had your photographs taken before? First you must tell me who Mr du Toit is. Then I'll tell you what this is.' I began to unfold the black cloth.

'He does the knives.' The child crept up to the camera, mesmerised by its strangeness. 'He brings a stone and sharpens the knives. Then he fixes things what are b-broken. How can that make a picture?'

I show her how. She hovers like a humming-bird, examining the lens, glancing at the plates. She pulls the black hood over her head and shrieks with excited terror.

I feel the years drop away from my tired body.

I position her in profile and she enjoys pretending to smell the odourless petals. I tell her Dodgson's story of the gardeners who painted the white roses red.

'Why?'

'Because the wrong roses had been planted. They were supposed to be red – for the Queen of Hearts, you see.'

Maria appears to have encountered neither the most famous children's book of the century, nor even a pack of cards. I resolve to put this right before I return to England in three days' time.

She soon understands what I require and freezes into

patient poses, gathering rosebuds, scattering petals, brushing a full-blown bloom against her cheek. She is quite wrongly dressed for a session of this sort, in her dark serge frock with inevitable white pinafore. I have not asked her to replace her boots and stockings, as bare feet seem more appropriate to the mood of the pictures.

It is growing hot. I wish I had a Panama hat, like Kipling's. The shadows are sharp and black. I try to adjust my lens to the brilliant light, and hope for the best.

This fully operational fountain has taken me by surprise. I can only assume that the Great Granary's gardeners keep it serviced. It is not an ambitious fountain: a large stone basin with central pediment releasing three fine jets of water. Perhaps it is a Netherlandish assertion of triumph over water; a nation which can reclaim land from the seas and reverse the flow of rivers can build a fountain on a mountain.

Maria's skirt is wet at the edges; splashes of damp stain her pinafore. I move the camera closer to photograph her as a tomboy Narcissus leaning over the water which shimmers back her image. The whites of her eyes and teeth flash in the wavelets. She sits on the edge of the basin and kicks her feet.

As I change plates I notice she has found something of interest on the basin rim. She bends over and exclaims in delight.

'What is it?' I move over to her side.

On her hand is a lizard-like creature with a face like an Oxford gargoyle. Its delicate, prehensile fingers cling to her flesh. Its long tail curls upwards with a Baroque flourish. Its bulging eyes are heavily hooded and remind me of Sir Alfred Milner.

'He can change he's colour!' she announces.

The chameleon is bright green, but even as I watch its

pigmentation starts to flush. 'He'll go the same colour as my s-sleeve,' she explains. The fact that her sleeve is dark blue and the chameleon is now a dusky pink seems immaterial.

I photograph her trying to establish eye contact with the shifty-looking creature. It begins to crawl up her arm, its two eyes rolling about in opposite directions. I can see its heart beating fast inside its rosy skin.

She plucks it from her shoulder and places it on an oleander bush. 'Now you can t-turn green again,' she says to it.

It occurs to me that we might as well be in the Gardens of Versailles for the degree of mountain in my pictures.

The octagonal summerhouse is built entirely out of mountain stone, and painted over with whitewash. The inevitable teak beams and benches make it seem like another room in the Great Granary. On either side, at a distance of some fifty yards, are two stone benches for the slaves who would have carried their lords and ladies up the mountain slopes and awaited their commands without making their presence felt. Did they, too, enjoy the view?

Maria cavorts in the dark cavern of the summerhouse while I turn my tripod round and ponder exposure lengths. The sun rises higher in the sky and beats against my head. I feel I am being strangled by my high collar. The child will not notice if I loosen it. Nor will she care if I remove my jacket and work in my shirt-sleeves.

She poses under an arch, leans against a column, sits demurely on a bench, plucking at rose petals. My head is in a black bag. I cannot breathe. Sweat begins to roll down my face and body in torrents. I struggle out of the cloth and run to the icy waters of the fountain. Oh, what exquisite relief to feel coolness on my face, my neck. I splash joyously. The slender fountain-spray murmurs lies about rain.

Maria has joined me.

'You hot, hey?' Her eyes are enormous with concern.

'Yes, I'm s-sorry,' I stammer. 'I'm not used to this heat, you see. Goodness me!' I am recovering. 'If this is your winter, I don't think I'd survive your summer!'

The child looks around her in astonishment. 'It's not winter! In winter it rains and the squirrels go to sleep.'

'Ah, but does it ever snow?' My fingers, spread out in fountain water, have become numbed by the brimming cold.

Now Maria climbs back into the basin and begins kicking arcs of water into the air with her brown feet. I have learnt that she answers questions in her own time, and wait patiently for a response.

'What's snow?' she enquires in a shower of self-made raindrops.

'Snow is what happens in England when it is very cold. White snowflakes fall out of the sky and cover the earth. Children go sledging and make snowballs.' I cannot put it more simply than that.

This is not good enough for Maria. 'But what does it l-look like?' she cries.

I rack my scientific brains miserably. 'I suppose, once it has fallen, it looks like whipped cream – or ice-cream!' I add in a flash of whimsical inspiration.

'Oo-hoo!' Maria jumps out of the fountain and runs round the rosebushes with her head thrust back and tongue stuck out. 'Ook!' she commands. 'I ee ing I eam!' This open-mouthed method of speech reduces her to a great deal of silly giggling, and I decide it is time to return to my camera and pack up. I have taken enough photographs.

I move into the coolness of the summerhouse where I pack and fold in meticulous order, out of the violence of the sun's rays.

When I raise my head, I cannot see Maria.

With a screech of terror, I run down to the fountain.

She has thrown her clothes off and her tender young limbs slip through the water like long, sinuous fins.

I cannot stop looking at her beautiful body.

She swims round and round, then rears up sharply and, laughing, threatens to splash me. Her tiny shoulders form a perfect right-angle with her neck, yet there is a curve in them that breaks my heart.

I back away. I find a voice which says: 'Maria, are you allowed to swim like that?' She looks at me slyly. 'I got all dirty from the ice-cream. So I had to have a barf.'

And in she plunges once more.

I return to the summerhouse and unpack my camera. In spite of the sun I drag the tripod, the black hood, the plates, down to the pool. I ask Maria to pose for me. She stands waist-deep in the water, hands held up high beneath the spray which slithers down her torso. *Snap!* She crouches on hands and knees, so that only her smiling face surrounded by hair that has quadrupled in size protrudes from the water. *Snap!* She stares pensively at the water-jet, a self-conscious forefinger on her chin. *Snap!*

I remove my head from the black bag and say as casually as possible: 'Would you like to pose for me again among the rosebushes?'

'Wif no clothes on?'

'Whichever you please.'

The child springs out of the fountain and streaks over to the roses. I hardly dare to follow her with my eyes.

Her buttocks would fit precisely into my cupped hands. The slit between her legs seems to have been drawn with a pencil. I can see the stripes of her ribcage. She begins to dance.

I wriggle my head into the hood and begin taking photographs. Maria points her toe, her hands in an arch above her head. *Snap!* Maria bends down and trails her fingers over her feet. *Snap!* Maria lifts one leg into the fountain. *Snap!* Maria bends her knees and prepares to dive. *Snap!*

Maria's hand extends slyly into the oleander bush. She plucks out the chameleon, a miniature dinosaur who has not moved from his twig for a millennium of micro-seconds, and places him upon her shoulder.

'Come closer!' I call out. 'So that I can photograph the two of you together.'

O, how Maria plays with the chameleon! She lies in the grass. I adjust my camera lens. He runs up and down her body. She giggles at the prickling sensation. He holds himself still, his own body now a diagonal slash across her navel. Maria's fingers explore the grass idly and release a cloud of small flies. From the chameleon's jaws a long coiled tongue thrusts, abruptly, but accurately.

My head under the cloth, I view the antipodeal scene, upside down, upon the plate glass. In the heat, my fingers tremble violently as I press the button to open the shutter.

And suddenly Maria is no longer there. I tear my head out of the hood and for a moment can see nothing with my dark-adapted eyes. I can hear bodies struggling. As my pupils dilate I can see that a woman has swept the child under her shawl, a woman whose frowning brow is now turned upon the extended lens which is fixed upon her like the barrel of a gun. Maria struggles and squawks but Mrs Kipling is used to dealing with children. She makes Maria don her abandoned clothes, ignoring me as I emerge from the protection of my hood.

I stand beside my camera, smiling sheepishly. She is already bustling Maria out of the rose garden, away from my contamination. Before descending into the gorge she turns to me with bitter eyes: *'For shame, Professor!'*

I have no reply to that.

Ujiji
1907

Dear Miss Schreiner,

You will no doubt be somewhat startled to receive this manu-script – a form of diary, I suppose – from someone you have undoubtedly dismissed with the greatest contempt as a man who did not keep his word. Eight years have passed since my peremptory departure from Cape Town, and not one day goes by without my resolving to write you an explanation, an apology, an excuse, call it what you will. For I live in hope of your forgiveness. Now Selous, who is visiting Central Africa, has very kindly agreed to deliver the enclosed to you on his return to Cape Town. It will reveal more than any letter ever could.

I still retain vivid memories of the last time I saw you – in the upper reaches of the Great Granary gardens, on the day before the Release of my birds was due to take place. In your arms you held two brightly painted toy automobiles which you had procured from a shop in the village below – I forget its name. (I often wonder whether you found it within yourself to present them to Salisbury and Chamberlain, even though my sudden exit meant it was no longer necessary for you to lure them away.)

I could have given you the telegrams then and there, and, bearing in mind the unmitigated disaster of the War that was to follow – a War that might just possibly have been prevented by the exchange of eight telegrams for two toy motorcars – I now regret most bitterly that I did not.

May I assure you that I had every intention of keeping to my side of the bargain.

However, an unforeseen chain of circumstances was to prevent this intention from being honoured. On returning to the Great Granary, I immediately shut myself up in the dark-room and spent the next hour developing and printing the photographs I had taken on the mountain slopes that morning. I pegged the pictures on the drying line and returned to my room to clean myself up and prepare for a light lunch. Imagine my astonishment when half an hour later, Huxley, the major-domo, knocked on my door and ordered me to join his master in the latter's magnificent bedroom, wherein he often conducted his interviews.

'And bring the telegrams with you!' he barked, in a voice entirely devoid of respect.

On entering the bedroom, I was further surprised to find the Colossus, Mr Jameson, Mrs Kipling and Huxley standing in a row in the great bay window, for all the world like a quartet of opera singers about to break into a four-part fugue.

The Colossus said (his thatch of hair more dishevelled than ever): 'You have completely betrayed my trust.'

Jameson said: 'Come on, old chap, hand them over. You know I know you've got them.'

Mrs K said: 'I have told them everything.' (Her nostrils flared as she spoke, as if I were emitting an unpleasant odour.)

Huxley merely grunted.

Miss Schreiner, if you read my document, you will understand.

My host said: 'I must ask you to leave this house within the hour.'

His best friend said: 'Sorry it had to end this way.'

Mrs K said, or rather, spat: 'You ought to be locked up.'

It seemed to me that, one after the other, the foursome then proceeded to lift their voices into an angry arpeggio – an accusing appoggiatura – an indignant discord – suspended in that great bedroom, requiring resolution.

'Paedophile!'

'Traitor!'   'Pervert!'

'Thief!'

I looked around for help.

Oscar was standing beside the bed. Once again he wore his martyr's arrows, and he was offering me his blackened smile.

Inside my ribcage a nightingale began to sing. The silver music slid around my fortressed heart, Miss Schreiner, and found some secret aperture into the very sanctum of my life's blood. Then how the thrushes trilled! the wrens fluted! the blackbirds crooned! the starlings warbled cakewalk and telephones! Out of my mouth bubbled the song of my birds, liquid as the stream in the mountain's cleft, potent as any wine. For my tormentors, I performed an entire dawn chorus.

'Professor Wills, please stop that whistling! You look quite ridiculous!'

Yes, I am a ridiculous person, I can see that. And always have been. Worthy of ridicule: a laughing stock.

Oscar caught my eye and pursed his lips. His life has always perched on the edge of ridicule, a stylish bird who depends on song rather than wings for survival. Now he threw back his head sideways in the manner of his favourite saint, and winked.

The laughing stock began to laugh. Almost immediately unused muscles round my diaphragm went into spasm, causing me to bend over in pain, clutching my stomach, stamping my feet. Yet in the midst of my physical discomfort I sensed the draining away of a great weight; I became a light thing, as if borne by wings.

'The man's hysterical,' said Dr Jameson.

'I cannot see that this is a laughing matter,' shrilled the Colossus.

'This has gone too far!' snapped Mrs K, and whirled out of the room, causing Oscar to jump sideways and raise an imaginary hat.

'The telegrams, please.' Huxley extended a hairy hand.

'And you can have your dirty photographs back,' smirked Jameson.

'And what of the Release?' I enquired.

The Colossus was towering above me. Had he suddenly grown or had I shrunk? His blue eyes, set within their red rims, had become transparent. 'The birds can be released without you.' He turned away to fiddle with papers on his desk.

I withdrew my hands from behind my back and placed the telegrams in Huxley's extended palms. I said: 'Tell me, Huxley, was it on your grandmother's or your grandfather's side that you are descended from an ape?'

A couple of hours later I stood on Cape Town station, surrounded by baggage and awaiting the Trans-Karoo Express. Mary the poodle pranced around my bags and left her mark upon them, while Challenger drew a map of the shortest route to his verandah-encircled house in Ujiji. He promised to join me within six months, a promise I am glad to say he has kept.

His Dodos turned out to be Whaleheaded Storks, more accurately known as the Shoebill species Balaeniceps rex. Though the bird looks like a stork or a heron it is neither, and has the honour of being the only species of its genus. I have become extremely interested in this clumsy wading creature, and somewhat concerned for its survival. It lives only among the local waterways and marshes, which hunters set on fire so as to flush out their prey. I fear that this can only result in the destruction of the habitat and the ultimate extinction of this *unique species. I plan to lend my support to the creation of a National Park.*

Mr Selous brings much news of Cape Town. He tells us that in the last year of the War the Colossus died in Jameson's arms, in his little cottage by the sea. A massive lump of ice was lowered through a hole in the ceiling in an effort to cool the unusually hot and sultry temperature. I hope he did not curse me as he lay dying.

It seems inconceivable that JimJam is now the Colony's Premier, attempting to unify a country riven with hatred. It does not help that Milner is busy anglicising the ex-Boer Republics. I am not surprised to hear he has been made a viscount out of gratitude for precipitating the Anglo-Boer War. Who gains by war? you once memorably asked him. We certainly know who the losers are: the British taxpayers who lost over two hundred million pounds in this venture, and more than fifty thousand British, Boer and Afrikaner men and women who lost their lives in bloody battle or in refugee camps (now referred to as 'concentration' camps, I believe), to say nothing of the thousands of black people who gave up their lives for what they thought was their country. Selous is convinced that JimJam will be knighted before long.

Selous also informs us that on the day of the Release, my songbirds flew off into the forest and were never seen again – except for the starlings, who have by now become a national pest. Some of them can sing like nightingales, he says.

Yours very sincerely, Miss Schreiner,

Francis Wills

The Impatient Imperialist

Today is the centenary of Dr Jameson's birth. This worthy man, who always acted from the highest motives, owes his immortality solely to an act of impatient folly. It was his ambition to be an idealistic builder of Empire; and he served Cecil Rhodes with sincere devotion.

It was largely thanks to Jameson that Matabeleland was won for British authority without bloodshed. He meant to rescue the Transvaal by a similar act of daring. The men who encouraged him – Rhodes at Capetown and those still more highly placed in London – may have been without scruples; Jameson himself was an idealist, however mistaken.

But when the plans for a revolution at Johannesburg misfired, Jameson launched the supreme blunder of the Raid. He thought the failure would fall only on himself. Instead it ruined Rhodes and more remotely Joseph Chamberlain. Still more it ruined all hopes of a reconciliation between Boers and Britons.

Jameson devoted the remainder of his life to trying to undo the effects of his disastrous act. He served as Prime Minister at the Cape, held out the hand of friendship to Botha, and died, a respectable baronet, in 1917.

But the Jameson Raid had made an ineffaceable mark on South African life; we see its working even at the present day. Yet it was not without its good consequences, though Jameson might have deplored them.

The Raid was the high-water mark of aggressive British Imperialism. The reaction against it first brought together the 'pro-Boers'; it was they, not Rhodes, Milner or Chamberlain who set their stamp on the modern Commonwealth of Nations.

Guardian, 9 February 1953

No gratitude

ZIMBABWE'S Marxist dictator Robert Mugabe is steadily removing all British names from streets and squares in Harare.

But if Cecil Rhodes and other British pioneers had not tamed the wilderness there would be no Zimbabwe and no towns.

And Mr Mugabe would not be sitting in state dressed in a smart western suit.

He would be roaming the veldt in a loin cloth and carrying a spear.

There ain't no gratitude!

Sun, 1990

A NOTE ON THE AUTHOR

Ann Harries was born and educated in Cape Town, where she worked in township schools and community centres. On moving to England she became active in the anti-apartheid movement. She now lives in the Cotswolds and is writing her next novel.